Beyond the Trees

Stories from Settlement of America

J. Laurie Byrne

Knoxville, Tennessee, USA
crippledbeaglepublishing.com

Cover art by Mimi Eichholz
Cover design by Maria Loysa-Bel Nueve-de los Angeles
Edited by Janice Laurino and Linda Albert

Paperback ISBN 978-1-965334-03-4, 978-1-965334-02-7
Hardcover ISBN 978-1-965334-04-1, 978-1-958533-99-4

Library of Congress Control Number: 2024915717

Printed in the United States of America

For my daddy, Arthur D. Byrne, who encouraged me to read and write by sharing stories with me when I was young about characters in Jackson County, Tennessee, including Aunt Polly, Matt, Sally "Sack" and Willie "Skillet" Hampton, Hub Haile at his grocery store on the square in Gainesboro, and the two-year stay in a house on Lawrence Byrne's property by John and Jane Clemens, the parents of Samuel.

Preface

As young students in the 1960s, we read textbooks that hit the high points of American history and listened to teachers who presented a version that mostly skimmed over the ugly. White men sailed the ocean in big, wooden boats, raised crops and children, built rustic log houses, fought with Indians, pushed into the wilderness, developed towns with wooden frame houses, battled the British and French to claim this land as our own, brought slaves over from Africa to help grow large acreages of crops, and fought a terrible Civil War to free those slaves. The truth was even harsher. It was traumatizing for those brave enough to venture over in the earliest days - tragic for many of them.

I began researching the history of my various families in 2015, first on ancestry.com. As a writer, I sniff out stories. I started making a list. I was amazed at how many accounts directly linked to my ancestors related to the history of this country. I realized I must share these stories.

I have three families. My father grew up in middle Tennessee. He came to Maryville College in East Tennessee, where he met my mother, who arrived from Massachusetts. They married in 1942. Ten years later, they adopted me as an infant. In the mid-nineties, when Tennessee adoptees could access their adoption files, I found that my birth mother came from the hills of West Virginia. There was no acknowledged paternity.

In telling these stories of my ancestors, they became flesh and blood, not just names. It gave me a whole new perspective on our history when they participated in an event, suffered an outcome, and achieved a victory. I became more than a spectator.

When Edward and Mary Hill hid in a natural culvert outside their village in Virginia on March 22, 1622, while members of the

Powhattan Confederacy were in the process of slaughtering 347 white settlers up and down the James River. When Josiah Bartlett, a New Hampshire delegate to the Second Continental Congress in 1775, became the second person to sign the U.S. Declaration of Independence, or, as Josiah Lambert found himself crammed in the dark, airless hull of a prison ship in New York harbor starting in 1776 for three years, where human waste mingled with the putrid smells of sickness and death. When Francis Hughes neared the crest of King's Mountain in South Carolina in 1780, and suddenly stared at a line of charging British bayonets. Or, when Cyrus and Ruth White, my great-great-grandparents, who were abolitionists on the Underground Railroad, sheltered four runaways for four weeks in 1851 because a large slave patrol roamed the Massachusetts coast.

These are the kinds of discoveries that can be made today through ancestry research. All the legwork has been done. In the 1980s, my parents searched Wicklow, Ireland, for information on Byrne's genealogy. It did not take my dad long to give up. He would be astonished and delighted at the stories I uncovered and that I traced his roots more than three centuries before the time William Terrell Byrne immigrated to this country in 1792.

Every family possesses undiscovered stories hidden in decades and centuries past. They are our links to history. Had those people not come and survived, we would not be here. All are important. That is not to say we take pride in every single ancestor. You will likely make discoveries you'd rather not. I did. Luckily, I uncovered far more nuggets of gold than rocks.

Regardless of location, I mainly discovered unbelievable resiliency in overcoming unimaginable hardships to endure and to survive against the odds.

Seeking religious freedom and economic opportunity, most of our European ancestors from the British Isles began their immigration to these shores in the early 1600s. They operated blindly, strictly on faith. They did not know what lay beyond the trees. Their backs were to the sea. They died of disease and starvation. They froze to death. They were killed by the Natives. More arrived. Out of necessity, they evolved into warriors in their own right. They persevered. They produced many children. They moved through the trees. They learned. More ships came.

Towns sprang up. They continued battling with the Indians. British and French soldiers vied for support among Native tribes in their attempts to claim North American territory, resulting in the death of many white settlers in wilderness areas. Terror reigned on the frontier. The Revolutionary War held the country hostage, which led to our independence from Great Britain. Starting in the late 1820s and continuing for the next forty years, Americans joined wagon-train migrations by the thousands, taking one of at least five major trails heading west of the Great Plains. Many perished on the long, treacherous journey. The American Civil War lasted from 1861 to 1865. It tore the nation apart and devastated many families, particularly in the South. The Panic of 1893 lasted for four years, staggered businesses nationwide, and left many families destitute.

Stories that follow focus on the 1600s, 1700s, and 1800s. I gained an understanding of what a short history we have. I had not put it into perspective until the day I realized that my mother, Jean W. Byrne, who passed away in July 2021, two months shy of her 102nd birthday, lived one-fourth as long as this country has been around, measuring it by when the *Mayflower* arrived from Southampton, England. Incredibly, she had six direct line ancestors on the *Mayflower* when it dropped anchor on the northern tip of Cape Cod on November 21, 1620.

What follows is historical fiction, although probably seventy-five percent is fact. Research does not provide enough details to bring characters to life, fill gaps, or complete any story.

These stories may inspire you to seek out your family genealogy. Discover not just who and where you come from but what surprises your past will reveal. Information might not lie on the surface. Look in the cracks and crevices. What you find can take you on quite a ride!

J. Laurie Byrne

Contents

WHITE families

Found Themselves on Ships

Ross/Levistone

While Thomas Ross swung his scythe, he considered that a man's circumstance is relative at any given time. Not yet a free man, somehow, by God's mercy or because the stars aligned in his favor at just the right time, he managed to escape not only death but the terrible conditions faced by many of his Scottish countrymen sold into indentured labor.

Thomas knew he was lucky. He freely mowed grass in the bog on the north end of Spy Pond in the village of Arlington, Massachusetts, six miles north of Boston. His indenture was served in Middlesex County, where he performed various tasks at his owner's sawmill.

One year remained on Thomas's contract to Edward Winship of Cambridge, who purchased him as a Scottish prisoner of war after the conclusion of the third and final English Civil War in 1651.

When Mr. Winship heard that Oliver Cromwell had taken more than 8,000 Scottish prisoners and would be selling them as indentured servants in the West Indies, Virginia, Massachusetts, and Maine, he determined to acquire a young man for his business. But he was not willing to accept any rogue. He wanted someone who came from nobility.

In August 1635, as a twenty-three-year-old, Edward Winship had left the safety of his Newcastle home on the upper northeast coast of England, boarded the ship *Defiance* in Harwich, and arrived in Boston the first week in October. Immediately, he bought three acres in the heart of Cambridge. Three years later, he purchased land in what became Lexington on Mill Brook and built the first sawmill in the area. He continued to acquire extensive tracts of land in Cambridge and Lexington.

Thomas Ross descended from Rosses in the west central Lowlands of Scotland in the historic county of Renfrewshire.

His father, Sir James Ross, 6th Lord of Halkhead, descended from Lord John Ross, born in 1501 in Halkhead. The title of Lord Ross was a Lordship of Parliament in the Peerage of Scotland, created in 1499 for Sir John Ross. The Rosses of Halkhead were considered a branch of Clan Ross, a Highland Scottish clan.

Thomas's mother, Lady Margaret Scott, descended from an old, colorful family whose exploits served the Scottish royals over the centuries in their defense against the ever-invading English. Included was Sir Walter Scott, Thomas's fourth great-grandfather.

Lord Walter Scott of Buccleuch and Lady Margaret Kerr of Cessford wed in 1586. They were Thomas's great-grandparents. A few decades earlier, a marriage between the two families would have been highly improbable.

Sir Walter Scott, a nobleman of the Borders, was known to be an "inveterate English hater." In the early summer of 1526, he was enlisted by fourteen-year-old King James V of Scotland to free him from the teaching of Sir Archibald Douglas, 6th Earl of Angus, husband of the Queen Dowager Margaret Tudor, mother of the king.

On July 25, Sir Scott led more than 600 Border raiders in an attempted rescue of the young king while he was being escorted on a journey to Edinburgh by Sir Douglas and his train. Included in the procession were many Kerrs of Cessford and Ferniehurst who pursued their attackers. About eighty of Sir Scott's men were killed. Sir Douglas's forces managed to prevail, but the cost was high. A rider in Sir Scott's service killed Sir Andrew Kerr of

Cessford, forty-one. His death precipitated bloodshed between the Kerr and Scott families over the next two decades.

King James V died on December 14, 1542, at age thirty. That day, his only legitimate child, Mary, just six days old, became Mary Queen of Scots.

On October 4, 1552, Sir Walter Scott, at age fifty-seven, encountered a band of Kerrs and their entourage on High Street in Edinburgh. John Hume of Cowdenknowes ran Sir Scott through with his sword as he shouted, "Strike! Ain strike for they father's sake!"

Oliver Cromwell was a devout Puritan who became a dictator after his role in the execution of King Charles I in January 1649. Scotland supported Charles II, who was proclaimed king a month after his father's death by the Covenanters, who had controlled Scotland since 1639.

The Parliamentarian New Model Army under Oliver Cromwell invaded and occupied Scotland beginning in July 1650. On September 3, the Scots sustained a resounding blow in the Battle of Dunbar when more than 14,000 of their forces were either killed, wounded, or taken prisoner.

In response, the Scottish Parliament passed an act requiring every burgh and shire in the Highlands and Lowlands to raise a quota of soldiers. This new round of conscription was called the Army of the Kingdom and included many men who had fought against each other in previous skirmishes. Then, the time to train was short. Morale needed raising. Their leader, the king himself, faced a formidable foe.

Nineteen-year-old Thomas Ross knew he must now step up and defend his country from yet another imminent threat from the English.

Clan Ross had been a Royalist during the ongoing Civil War. Thomas heard that Sir David Ross, 12th Lord of Balnagowan and current Chief of Clan Ross, was gathering his kinsmen to fight.

Thomas secured his weapons and rode north to County Ross, where he joined nearly 1,000 men.

Led by Sir Ross, Thomas, and his kinsmen headed west to merge with King Charles II and his troops, then south into England. On September 3, 1651, an estimated 28,000 soldiers enlisted in Oliver Cromwell's army defeated around 16,000 Royalists, mostly Scots, in the Battle of Worcester. Fierce fighting resulted in the death of some 3,000 Royalists. About 10,000 were taken as prisoners. Twelve hundred went to prison camps around London, where many died from disease and starvation. Chief David Ross was jailed in the Tower of London. He died after two years of imprisonment. The rest found themselves on ships sailing to the Americas, destined to be sold as indentured servants. Included was Thomas Ross.

✦ ✦ ✦

William Holman, forty-one, his wife, Winifred Henchman, thirty-five, their first five children, and Alice Ashbey, a twenty-year-old maidservant from Northamptonshire, England, sailed from Harwich on the *Defiance* in June 1635 as passengers bound for Boston. Edward Winship was a fellow passenger. William, a free tenant farmer, began acquiring small parcels of land around Cambridge. By the year 1645, he held twenty-eight acres.

The Praying Indian village, Shawshin, later spelled Shawsheen, along the Shawsheen River, was granted to Massachusetts Governor Thomas Dudley in 1638. Families from Cambridge and Charlestown Village started occupying Shawshin, which was renamed Billerica.

On June 4, 1652, William Holman received a fifty-acre lot on the west side of the Monotamye River as part of the division of the Shawsheen lands.

The Holman family remained in their six-acre home in Cambridge on the Old West Field. Nearby, William worked another six acres he owned on the south side of the Charles River. In the spring of 1642, the oldest son, Jeremy, thirteen, joined his father working in the fields.

Seeth, the Holman's seventh child, had arrived on May 19, 1640. At the same time, smallpox ravaged Boston. Everyone in Cambridge and other surrounding areas remained fearful and tried to stay as isolated. Mercifully, the highly contagious disease skipped over the Holman's household.

On the first Monday of May 1659, Jeremy Holman and his brother, Abraham, drove a load of rough-cut logs up to the Winship sawmill in Lexington. There, they met Thomas Ross, who processed their order. A rather lengthy conversation ensued. The Holmans discovered that Thomas came from the Scottish Borders and had been imprisoned and indentured as a result of the war. Coming from northeast England, the Holmans had been Royalists as well.

"My service for Mr. Winship has been quite tolerable," said Thomas. "In another couple months, 'twill be a free man. He has offered to put me on his payroll. I'm unmarried and not yet burdened with responsibilities."

"Ye ken ye are blessed with options," Jeremy replied.

"Aye, I suppose I am. But at twenty-eight, I probably ought to be thinking about finding a wife."

"It has been six years since we lost our father. Just before he passed, he reminded us that life slips by before ye know it. Told us not to put off raising a family too long."

Thomas walked his customers out to their empty wagon.

"I'll have this load cut to your specifications tomorrow," he said as he shook the brothers' hands. "Wednesday, I'll be in Cambridge to work with the manager of one of Mr. Winship's acreages. I will be happy to deliver your lumber to ye."

"That would be grand, Mr. Ross. If I'm not at the house when ye arrive, one of our siblings will fetch me or Abe. One of us can help ye unload."

"Good enough. And, please, call me Thomas. Latha math."

In two days, Thomas arrived at the Holman's mid-morning. Seeth, who had just turned seventeen, walked out of the house to greet him. He wished every delivery included a smiling, radiant face on a young English lass. He jumped off the wagon seat and saw she lacked an inch from meeting his 5-foot, 10-inch height. Strawberry blond, curly locks spilled out from around her simple, white linen cap.

"And ye would be Mr. Ross," she asked as words failed him.

"Thomas, if you please. And ye are?

"Oh, right, then. I am Seeth Holman."

"Are yer brothers about? These planks need unloading."

"Ah, dinnae ken. Let me ring the bell."

Seeth walked to the roof's eave, where a large brass bell hung. She rang it three times.

"Led thoil, come in the house. Jeremy will be here shortly," Seeth said as she opened the front door. "Would ye like some tea?"

Thomas met Mistress Holman, fifty-nine, daughter Mary, thirty, a spinster, and her youngest, Elizabeth, fifteen. Mary removed three loaves of dill bread from the oven. She then excused herself to go out back to clean fish as she busied herself preparing a noon meal of scup with fava beans and new potatoes. They asked him to stay and share dinner with them. He readily accepted the invitation.

Thomas discovered that two of the five Holman daughters were married. Hannah Johnson, thirty-one, lived in Sudbury, located in west Middlesex County, with her husband, Soloman, and three small children. Sarah Parker, twenty-seven, and husband, Samuel, had a one-year-old daughter, with the birth of their son imminent. They lived just south of Cambridge in Dedham.

The youngest Holman son, Issac, twenty-three, still lived at home and helped his two brothers work their farm properties.

Thomas received his papers as a free man from Mr. Winship in July. He continued living in his quarters on the Winship estate in Cambridge. He planned to save enough money to buy land and start a family. Therefore, he wanted to focus his efforts on agriculture. Mr. Winship now considered Thomas to be his protégé. He agreed to make Thomas assistant manager of his overall farming operations.

The Holmans often invited Thomas to their house since he and Jeremy had struck up a friendship. He helped them with projects around their property in his spare time, they fed him, and twice before the weather turned, he went with the family on outings into Boston. An immediate attraction developed between him and Seeth.

Winifred Holman was one of the first in America to observe the Christian Scientist denomination. When the Holmans arrived from England in the mid-1630s, the religious fervor of the Puritans allowed for little tolerance of outside religions in their midst.

Christian Scientists were emphatically Christian. They believed in the Bible and Jesus Christ as the Son of God. They believed that God is all-good, all-encompassing, always present, and that God loves each individual.

Naturally, Winifred began sharing what she considered the healing power of God's love with those in their community who chose to discuss their problems with her. By the 1640s, it was rumored that the Holman family were not Puritans. Winifred was singled out, arrested, and briefly imprisoned.

"Is freedom of thought not a primary reason so many of us came across the ocean to this new land?" asked an incensed daughter, Hannah, seventeen after her mother was taken away to be questioned. "Are the English and the Dutch not supposed to be the most tolerant of societies? As the founding peoples of this new nation, should we not be setting an example of acceptance?"

"I could no have said it better meself, daughter," replied William Holman. "I will speak with Reverend James and see if we cannot discover the source of this misunderstanding. Stay put. Do not fan the flames. Ye hear me?"

In the summer of 1659, Winifred and Mary became the target of neighbors who sought retribution for the unexplained illness of their adult daughter. They latched onto the mysterious phenomenon of witchcraft, which had surfaced in the Massachusetts Bay Colony when Margaret Jones, a Puritan nurse midwife, was hung on June 15, 1648, in Boston after being accused of witchcraft.

The Holman's neighbor, John Gibson, said his married daughter, Rebecca Stearns, began having fits and screaming that Mistress Holman and Mary were witches. The Gibsons claimed in an indictment that Winifred had offered their daughter herbs after a previous fit, which only seemed to make matters worse. The Holmans had also tended to the woman's child, who became sick. The treatment failed to produce results.

Winifred Holman submitted signed statements by two church deacons and other neighbors in her defense, stating she was a "good Christian woman" who regularly attended church, and they were not aware of any behavior on her part that would indicate she might be guilty of actions associated with "witchery."

The family realized the seriousness of the accusations even though they considered the charges to be ridiculous. In the past eleven years, fourteen women and six men have been accused of witchcraft by the courts. Two of the women suffered the hangman's noose.

Winifred and Mary were apprehended and brought to the county court in Charlestown, along with their maid. After several court sessions in 1660, the recorder of the court appended the following memorandum:

"John Gibson, Jr. acknowledged in Court that whereas he is legally convicted of a slanderous speech concerning Mary Holman, he is heartily sorry for his evil, thereby committed against God and wrong done to the said Mary Holman and her friends, and doth crave forgiveness of the said Mary Holman of the trespass."10

At the end of March 1660, the Holmans brought two suits in county court against Mr. Gibson and his daughter for defamation.

Neither mother nor daughter ever again found themselves involved with the courts. Nor were they in disrepute among their neighbors in Cambridge, where they lived until Winifred died at age seventy-one in October 1671. Two years later, Mary was killed in a carriage accident en route to Dedham to visit her sister, Sarah, and her family.

In May 1661, Thomas and Seeth married in beautiful Fresh Pond Meadow. William Holman had purchased two and a half acres beside the large pond in Cambridge in the early 1640s. The land lay dormant. But Seeth always thought she would like to live there when she wed.

When Thomas proposed marriage, Seeth's three brothers, who had already welcomed Thomas into the family, celebrated with her. The four men built a cabin in the meadow to Seeth's specifications, which looked due east over the water into each sunrise. They completed their work two weeks before the early morning ceremony.

The following year, in December, Thomas and Seeth welcomed wee Thomas II into the world. Thirteen months later, the infant inexplicably died during his sleep.

Jeremy Holman was not far behind his friend in securing a wife. When he married twenty-year-old Mercy Pratt in the early fall of 1662, he inherited a father-in-law who would wind up in the history books.

✦ ✦ ✦

Phineas Pratt, from London, worked as a joiner and an artisan who built things by joining pieces of wood. At age twenty-nine, he came to America with ten other men on the fishing vessel *Sparrow* as part of Thomas Weston's company. Mr. Weston had been an agent for merchant adventurers' investment in the *Mayflower*'s voyage two years previously. He now looked to establish his own colony.

The *Sparrow* mistakenly sailed to the coast of Maine in 1622. They then sailed down to Plymouth Plantation to await the arrival of their other two ships, the *Charity* and the *Swan*. The Pilgrims supported the small, poorly supplied group through the summer. With the arrival of the other ships, about sixty men sailed back north around the small islands into what would become Boston Harbor. They built a trading post-stockade in the abandoned Indian settlement of Wessaguscus. It was renamed Weymouth in 1635.

A harrowing seven months followed. The group was ill-prepared for both growing and hunting for food. Many starved to death. The others barely escaped their misery after stealing from the Natives in an attempt to survive.

Phineas correctly suspected that both his group, at what they now called Wessagusset, and very probably the people at Plymouth Colony were in danger of attack because they failed to appease the local sachem. He knew he had to warn Captain Myles Standish in Plymouth. No one would join him in trekking twenty-five miles in the March snow, so he went alone: virtually without food, being uncertain of the way, and getting lost.

In describing part of his experience, Phineas wrote:

> ". . . running down a hill, I saw an English man coming up the path before me. Then I sat down on a tree. Rising up to salute him I said, 'Mr. Hamdin, I am glad to see you alive.'

He said, 'I am glad and full of wonder to see you alive; let us sit down. I see you are weary.'"

Thus warned, Captain Standish and his company traveled to Wessagusset. Once there, a sachem, several of his tribe and a handful of colonists were killed in a brief battle. Those who remained were divided. Some returned to England. Others settled in Plymouth.

Phineas spent the next quarter century in Plymouth. He married Mary Priest at seventeen in 1630.

On November 21, 1620, Mary's father, Degory Priest, forty-one, from London, signed the Mayflower Compact. This agreement established a starting government for 102 Separatists coming to the New World seeking religious freedom. That day, the *Mayflower* dropped anchor near the tip of Cape Cod. Mr. Priest survived the overseas journey but died on January 1, 1621, forty-one days after arrival.

Phineas Pratt sold his estate in Plymouth in 1646, and two years later, he moved his family to Charlestown on Windmill Hill. Their house and gardens sat very near a Dutch-style windmill for grinding grain and close to a fort built in 1629 for protection against the Indians.

In 1662, Phineas, then sixty-nine, submitted a comprehensive narrative of his settlement to the General Court of Massachusetts called *A Declaration of the Affairs of the English People That First Inhabited New England*. He sought financial assistance available to those who established themselves as a "First Comer," the earliest settlers of Massachusetts, entitled to benefits as afforded by law.

The court rewarded Phineas 300 acres of land east of the Merrimack River near the upper end of Naticook Brook near the border of New Hampshire. Nearly 200 years later, the full text of the narration would be published.

✦ ✦ ✦

By 1669, Thomas Ross felt the need to find more land for his agricultural pursuits. Acreage around Boston became scarce as the population grew. He wanted to take his family inland.

None of the Holman siblings had claimed the land in North Billerica purchased by their father in 1652. All agreed that sister, Seeth, and her family should inherit the property, which lay about fifteen miles northwest of Cambridge.

As soon as crops were harvested in the fall, Mary and the children joined Thomas, who had already started clearing land to build a cabin. Another worker from Mr. Winship's sawmill volunteered to come and cut boards on site. With six workers, they finally managed to get a roof on before the first serious snowfall.

The Rosses moved the first wagon load of their possessions into their new home as the first signs of spring green appeared. There would be no spring planting since there had been no time to prepare a field. But Thomas thought that maybe, with help from new neighbors, he might get summer crops in. Seeth had plenty of space to start a vegetable garden.

Seeth's sister, Hannah, her husband, and their eldest son, Nathan, thirty, who would soon marry, came up from Sudbury for several days. Thomas needed their help to start a small barn for a couple of cows and chickens.

The Rosses brought their oldest child, Margaret, five, and son, Thomas III, three, when they moved to Billerica. Daughter Sarah was born the next year. In March 1679, daughter Hannah joined the family. Seven years later, they were surprised when twins John and Benjamin arrived.

They quickly integrated into the town, which was made up of many families originally from England who had also relocated from Cambridge over the past several years.

By the mid-1670s, when King Philip's War started, forty-eight families lived in Billerica. Miraculously, the town escaped attack in a nearly three-year bloody assault between Native tribes in southern New England and white colonists. By the time Metacom, the Wampanoag chief, known as King Philip, was killed on August 12, 1676, more than half of New England's towns had been attacked by the Natives. Twelve towns were destroyed.

John Levistone, twenty-two, found his way from East Lothian in the east central Lowlands of Scotland in 1677 to Boston. In his short lifetime, Oliver Cromwell died, King Charles II became the undisputed king of England, Scotland, and Ireland, and a tenuous peace existed in the British Isles. He lost his father when he was nine. He kept hearing the word "independence" when people referred to this big new country far to the west, and he thought it had a nice ring to it.

John stayed in Boston for a couple of days to get his bearings, then started walking northwest. He crossed the Charles River and walked through Cambridge. As he headed out the other side of town, a loaded wagon pulled up beside him with a man and boy in it.

"Halo," said the man. "Are ye goin' far?"

"I don rightly know," John replied.

"Is that a Lowlands accent, then?"

"Aye," said John as he grinned and extended his hand. "I'm John Levistone from Linlithgow, and I just got off the boat."

The man laughed, jumped down from his seat, and hugged John. Good to meet ye. Our families were practically neighbors. I am James Paterson from Dumfriesshire, and this is me ten-year-old son, James. We live up the road a piece in Billerica. We'd be pleased to take ye home with us. Jump up. I'll make a space for young James in the back."

In less than an hour and a half that it took to reach North Billerica, Mr. Paterson explained that they occasionally came down to Cambridge to see his in-laws, the Stevensons. They said they nearly always picked up supplies when there.

It turns out James Paterson fought against Lord Cromwell's forces during the Battle of Worcester, was captured, and sold into bondage. He was among prisoners who sailed on the *John and Mary*, arriving in Boston in May 1652 when he was nineteen years old. A blacksmith by trade, James found his contract bought by Andrew Stevenson, a Cambridge merchant.

By 1658, James received a grant of land from the town of Billerica. Over the next twenty-seven years, he received sixteen land grants from the town.

James married Andrew Stevenson's daughter, Rebecca, nineteen, in 1662. Eight children followed over the next twenty-one years. Tragically, young James was killed in an accident while hunting with his father and an uncle outside Billerica very shortly after John Levistone met him.

The Paterson's house was one of twelve garrisons formed in Billerica during the King Philip War. James participated in the fighting to quell the Native uprising.

A period of uneasy peace lasted from the end of the actual fighting during King Philip's War in 1677 to 1691, after the start of King William's War, also known as the Second Indian War. Four residents died in an attack in nearby Dunstable on the first of September.

The following August, two households suffered Billerica's first massacre. Johanna Dutton, thirty-six, whose husband, John, died of smallpox in 1690, lost her life along with children Mary, sixteen, and Benoni, two. Five of her children survived. Her neighbor, Ann Shed, also thirty-six, was killed along with daughters Hannah, thirteen, and Agnes, two. She left her husband, Zechariah, with four boys.

In the late 1650s, a mysterious man arrived in Billerica. Although Thomas Carrier kept to himself, the man was hard to miss. He dressed neatly, appeared to be quite learned, and seemed financially secure. And he stood 7 feet, 4 inches tall.

Thomas Morgan was born in Wales in 1626. He served in the Royal Army and belonged to the bodyguard of King Charles I of England. Rumors circulated that he was one of two regicides who stood on the scaffold before Whitehall in London and executed King Charles I in January 1649. By 1655, he had arrived in Cambridge, Massachusetts, under the assumed name of Thomas Carrier and, shortly thereafter, in Billerica.

Research suggested that rumors reaching Massachusetts about his possible background may well have been accurate. The inferences of such a scenario might have scared town leaders enough to vanquish the man.

Mr. Carrier married Martha Allen from nearby Andover in Billerica on March 4, 1674, after she had named him as the father of the baby she carried. Richard Carrier was born four months later.

To the surprise of the townspeople, in 1676, the Billerica selectmen told the Carriers to leave town immediately or pay twenty shillings a week. Smallpox circulated through various New England communities at the time, but there was no sickness in the Carrier household. The reason for the dismissal remained a secret for a time.

The Carriers moved to North Billerica. The next year, when John Levistone showed up at the Paterson's house, Mr. Carrier went to his new neighbor and told him that he could use assistance on his property. He asked permission to talk to the new, young Scottish arrival.

John appreciated the opportunity for immediate employment and accepted the offer.

Annually, the town of Billerica summoned squadrons of men to cut brush along its highways. It was one of the first services that John helped his new employer perform.

The Carriers moved to Martha's hometown of Andover by 1685. Smallpox soon afflicted the family, and authorities again encouraged them to leave. Mistress Carrier refused. She stayed to nurse several members of the immediate and extended family who were sick.

Martha Carrier exhibited bold independence. She was outspoken and argumentative. She was the perfect target when the witch hunt intensified in northeast Massachusetts. She became the first person in Andover to be charged as a witch. To her horror, two of her sons were arrested and tortured until they agreed to testify against her. Her eight-year-old daughter was also taken into custody and coerced to take the stand against her.

On August 19, 1692, the defiant woman shouted her innocence from the gallows before being hung, along with four accused men in Salem.

People who lived in North Billerica lived within striking distance of each other and grew close quickly. They depended on the cooperative, neighborly spirit that James Paterson first extended to John Levistone before he even knew him.

John soon discovered that Thomas Ross, from Scotland, had also been a prisoner after the Battle of Worcester, indentured to the Americas. The Rosses and the Patersons became good friends. The men often compared notes of their survival. The details fascinated John. So much death. So much suffering before their arrival. And yet, here they were. Building families and new lives. He considered it an amazing story.

The first time John saw fourteen-year-old Margaret Ross when her father invited him to supper one night not long after they met at the Paterson's house, he knew he could not show what he felt. She was the oldest of three but already assumed much responsibility around the house, and she acted like it.

She had big, brown, sparkly eyes and thick, naturally wavy light brown hair that fell past her shoulders. Her simple cotton dress with a light shawl loosely tied over it did not particularly show off her splendid figure, but neither did it hide it. He focused on looking at her face. But not too often that first evening.

As the meal of fricassee of chicken served over dumplings, with small onions, and biscuits with currant jelly progressed, he realized that Margaret's sense of humor mirrored that of her mother. In fact, there was a lightness in this household that helped him relax.

Finding yet another Scottish family, hearing his Native Lowland dialect, made him sense that fate had directed him into the arms of his future family.

John and Margaret married in the early spring of 1681. Margaret's father gave them twenty acres of his property. John had plenty of help building a house and barn and clearing the property to begin farming operations.

Thomas Carrier sold the Levistone's ten acres of his property when he and Martha left Billerica.

The beloved grandfather of the six Levistone children passed away from consumption on March 20, 1694. Even though Thomas and Seeth Ross lived close to their daughter's family, John decided to add a room to their house and move his mother-in-law in with them because of insecurity over continued Indian threats.

On a sunny Monday afternoon, August 5, 1695, devastation reigned upon the Levistone household and their close neighbors.

John III, ten, had gone from North Billerica down to Billerica a couple of nights previously to stay with his friend, Sam Ruggles, also ten. The boys met the previous fall at a town picnic after the harvest and quickly bonded. Young Sam sometimes came to Billerica with his mother, Martha Ruggles, and an escort from Boston to stay with his maternal grandparents, the Reverend John and Mercy Woodbridge.

Mercy Woodbridge was the daughter of Thomas Dudley, who served for several terms as governor of the Massachusetts Bay

Colony. Her sister, Anne Bradstreet, became the first notable American poet and the first woman to be published in Colonial America.

That Monday around noon, John took Margaret to Billerica to run a few errands and to collect their son, John, at the Woodbridge home. He figured she would like a break from the younger children who were home with their grandmother.

Early afternoon, a group of Indians on horseback quietly crossed the Concord River, which ran through North Billerica. They first entered the house of John Rogers I, fifty-three, a neighbor of the Levistones. After working in his field, Mr. Rogers was taking a nap when an arrow entered his neck. He immediately sat up and pulled out the arrow but died within minutes from blood loss. His brother, Thomas I, forty-nine, and his son, Thomas II, eleven, also died in the attack. The oldest of Mr. Rogers' sons, Daniel, twelve, and his sister, Mercy, ten, were both kidnapped.

A neighbor woman, who was in the room at the time, jumped out of a window, hid under some flags, and managed to survive. Another woman who lived nearby survived several years after being scalped.

Seeth Ross was in the house with the door cracked, holding her two-month-old youngest grandchild, Alex, who became fussy because his mother was not back. Four-year-old Mary and two-year-old Margaret kept themselves occupied with strips of fabric their grandmother kept in a basket. Sarah, ten, sat at the dining table, shelling beans.

Suddenly, one of the seven-year-old twin boys, who were both outside in front of the house, let out a high-pitched scream that was almost immediately muted. It took Seeth's breath. She barely had time to stand before the door slammed open, and two Natives, one with a blood-soaked tomahawk and the other with blood dripping from a hunting knife clenched in his right hand filled the room.

Seeth knew she was taking her last breaths. Paralyzed with fear, she figured Seth and Thomas surely lay dead in the yard. She clutched the now squalling infant to her breast and silently prayed, "God, have mercy on us all."

Suddenly, she heard a gunshot. Sarah had cocked the pistol that lay on a chair beside her and, somehow, in the same moment, stood, raised the gun, and shot at one of the invaders. The bullet grazed his left arm.

The Indians spoke a few words. One walked over to the young girl, restrained her, secured her arms behind her, and led her outside. Another entered the house, grabbed tiny Alex out of his grandmother's arms, and bashed his head against the wall. Little Mary screamed. She immediately lost her scalp.

At that, Seeth found her voice. Whimpering, little Margaret reached for her grandmother's hand.

"Take me. Don kill this wee lass. Let her live. I beg ye."

As the savage walked behind Seeth, she uttered, "Chruthaich Dia mi." He then cut her throat and took her scalp. Finally, he collected the last child's scalp.

They then proceeded to the house of Mary Toothaker, a sister of Martha Carrier. Her husband, Dr. Roger Toothaker, fifty-eight, died of natural causes in the Boston Gaol in June 1692 while awaiting trial for witchcraft.

Mary lost her life in the North Billerica assault. Her daughter, Margaret, twelve, became a captive, and, like Daniel and Mercy Rogers and Sarah Levistone, she was never seen or heard from again.

The surprise daytime attack stunned Billerica and the surrounding area for weeks. The killers stealthily left the area as quickly as they came. A rescue could not be organized quickly enough.

Lieutenant Colonel Joseph Lynde of Charlestown was commissioned to pursue the enemy. In a report dated August 23,

1695, he stated that he found about 300 men in arms from Woburn, Reading, Malden, Medford, Charlestown, Cambridge, and Watertown collected at Billerica. Despite marching up to where the Merrimack River meets the Concord River, guarding the fords between Andover and Chelmsford, and trudging through the Great Swamp north of Billerica, they saw hide nor hair that led them to identify what tribe committed the atrocities.

On September 11, 1697, the Treaty of Ryswick was signed, officially ending King Williams's War. There was no peace. Five years passed, and Queen Anne's War broke out, a conflict characterized again by frequent Indian raids resulting in many deaths of Massachusetts colonists.

Margaret and John Levistone added four more children to their household over the next seven years. On February 14, 1705, their six-year-old daughter, Hannah, choked on a chicken bone and died. Her mother went into a debilitating depression. On June 16, Margaret, forty-two, did not wake up. Her husband always claimed she died of a broken heart.

Just before Thanksgiving, John married Eunice Shed, forty-one, youngest daughter of Daniel II and Mary Gurney Shed, an English immigrant, who raised ten children to maturity. The Sheds were one of eight families from Braintree, which acquired a land grant in May 1655 when Billerica incorporated.

Eunice's oldest sister, Mary, had been married to John Rogers, the Levistone's neighbor, who was the first to die in the 1995 Indian attack on Billerica. The Roger's oldest daughter, Mary Jr., twenty-seven, was captured and vanished. Another daughter, Sarah, married Roger Toothaker Jr., the only son of Dr. Roger and Mary Allen Toothaker, who were caught up in the Salem witch trials.

Zechariah Shed, Eunice's brother, had been married to Ann Bray Shed when she and their two daughters were murdered in the first Indian attack on Billerica in 1692.

John and Eunice got precious little time to enjoy life together. Between the absurdity of the witch hunt the preceding decade, what seemed a never-ending threat of violence from Natives kept stirred up by both the English and French, and sudden responsibility for three growing children, Eunice's anxiety mounted after her marriage. On June 16, 1709, while she was visiting a sister in Chelmsford, Eunice Levistone suddenly passed away from what was suspected as apoplexy.

Although both the Levistone and Shed families suffered immeasurable losses over the years, a bright spot shown on the horizon. John Levistone III and Ruth Shed, daughter of Daniel Shed III and Ruth Moore Shed, held a marriage ceremony on the Shed's property in late September 1709. Many Shed family members and friends gathered to celebrate.

A second parent missed the occasion. Daniel Shed III died of smallpox on Christmas Eve, 1690, at the age of forty-one. The disease had claimed his three-year-old daughter the previous day.

Eunice Levistone, born in May 1719, was the second of three daughters born to John and Ruth. Through her brother, Daniel, who, in 1736, at age twenty, went just north to Lowell to work on a logging crew, Eunice met Ephrain Hall. The Halls had fairly recently moved from Bradford to Dracut on the north edge of Lowell, so father, Richard could lend his expertise on the construction of mills along the Merrimack River.

Eunice and Ephrain married in Tewksbury in May 1738, a convenient meeting point intersecting North Billerica, Drucut, and Andover, where Ephrain's mother's people were.

Two children of Eunice and Ephrain Hall, Ephrain Jr., and Martha, ended up with children who married each other in 1798. Phineas and Patty Cheever Hall were both born and died in Dracut.

Phineas' maternal grandfather, Captain Stephen Russell led Phineas' father, Private. Ephraim Hall Sr, in the same company of Minutemen as they marched and fought for the relief of Boston in the Lexington Alarm, April 19, 1775. It was the first battle of the Revolutionary War.

Patty Hall was the great-granddaughter of Ezekiel Cheever Jr., infamous for his role in the 1692-93 Salem witch trials. She lived to be ninety-eight years old.

Patty and Phineas Hall's great-granddaughter was Alice Gage Currier, who wed Edson W. White in Wakefield in 1884.

The Scots brought their resiliency across the ocean to the fledgling new country to become among the most persistent in putting down roots. Whether they arrived as indentured servants or free men, they quickly demonstrated a fierce determination to fight the odds and endure tragedy in helping to build these United States.

A Wild Place Full of Danger

Lothrop/Cheever (White)

Nine-year-old Ellen Lothrop quietly sat in a chair by a window in her father's dining room. She sensed her life might be influenced by the discussion taking place.

Seated at the table was the girl's father, Mark Lothrop Sr., thirty-six, and his oldest son, Thomas, twenty, along with Mark's brother, Reverend John Lothrop Sr., forty-nine, and his four older children, including Thomas, twenty-one, Jane, nineteen, John Jr., sixteen, and Barbara, fourteen. His two younger children, Joseph, nine, and Benjamin, seven, joined their cousin Ellen, sitting against the wall.

The Lothrops descended from the central Yorkshire County gentry. Mark's great-grandfather, Sir John Lowthroppe, born in 1480, possessed extensive landed estates in both Cherry Burton and other parts of the county. Mark Lothrop raised his children in a valley just south of Cherry Burton on a portion of this land.

The family recently faced a crisis, starting with the death of Mark Sr's wife, Mary, immediately after the birth of their last son, Mark Jr., in 1630. Two years later, Reverend John, a Separatist preacher in London, was arrested. In February 1633, just three months prior to this family meeting in his brother Mark's home, Hannah Lothrop, thirty-eight, John's wife, died of a malignant fever.

Reverend John Lothrop and other Separatists operated as a religious minority in England. Protestants forming independent local churches, separate from the Church of England, did so at their peril. Their desire for freedom of religion, the right and responsibility of each congregation to determine its own affairs without having to submit those decisions to the judgment of any higher human authority, set the stage for persecution.

Reverend John ministered in an English church for a number of years after obtaining an education at Queens College, Cambridge, with an M.A. in 1609. He received an invitation to join the Independents and to preach in the First Independent Church in London in 1623. Shortly thereafter, King Charles I harassed the Separatists into hiding.

Reverend John was arrested by the king's officers, along with twenty-three of his congregants, at a private meeting at Southwark in the summer of 1632. Eighteen members of their group managed to escape. Apparently, some of those arrested were housed in Clink Prison, others in Newgate Prison. The public sided with the much-respected reverend, especially after his wife died. People considered those imprisoned to be martyrs.

Not only did Reverend John find himself separated from his family when he was jailed, but the Crown confiscated his property. Hannah took their five youngest children up to Yorkshire County to live with family. Thomas and Jane were welcomed into a friend's home in London so they could closely monitor developments with the religious nonconformists in prison. Thomas found abysmal conditions on a couple of occasions, but he managed to see his father.

Thomas and Jane traveled to their Uncle Mark's home in May 1633 with news of the impending release of their father. Word circulated that the Separatist prisoners would be offered their freedom in exchange for an agreement to leave the country. Before her death, Hannah and John had discussed the possibility of taking their family to America. If this offer, in fact, became a reality, there was no doubt the move would now happen. Even without their mother, the children were mature enough. They would make it work.

Unbeknownst to all seated in Mark Lothrop's dining room that day, other than his father and sister, someone else planned to walk onto American shores first.

Thomas, Mark's son, thought he might burst with excitement at his cousin's news. "I cannot wait another second to share this with ye," he almost shouted.

"I, or rather Father, booked passage on the *James* sailing out of Gravesend to Salem on the coast of the Colony Massachusetts in mid-August. We have your father to thank for Captain Wiggin accepting us as passengers. How thrilling to know I may have family coming soon as well."

At that, young Ellen jumped up and emitted a loud squeal. Every head in the room turned to look at the beaming girl. "Aye, and he's taking me with him!"

Her father threw back his head and laughed out loud at his daughter's exuberance. "Indeed, he is, me miting."

"But Uncle, ye are not leaving with your children," asked Jane. "It will just be Thomas and Ellen?"

"We have discussed this since their mum's death. I cannot depart with wee Mark, nor could I survive the journey with my acute seasickness. I suspect that we, in this country, might very well face a civil war in the near future. I don want my children living in the midst of such horror. The New World offers a clean slate and freedom to be who ye want to become. Yes, 'tis a wild place full of danger, but Thomas is smart, strong, talented . . . brave. He will do well there. And me Ellen has a resilient spirit and strong faith she inherited from her mum. What Psalm do ye like so much, daughter?"

"Psalms are full of wise advice," Ellen said, "but I especially like, 'Trust in the Lord forever, for in God the Lord, we have an everlasting Rock.'"

"Amen to that," Jane said.

Captain Thomas Wiggin, of Warwickshire, was twenty-nine years old when he arrived among nearly 1,000 passengers on a fleet of eleven ships leaving Southampton and arriving on the New England coast in May and June 1630. Organized by John Winthrop in response to ongoing internal conflict in England in the early decades of the seventeenth century, migration became a desirable option for many since there had been preliminary exploration and settlement of the coast.

Many of these new arrivals were Puritans from Boston, England. The religious reform movement began in England in the late 1500s. They opposed Catholicism and thought the Church of England, too, conducted practices and performed ceremonies not rooted in the Bible. These families believed they had a binding contract with God to enact reforms designed to align their lives with His will. The more radical among them claimed autonomy for their individual congregations, as did Reverend John Lothrop. As the movement gained popularity, new professional classes realized it corresponded with their growing discontent with economic restraints being imposed.

Reverend Lothrop was among those men with a Cambridge degree who became dynamic speakers versed in reform theology. They brought the wrath of the Archbishop of Canterbury upon them and ultimately the ire of the king.

Once they landed in America, The Winthrop Fleet first settled in Charlestown, located on the Shawmut Peninsula between the Mystic and Charles rivers, near what would become Boston, Massachusetts. Over 200 died in the first eight months.

Known first as the Massachusetts Bay Company, it had been granted a charter by King Charles I on March 4, 1629, to officially engage in trade in New England. Soon after arrival, the company renamed itself the Massachusetts Bay Colony and determined to establish a self-governing religious commonwealth. Leaders envisioned a "City of God in the wilderness." They wasted no time inviting hundreds of other colonists from their homeland.

A year after his arrival, Thomas Wiggin settled in what would become Stratham, New Hampshire. The proprietors of the Upper or Dover Plantation appointed the young man as governor of the plantation. He became a landowner and close ally of Governor John Winthrop of the neighboring Massachusetts Bay Colony. In 1632, he ventured back to England, announcing that he planned to return the following year to transport a shipload of colonists to America.

While in prison, Reverend John Lothrop stayed advised of ships transporting immigrants to Massachusetts. He contacted his family in Yorkshire when he heard that the *James* would set sail the following summer twenty miles east of London on the south bank of the Thames Estuary in Gravesend, a maritime town on the English Channel. His brother, Mark, quickly replied saying he wanted passage for two.

Shortly after Christmas, Mark traveled to London to visit Thomas and Jane and managed to see their father in prison. Then, he met with Captain Wiggin's London contact and paid the fee for his two children to sail West.

With a mostly heavy heart, Mark Lothrop took his Thomas and Ellen to London on Tuesday, August 17, 1633. The following day, they rode over to Gravesend. Mark wanted to meet Captain Wiggin and properly introduce his children. At mid-morning the next day, after watching horses, cattle, goats, various provisions, and over ninety passengers board the relatively small but sturdy ship, he stood transfixed as his two older children slipped out of sight under what would be a full moon that night.

"Lord, may Your grace be sufficient to protect them," he silently prayed.

After a relatively smooth voyage, Thomas thankfully spied the Massachusetts coast just after noon on Monday, October 10th.

They pulled into what would become a significant seaport north of Boston and Massachusetts Bay. Located at the mouth of the Naumkeag River, Salem had been settled seven years earlier. It was now part of the Massachusetts Bay Colony.

The Lothrops were among sixty passengers who stayed in Salem. Captain Wiggin and the other thirty or so sailed up the coast to Hilton Point, where they started a new settlement. It became known as Dover, New Hampshire.

Young Thomas wasted no time integrating himself into the developing Town of Salem. On May 14, 1634, he was admitted as a free man. Around the same time, he was admitted by other Puritans to the First Church of Salem. Before the construction of the church the following year, members gathered in a building near Town House Square. It would become one of the oldest continuing Protestant churches in North America.

Coming from a family of landowners across the ocean, Thomas ingratiated himself with leaders who owned property and offered his services to learn needed skills, including farming and construction. He made friends with a few local fishermen, some also in their twenties, who persuaded him to go out with them during mackerel season that first summer. He never imagined such a seafood bounty in one place.

Thomas's family wrote to advise him that Uncle John obtained his release from prison. He agreed to leave England permanently with his family and as many congregation members as he could take, who had refused to accept the authority of the Church of England. Reverend John Lothrop and six of his seven children would leave the country on August 1, 1634. Traveling on the *Griffin* with about one hundred other passengers and cattle for the plantations, they expected to arrive in Boston in mid-September.

Once there, the Lothrop family planned to head south along the coast to Plymouth. Instead, they stopped about halfway in Scituate [sit-choo-it], bordered by Massachusetts Bay. To their surprise, nine other families from London and Kent, most of whom they knew, preceded them and had constructed homes. In fact, they prepared the way for Reverend Lothrop to join them.

In 1855, Amos Otis wrote the following testimony of Reverend Lothrop in *Scituate and Barnstable Church Records*:

"The kindly reception which was extended to him, and the cordial welcome with which he was greeted, were most gratifying to his feelings, and he resolved that Scituate should be his future home—the fold into which he would gather together the estrays of his scattered flocks. His grateful heart believed that the hand of God had opened this door for him; had at last given him a resting place from his tolls. Here, protected from the law, he could build up church institutions, and here he and his family could dwell together in peace, surrounded by the loving friends of his youth."

Families of Scituate formed a covenant to develop a Church of Christ. Word reached back home of the Lothrop's arrival. Soon, a new immigration group, many of whom were from Kent County, joined the population. In January 1635, Reverend Lothrop was formally selected as minister of the settlement.

A month later, Reverend Lothrop married Anna Hammond Dimmick, a thirty-one-year-old widow whose husband drowned two years previously after getting tangled in his fishing net. In June of the following year, a son, Barnabas, came along, the first of six children born to the couple.

When the reverend first agreed to settle his family in Scituate and lead the ministry, the court granted him a farm southeast of Coleman Hills. Their young children loved being in the country, on the sea. They picked wild blueberries in the hills and plums on the beach. The family's minimal house sat between the New Harbor Marshes and the North River. The young Lothrops went to the river's flats in the spring with their father to fish the shallows, where striped bass and bluefish got trapped as the tide rapidly changed.

More than a handful of worshipers were welcomed into the fold at Scituate after being dismissed by other churches. Reverend Lothrop's commitment to freedom of religion and his sacrifices to humbly bring the word of God to the people preceded him.

Yet, strife developed in the Scituate church. Within five years of his family's arrival, the reverend realized the time had come to move on. An unresolvable conflict on the question of baptism had developed between him and some of the other congregants.

On October 11, 1639, after heading south with crops needed to sustain them through the winter, the Lothrops and a large contingent of their followers arrived in Barnstable. They settled in the shelter of Barnstable Harbor. The narrow peninsula of Sandy Neck protects the harbor from Cape Cod Bay. On the other side of the Cape, to the south, lays Nantucket Sound.

Ten days after arriving with no house of prayer and in the midst of building crude pioneer houses of their own to shelter against approaching bitter cold, the people gave a day to fasting, humiliation, and prayer. As Reverend Lothrop was quoted to say, "For the grace of God to settle us here in church estate and to unite us together in holy walking, and make us faithful in keeping covenant with God and with one another."

On November 8, 1653, Reverend Lothrop passed away of an undetermined cause at sixty-nine. Five of his children stayed in Barnstable with families all their lives. His wife, Anna, found happiness in a third marriage with a member of their congregation and died in her sleep at ninety in the spring of 1694.

❦ ❦ ❦

Thomas and his sister, Ellen Lothrop, lived on a strip of land between Collins Cove off Beverly Harbor and the North River, just north of Salem. Within a couple of years, a portion of the population of the town began moving in that direction to interior lands. At the time, the area had no separate identity from the Town of Salem, but residents started referring to their little community as Salem Farms. Members of the community wanted greater freedom from the town in regard to their personal interests. The town resisted. When Salem Farms petitioned for autonomy in the mid-1660s, the Town of Salem refused to grant the request.

The people of Salem Farms changed its name to Salem Village. Because of the five-mile distance to the church in the Town of Salem, the general court agreed that the village should have its own minister. No action was taken for three years. Meanwhile, the town levied a special tax to construct a new church. Residents of the village refused to pay the tax until the court agreed to share the monies when the new church was constructed.

Thomas Lothrop was among the tax payers supporting the new parish in Salem Village. He quickly became a trusted servant of the community, representing their affairs in the general court. Thomas provided a voice of reason in a time of increasing political instability and rigid societal norms that seemed to clash with what many sought when they came to the New World.

When young Thomas became a member of the First Church of Salem in 1634, he unknowingly met his future in-laws, Daniel and Bethiah Rea, who immigrated from Suffolk County, England, in 1630. Their youngest of three children, Bethiah, four, would become his wife eighteen years later.

Thomas first participated in military service in 1636 during the Pequot-Indian War in Southern New England. He was horrified at the brutality exhibited by both sides. His eyes opened to the danger that dwelled beyond the trees. It became clear to him that the Natives would not voluntarily accept concessions. They were great warriors who would fight to the death to keep the white settlers right where they were with their backs to the sea. He reckoned that when all new or occupied lands were first explored or invaded throughout history, battles with predecessors must have ensued. Sacrifice in claiming land came colored in red.

Prior to King Philip's War in the summer of 1675, tension fluctuated between several Native New England tribes and the increasing colonial population. In general, relations remained tolerably peaceful. Massasoit, the sachem of the Wampanoag Confederacy, formed an alliance with settlers at Plymouth Colony for protection against the Narragansetts.

Wamsutta, known as Alexander by the colonists, succeeded his father for one year in 1661 before his own death. Then, his brother, Matacomet, called Philip, became the grand sachem of the Wampanoag Confederacy. He did not trust the white settlers. He conspired with other Algonquian tribes who spoke the same language against the Plymouth colonists encroaching on their lands.

At the time, there were more than a hundred towns in New England with about 16,000 men of military age. Those who were neither too old, too young, disabled, or clergy were expected to volunteer for local militias and supply their own arms. Many towns constructed secure garrison houses. Others built stockades around the houses for defense as hostile action by Indians escalated.

Thomas quickly rose through the ranks as a soldier. His difficult assignments put him in dangerous positions fighting both the Natives and the French. On May 14, 1645, he was promoted to sergeant of the Company of Salem and Lynn. He was then commissioned lieutenant of the Salem Company on May 6, 1646. After receiving a commission as captain, he participated in a successful expedition in 1654-55 in Acadia at St. Johns and Port Royal against the French. On July 7, 1662, he served as captain of the Foot Company on Cape Ann.

By September 1675, King Philip's War centered along the Connecticut River Valley. On the first of the month, Natives burned the town of Deerfield, Massachusetts, and killed one resident. Two days later, in Squakeag, later called Northfield, ten settlers were killed in an attack. The next day, Captain Beers marched with his company from Hadley to relieve the garrison at Squakeag. They did not know of the attack the previous day. Captain Beers and thirty-six of his men lost their lives in a second ambush. Several of their heads were displayed on poles along the road.

Captain Thomas Lothrop, then sixty-two, commanded a company of about a hundred soldiers, mainly from around his home area in Essex County, some from Boston and vicinity. His company had joined forces with that of Captain Beers until Captain Beers marched from Hadley on the 3rd.

On Sunday the 15th, twenty-two soldiers passing from one garrison to another were attacked by Indians. None died in the assault, but one was kidnapped. Warriors burned two houses, stole several horses packed with beef and pork, and killed several other horses. Upon receiving the news, soldiers from Northampton joined others from Hadley, along with some of Captain Lothrop's company. They pursued the transgressors who were reported to be on a hill in a large Deerfield meadow. But the Natives had fled.

Although Deerfield was then vacated, crops had been gathered. About 3,000 bushels of corn were loaded on eighteen wagons, with ox teams and drivers provided. Captain Lothrop and his company volunteered to guard the procession on the fourteen-mile trip to Hadley, where the crop would be stored.

The group left on the morning of September 18. They were not on high alert. No Indians were known to be in the immediate area. Captain Mosely and his company rode a distance behind, scouting for signs of danger. About five miles out of Deerfield, the train of wagons proceeded to cross what was then known as Muddy Creek. Most of the soldiers had already crossed the creek and waited on the remaining lumbering wagons. A few put their rifles up on wagons and picked wild grapes along the road.

Suddenly, they fell under a hail of bullets from hundreds of the enemy, who had quietly managed to almost encircle them. Many dropped in the first volley. Captain Lothrop and more than forty of his troops died in the massacre. Captain Mosely lost eleven of his men when they approached the scene. Eighteen teamsters were slain, and only seven escaped.

A pall fell over Massachusetts Bay Colony. Terror swept through the region as nearly every village and town lost at least one man to the savagery.

A single burial plot contains the bodies of all those killed in what became known as the Battle of Bloody Brook.

Settlements and towns all over New England, including those in Maine and Acadia, continued to be raided by various tribes supporting Metacomet's campaign to retaliate against the colonists for major concessions forced on the Wampanoag. The Indians had been humiliated by the demands made by those encroaching on their lands.

On August 12, 1676, at Mount Hope in Bristol, Rhode Island, Metacomet was finally shot and killed by John Alderman, a Native. His corpse was then beheaded, drawn, and quartered. His head was later displayed in Plymouth for many decades. King Philip's War did not officially end until the Treaty of Casco was signed in 1678 to end fighting in the northern theater.

The war devastated New England just as it struggled to get a foothold. An estimated 2,500 white settlers lost their lives. Around 2,000 Indians died in battle. Another 3,000 were thought to have perished from sickness or disease. Approximately 1,000 more found themselves sold into slavery in the Caribbean Islands.

✐ ✐ ✐

After nineteen years living in the colonies, Ellen Lothrop, twenty-seven, moved from her brother's house within sight of Collins

Cove in Beverly to Ipswich in November 1652. She had just married the respected schoolmaster and occasional preacher, Ezekiel Cheever. The two met the previous year when he came down to the First Church of Salem, where the Lothrops were in attendance.

Mr. Cheever's first wife died in 1649 and left him with five children. The following year, he moved his children from New Haven, Connecticut, where he had spent the past twelve years teaching and serving as one of twelve foundation members of its church, to Ipswich.

Ellen did not think him handsome. But his kindness to her made up for it. He was greatly respected for his intellectual insights. Although he was by no means well off, she believed his strong faith would provide them with the security needed to raise a family in a world that seemed less certain every day.

Mr. Cheever became headmaster when he agreed to establish a grammar school in the town of Ipswich, which lies twelve miles north of Salem. It sits on the Ipswich River and includes the southern end of Plum Island. Two years later, at age thirty-eight, he brought his new wife to this more northern end of Essex County. Ellen settled into their home fronting the Ipswich River.

In October 1653, their first of five children, Abigail, was born. Ellen had not lived in a house with children since she left her three-year-old brother, Mark, in England with their father. Brother Thomas and his wife, Bethiah, produced no children. She had no choice but to adjust to motherhood quickly. It helped greatly that Mr. Cheever, which is what she always called her husband, worked around children every day. She spent the colder months upstairs entertaining their younger children during the day.

Shortly after the Cheevers moved in, Ava Digby, a neighbor two doors down, stopped in one late afternoon with a generous pot of corned beef and cabbage carried by her sixteen-year-old son,

Farrell. The following day, they returned to visit along with Farrell's twin sister, Frances.

Ellen discovered that Ava came from Dunbar on the southeast coast of Scotland. Her father, Leslie Gibb, worked with his two brothers as a fisherman out of Cromwell Harbor. They did better than many, eventually buying two boats. Ava met Charles Digby, an English silversmith from Newcastle in Northumberland, about ninety miles down the coast in 1629. Her father, also an artist, had always drawn pictures of what he found in and around the sea. He and Charles Immediately liked each other.

Charles felt uneasy with the political unrest in England and looked toward America. He and Ava decided to marry and immigrate as soon as possible, along with Mr. Gibb, who by then was a widower. In September 1632, they sailed into Boston Harbor.

The following spring, they choose to locate in Ipswich, away from an area the size of Boston. Charles assumed a growing population wanted locally crafted silver objects for everyday use. Ipswich put them on the coast and was close enough to Salem and several smaller towns for the distribution of his product.

The area teamed with marine life. Mr. Gibb bought a quantity of paper, pencils, pens, and ink in Boston in much anticipation of drawing what he would find in and around the water on this side of the Atlantic. He carefully bound his large collection of drawings. As the four Digby children were born over the next few years, their granda anticipated his role in their education. During the long, cold winter months, he showed his grandchildren each print, explained what was illustrated, shared details about its life, and had them memorize the information. When the ice melted, they headed outdoors and found every species of bird, fish, arthropod, mammal, amphibian, and reptile in his collection.

Both Farrell and Frances, as well as their older brother and sister, thought they were the luckiest children in the world to have grown up under their granda's wing learning all about Mother Nature's bounty. Now, the twins offered to take that same information and share it with the Cheever children.

Ellen felt like pinching herself when the younger Digbys made their offer. She looked at their mother, who smiled and nodded.

"I feel like it's Christmas," said Ellen. "You two are offering to take part of our brood into this wonderful environment and teach them all about what lives here? May I come too?"

"Of course," laughed Frances. "We both want to pass along Granda's legacy of teaching and believe this would be a wonderful start."

"Sometimes, one or the other of us will be with them. Sometimes both will go depending on where we go and what we plan to do that day," explained Ferrell.

As the weather thawed in early spring, Ellen, several of her children, and the Digbys happily began their quest outdoors. Songbirds in the meadows, such as bobolinks, Eastern bluebirds, and Baltimore orioles, gripped small branches. Each offered unique calls or songs. Wading birds in the marshes, such as ibis, egrets, and herons with long, thin legs, probed the soft sediments for prey with their long bills. The children also discovered frogs and various kinds of snakes in the marsh. They spotted big predatory birds, like the osprey and hawks, and occasionally a bald eagle, with their hooked beaks and sharp "claws," as the children called them, looking to feed on mice, reptiles, and fish. If they went out early enough in the spring, they sighted ducks, loons, and grebes. On the shore, there were always terns, gulls, and sandpipers. Sometimes, they saw purple sandpipers on the rocky shore, along with seals. They never tired of watching dolphins play in the water and were thrilled to see whales not far offshore. Occasionally, sea rays and jellyfish washed up. Now and then, they examined a dead shark that rolled in with the tide. They found sea stars, sea urchins, crabs, and shrimp in tidal pools.

Sometimes, they ventured onto Plum Island, where dunes were covered with wild beach plum thickets, bogs, a freshwater marsh, shrubs, and a forest to explore. The mainland was mostly grassland laced with tidal creeks and mud flats filled with shellfish.

Right at their back door, they caught bream/bluegill, crappie, perch, pickerel, and other freshwater fish from the riverbank for supper. Perhaps their favorite activity was digging clams in the mud in the salt marshes along the Ipswich River.

The family reluctantly left Ipswich and moved down to Charlestown in November 1661, where their husband and father accepted another teaching assignment. Nine years later, they crossed Boston Harbor, where Mr. Cheever then spent thirty-eight years as headmaster of the Boston Latin School. The school became a highly regarded classical academy under his tutelage. Several of his students became respected politicians, ministers, businessmen, and educators in their own right.

When Mr. Cheever taught in New Haven, beginning in 1638 and through most of 1650, he wrote the acclaimed *Accidence, A Short Introduction to the Latin Tongue*. Published in 1650, it is considered the earliest American school book and became the standard Latin textbook throughout colonial New England. Twenty editions of the book appeared by 1785 with another republished in 1838.

Most years, regardless of where the family lived, the largest room downstairs of their various homes became a classroom. Mr. Cheever taught Latin, writing, and arithmetic. His teaching style could hardly be called progressive. He kept a basket of hickory sticks by his desk, which he used on his students often enough to maintain control and encourage greater effort. To the relief of the children, their teacher hated periwigs. Most Puritans believed the highly styled wigs being popularized and imported from Europe detracted from focusing on God's will. Mr. Cheever wore a black skull cap instead.

Ezekiel Cheever Jr. arrived on July 1, 1655, the second child of Ellen and Ezekiel Cheever. In the early 1670s, young Ezekiel moved to Salem, where he established himself as a respectable tailor. Soon, he connected with town leaders. In 1678, he was among the primary signers of the Salem troop of commissioned officers.

Ezekiel Jr. met Abigail Leffingwell at a late spring wedding in 1679 when they were both twenty-four. She and a brother rode the fifteen miles from Woburn to Salem to see one of their Benjamin cousins marry. Abigail came over two or three times a year to visit with this family. She continued these trips the following year but now added Ezekiel Cheever to her list of reasons to come. She thought he demonstrated a quick wit. He could hold his end of a conversation with anybody.

Abigail Leffingwell descended from the Benjamin family, who arrived during The Great Migration spirited by John Winthrop. John Benjamin, her maternal grandfather, developed a close friendship with Mr. Winthrop when they attended Cambridge University together. Their families lived near each other in Heathfield, Sussex County, England.

Both men decided to flee to the New World when, in 1629, friends were being sent to prison under King Charles I. Committed English Presbyterians and other congregations that sought to become more independent faced immediate threat. Mr. Benjamin believed it was only a matter of time before a violation of religious liberty would result in the Crown dipping into his purse.

John Benjamin, his wife, Abigail Eddy Benjamin, and their four children were among 123 passengers, including fifty children, who sailed from London on the *Lyon* on June 22, 1632. They cast anchor in Boston Harbor on September 16. In November, John became a free man and settled his family in Newtown, which later became Cambridge, three miles inland from Boston. Unaccustomed to living on the sea, he sought a slight physical distance from the storms he knew blew in off the coast. He was one of the first to settle in Newtown. A year after arriving, the general court chose him as the town's chief executive officer.

Mr. Benjamin built a house on six acres of land. His friend, John Winthrop, then governor of the Massachusetts Bay Colony, who lived in Boston, described the home when he said, ". . . a mansion unsurpassed in elegance and comfort by all in the vicinity. It was the mansion of intelligence, refinement, religion, and hospitality."

Abigail shared what she considered unfortunate news with Ezekiel in March 1680. She was with a child. Somewhat to her surprise, he seemed delighted. She knew about his rather strict Puritan background. In fact, they lived in the heart of Puritan worship with what she considered their exaggerated emphasis on morality. There was right. There was wrong. And, in their minds, ne'er the twain shall meet. Sexual transgression outside of marriage, especially by a woman, was not to be tolerated.

They had already discussed marriage. Love bloomed almost from the first time they met. The development of a baby would push their timetable up, though.

Abigail knew who she must go to for advice. Her beloved grandmother and namesake, Abigail Benjamin, seventy-nine, now widowed for thirty-five years, lived in Charlestown. She was always there to walk her grandchildren through their problems. She could just hear her saying, "This too shall pass."

Two of Abigail's Salem cousins drove her down to Charlestown to see Grandmother Benjamin. She brought Ezekiel with her. The two women spent the better part of the next day alone in Grandmother Benjamin's spacious house, talking and eating a noon dinner of cod fish cakes, egg ring salad, and hot cross buns served by her cook.

"This man loves you. I see that," said her grandmother. "And his father has been a renowned educator in Boston for decades.

That bodes well for the intelligence and future success of your children.

"You certainly will not be able to marry in a church if you wait much longer. In three months, I don't know whether a dress will hide your secret."

"Yes, Grandmother, I know. And we don't care whether the ceremony is held in a church. We understand the condemnation we will surely face. I wish it were not so. I do understand we sinned in the eyes of God. I wish we had waited until after marriage too . . . procreate. Believe me, it was not planned. Neither of us meant to err. We should have been more vigilant."

"Ha! My dear girl that has been said millions of times by couples just like you. It is what makes you human. The Bible says: 'For all have sinned and fall short of the glory of God.' I have a secret of my own. No one else knows this. When I was eighteen, back in Sussex, your grandfather and I took a roll in a meadow one day. Mercifully, no baby resulted. But we were not married until the next year.

"Stiffen that spine of yours. Yes, you might hear ugly words spoken outside the family and maybe by some within the family. But never mind. Not one of those people, and I mean not a single one, fails to sin. None of them have any business throwing stones at you or anyone else.

"Now, you and your young man can jolly well wed in my yard. Look! There is more than ample space to entertain however many guests you choose to help you celebrate."

Grandmother Benjamin hosted the wedding on a lovely morning in mid-June. Abigail's father, Michael Leffingwell, accompanied nine of his eleven daughters, who came to see their sister married. Her cherished brother, Thomas, the only son in the family, arrived with his wife. Ezekiel Cheever Sr., on the other hand, struggled to come to terms with what he considered a serious lack of discretion in his son's decision to marry a woman conceiving a child before marriage, even if it was his own child.

"It shames our whole family," he said to his wife, Ellen. "They cannot keep this a secret."

"So you are a little concerned about our son, his Abigail, and our soon-to-be grandchild," Ellen responded. "You worry about public sentiment, what others might think. You accuse Ezekiel and Abigail of sin. Yet, need I remind you, husband, that pride is one of the Seven Deadly Sins."

"How dare you lecture me on morality!"

"I will be disobeying you, Mr. Cheever. If you cannot see your way to attend our eldest son's wedding, it will be your burden to bear. I am going to Charlestown along with my daughters Abby and Susanna. We will ride to Grandmother Benjamin's from here. Daughter Elizabeth and her husband, Samuel Goldthwaite, plan to sail around from Connecticut."

Young Ezekiel thought that when he brought his bride back to Salem, there might be a few rough spots for the first few months. But he was not worried long term. After all, Abigail came from a family that arrived early in New England and immediately began distinguishing themselves. Her grandfather knew Governor John Winthrop when they were young men in England, and they remained close friends all their lives. They were practically colonial royalty. Who would fault him for marrying well? Abigail would be a good wife and mother. He planned to distinguish himself through service, and all would be well.

The same year Ezekiel Jr. and Abigail married, a lawsuit over Thomas Lothrop's estate was settled. When he died intestate in the Battle of Bloody Brook in 1675, his wife, Bethiah, was appointed administrator of his estate. But Ezekiel Cheever Sr. petitioned that his wife, Ellen, the sister of Thomas, deserved a portion of the estate. In the end, Bethiah received the whole estate, "the use of the houses and lands was hers for life, then to revert to the wife of Mr. Ezekiel Cheever and her issue, heirs of Lothrop."

In 1684, Bethiah, Thomas Lothrop's widow, who had married William Goodhue Sr., deacon of First Church of Ipswich, two years previously, agreed to give the old Lothrop Farm in Salem Village to Ezekiel and Abigail Cheever. After bearing three children in rapid succession, the family's modest home in the Town of Salem became cramped and loud.

Ezekial became a charter member of the Salem Village Church in 1689. That same year, Reverend Samuel Parris accepted the vacated churches' ministry. In October, Ezekial traveled with Reverend Parris, as the church representative, along with other ministers and deacons, across the ocean to Cambridge University to discuss God's judgment for New England.

One of the most bizarre chapters in American history happened in northeast Massachusetts in 1692 into 1693. Ezekiel was inadvertently pulled into it because of his role in Reverend Parris's church and because he had been promoted as an official of the county court in Salem.

Many people quickly became disillusioned with Reverend Parris's overbearing disposition in Salem Village. There was already contention in the village before his arrival due to property line disputes, grazing rights, personal feuds, and church privileges. His evangelical enthusiasm, combined with what some described as "psychological rigidity and theological conservatism," did not sit well with everybody at a time when Puritan churches had begun relaxing their standards for church membership.

The reverend's nine-year-old daughter, Elizabeth Parris, and her cousin, Abigail Williams, started experimenting with fortune telling in the winter of 1691, even though it was considered to be demonic activity. By January, Elizabeth started exhibiting strange behavior. According to her father, the girl would bark like a dog when he scolded her, scream wildly when she heard the "Our Father" prayer, and throw the Bible across the room.

"After these episodes, she sobbed distractedly and spoke of being damned," explained Reverend Parris. "Soon, she was contorting her body in strange positions, consistently spouting foolish and ridiculous speeches, and generally having fits."

Before long, her cousin, Abigail Williams, and a few of their friends also started having fits. A doctor suggested Elizabeth must be influenced by the devil since he found no physical reasons for her symptoms. It was believed that witchcraft victims suffered if it was the result of a crime. Naturally, the community set out to find the perpetrators, and it did not take long. Accusations against women and men from Salem Village, the Town of Salem, Beverly, Ipswich, Andover, and Wenham were made. By May, more than 150 people had been jailed. According to a special Court of Oyer and Terminer formed to handle the cases, a person could be indicted on charges of afflicting witchcraft or for making an unlawful covenant with the devil.

Ezekial Cheever Jr. had become a court clerk because he knew shorthand. He served as notetaker for many of the infamous witch trials, which resulted in nineteen deaths by hanging. He sometimes included his personal opinion in his notes. As a church deacon, he visited the homes of the accused, conducted interviews, and examined people for marks of the devil. He presented depositions and complaints before the court. Of those Ezekial testified against, Bridget Bishop, Sarah Good, and Martha Corey died on Gallows Hill. Giles Corey, Martha's husband, was crushed to death with stones. Abigail Hobbs pled guilty and was later pardoned. Mary Warren confessed and avoided the death penalty by testifying against others.

One of the families most impacted by the hysteria of the witch trials was that of John Proctor Jr. of Salem. Born in Suffolk County, England, he immigrated with his parents, John Sr. and

Martha Harper Proctor, in April 1635 aboard the *Susan and Ellen*. The family soon became known as one of the wealthiest in Ipswich after purchasing several properties in the area, which included shares on Plum Island.

John Jr., twenty-one, married Martha Giddens in 1653, who died six years later during the birth of their fourth child, Benjamin, the only one to survive childhood.

In December 1662, he wed Elizabeth Thorndike, whose father, John Thorndike, founded the town of Ipswich. The Proctors moved just south of Salem Village in 1666, where they leased a 700-acre estate from a brother-in-law of Governor John Winthrop. Two years after their relocation, John received an annually renewable license to operate a tavern one mile south of the village line. Elizabeth passed away shortly after the birth of their seventh child in the late summer of 1672.

Elizabeth Bassett became John's third wife on April 1, 1674. She, along with the older children, tended the tavern. At the same time, John and son, Benjamin, fifteen, worked the large farm outside Salem Village, as well as a portion of his father's property in Ipswich, which he inherited when Mr. Proctor died in 1672.

Charges involving witchcraft started soon after their neighbor, Giles Corey, filed a lawsuit against John Proctor. Mr. Corey said that Mr. Proctor accused him of setting the Proctor's house on fire. In fact, one of the Proctor's sons accidentally caused the blaze.

Elizabeth Proctor suffered accusations from young women in the community, including Abigail Williams, niece of Reverend Parris, Mary Walcott, and Mary Warren, the Proctor's former servant. Of course, Mr. Proctor vigorously defended his wife and challenged the charges he claimed were based strictly on spectral evidence. Thirty-two neighbors signed a petition stating that John Proctor had lived a "Christian life and was ever ready to help such as they stood in need." More than a few thought claims were leveled at him as well because he challenged the credibility of the

Court of Oyer and Terminer. On August 5, 1692, both John and Elizabeth Proctor were tried, found guilty, and sentenced to be executed.

Out of 141 complaints received by the Court that year, twelve were leveled against the Proctors and their family members. Two of those people, John Proctor himself and Rebecca Nurse, an elderly, respected member of Salem Village and relative of a son-in-law of John and his second wife, Elizabeth Thorndike, were hung. Because Elizabeth Proctor was pregnant when she went to prison, she received a reprieve. It saved her life. She delivered a healthy son, John, in January 1693. Then, in May, she, her new baby, and all those remaining in jail were freed.

While their parents were imprisoned, the Proctor children found themselves with no means of support. The county sheriff seized all of their household possessions. Their cattle were sold. Beer barrels at their tavern were emptied. Thus, upon her release, their mother found she could not claim any of her family's estate. She was a condemned woman who waited until 1709 to receive a monetary settlement after those executed had finally been exonerated of all convictions during the frenzied spectral of witch trials in Essex County more than a decade earlier.

Lessons evolved from the tragic 1692 prosecutions in Massachusetts. One lesson: be wary about making enemies. Ezekiel Cheever Jr., an accuser, and John Proctor, who was hung as a witch in Salem, both became ancestrally linked to Alice Gage Currier White of Wakefield, Massachusetts. She could claim Ezekiel Cheever Jr. as her 4x grandfather. She was related to John Proctor through his 5x granddaughter, Dorcus Gage Hobbs of Pelham, New Hampshire.

And so, it goes 'round.

Something Special Lay Ahead

Bartlett (White)

Walking along the Pemigewasset River, Joseph Bartlett, twenty-two, thought he'd enjoy the day if his hands were not tied together. Early September yielded the start of fall leaf colors, yet temperatures stayed pleasant. He'd seen otters at play in the water, observed beavers building their dam, and heard black ducks and loons this morning.

He assumed they would soon be heading west toward the Connecticut River. He could not imagine that their captors would take a group of mainly women and children up and over New Hampshire's White Mountains. But this was a forced march. Joseph estimated that as many as two dozen people had been killed since the attack nearly two weeks ago. Those captured now numbered twenty. They started with twenty-six. The Indians killed women and children who could not keep up. To his dismay, the French soldiers who accompanied them did nothing to stop the butchering.

On August 29, 1708, as part of Queen Anne's War, about 160 French soldiers and fifty Abenaki and Algonquin Indians attacked the town of Haverhill, Massachusetts, located near the state's northeastern border. Joseph, from nearby Newbury, on the coast, was drafted into the state militia late in the previous year specifically to defend Haverhill against a suspected attack.

Residents knew the seriousness of the threat. In March 1697, during King William's War, Abenaki Indians attacked Haverhill and killed twenty-seven people. In February 1704, the French and Indians attacked the settlement of Deerfield on the northwestern Massachusetts border. They burned part of the town, murdered forty-seven residents, and captured 112, who marched 300 miles to Montreal. Many died in the harsh winter conditions or were slain along the way. Sixty were ransomed by family members. Others became assimilated into the Mohawk tribes.

When the second attack on Haverhill occurred, Joseph and a handful of his fellow soldiers had gathered at Captain Simon Wainwright's house, which had a view of the entire village. The captain was killed when gunfire passed through his front door.

At first, soldiers fired on their enemy out of windows as the town was set ablaze. When Joseph realized the only way to safety was to surrender, he hid his rifle up the chimney of the fireplace. On a whim, he asked Mistress Wainwright if he might take her dead husband's wool coat in the closet.

"Of course, you can have the coat. God forbid if the savages take you captive," she said. "I believe his gloves are in the pocket. You are about his size. They should fit. And take this scarf as well. Bless ye, young man."

"Madam, you are too kind," said Joseph. He then went outside and gave quarter.

Mary Wainwright unbarred the door and let the predators in after the soldiers left. Attempting to be gracious, the brave lady promised to give them whatever they wanted. They demanded money. When she left the room to retrieve it, she fled with all of her children except her daughter, Mary, twenty-one, who was captured.

The raiders left with prisoners and looted as they heard the distant arrival of militia from surrounding areas. One party collected packs when they discovered the raider's baggage camp several miles from town. Another group set out after the retreating raiders. Nine of the enemy were killed and eighteen wounded. A few of the traumatized captives managed to escape.

Five other soldiers, a handful of older boys, eight young women, and eight children started on what would be a long, miserable, scary journey that pushed the physical and mental limits of the women and children, who survived nearly 300 miles and more than five weeks in the wilderness.

Although the Merrimack River flows through Haverhill, Joseph figured they would move northwesterly to meet the river in New Hampshire to avoid detection. There were plenty of ponds between here and there to sustain them. He felt certain their destination was Quebec.

Joseph aimed to live. He needed to determine how to make it happen. First, he thought, he must eliminate stupid mistakes. There had to be a reason they kidnapped six soldiers. The French must want them for purposes of negotiation. He considered that to be a positive.

Perhaps as militia, they might be expected to band together and attempt some kind of escape in this situation. Their captors kept the six men separated. No interaction took place with the women or children. Their hands were bound except when they ate once a day. They were under scrutiny at all times. When the Natives sacrificed a prisoner who was too slow or who became sick, they forced the group to watch. Joseph had never seen a person scalped alive. Such an atrocity against a woman or a child fits Joseph's definition of barbarity. Maybe the Indians hoped to elicit a response to their cruelty among the soldiers. Any such action would have resulted in another death. Joseph decided to bide his time.

Once the party reached a point west of the White Mountains, most of the Indians took the women and children and headed northwest across New France toward Lake Champlain. They were shared among different tribes to be assimilated or, when that did not work out, sold as slaves.

French soldiers met the men and their French captors with horses. They rode to Quebec. When Joseph and his fellow soldiers approached what was to be their new home, he immediately abandoned all thoughts of possible escape. The military installation, which the French called la Citadelle de Quebec, sat on the St. Lawrence River atop Cap Diamant, adjoining the Plains of Abraham in Quebec City. Engineers designed and built a heavily fortified protective stone wall on the west side, the only side not naturally protected by the steep promontory. It was completed in 1690, just in time for the Battle of Quebec.

Other American prisoners shared their accommodations. The French thought it useful to keep American as well as British soldiers imprisoned to use as bargaining chips for the release of their captive soldiers.

Although the French fortress in Quebec harbored political prisoners, overcrowding was not a problem. Joseph knew there were far worse places to endure imprisonment. They were not physically abused. Food, such as it was, appeared twice a day. He requested books and received French novels. He learned to speak the language while there. Every day, he remained grateful for the warm coat, gloves, and scarf received from Captain Wainwright's widow because others, not so fortunate, suffered from the cold worse than he did.

Joseph Bartlett, the Massachusetts militia, and residents in small English settlements along the state's northern border found themselves players in hostilities between the French and English over control of North America that started with King William's War (1688-1697). Events moved right into Queen Anne's War (1702-1713), Father Rale's War (1722-1725), King George's War (1744-1748), and the French and Indian War (1754-1763), in which France was removed from the equation. Both the French and the British used local Indian tribes to wreak havoc among the white settlements. Border disputes between Britain's northern colonies and the southern part of New France in Canada and the western Ohio River Valley remained unresolved. All the warring, killing, and pillaging failed to shift major power on land until the thirteen

American colonies overthrew British rule after the Revolutionary War in 1783.

On October 5, 1712, almost four years after arriving, Joseph inexplicably received his release. He longed to board a ship heading up the St. Lawrence River out to sea so he might sail to Boston and arrive close to home. Having been stripped of the coins he possessed in Haverhill, he had no means for such a trip. He would return the same way his captors led him north, believing it to be the easiest, most direct route. He thought he might get lucky and find a boat to take him part of the way down the south-flowing Connecticut River.

Joseph desperately needed a weapon. He had to eat. A guard who helped him learn French and with whom he became friendly gave him a sharp hunting knife in a sheath, a bundle of food, and a leather canteen once he got outside the wall to help him get started. "Merci, mon ami," replied Joseph. He received his papers, was taken across the wide river, and set his feet on a path south.

On an unusually sunny morning, November 12, Joseph walked into the yard of his family's house in Newbury. His sister, Mary, fifteen, Richard Bartlett's youngest child and second girl among ten boys, stood bundled at the clothesline with her back to him.

"That wouldn't be my little sister all grown up now, would it," Joseph asked, grinning.

Mary whirled around, dropped the sheet she held, and stared wide-eyed with her mouth hanging open. "Oh, my stars! Joseph, is that really you?"

He laughed out loud for the first time in many months. "Tis, sweet girl."

She ran to him and jumped with her arms around his neck and legs wrapped around his body, knocking his hat askew and nearly toppling them both to the ground. Their tears intermingled. He looked into big, brown eyes and wavy light brown hair cascading past her shoulders and regretted that he had missed her turning into the swan before him.

"I never thought I'd see ye again in this lifetime, Brother. I was sure those savages had killed ye. My heart broke when I heard what happened. Come. Father should be in his shop. Stephen will likely be there as well. I'll find ye something to eat. You're thin as a lath."

# # #

The name Bartlett became synonymous with fine leatherwork in the upper coastal area of Massachusetts. Richard Barlett, I worked as a cordwainer and a shoemaker. He curried leather when he immigrated from Sussex, England, to the Colony of Virginia in 1624 with his wife, Joane, three-year-old son, Richard II, and four other children.

The family settled in Jamestown, which constructed a fort against Indian attacks. They stayed for twelve years before boarding a ship north to Boston. In 1636, they found their way to the newly established Newbury Plantation about thirty miles up the coast from Boston, situated just south of the mouth of the Merrimack River.

Early Newbury settlers were not fleeing religious persecution. Rather, they sought to establish a stock-raising company because of England's high prices for horses, cattle, sheep, and hogs. The salt marshes of the area provided plenty of hay. An early mill on Newbury Falls ground their corn. A tannery gave Richard Bartlett all the leather he needed to craft shoes and boots.

A record dated December 1642 listed ninety-one of the first known settlers of Newbury. Three Bartlett sons appear on the list: Richard II, Christopher, and John.

Like most families in the 1700s, the Bartletts maintained a small sustenance farm. However, their primary income was generated in a well-equipped leather shop that could hardly turn out products fast enough to keep up with demand.

When Joseph returned from Canada, he discovered that his brother, Stephen, twenty-one, who worked alongside his father in the shop, would marry Hannah Webster the following month on December 18. The young couple planned to move to Amesbury below the New Hampshire state line. There, Stephen would open his leather shop. Although another brother, Sam, also worked with his father, Joseph's skills as a cordwainer were now needed again by his family.

Richard II had worked beside his brother, Christopher, in the same shop, although it had since been expanded. Their brother, John, became known as "John the Tanner." The brothers learned the craft from their father, Richard I, who apprenticed under a leather worker in Ernley, England, when he was a young man, to the distress of his father, Sir Edmund Barttelot.

Up to that point, the family had been members of the English gentry. Sir Edmund's great-grandfather, Sir Richard Barttelot, twenty-five, in June 1503, went to France with King Henry VIII in the retinue of Cardinal Thomas Wolsey. In September 1514, he was killed in battle at Tourney, France.

As the 1600s approached, young Richard I heard of British explorers searching suitable locations on the coast of North America for settlement. He surmised it was only a matter of time before ships would start taking people who wanted to immigrate. He set his sights on a new life. He knew he needed to acquire a skill that would enable him to survive in the new country, which fueled his desire to learn as much as he could about handcrafting leather. He worked with Thomas Reed for thirty-one years, primarily making shoes, before he and his family finally thought the timing right to cross the ocean. By then, he was forty-nine.

Over the years, the war created much demand for leather products. In addition to sturdy boots and shoes, soldiers needed holsters, belts, bags, and packs, including saddlebags, bridles, and saddles for horses of those in the cavalry.

Soon after Queen Anne's War started in 1702, state militia discovered Bartlett's shop to be a reliable source for its leather needs. The Bartlett family worked tirelessly to fill the orders.

In May 1704, Hannah Emery Bartlett did not survive a bout of pneumonia. Her death left daughter Hannah, twenty-one, to care for her father, Richard, a house full of brothers, and six-year-old little sister, Mary.

Joseph did not know it until after he returned home, but France and Britain declared an armistice shortly before his release in the fall of 1712. A final peace agreement was signed after the first of the year. Under the Treaty of Utrecht, the English gained Acadia, which would become Nova Scotia, sovereignty over Newfoundland, the Hudson Bay region, and the Caribbean Island of St. Kitts. France recognized British sovereignty over the Iroquois tribe and agreed that commerce with American Indians farther inland would be open to all nations.

One July morning in 1713, Joseph was in the shop when two nicely dressed men somewhat younger than he and two even younger women walked in. The men introduced themselves as brothers, Lloyd and Marcus Nelson, from Boston. The older of the young women was their sister, Mistress Christine Nelson, and the younger was Mistress Lydia Nelson, their cousin from Plymouth, who was staying with their family for the summer. They brought their sloop up the coast for a few days and heard they could get handsome boots crafted at the Bartlett's shop in Newbury.

"Now that the British and French have put aside their arms, we wanted to escape. Get the sea breezes in our faces again. Have some fun," explained Mr. Marcus.

"Trust me, I know all about the need to get out," Joseph replied.

"Do you, then?" Mistress Lydia asked.

"I spent four years imprisoned by the French in their fortress in Quebec. Was, mercifully, released last year."

"Oh, you poor man," said Mistress Christine.

"Yes, we can make each of you very fine footwear. It would be our pleasure. Tell me what you have in mind. Then we'll take off your shoes and measure your feet."

The Nelsons visited for nearly two hours while Joseph introduced them to his father. They determined what each person wanted, carefully measured each foot, and showed them suitable leather they had in stock. They remarked on the beauty of sailing into Plum Island Sound, a tidal estuary, at high tide to reach Newbury.

Joseph explained that the mouth of the Merrimack River reached the Atlantic on the north end of Plum Island. He told them his brother, Stephen, took his new bride to Amesbury, accessible on the Merrimack, where he had opened his own leather shop.

When the Nelsons got ready to leave, Marcus suggested they head to Amesbury and invited Joseph to go with them. Said they could find somewhere to stay the night, Joseph could visit his family, and they would return to Newbury.

The idea of spending a couple of days sailing with two attractive young women and, undoubtedly, a hospitable cousin and brother thrilled Joseph. He jumped at their invitation.

As fate would have it, Joseph traveled to Plymouth to marry seventeen-year-old Lydia Nelson on December 9, 1714. The marriage proved short-lived. Tragically, Lydia died of puerperal fever, or childbed fever, the following year.

Stephen and Hannah brought infant Hannah down to Newbury for Christmas 1715 to visit with family. Joseph decided to return to Amesbury with them. He needed a change of scenery after the loss of his wife and baby. Stephen said he would be glad to accept help in the shop.

In early spring, Joseph met Elizabeth Tewksbury while staying in Amesbury. Her parents were first-generation residents of the town. The couple married December 5, 1717, in Amesbury, where they stayed to celebrate Christmas with Elizabeth's family and with Stephen and Hannah, little Hannah, and four-month-old Stephen Jr.

Joseph Bartlett Jr. arrived on September 23, 1718. Less than two weeks later, his mother succumbed to a late postpartum hemorrhage. Twenty-seven days later, the infant slipped away. He could not ingest the milk given to him.

Struggling to make sense of his losses, Joseph spoke with his brother Stephen, a deacon of the First Church of Christ in Amesbury. His brother implored him to talk to Reverend Thomas Wells.

He expressed his grief to Reverend Wells, who agreed that his losses were tragic but no fault of his own. The reverend sympathized that Joseph had endured undue burdens in his young life but told him there would be rewards in the coming days if he walked in the light.

Losing two wives and two children in three years tested Joseph. He knew he must pick himself up and move forward. He could not help but feel that something special lay ahead. Perhaps the Divine needed to intervene to get him there.

The reverend read 1 Peter 5:7-10 to Joseph:

"Casting all your cares upon Him; for He careth for you. Be sober, be vigilant; because your adversary the devil, as a roaring lion, walketh about, seeking whom he may devour: Whom resist stedfast in the faith, knowing that the same afflictions are accomplished in your brethren that are in the world. But the God of all grace, who hath called us unto His eternal glory by Christ Jesus, after that ye have suffered a while, make you perfect, stablish, strengthen, settle you."

Joseph appreciated the gentle, caring nature of Reverend Wells. He had attended the church for the past couple of years. Not only was Stephen a deacon, but his late wife's father, John Tewksbury, also served as a deacon.

Another family he met through the church were distant relatives of the Tewksburys. Thomas and Elizabeth Hoyt had a daughter, Sarah, who was a couple of years younger than Elizabeth had been.

The Hoyts expressed more than kindness to Joseph after he lost Elizabeth. She and Sarah had been close growing up. During that winter of 1719, Mistress Hoyt, Sarah, and younger sister, Liz, brought much appreciated food and conversation to Joseph's small house. Sometimes, the girls dropped by the shop with unexpected lunch for the Bartlett brothers.

On a chilly but sunshiny Sunday afternoon, April 27, 1721, Joseph and Sarah became man and wife. The Bartletts, Hoyts, Tewksburys, and the rest of the First Church of Christ congregation attended. Inexpressible joy filled Joseph's heart.

♦ ♦ ♦

In 1728, after the birth of their fourth child, Gershom, the Bartletts moved into a larger house in Newton, a section of North Amesbury. It was destined to become part of New Hampshire in 1746.

In Stephen and Hannah Bartlett's household, Josiah, their seventh child, came along on November 21, 1729. Three years later, their last child, Levi, who lived to be ninety-six, completed the family.

Twelve children would be born into the Joseph Bartlett family. Five died as infants. Christmas 1730 was interrupted by impending birth. Sarah went into labor that night, and early the morning of December 27, Mary and her twin brother, Benjamin, arrived.

These cousins spent countless hours together growing up. They lived in a world of water. Much of their diet came from rivers, ponds, and the sea. The children eagerly sought to contribute.

The Merrimack River ran practically past their back door and emptied into the ocean just east of Newburyport. The Powwow River and Back River joined near the center of Amesbury. Lake Gardener and Lake Attitah were right there, as well as Tuxbury Pond, Meadowbrook Pond, and Pattens Pond. Crappie, white perch, pickerel, and bluegill, all freshwater fish, swam in the ponds and rivers. Sometimes, they went down to see their cousins in Newbury in the summers. In June, the shallow tidal mud flats provided early-season bait fish. The youngsters caught striped bass and blue fish from the waters of Plum Island River. And clams and mussels from the marshes and coastal ponds.

When Josiah Bartlett was sixteen, he began his medical studies with Dr. Nehemiah Ordway of Amesbury, a first cousin, who was eighteen years older. Five years later, in 1749, he began his medical practice in Kingston, about twelve miles northwest of Amesbury in Rockingham County, New Hampshire. He quickly became a prosperous young country doctor. Because of his integrity, he earned the esteem and trust of area residents.

Mary and cousin Josiah grew close as the years passed. Both felt a void when Josiah moved to Kingston. Of course, he was busy establishing his new medical practice. Mary, the youngest daughter of Joseph and Sarah Bartlett, helped her mother with cooking and other household chores. She was educated and, thus, volunteered to substitute teach at the overcrowded school within walking distance from their home.

Sometimes, Mary went up to Kingston with Josiah's close brother, Simeon, who had recently lost his new wife during childbirth. Other times, she rode with cousins Hannah and Levi when they went to see their brother.

It soon became obvious to family members that Josiah and Mary had developed a much more intimate relationship. A deep love blossomed based on mutual respect.

The cousins married in a private ceremony on January 15, 1754. The air was frigid, and the sky was overcast. The good reverend agreed to perform a brief ceremony at what was to be Josiah and Mary's home. Prepared food and Madeira wine sat in the kitchen. Finally, the waiting was over. In the spring, they planned to celebrate with family and friends.

Josiah's participation in public affairs began after their first two daughters, Mary and Lois, were born nineteen months apart. He became a civil magistrate and was then given command of a regiment of militia.

In 1765, he was chosen as a representative from Kingston to the Provincial legislature. The following August, John Wentworth, from Portsmouth, a son from the upper echelons of New Hampshire society, was commissioned as governor and vice admiral of the state.

Concerned about his patients' perpetual long-term medical care, Josiah turned to a man he greatly respected, who had served an apprenticeship under him in the early 1760s. Dr. Amos Gale was now also a practicing physician and surgeon in Kingston. In June 1765, Drs. Bartlett and Gale signed articles of agreement, possibly representing the first contractual medical partnership in American history. Amos Gale Jr. would marry Sally Bartlett, the tenth child of Josiah and Mary Bartlett, in 1796.

Josiah's natural sense of justice and philanthropy toward the people immediately left him uncomfortable with Governor Wentworth's mercenary views and actions. It surprised him that most of the legislature acquiesced to the governor's will. He quickly found himself in a small minority, obliged to vote against unjust violation of rights. He was devoted to the good of his country.

"I don't understand how Governor Wentworth can conscientiously serve as governor to one of the thirteen colonies while aggressively pursuing policies that will benefit the Crown," said Mary after Josiah had returned from Portsmouth one afternoon. "Clearly, he and his family stand to benefit."

"Ha! Such a precedent was set by his uncle, Benning Wentworth when he was governor," Josiah replied. "He lined his pockets by selling land grants to the west of the Connecticut River, and it was questionable even then whether New Hampshire owned that territory. As you know, three years ago, the Lords of Trade ruled that New Hampshire's western border ended at the Connecticut River, decisively awarding the territory to New York.

"Their family's merchant interests are closely tied to London, I'm afraid. We need to keenly monitor his reaction to New England's response to British goods coming in."

In 1774, Josiah headed a "Committee of Correspondence," on which other New Hampshire legislative patriots served. The purpose of the committee was to coordinate discussions and responses with other colonies as America moved toward war with England. Another function was to inform voters of the common threat faced by all the colonies and disseminate information from the main cities to the rural, outlying areas where most people lived.

Although the first formal committee was established in Boston in 1764, Samuel Adams, who had been a classmate of John Wentworth at Harvard College in the mid-50s, formed another committee in 1772. The Boston Committee under Mr. Adams became a model for other patriot groups.

About 7,000 to 8,000 men served on these committees in cities, seacoast towns, as well as those in the interior. The committees became the leaders of the American resistance to British actions and largely determined the war effort at the state and local levels. They were the forebearers to the First and Second Continental Congresses.

Josiah's fellow patriots elected him to the First Continental Congress in Philadelphia, which convened on September 5, 1774. He would have been among the fifty-six deputies representing every colony except Georgia. When his appointment was announced, Governor Wentworth, backed by his Troy allies, revoked his title of justice of the peace, and his commission as colonel of the local militia was taken away.

After Josiah received a warning to cease his "pernicious activity," the Bartlett's house mysteriously burned to the ground on Sunday, August 28, one week before the Continental Congress was to meet. All twelve members of the family were in church when the fire was set.

Mary did not flinch. As they stood on the street facing the remnants of their smoldering house, she said, "The miscreants who did this spared our lives. They timed it perfectly.

"Thank you, God. Every one of our children is here with us.

"We are in a battle, Josiah. And we stand on the side of justice, of liberty, of freedom. You are in a position to make a difference. The price for all that is liable to be high. We've discussed it."

"Yes, wife, but I never thought it would come so close to my family. You and our children have lost their home."

"Our house will be rebuilt," Mary replied. "With winter coming on, this is not ideal timing. However, we are surrounded by people who love us. This will be an inconvenience, yes. But this family will go right on.

"You will stand strong against those who try to cause you to stumble. We'll let Samuel Adams, Joseph Warren, and Patrick Henry know right away what has happened here. This will not bode well for John Wentworth."

Josiah immediately sent word about the fire to Nathaniel Folsom, from nearby Exeter, a close political ally in the state assembly who had become another one of the principal opposition leaders in the House. He had also been invited to the First

Continental Congress. He would return as a delegate in 1777 and 1779. Since the two men planned to travel together to Philadelphia in the next few days, Josiah wanted to let him know he would not attend the proceedings due to his unexpected personal situation.

The Bartletts immediately retired to their small farm outside of town, much to the delight of most of their ten children. Their youngest, Sarah, whom they called Sally, was a fourteen-month-old infant, and little Ezra, a three-year-old toddler, but Mary had plenty of help. Their seven oldest were teenagers or close to it. Nate, 18, had a lean, wiry, strong frame. When a couple of men came to help his father shore up the farmhouse for approaching winter conditions, the boy provided considerable assistance.

Josiah was again chosen as a delegate to the Continental Congress the following summer. He traveled to Philadelphia in September. American and British troops had already clashed at Lexington and Concord, Massachusetts. The Congress appointed George Washington Commander-in-Chief of the American Army on June 15, 1775, and began acting as the provisional government of the thirteen colony states.

Josiah returned home briefly in March 1776. He went back to Philadelphia, where he stayed until May 17th. After another short break at home, he again met with Congress for a historic session.

The topic of America's independence had been freely discussed among delegates for some time. As an ardent Patriot, Josiah's mind had no other open path. On July 1, supporters found they could carry a majority with a vote. Talks continued until July 4, however, in order to obtain as close to a unanimous vote as possible.

It was decided to take a vote on that day, starting with the northern most state ¬ New Hampshire. Josiah Bartlett's name was the first called, and he answered in the affirmative. John Hancock, president of the Congress, first signed the Declaration of

Independence. Josiah, being the first to vote for independence, was the first to sign the document after Mr. Hancock.

Josiah came home to Kingston fatigued from that session of Congress. He did not resume his participation until 1778.

Meanwhile, he engaged in his public duties and happily stepped into his role as physician and surgeon with Dr. Gale. He could now assist Mary in delegating to their adult children and others who could contribute to the many functions of running a farm and a large household.

On December 13, 1776, Mary gave birth to Hannah. The child lived for four months. Mary had not meant to bear another baby. This would be their last.

In August 1777, with the Revolutionary War underway, Josiah responded when the call went out for help by Gen. John Stark, a New Hampshire Native in the Continental Army. British troops were heading to Bennington, Vermont, to capture American supplies. General Stark needed local militia to join his force.

Josiah and others hurried to the southwestern border of the state. He knew his medical skills would be needed.

In bloody hand-to-hand combat, the New England militia, which was, for the most part, lacking in military training, undisciplined, and unenthusiastic about getting shot, managed to kill more than 200 British Regular soldiers. Reportedly, thirty Americans died.

General Stark's reputation preceded him in this battle. He did nothing to diminish it when he rallied his troops by crying, "There are your enemies, the Red Coats and Tories. They are ours, or this night, Molly Stark sleeps a widow!"

The Continental Congress convened in May 1778 in Yorktown as the British occupied Philadelphia. Josiah attended. He worked in Congress to build the American Navy. He also worked on a committee that drafted the Articles of Confederation. This proved to be his last federal service.

In 1779, Josiah served as a judge in the Court of Common Pleas. Three years later, despite not having a law degree, he was appointed to the New Hampshire Supreme Court. In 1788, he became Chief Justice of the state Supreme Court and served for two years. That same year, he chaired the state convention for adopting a state constitution.

A rabid red fox bit Mary Bartlett on her hand in mid-June 1789 while she was at their farm. Flu-like systems developed. She became extremely fatigued and experienced double vision. Hallucinations began days before she died on July 14.

Josiah was devastated. Not only had Mary been his closest friend, but she served as his counselor in all he undertook. Lois, then thirty-three, who never married, proved invaluable in helping to run the household for the rest of her father's life.

In 1790, Josiah was chosen as President of New Hampshire. The state's constitution finally took effect in 1792, and he continued as chief executive, now New Hampshire's first governor since it became an independent state. He resigned in 1794 due to poor health.

Josiah practiced medicine for forty-five years. He founded and was president of the New Hampshire Medical Society. He remained most pleased that his sons Levi, Josiah "Jesse" Jr., and Ezra also became acclaimed physicians. Each played significant roles in public affairs as well.

On May 19, 1795, Josiah Bartlett Sr. passed away at his home in Kingston due to paralysis at the age of sixty-five. One day, a bronze statue would stand in the square of his hometown of Amesbury, Massachusetts, in honor of his many lifetime achievements.

Took to the Sea

Pitts (White)

Although Captain George Pitts owned two transatlantic merchant ships, he enjoyed sailing his small sloop down the Taunton River and occasionally into the tributaries of Narragansett Bay to fish. One April day, he and Seth Hodges rode the incoming tide back up the Taunton River from Newport, Rhode Island, into a stiff northeast breeze. Increasingly dark clouds on the afternoon horizon promised rain before they docked in their home port of Dighton, Massachusetts.

The pair had come the day before to meet a couple of rum distillers with whom George had developed a good working relationship. He expected his ship, *Amphitrite*, to depart for England within two weeks. His rum supplier from the town of Taunton, just north of Dighton, was delivered to his wharf the previous week. He wanted to make certain the two in Newport would be ready when his ship arrived.

It was 1760, and George Pitts, forty-five, owned one of the finer homes in Dighton. He was a third-generation Pitts in Bristol County. The family became well-known with the arrival of his grandfather, Peter Pitts, who came west to Taunton from Plymouth as a young man looking to prosper.

Ebenezer, a son of Peter Pitts, left his son, George, several real estate holdings. Over the years, George had purchased a substantial amount of additional property in and around Dighton.

George operated a boat that works along the waterfront, just south of Muddy Cove. He also owned a ferry, which crossed the river onto the east shore, where there was a towpath up to Taunton. North of Dighton, the Taunton River becomes prohibitively shallow for ships.

Goods unloaded from ships on Dighton's wharves could be transferred to smaller boats for transport to surrounding towns or towed by oxen along the towpath.

The rum industry prospered in New England thanks to trade established in the Atlantic Ocean route known as the Bermuda Triangle in the seventeenth and eighteenth centuries in British colonies of the Americas. Slaves were brought from Africa to sugar plantations in the Caribbean and islands controlled by England, Spain, and France. The juice from crushed sugar cane was boiled down, and crystals formed to make sugar. The remaining sticky, dark substance was called molasses. This by-product was fermented with yeast and water and distilled into rum in copper pot stills. English colonists along the Atlantic coast, primarily those in New England, purchased the molasses to produce rum. It was also used in such foods as baked beans and brown bread.

The British soon acquired a taste for the product, and ships transported wooden barrels containing molasses that originally came from the West Indies. George Pitts offered his English buyers rum aged in molasses barrels with a deep copper-brown color; the flavor was extracted from barrels jostled around in the hold of a rocking ship crossing the ocean.

The region became one of the leading rum producers in the world in the 1700s. Rhode Island supported thirty rum distilleries, twenty-two in Newport alone, while sixty-three distilleries operated in Massachusetts. Some say the coastal New England shipbuilding industry prospered originally because of the need to run molasses and rum.

At its height of popularity, colonists supposedly consumed more than five gallons of rum per person annually, paying mere shillings per gallon.

A man might walk into a tavern and see a sign with a simple rhyme such as: "One of sour, two of sweet, three of strong, four of week." Maybe one customer would order a stone fence, a second a flip, another a rattle-skull, a fourth a kill-devil—all rum drinks were mixed with tonics, citrus juices, freshly grated spices, beers, cream, hot butter, or frothy eggs. Recipes varied widely.

Of course, the British Parliament wanted to get its cut of the profits, thereby imposing a tax of six pence per gallon on imported molasses. Its action caused an outcry years before the Sugar or Tea Acts were drafted. Localities passed bans to limit rum distillation.

Colonists banded together as rum runners and smugglers to ensure widespread distribution. New England merchants reputedly smuggled about one and a half million gallons of molasses a year. Corrupt officials collected about 2,000 of the 37,000 pounds due, less than one-quarter of what was needed for their salaries.

Early on, George decided not to trade in human cargo. Therefore, his ships, *Amphitrite* and *Calypso*, did not make runs to Africa. They also did not sail to the Caribbean. Many others picked up the sugar and molasses produced there. His captains and crews would then carry the secondary product, rum, to England. On return trips, his ships brought mainly woolen textiles and various manufactured goods, including furniture, which was easy to sell to the growing New England population.

＃＃＃

When George got into international trade, iron proved to be the most natural product for export. Ore lay virtually in his backyard. The Pitts family fortuitously found itself among a group of men who seized the opportunity to purchase shares when a joint stock company was formed in 1652 to develop what would become the Taunton Iron Works.

Settlers had moved into an area west of Plymouth in the 1630s. In 1637, a small group purchased what was then known as Cohannett from the Nemasket Indians. They named the area

Taunton as a tribute to the town in Somerset County, England. The new arrivals soon discovered large amounts of bog ore in streams and ponds.

Henry Andrews was among seven original purchasers, the first to become free men, on December 4, 1638. Hezekiah Hoare was among a group of sixteen arriving within another year. Both men liked the prospect of a local ironworks as talk circulated.

Brothers James and Henry Leonard immigrated from Pontypool in County Monmouth, Wales, a place known for working iron. The two found iron works established in Saugus and Braintree, Massachusetts. When residents in the Taunton area voted to establish their own iron works, they invited the Leonard brothers to set up a bloomery on Two Mile River in what would later become incorporated as Raynham.

James Leonard moved south to the newly established territory, where he built a two-hearth water-powered forge and furnace. In 1656, it began producing bar iron directly from ore, yielding about twenty to thirty tons annually. He quickly became known as a master workman.

James learned the languages of local Indian tribes and developed a warm friendship with Chief Massasoit, ruler of the Wampanoags, who frequently slept under his roof. Because of James's knowledge of iron and skills as a blacksmith, he repaired Massasoit's guns and made weapons for him. Before the older man's death, he extracted a promise from his son, Metacomet, who had now adopted the name Philip, that he would never harm a Leonard. In 1675, in a meeting in Taunton Church, with James present, Philip affixed his mark to a document promising peace with the men of Taunton.

No one that day could have imagined just how significant that promise would be. What became known as King Philip's War flared between most of the Native tribes in the New England territory and white settlers. The bloody conflict raged for three years. It ended shortly after King Philip was killed at Mount Hope in Bristol, Rhode Island.

Henry Andrews was among the original group of proprietors in Taunton's Iron Works Company. Many of these men became friends whose families intermarried over the years. In their own ways, their sons and grandsons contributed to the 220-year longevity of Iron Works Company, commonly called Taunton Iron Works, and the successful production of iron throughout the region.

In 1648, Henry's daughter, Mary Andrews, married William Hodges, another proprietor in the company. William was killed on April 2, 1654, on his thirtieth birthday, while harvesting trees.

Three years later, his widow, Mary, married Peter Pitts. By age twenty-six, Peter had accumulated more than adequate capital to become one of the original shareholders in Taunton's fledgling iron works. He and other investors received annual dividends, paid in iron ingots, which yielded for many years due to the successful operation.

One of Mary's first two sons, John Hodges, became one of the original purchasers in 1672 of what was known as the Taunton South Purchase, which became Dighton. The land was bought from King Philip.

John Hodges and his brother, Henry, stepchildren of Peter Pitts, were half-brothers to the six children born to Peter and Mary. The youngest Ebenezer married Elizabeth Hoskins in 1698, and the couple moved down to Dighton.

When George Pitts, son of Ebenezer and Elizabeth, bought his first ship in 1741 at the age of twenty-six, with help from his father, he hired Sam Hodges, who was a year younger, to manage his warehouse. He hired Sam's twenty-two-year-old brother, Seth, four years later, who eventually handled the books. The Hodge brothers' grandfather was John Hodges.

Another loop in the Taunton Iron Works circle as it related to the Pitts family centered around Seth Hodge's wife, Anna Hoare. Her great-grandfather, Hezekiah Hoare, was the first signer of the articles of agreement of the Taunton Iron Works.

The most direct hereditary connection between the Leonards and the Pitts started when James Leonard's daughter, Hannah, married John Crane in Taunton in 1686. Hannah and John's great-grandson, Ebenezer Crane Jr., married George Pitts's daughter, Silence, in Taunton ninety-one years later.

Taunton Iron Works manufactured merchant iron bars. These were sold to blacksmiths, who turned them into castings for family furniture, anchor chains, horseshoes, cookware, musket barrels, and tools and hardware, such as nails, files, saws, and plows. George Pitts supported a network of these craftsmen, who brought and sold him their finished products. He then shipped and resold them to England.

Being a port city, Dighton was susceptible to diseases from ships' crews who sailed from Europe, Africa, the Caribbean, and even South America. Working along the waterfront, illness remained a risk. George Pitts and other merchants tried to keep their families away from the wharves and the hubbub of activity amongst strangers. Doctors stayed on call and were busy.

To the distress of the Hodge and Pitts families, Sam Hodges contracted dysentery and passed away in August 1745 at the age of thirty-one. He had been George's sounding board for the first four years of the business. Since George had been the only boy among nine girls in the Pitts household, the Hodge boys felt like brothers to him, perhaps because their grandfather had been a half-brother to his father.

It worked out that Elisha Crane, a year older than Seth Hodges, Sam's brother, was available and willing to learn the crucial details of managing the warehouse. Elisha was one of six sons of Gershom Crane, a Dighton family well-known to the Pitts. His older brother,

John, captained a ship making runs to the British Isles. The previous year, Elisha went as a member of his brother's crew but decided that he'd rather stay on firm land because he had a good head for figures.

George Pitts married Elizabeth Brightman in 1748 in Dighton. Her grandfather, Henry Brightman, fled from Bedfordshire, England, during Cromwell's War when he was about 10 years old. Henry arrived in Rhode Island and became a free man in Portsmouth in 1670. He was a grantee of 5,000 acres of land and became a prominent citizen serving on grand juries and as a deputy in Portsmouth and Newport.

Elizabeth's father, Joseph Brightman, experienced a heartbreaking situation after his first marriage to Mary Alden in October 1714 in Boston. (Mary was the great-granddaughter of John and Priscilla Mullins Alden, both passengers on the *Mayflower*.) The Brightman's first child, Mary, arrived in July 1715. Mary labored for hours with the breeched birth. The midwife said she was lucky to have survived the ordeal; most of the time, the situation results in either the baby or the mother dying or both. Their son, Joseph Jr., was born eighteen months later. Complications developed almost from the start of the pregnancy. Mary lay in bed for five of the eight months until Joseph was born. Although four weeks early, little Joe survived. His mother, however, did not intend to put her life at risk with childbirth again. The midwife told her another pregnancy might very well kill her. Mary was twenty-four years old.

The news stunned Joseph. No more conjugal relations. Mary told him he would have to move into a separate bedroom. But he loved his wife. He would certainly not kill her intentionally. So he moved.

Two years later, Joseph met Susannah Turner on a trip to Newport to visit his family. Mary agreed to release him from his marriage obligations due to their situation, but guilt kept him in Boston. On February 8, 1721, Mary died of apoplexy.

In the spring, Joseph took his two young children to Middletown, north of Newport, where his father's sister, Sarah, lived with her husband, Hezekiah Hoare II. They invited the family into their home despite a house full of young'uns.

Susannah agreed to become Joseph's wife after an appropriate period of grieving. It gave him time to recruit family members to help build a house on property given to him by his father in Little Compton, across the Salonnet River from Newport. That same month, in April, Susannah's sister, Hannah, married Jeremiah Lawton. He agreed to take his new bride to Little Compton to help Joseph build his house. In exchange, Joseph said the newlyweds could live there with Susannah until he and Susannah married early in 1723. Five months later, Susannah gave birth to George Brightman, the couple's first child. She and Joseph wed seventeen months after that. Their in-laws ended up sharing their new home.

***

Joseph and Susannah Brightman had their second child, Mary, in August 1727. They left Jeremiah and Hannah farming the property in Little Compton while they moved north to a section of Fall River purchased from the Wampanoags. What would become known as Freetown sits on the banks of the Assonet River along an old Indian trail that led to Boston fifty miles to the north.

Elizabeth was born in July 1730. She became an inquisitive child enthralled by the natural world. As an infant, Lizzy, as they soon called her, seemed fascinated by the cradle boards used to carry the Native papooses. Susannah let it be known that she would trade a quilt for one of the child carriers. The next month, she received one.

Susannah became friends with a Wampanoag woman, Shikoba, who had two small girls of her own. Shikoba's grandfather had been a healer in the tribe. He passed his knowledge of spiritual and medicinal healing down to his daughter and, through her, to her daughter, Shikoba. Susannah eagerly foraged the woods with her new friend for the wealth of plants and trees, offering relief from many physical ailments. The three girls almost always went along. Lizzy seemed unusually attentive for a five-year-old to the woman's explanation of the flora's benefits. She and her young friends, Tel-e-ka, six, and Kim-ki-ai, seven, carried sacks to collect the harvested leaves, roots, and/or bark. Sometimes, they went back to Shikoba's village. Occasionally, they spent the night to have more time to learn what their host did with the collected plants.

"Brother, take me. I want to go," Lizzy said as the light of dawn hinted at breaking through the house's kitchen window.

George, now seventeen, took another slug of tea after biting a chunk out of his hard roll. He smiled at his precocious eight-year-old sister. He liked her. Had always admired her spunk. She did not want to stay home when fishing, hunting, or exploring of any kind was about to commence. Yet father was gone. He left the previous day to go to Swansea to meet his brother. George had never taken Lizzy, not even on a short trip by himself. Today, he and two friends would go just north to Assonet on a tributary of the Taunton River to fish.

"Well, Missy, it will be a long day. Might rain," said George.

"Might not," she shot back. "I have covering to put on if it does. It will not take us long to get there. I won't be any bother. Your friends both like me. They won't care if I go along. We can take the wagon. Throw all the fishing gear in there."

Right then, their mother walked down the stairs. "I thought I smelled sassafras and heard chit-chat," said Susannah Brightman. "George, please don't lean back in your chair like that."

"Liz is thinking she wants to go up to Assonet to fish the Taunton with Carson Greene, David Cornell, and me today."

"Is that right? I'm not quite sure what your father would say. It will be warm enough. If it should rain, I suppose you could take the wagon with the top in case you need it. And your guns, of course. When are the boys supposed to be here?"

"Any minute now," George said. "They're both used to being around Lizzy. I do not think it would be a problem. You know I'd guard her with my life, Mother."

George hitched the team of horses while his mother put together dried venison, cheese, and bread for their lunch. The other boys arrived, and fishing rods, buckets, and scrounged bait went into the wagon. Weapons were collected and loaded, and they were off within the hour, much to young Lizzy's joy. It was an unusually warm Massachusetts morning to be so early in May. Mist still shrouded the woods as they rode along, but George was optimistic that a fine day of fishing lay ahead when it soon burned off.

They stopped at a spring just shy of the village to fill containers with fresh, clean drinking water for the day. A man at the spring said he had been fishing the day before. He said the water was cool, and largemouth bass were hungry. He suggested a location where he thought they would have good luck and where they could keep an eye on the wagon and horses.

Under intermittent sunshine, they stayed about one hundred yards apart, moving to work about half a mile from the bank until early afternoon. Lizzy seemed to have a mess of bluegill in front of her all morning as her brother kept an eye on her. She focused on pulling in one after another of the small fish ¬ eleven keepers in all. The boys, meanwhile, concentrated on largemouth bass and pickerel, which were not so easy to lure in, but they were biting. They hauled six good-sized fish of each species between the three of them. All three families would eat well that night. George knew he'd never hear the end of his little sister catching more fish that day than he did.

✐ ✐ ✐

Medical science in 18th-century New England was virtually non-existent. It retained a provincial character. Mothers and fathers were part-time medical practitioners. Ministers in those decades often exhibited the "Angelic Conjunction," a term used by New England Puritan Cotton Mather to denote the mutual affinity of medicine and religion. So-called physicians were not generally called doctors because few earned medical diplomas. Then, there were Indian healers whose knowledge was called upon by the white settlers. Indian midwives especially received requests to assist with the births of white babies.

Ever since she was a child going out with her mother and Shikoba to collect medicinal plants, Lizzy had known that she wanted to help heal people. The need far exceeded available assistance; a wide variety of accidents happened, people developed all manner of sickness and afflictions, and disease circulated through towns and villages.

When Lizzy was sixteen, she let it be known that she wanted to be a "doctoress." There were other female midwives, nurses, and female doctors who traveled to attend to the scattered population. The next year, she met Mercy Renfro, a twenty-eight-year-old "doctoress", whose home base was New Bedford, a port city on Buzzard's Bay just to the southeast of Fall River. Mercy worked the territory east of New Bedford into the heart of Plymouth County. She invited Lizzy to go along on one of her rounds that spring. The experience fixed the mission in her heart.

When they returned to New Bedford, Lizzy headed to Middletown, where brother George lived with his wife, Hannah Peckham Brightman, whom he had married two years previously.

George now worked as a wood crafter, making mostly doors and windows.

Hannah took Lizzy to George's shop to meet his business partner, Louis Talbot, and to show off his workmanship. While she was there, a man walked in who appeared somewhat older, close to six feet tall, with a red tint to mostly blond hair, blue eyes, and a square, shaved jaw. He wore a casual but not inexpensive suit and introduced himself as George Pitts.

"This morning, I visited a Mr. Mason, a small tobacco proprietor with a shop near the wharves," explained Mr. Pitts. "I was admiring the door to his storage area outside. He told me you recently made and installed the door for him.

"Aye, we finished that door for Mr. Mason about six months ago," George said. "Thankfully, we've received a handful of referrals from him. A satisfied customer he is."

George explained that he wanted two large new doors for one of his warehouses in Dighton. Asked if he could take Mr. Brightman and the Mistresses Brightman to lunch to discuss the details.

At the end of the week, Lizzy asked George if she could accompany him up to Dighton to inspect and measure his new job at Captain Pitts' shipping warehouse. She reasoned it would bring her close to being back home.

"That way, I would not have to ride all that distance by myself," she explained. "That is if you could get away soon."

"Now, why on earth would you want to go up Dighton and then down instead of going back over the Sakonnet, which would put you practically in Freetown?" George asked.

"Perhaps I'd like to see the good captain again. I rather enjoyed the brief conversation I had with the man. There is no wife at home, you know."

"Am I hearing you right, Liz Brightman? You are interested in a man? I never knew you to show the slightest inclination to pursue further conversation with any man. Ha!"

"And if I am? There has to be a first time for us all, does there not?"

"Indeed, there does, dear sister. And my answer is, 'yes.' I'll go to Newport tomorrow and send Captain Pitts a message. Boats go daily to Dighton. We should get a reply in a few days. If he agrees to see us within the week, we'll arrange transportation for us and your horse."

George Pitts welcomed the quick response from George Brightman. He was particularly glad to hear the man would be bringing his personable younger sister along. She did not shy away from contributing insightful, intelligent observations to their conversation. Her enthusiasm for her new mission in life was infectious. He admired a woman with a goal. And he liked her wit. He walked out of their wood shop happier than when he went in, and, he thought, by golly, on the trip back up the river, it was young Elizabeth Brightman who lifted his spirits.

The meeting between the Brightmans and George Pitts at the end of the week in Dighton went well. They saw the *Calypso*, which was sitting in port, and toured the warehouse. It was the start of a two-year courtship between Liz and George.

Liz spent much of that year collecting and drying plants from the woods and herbs cultivated from their garden. She would introduce people to medicinal teas made from echinacea, lemon balm, sassafras, chamomile, cardinal plant, hyssop, lupine, turtlehead, and wild blue indigo. Her apothecary included, at various times, Indian tobacco, St. John's wort, skull cap, blazing star, American spikenard, jewelweed, rattlesnake plantain, white hellebore, great blue lobelia, partridgeberry, bloodroot, fleabane, horse balm, feverwart, and Joe Pye weed. Her plant medicines could help with a range of conditions, including menopausal symptoms, menorrhagia, chronic pain, diarrhea, common colds, chronic coughs, asthma, arthritis, itching and rash, gout, high blood pressure, inflammation, respiratory difficulty, digestive problems, kidney stones, and snakebite, among others.

Mercy Renfro had graciously supplied her with what she needed to stitch up wounds and demonstrated on an injured boy when they made their rounds together. Liz put the supplies to good use.

Liz was not experienced with childbirth. Did not offer her services as a midwife. But on two occasions in that first year alone, she encountered emergency deliveries and, with instructions from the mothers, she managed to help birth healthy babies.

Leather satchels and a small, secure wooden chest held her supplies. After talking with other physicians in Bristol and Suffolk counties and the nearby Rhode Island area, Liz set out the following spring to see patients. Roads were rough and, often times, little more than wide trails. She rode one sturdy horse and used another to carry her supplies. She figured most of her compensation would come not in coin but in trade, including care for her animals.

Liz kept a loaded pistol and a hunting knife on her person at all times. She was 5 foot 9 inches tall and strong from walking in the woods all her life and working in the family's large garden. Her Indian friends taught her how to use her hunting knife effectively for self-defense. She knew how to kill an animal or a man and would not hesitate to do so if her life was threatened. Her family maintained good relations with the Natives; however, there were a multitude of other dangers a young, attractive woman might encounter traveling alone. She knew her trips into the wilderness presented possibly compromising situations. However, the very nature of her mission provided somewhat of a shield as word got out and people became familiar with who she was and why she was there.

At one time or another, Liz rode and doctored between Newport and Boston. For the most part, though, she stayed between Little Compton and Westport (south of Fall River); west to Swansea, what become known as Somerset, Rehoboth, North Attleborough, Norton, Mansfield; the village of Norwood; then back south to Stoughton, Eaton, the Taunton area, Berkeley, Dighton; then Assonet and home. She did not go out from November through April. New England winters posed a danger, and she was not willing to negotiate.

On July 7, 1748, Elizabeth Brightman married George Pitts at her home in Freetown. It remained a mystery to Liz why he chose her to be his bride. Numerous ladies of a higher social standing would have been happy to become the wife of Captain George Pitts. George had never seriously considered anyone else, though. Liz Brightman made him laugh. He admired her adventurous spirit. She was well-read. He figured she should bear up well to childbirth. He loved the woman.

George and Lizzy's Brightman's maternal grandmother, Mary Turner, had moved to Middletown from Newport a couple of years after her husband, Lawrence, died in 1719. At that time, a neighbor and close friend, Gwenevere Adams, also lost her husband. Lawrence Turner purchased land around Middletown to move to what he considered a safer inland location on the island. Grandmother Turner traded that piece of property for a tract with a house in town. She invited her friend, whom she called Gwen, to come and live with her. Both ladies thought the port city had become a bit noisy for their tastes.

Liz's brother, George, and his wife, Hannah, brought Grandmother Turner, seventy-three, up from Middletown for the wedding. Grandmother Turner's daughter, Sarah, a younger sister of Susannah Brightman, married George Bliss. Their family were neighbors of the Brightmans in Freetown. Amazingly, Sarah Bliss lived to be one hundred years old, while her husband, George, died three months and five days short of his one-hundredth birthday. They both passed away on July 20, 1793.

Three of Liz's other four remaining siblings were home for the wedding. Joe, Joseph Brightman's first son, died seven years earlier in Boston of "throat distemper" at the age of 24. Cousins came up from Little Compton and other aunts and uncles gathered from the surrounding area. Elizabeth Haskins Pitts, sixty-eight, George's mother, and two of his sisters, Elizabeth Paull and Mary Andrews, came from Dighton. The Wampanoag's were well represented. Shikoba presented Liz with a wampum pendant on a necklace for a wedding present, which she wore for the ceremony and thereafter during her travels.

When Sarah Turner married George Bliss in 1717, their descendants were assured of ancestry to Benedict Arnold I, who died with distinction, and his great-grandson Benedict Arnold IV, who would become one of America's most infamous traitors. George's mother was Damaris Arnold Bliss, Governor Benedict Arnold's daughter. His descendant and namesake, Major General Benedict Arnold IV would soon become the notorious American Revolutionary War general.

Benedict Arnold, I immigrated from Somerset, England, and married Damaris Westcott in December 1640. Her father, Stuckeley Westcott, was one of thirteen owners of Rhode Island and Providence Plantations. The couple moved to Newport in 1651, and two years later, he served as president of the colony until 1660. In 1662, he was again elected president. The following year, King Charles II appointed him governor. He was re-elected several times and died in office in 1678.

Benedict Arnold IV, born in 1741 in Norwich, Connecticut Colony, operated merchant ships on the Atlantic Ocean when the Revolutionary War broke out in 1775. He joined the Continental Army outside of Boston and quickly distinguished himself through his intelligence and bravery. He gained the trust of General George

Washington, who assigned him to lead campaigns and battles. In 1779, he married young, pretty Peggy Shippen, daughter of Judge Edward Shippen of Philadelphia, a Loyalist sympathizer. In 1780, Major General Arnold planned to surrender the fort at West Point, New York, to the British. The plan was discovered, and he fled. He then led the British army in battle against the men he had once commanded.

Two summers after Liz and George Pitts married, baby Elizabeth, who they called Betsey, arrived. Over the next ten years, Liz birthed nine healthy babies, including two sets of twins. All lived to adulthood.

For the first six years, Liz had a baby every other summer. When the midwife visited in March 1756, she advised Liz that she was probably carrying twins. It did not come as a complete surprise. Her first three pregnancies presented no problems. This one felt heavier and more awkward. George's mother experienced the birth of two sets of girl twins. It was decided that it would be best if she did not go out on her doctoring rounds that spring. Silence and Susanna arrived on June 15. With five children now in the house, Liz knew the time had come for her to stay home. She sent notices to at least one family in each community she served, asking that they spread the word of her retirement.

Ebenezer, the second and last boy, was born the following year. Hannah the year after. In early April 1760, twins Mary and Sarah completed the Pitts' busy household.

In early October, a ship arrived in its home port of Dighton after unloading Africans from Senegambia in Newport to be sold as slaves. Nearly two weeks after docking, three crew members started exhibiting the initial symptoms of smallpox. Doctors notified town residents, but it was too late. One of the three originally infected died. Reportedly, about seventy people in the immediate vicinity contracted the contagious disease, which spreads from one person to another. Twenty-five would die by the end of the year.

Massachusetts knew all too well about smallpox. It was thought to have decimated the Native population before the *Mayflower* landed in 1620 and then shortly after. In 1633, Boston suffered a severe bout of the disease, and again in 1721. It seemed the sickness would ravage certain areas every ten years.

As soon as their father started exhibiting symptoms toward the middle of November, Liz Pitts found family members and a friend willing to take all of the children into their homes. She cared for George by herself because she did not want to expose anyone else. She wore gloves to handle his clothes and bed linens and took care not to touch his abscesses. Women brought food to the back kitchen door to help relieve her from that responsibility. Men stacked wood for the fires, which needed to be continually fed.

On December 10, 1763, the unthinkable happened. George Pitts, forty-eight, died at home from smallpox. George lost his fight in the early morning hours on a Saturday. Liz left him as he was, laid down, and fell into a deep sleep. An insistent knocking on the kitchen door woke her. George's sister, Mary Andrews, offered breakfast. Liz asked her to fetch the undertaker.

Even though Christmas was approaching, Liz decided to leave the house after they buried her husband two days later. She felt exhausted. She did not want the children to return with the possibility of the sickness lingering. Even though it was winter, she opened the upstairs windows and left to stay the rest of the month with Mary and her family, who were already keeping Hannah, five, and the Pitts' second twins, Mary and Sarah, three. Just three of the Andrew's six children were still at home, and Zeph, twenty-four, would be gone in a couple of months when he married.

For the most part, people in Dighton tried to remain sequestered in their homes. Red flags still dotted houses throughout the town to recognition those sick with the disease. Liz remained tired as her young family moved back into their home after the first of the year, but she thanked God for apparently sparing her from what she feared.

Then, on February 27, an intense headache was followed by a high fever, chills, and severe back pain. That morning, she immediately sent her son, George, eleven, to the Andrew's for help. Once again, she needed to remove all her children from the house. Someone immediately retrieved her sister, Mary Brightman, from Freetown, and came to nurse her. Days later, she experienced the onset of an early rash. When the rash progressed to fluid-filled abscesses, Liz's strength waned. She fought to make it through each day.

On March 20, 1764, she, too, left them all. The town was stunned that George and Liz Pitts were both taken down by the disease. Nine more children would be raised without a parent.

Sam Andrews agreed with his wife, Mary, that they should permanently take in the youngest three Pitts girls since all went well over a couple of months during their stay when the parents were sick. The Andrews had six boys, one of whom, Stephen, died at three years of age, and one girl. They thought raising three extra little girls might spice up their rapidly emptying nest.

Young George played with Ebenezer Crane Jr. growing up; his father often came down to Dighton from their home in nearby Berkley to visit his brother, Elisha Crane, who worked for George Pitts Sr. for eighteen years. Elisha had even taken George Jr. with him occasionally when he went to see his brother's family. The boys were a year apart and loved to fish together. Ebenezer Jr. was stuck with three sisters. When Liz Pitts died, Ebenezer Sr. petitioned the family for custody of young George, thinking a brother for his son, under the circumstances, would be ideal. The Pitts family knew several members of the Crane family, which was well-established in the county. Sam Andrews told the Cranes they wanted George to be raised with his younger brother. Both families agreed. With two boys named Ebenezer under the same roof, they started calling young Ebenezer Pitts E.P., and it stuck.

Ebenezer Crane frequently went to Dighton to meet with business associates. Often he took George and E.P. down with him for the day to stay with the Andrews family and see their little sisters and cousins.

Betsey Pitts mourned the breakup of her family. She understood no one would take on the responsibility of raising nine children. But sending her siblings off in four directions frightened her. The powerlessness weighed heavily on her thirteen-year-old soul.

The good news was that she and her sister, Mary, nine, were going to Freetown to live with Grandmother Brightman and their Aunt Mary. They had lost Grandfather Brightman ten years earlier, but Betsey barely remembered him. Her grandmother, at sixty-eight, still had plenty of stamina to keep up with two energetic girls. She and her one daughter, who never married, were heartbroken over the loss of their Lizzy. They insisted that her oldest two daughters come and share their lives. The Brightman matriarch would live another twenty years.

George and Hannah Brightman were raising four children in Middletown ages ranging from sixteen to three. They offered to take in the older Pitts twins, Susanna and Silence, now seven, as part of their family. The parents figured adding two girls between the ages of their two daughters would be helpful for everybody. They made at least three trips a year over to Freetown to see family, especially Grandmother Brightman. Therefore, the girls would get to visit with sisters Betsey and Mary fairly often.

♦ ♦ ♦

The Great Britain Seven Years' War, known as the French and Indian War in British America, raged between the British and French Canadians, who fought to control the colonies. Indian tribes aligned with the side most likely to protect their lands. Colonists were being conscripted into state militias to fight encroachment and attempted control of the budding nation by what many now consider to be foreign powers.

A major battle took place in the summer of 1758 on the approaches to the St. Lawrence River at the fortress at Louisbourg on Cape Breton Island. (It later became known as Nova Scotia.) To capture French-controlled Quebec, which led to French holdings in North America, the British had to open up the system of waterways between the St. Lawrence River in the north and the Hudson River in the south, with Lake George and Lake Champlain completing the circuit. It formed a resupply channel for French troops.

Jacob Haskins enlisted in the militia on April 6, 1758, and "passed muster" on April 8, meaning he was fit for duty, formally enrolled, given an oath, and read the Articles of War. He received 14 pounds with his bounty. Many went into the militia because of the good pay: two shillings a day, which was twice the pay of British Regulars.

He also received a blanket as part of his bounty. Jacob had become a skilled weaver of wool. He worked at his loom all winter, farming his family's land in Taunton, Massachusetts, during the warmer months. Therefore, he left home with one of his hand-crafted blankets, anticipating the freezing temperatures inside the fortress. Now, he had two. In addition, he wore a long, hooded woolen cape her sister, Hannah, fashioned from his weaving. He also took four pairs of wool socks, a pair of mittens, a pair of gloves, and two wool caps.

Jacob said goodbye to his father, stepmother, eight younger siblings and step-siblings, and friends before walking with his company of nearly ninety men the roughly forty miles to Boston in three days. Led by Captain Glover, a lieutenant, and an ensign, plus seven non-commissioned officers, including three sergeants and four corporals, the company received basic training in using a musket. However, few among their ranks would experience actual fighting. They boarded the *Wolfe* on May 24, 1759, and sailed north.

The short sea voyage turned Jacob inside out. He was not destined to become a sailor. As they approached the looming stone fortress at Louisbourg, he thought he had never seen any building quite so large. Add sickness to freezing weather on top of snow and "plenty of ice," their mid-April arrival promised challenges ahead.

Jacob and his company were used primarily for guard duty. They stood guard in twenty-four-hour shifts every three to four days. In addition, they worked "fatigue duty," building roads and bridges, digging trenches, and other skilled jobs offering extra pay. They might be requested to shovel coal for the officers, go out of the city to gather firewood, or maybe help to build a battery.

Between the American Provincial troops and British Regular forces, which remained stationed there, the barracks were densely populated. Because of crowded and unsanitary conditions, illness and subsequent deaths started virtually as soon as the Americans arrived. Punishment for British Regular soldiers was severe. Suicides were not uncommon. Accidents claimed other lives.

On June 5, Jacob began feeling sick with lung inflammation and pain from what he thought was pleurisy. He stayed in the infirmary from June 14 to the first of July. By August 6, Captain Glover had lost twelve men to sickness.

After failing to overtake Quebec the previous year, the British succeeded in two big battles on July 23rd and 25th in their siege of

Louisbourg. Provincial soldiers from Massachusetts were shipped not only to Louisbourg but to other area forts to free up the so-called "Regulars" to move on Quebec.

Jacob reported in his diary on September 22, 1762, that British forces under Maj. Gen. James Wolfe had crossed the St. Lawrence River on the night of September 12, established a position on the Plains of Abraham, and the next day successfully moved into Quebec to defeat the French. The victory opened a path into the American West for the British.

The conflict ended in February 1763, with France, Britain, and Spain signing the Treaty of Paris. In the Treaty, France lost all claims to Canada and gave Louisiana to Spain. Britain received Spanish Florida and Upper Canada. The thirteen American colonies were strengthened by removing their European rivals to the north and the south.

Work remained for the Provincials. With much discontent, the men spent the winter months in Louisbourg. It was not until May that they discovered their ultimate assignment. The following month, they began demolishing the walls of the fortress. The project took five long months to complete.

On December 5, after boarding the *Squirrel* and suffering through twelve days of a mostly stormy passage, now Captain Jacob Haskins and his fellow soldiers landed off of Casco Bay, Maine. Troops spent a miserable Christmas aboard the ship. It took twelve additional days for Jacob to arrive at the Homestead in Taunton.

He discovered that his brother, John, who was two years younger, had married Miriam Caswell from Plymouth in March. As his father's oldest son, Jacob felt obligated, especially with John gone, to stay and help manage the farm. He had no prospect of a wife. The family kept the "east, back chamber" set up with the loom for his weaving.

Jacob rode down to Freetown in April with his father and stepmother, Henry and Mary Rounseville Haskins. They had married in January 1745, after Jacob's mother, Hannah Packard Haskins, twenty-seven, was killed the previous winter by a large falling icicle. Mary's father, Phillip Rounseville, eighty-six, a wealthy and respected member of the Freetown community, died on Sunday, November 6. Now that the weather was clear for traveling, the family gathered for a memorial. They looked forward to visiting with Jacob's sister Hannah and husband, Thomas Chase, and other friends. They did not anticipate returning to Taunton until early the following week.

Phillip Rounseville immigrated from Devonshire, England, in 1704 and settled in East Freetown, a part known as Freemen's Purchase because purchasers were all freemen, not indentured to anyone. The names Brightman and Chase also appear on that list of purchasers. Mr. Rounseville owned a dam and water power plant, where he operated a mill for his business as a cloth dresser, a foundry that specialized in molding farm implements, and, later, a sash and door factory.

Henry Haskins conducted business with the Rounseville foundry over the years. That is where he met the daughter, Mary Rounseville. Phillip lost his wife and Mary, her mother, three months after Hannah Haskin's accidental death.

Captain Jacob Haskins first saw Mercy Pitts, whom they called Mary, in late June of 1763 when he went down to Freetown to visit his sister, Hannah, and her husband, Thomas Chase. Married in 1757, the couple welcomed their fourth child, Roby, in the spring of that year.

Hannah took Jacob to the Brightman's house one afternoon, right after the Pitts sisters returned from a day scouring the woods, with Tel-e-ka, daughter of Shikoba, their mother's Wampanoag friend, and her two daughters, Mikula, fifteen, and Firaki, ten. When Shikoba and Tel-e-ka heard about Elizabeth's girls relocating to Freetown after her death, they went to Grandmother Brightman's house and introduced themselves. They told stories about the old days when they took Lizzy out with them to collect medicinal plants before she became a doctress. They invited the young Pitts to go with them so they could learn about the wonders of plants as their mother had. Both Betsey and Mary eagerly agreed.

The day Jacob met them, they had gathered mainly edibles, including morel mushrooms, early black raspberries, mulberry fruit, wild carrot shoots, and wild radish tops for that night's supper. He liked the twinkle and excitement in young Mary's eyes as she described their day in the forest.

"Mary, is it, then?" asked Jacob.

"My real name is Mercy. But they have always called me Mary. I don't know why. My father's sister in Dighton is Aunt Mary Andrews, and, of course, we now live here with our Aunt Mary Brightman, my mother's sister. Seems to me there were enough Marys already."

"I think Mercy fits you very well," Jacob said.

"You can call me Mercy. I believe I would like that," she laughed.

"I think it's fine that you and your sister are learning cures for various ailments from the Natives. I believe Mother Nature holds many more secrets for restoring our health than we know. I admire the fact that your brave mother was a healer."

"We don't know nearly enough about medicine, do we?" Mary asked. "No one knows enough to save people from smallpox."

"No, my girl, we do not. Four years ago, I lay very sick in the fortress of Louisbourg with men dying all around me. Human intervention did not save me. It was only through the grace of God that I survived."

"I'm glad you did, Captain Haskins. Why do men feel like they have to fight all the time?"

For the next seven years, Jacob managed to visit Freetown fairly often to see Hannah and Thomas and their growing family, the Rounsevilles, the extended Chase family, and the Brightmans and Pitts. He thought Mistress Brightman retained an impressively sharp mind as she aged. Daughter Mary handled two teenage girls as if she had been a mother all her life. Betsey and Mercy, as he called her, both seemed to relish their roles as important contributors to this happy household and the community. When they asked him to come with them on one of their day-long foraging expeditions, he knew he had been accepted as one of their own.

In 1769, Jacob realized that Mercy Pitts, the girl, had blossomed into a young woman who had managed to steal his heart. Now fifteen, she was aware of her surroundings; like her mother, she was brave, smart, concerned with other people, had gained the respect of the Indians, spoke their language fluently, and possessed a loving spirit. The eighteen-year age difference did not bother him. He knew she would grow into her own person.

Just before Christmas, Jacob asked Mercy if she thought she was ready for marriage. He told her he loved her and wanted her to become his wife. Somewhat to his surprise, she agreed.

They decided to wait until spring to let the weather clear so their many family members could gather to help them celebrate. On May 3, a large, happy crowd congregated at the home of Captain John Rounseville, brother of Mary, Jacob's stepmother. Captain Rounseville, along with his wife, Sarah, had moved into his deceased father's house, which was the largest property in Freetown. They graciously offered their home to Jacob and Mercy for their wedding.

All four Haskins siblings and four half-siblings attended, as did all five of the Rounseville siblings. There were now seven Pitts brothers and sisters. Mary, the youngest of the twins, died of pneumonia two years earlier when she was eight years old. Thomas

Chase's parents and a couple of his brothers came along with several Brightmans. A couple of Burt families from Taunton made it down, and cousins from Little Compton rode up. Neighbors, including Wampanoag friends, brought food to add to a table loaded with bounty.

Betsey Haskins came into the world on February 22 of the following year. Her sister, Hannah, completed the family when she was born in December 1774.

Four months later, the Revolutionary War got underway in the battles of Lexington and Concord just northwest of Boston. Jacob volunteered in one of twenty-six regiments authorized on April 23 by the Massachusetts Provincial Congress. His first stint of service started on August 1 under Colonel Benjamin Woodbridge. Among the regiment was Colonel John Parker, who had commanded the Lexington militia.

In October, Jacob was promoted to Captain after his early service. He led two companies of soldiers from Taunton, one in 1778 and another from March 13 to April 15, 1779. By 1781, the war had, mercifully, moved South. Jacob received his discharge on March 14 of that year.

The next year, the Haskins family moved into their elegant Georgian L-shaped dwelling on sixty-four acres (with buildings), which lay on a bend in the Taunton River. Jacob paid 1,425 silver milled dollars for the Homestead. Five generations of Haskins and Burts would live in the house into the 20th century.

Simeon Burt married Betsey Pitts in 1769. Twelve years later, Stephen Burt Jr. claimed Hannah Pitts as his bride. In February 1792, the youngest Haskins daughter, Hannah, wed Enos Burt, younger brother of Simeon and Stephen Jr.

The Burt brothers had been the children of Stephen Sr. and Abigail Paull Burt, both Taunton families from the town's beginning. Richard Burt, Richard Paull, and John Richmond, father of Mary, who married William Paull, Richard's son, were among the forty-six purchasers of Taunton in the late 1630s.

When Hannah married Enos, Jacob wanted them to stay at the Homestead. Enos raised the south part of the house, in effect, making it two stories, added a large chimney, and built on a porch.

Jacob died in his sleep at age eighty-two in January 1819. Enos drowned trying to rescue a couple of calves in April three years later. He was sixty-one. Jacob's will left the Homestead to Mercy in her lifetime, then to daughter Hannah. Mercy applied for and received Jacob's Revolutionary War pension in September 1836, the first year widows became eligible for the funds. Proceeds went back to 1818, when Jacob first applied, which would have amounted to a considerable sum going into the Homestead. Major renovations were undertaken on the Burt's big house the following spring under the direction of eighty-three-year-old "Grandmarm" Mercy Burt. She broke her shoulder in a bad fall in December 1834, becoming progressively weaker thereafter. She died on February 17, 1839

William, the third son of Hannah and Enos, took to the sea as a young man. It did not hurt that great-grandfather George Pitts owned a wharf and two transatlantic merchant ships in Dighton in the last century. His name opened a door. William loved being on the open sea. He was blessed with good equilibrium and a strong stomach and did not mind hard work.

By the time William married Lydia Waldren in Taunton in April 1832, he no longer rode ships. He worked in an office, sorting accounts. Many local people in Taunton and Berkley invested in ships. He worked hard in tracking ships, where they moved, what they moved, and prices of goods. He did not yet have much money to invest, but he was close to the action, and he figured if he could offer sound advice to those who did, he stood to benefit.

After the Homestead lost its matriarch, William moved Lydia into the refurbished house to help manage the large farm. He knew he could get back into merchandising later to help support their growing family. Assistance stood at the ready. His brother, Enos Jr., commanded a ship, and his younger brother, Hiram, hoped to follow his lead.

The family of William's future son-in-law, Hathaway Tew, knew well the potential perils of life on the sea. His grandfather, Benjamin Tew, of Dighton, sailed in a merchant vessel whose crew was homeward bound from Hamburg, Germany, in 1795 and was never heard from again. His father, Philip Tew, of Freetown, was ten years old at the time. He lost his own life at sea in 1821, about a year after Hathaway was born.

William's sheets of accounts first mention buying supplies for a sloop, the Samuel, which he had apparently invested in 1837. Early on, he transported food. On August 28, he purchased twenty-eight pounds of pork, twenty-eight pounds of codfish, "a lot of cheese," a bushel of rye, thirty gallons of molasses, and fifty pounds of sugar.

The War of 1812 again staggered the region just as it regained its footing going into the new century after the war for independence. British interference in American trade and forcing American sailors into the British navy precipitated the war. The U.S. government declared war on Great Britain on June 18, 1812. The people of Massachusetts, for the most part, condemned the war.

Located thirty miles off the Massachusetts coast, Nantucket Island residents have always been at the mercy of the sea. When the war broke out, most of the wood for fuel and food for the 7,000 residents came by boat from the mainland. Most island men earned their living from whaling. This war also proved to be a disaster, as had the Revolutionary War, because the British again blockaded Nantucket. The people suffered.

Seth Cleveland and his son, Zimri, who was in his early twenties, bravely stepped up. Their whaling boat sat beached, and they decided to put it to good use.

The pair rendered valuable service to the inhabitants of Nantucket from 1813 until August 1814, when the island's residents and the British worked out an exchange for Nantucket's neutrality in the war to receive supplies. British cruisers blockaded the waters around the island. On nights, when it was dark and/or rainy, father and son ran their boat to the mainland to pick up supplies. If delayed until daylight, they sailed to the nearest land, hid their cargo in bushes, and sunk the boat in shoal water until dark, if necessary.

Enos Burt Jr. went down to Nantucket a couple of years after the conclusion of the war when boat building and fishing were on the rebound. He met Winifred Luce in 1818 and married her three years later. Winnie's parents were Elijah and Love Cleveland Luce. Both the Luce and Cleveland families, along with the Folgers (who connected with the Clevelands when Love's mother, Susanna Folger, married Ebenezer Cleveland in May 1724), had inhabited either Nantucket or Martha's Vineyard since Europeans first occupied both islands in the mid-1660s.

Winnie Burt's uncle was Seth Cleveland. Enos became good friends with his cousin, Zimri Cleveland, and his brother, Henry, who was the same age as Enos.

The Clevelands refurbished their whaling ship and got right back on the sea as whaling again became a highly lucrative deep-sea industry for those with bases on Nantucket, Cape Cod, or New Bedford with its deep harbor on Buzzard's Bay. Enos went out on an extended whaling venture but decided that the end of the business was not for him.

Whale oil was in demand primarily for lamps, illuminating homes, and businesses. It also lubricated the machines of the Industrial Revolution. Enos talked the Clevelands into investing with him in the construction of a coasting vessel. He wanted to captain such a vessel and profit in transporting the vast amount of whale oil being produced. He named it the *Candlemarsh* to honor Richard Burt, the first Burt ancestor to have come to America from Candlemarsh in Dorsetshire, England, in 1639.

In the mid-1740s, Henry Cleveland relocated to New Bedford, where he began manufacturing whale oil. Enos's vessel carried Henry's oil and large amounts of oil from other manufacturers in New Bedford down the East Coast to Charleston, Wilmington, Norfolk, Baltimore, Philadelphia, and New York.

The third son of Enos Sr. and Hannah Burt, who was to captain a ship, was Hiram, their youngest boy, born in 1812. He commanded a merchant brig, the *Marine*, in the 1850s out of Newport. In early September 1857, he set out with a crew of ten headed for the Caribbean. By late Thursday, September 10, howling winds blew them off course, causing Captain Burt to rethink his decision to start into what was known as hurricane season. The wind and sea worsened Friday, and their smaller mast snapped about 125 miles off the coast of Wilmington, North Carolina. His veteran crew grew concerned. The sinking *S.S. Central America* appeared on the horizon around 1 p.m. Saturday. By this time, the ships had drifted about 160 miles off the coast of Charleston, South Carolina.

The side-wheel steamer was bound from Panama to New York loaded with miners and their families returning home to the East coast from San Francisco, along with $1.6 million in gold, thousands of freshly minted 1857-S double eagles, some earlier $20 coins, as well as ingots, and gold in other forms. It rapidly took on water in thirty-foot waves, and her sails were ripped to shreds by ferocious winds.

Cmdr. William Herndon of the *S. S. Central America* ordered all women and children on deck in preparation for boarding lifeboats in an attempted rescue by the Marine, which kept drifting further away in the storm. Numerous trips were necessary. Out of 596 passengers, including thirty-two women, twenty-two children, and 105 officers and crew, only 101 people were saved, most by the *Marine*. They nearly starved before the brig limped into the port of Norfolk, Virginia. It was the greatest American peacetime maritime disaster up to that point. It contributed to the Panic of 1857 and led to a severe recession.

Captain George Pitts undoubtedly would have been proud of his three great-grandsons, who carried on the New England tradition of becoming seafaring merchants and/or captains. Like him, they exhibited a sense of adventure, independence, shrewdness, and bravery.

Hiding Places for Freedom Seekers
(Shepardson)

Even four generations later, stories get passed down hesitantly, as if secrecy remains necessary. The soul of discretion dies hard.

Captain Thomas White and his wife, Hannah, whom they called Ann, immigrated from Fiddleford in Dorsetshire, England, in the mid-1630s to help found Weymouth, located on the new Colony of Massachusetts coast. They and their fellow Puritans set the tone for generations of New England descendants by maintaining their strong Christian faith and convictions. They focused on their large families and heeded what they believed to be God's calling to a particular vocation as a means of serving their community.

Defying the law to help usher other people to freedom seemingly broke the mold of the conservative, responsible, and respected family members in the direct line leading from Thomas White to his sixth great-grandson, Cyrus Newell White of Wakefield. Yet Cyrus and his wife, Ruth Shepardson White, were abolitionists whose home became a station on the underground railroad.

They believed their mission to be sanctioned by an authority higher than the law of man. There were dangers inherent in the operation, to be sure, both for their family and for the families of the escaping slaves they sheltered. However, they were surrounded by a solid network of other avowed abolitionists, including family members.

The Whites lived in the middle of a hotbed of anti-slavery activity. They were not only Massachusetts residents but also lived just north of Boston, which was the epicenter for abolitionist activity in the mid-1800s. Wakefield, located in Middlesex County, sat between two of the four main routes of the underground railroad coming out of Boston. One ran through Medford up to Woburn, then Andover, and north just to the west. The other skirted east of Wakefield through Saugus, up to Danvers, to Topfield, and on through Essex County. Each route proceeded through New Hampshire and then into Canada, the slave's "promised land."

Generations of Whites, Shepardsons, Pratts, Blandins, Paulls, Reeds, Macombers, and Allens — Cyrus and Ruth's extended families — lived in counties immediately around Boston. Ancestors of every family were Massachusetts pioneers who immigrated from England in the 1600s. "We may be regarded as thoroughbred Yankees," said the spouse of one White.

Ruth's great-grandfather, Nathaniel Shepardson, was born in Attleboro in 1731 and settled in neighboring Cumberland, Rhode Island. He became a member of the state legislature for several terms and became known as Squire Shepardson. Two of his sons, Nathaniel Jr. and Otis fought in the War of 1812.

His middle son, Issac, at age fifty-two, left ten children behind when he inexplicably hanged himself in his barn on April 9, 1816, in Wrentham, Massachusetts. He said nothing to anyone. Left no note. He had become melancholy and reclusive over the past decade. His wife, Lucy, found his body. Eight of their children were still living at home. Son, Aaron, was so ashamed of this final act by his father that within months after his death, he started using the alias Aaron Woods.

John B. Shepardson was the seventh child of Issac and Lucy. He began courting Sarah Pratt after the Shepardson and Pratt families met at a large Congregational church meeting in Attleboro. Although he lived in Wrentham and Sarah in Taunton (about twenty miles south), they kept up regular correspondence.

John found the Pratts to be intellectuals who were full of lively conversation about the events of the day. Their father, Dier Pratt Sr., fought with the Massachusetts militia in the War of 1812, which proved extremely unpopular in New England. He talked about being among troops defending Boston as the British unsuccessfully attempted to attack the coast of Massachusetts.

Dier Pratt's father, Micah Pratt Jr., and his grandfather, Micah Pratt Sr., had been doctors in Taunton. His great-great-grandparents became deaf as children: Matthew Pratt when he was twelve years old and Sarah Hunt when she was three. Their parents made sure they were well-integrated into their church and community despite this disability. The children were capable of communicating abstract thoughts about highly complex subjects through sign language. Increase Mather, a well-known Puritan clergyman, considered Sarah's conversion to be an "illustrious providence" since she had given a full account of her profound experience with God to the church elders.

Dier Pratt's mother, Sarah Dyer Paull Pratt, descended from a family that paid a steep price for standing up for their principles. Her immigrant grandfather, William Dyer, was a founding settler of Portsmouth and Newport, Rhode Island. He and his wife, Mary, had been disenfranchised and banned from Boston after becoming supporters of dissident ministers. Mary went back to England, where she became a zealous Quaker convert. She returned to Boston five years later, in 1659. The following year, she became a martyr when she refused to repent for her Quaker activism and was hanged by authorities.

Indians killed William Dyer at his home in Sheepscot, Maine, in August 1689. Four months later, the Dyer's son, Christopher, Sarah's father, was also murdered by vengeful Natives at his home in Sheepscot.

Within a year after John Shepardson's periodic forays to Taunton, everybody realized that Sarah's sister, Mary, and John primarily had long conversations with the elder Pratts about politics. Boston had become the center of politically progressive movements, including the abolitionist, women's rights, and temperance movements. The liberal Pratts educated their children about the freedoms at stake. All could converse about ongoing developments. Mary seemed to thrive on analytical discussions; she enjoyed challenging John to debates. Her attempts humored him because he almost always agreed with her position, whether or not he showed his hand.

The Dier Pratt family invited John to a family picnic on the Taunton River on Saturday, July 4, 1818. Mother Zilphia and her girls spent Friday preparing food for the holiday outing. They baked anadama bread for sandwiches, baked and sliced a ham, sliced farmstead cheese from a local dairy, made egg salad with crisp celery, put together a thick fig sauce, made a coconut cake and a huckleberry pound cake, and picked strawberries.

Their five youngest children went. John and James Pratt rode horses while the others piled into a three-seat carriage.

John remembers exactly when he knew. It was a warm day, so everybody was in the water. John and James got out to play with a ball and bat that James brought. The ball sailed over John's head, and when he turned around, he saw Mary stroll up to it about twenty yards away. She picked it up and, to his complete amazement, threw it right to him.

As Mary walked toward John laughing, she said, "Toss it to me."

He lobbed it back maybe fifteen yards, and she caught it. Mary then walked up and handed the ball back to John, who was speechless.

"Ha! You should have seen your face. You were flabbergasted that I could throw the ball that far."

"I was, indeed," John said. "You are full of surprises. Wouldn't put much past you, though, Miss Mary."

She then held his gaze with brown, gold-flecked eyes inherited from her grandmother Reed. She and her brother, Dier Jr., were the only two among the ten siblings to have acquired the Reed's brown eyes and darker brown hair. For the first time, with her damp hair almost in ringlets touching her shoulders and the bright noon sun shining on full lips that broke into a slightly mischievous grin, John's heart involuntarily lurched. Mary lightly touched his arm and said, "There may be another surprise: you never can tell."

She turned toward her brother and told him, "James, go round up the others. John and I are going to the carriage to start pulling out the food and getting it set up. After swimming, I've worked up an appetite. How about you two?"

John returned home to Wrentham, knowing he was in a quandary. He had never looked at Sarah, seventeen, a year younger, as a future wife. She was a wonderful person who never criticized him, laughed at his jokes, loved poetry, and enjoyed reading to him. Others considered her his first youthful belle. He knew her feelings for him ran deeper than how he felt towards her. However, what little time they spent together remained unencumbered with requests or demands.

At twenty-four, Mary looked and acted like a grown woman who nurtured her playful side. She also loved the written word. Not only was she a voracious reader, but she wrote every day. John thought her intelligence and personality could make a difference by improving the quality of life for others. He loved their political discussions around the Pratt's big dining room table. Suddenly, he loved her with a feeling of intimacy not yet experienced in his young life. He knew this was the woman he always wanted to be by his side.

These concerns would have to be put aside for the next few months. Brother Aaron, who would be twenty-nine at the end of the month, looked forward to his wedding on the first of September. He and his youngest brother, Jonathan, fifteen, had worked hard to sustain the farm since their father died over two years ago. John knew his periodic disappearances did not help the situation. Since it was mid-summer, his assistance was needed through the fall harvest. He felt obliged to remain at home.

The disastrous 1815 eruption of Mount Tambora on the island of Sumbawa, part of the Dutch East Indies, impacted the Shepardson farm. One of the most powerful volcanic eruptions in history, it triggered extreme weather and harvest failure in Europe. Hops from the United States reached England in 1817 for the first time. The virtual destruction of the country's hops crop forced the British to lower the import tax. This proved to be fortuitous to the Shepardson's crop decision after losing their father.

Hops was one of the first crops planted by the Pilgrims who first landed in Massachusetts. They considered beer to be a necessity in everyday life. Even Increase Mather, a renowned minister and a leader in governing the colony nearly one hundred years earlier, described alcohol as "a good creature of God."

In the spring of 1817, John and his brothers planted thirty of their fifty acres in hops instead of the Timothy hay Isaac Shepardson sold to area dairy farmers and clover he fed his sheep. They sold the sheep over the winter. Their father undoubtedly would not have risked cultivating such a large new crop. His sons, though, saw an opportunity for profit in hops and jumped at the chance. Not only was England starting to purchase large shipments, but in 1789, Massachusetts enacted a law that encouraged the manufacturing and consumption of beer. By the 1800s, Boston would become one of the leading beer-brewing cities in the country. (Beer is made from malted grains, hops, yeast, and water.)

Even with advice and help from other area farmers on varieties and field location, the Shepardsons would be on a learning curve this first year. They had to figure out growth rates, bloom dates, cone development, targeted irrigation, and other critical factors. From fall through the winter, they devoted their time to trellis construction. They had to purchase rhizomes and potted plants from established hops growers to get them in the ground in the spring since they did not have a greenhouse built by the winter.

Varieties recommended for New England started blooming in early July. If all went as hoped, they would start harvesting the crop by the first of October. The process required helpers willing to commit several days of hard labor. The hops would be dried and then tied into 200-pound bales for shipping. A Bristol County cooperative of hops growers promised to accept the Shepardson's harvest in their allotment if it was determined to be a quality product.

In mid-September, John received a letter from Dier Pratt offering his service, along with his son, James, during the approaching harvest. John readily accepted. He invited the Pratts to be their house guests that week. Not only did they need the help, but it would also give him an opportunity to discuss his personal situation with Mr. Pratt. This was a discussion a man had with his father. He felt as though Mr. Pratt was as close to a father as anyone in his life.

On the third night of the harvest, after supper, John took Mr. Pratt down to the spring house, where there was a large, comfortable bench. He knew they would not be bothered there.

"Sir, there is a situation I need to discuss with you. This may put you in an awkward position, but I value your opinion and want to do the right thing."

"I'm glad you trust me enough to confide in me, son. I will help in any way I can."

"Sarah is not going to be the woman I marry. We have never discussed marriage. I hope she doesn't assume that to be the case. I like her very much, and I consider her to be a good friend. I don't know how to do this. What is proper? Do you learn as you go?"

Mr. Pratt sat back and chuckled. "You are what now, John, eighteen? You're just fine. It takes a while to figure out the intricacies between men and women. There is no right and wrong.

Everybody is different. You'll know when the right one comes along."

"My heart is telling me I have found the right one. On the one hand, I'm joyful, and on the other, I'm, well . . . It's Mary. I don't know how it happened."

"Oh, that creates a bit of dilemma, does it not? Does Mary know about this?"

"I'm certain she does," said John. "We have not talked about it."

Mr. Pratt put a pipe in his mouth, which he had been holding, and lit it. Then he said, "I was in a somewhat similar situation when I was about your age. I was nineteen when I started courting Zilphia's cousin, Mercy Woodward, who was seventeen and lived up in Norton. She was the daughter of Hannah Woodward, the sister of James Macomber, Zilphia's father. I met Mercy at the Macombers because they lived in Taunton. Zilphia was twelve years old at the time. Eight years later, I married Zilphia.

"Things work out as they should. You're not in any hurry, John. I believe I would talk to Mary face-to-face when the opportunity presents itself and honestly tell her how you feel. Go from there."

Things did work out. Mary was quite happy when John finally made it back down to Taunton in December after the Shepardsons completed the construction of a greenhouse. After a five-month absence, when she learned of his passion for her, it confirmed that her obsessive thoughts about him were justified. She was not surprised, as the two of them sat down with Sarah and confessed their love for each other. Sarah realized they were kindred spirits and suspected it was only a matter of time until love bloomed between them.

On Wednesday morning, March 21, 1821, John and Mary wed at the Congregational Church in Taunton. They trusted God and sought His love and support for their life journey as man and wife.

The windy, cold, overcast day did not discourage friends and family members from packing into the small church. From the Pratt side, Burts, Blanchards, Paulls, Macombers, and Reeds came to honor the couple. Follet and Fuller family members joined the Shepardsons to support John.

Afterward, the family went back to the nearby Pratt home for a seafood wedding feast that lasted into the afternoon. Rolls, onion pie, cheese quiche, potato puff, clam chowder, crab stew, scalloped oysters, baked stuffed shad, and maple-walnut cakes added to the warmth of the cheery crowd on this memorable late winter day. John and Mary took off to Wrentham, where they spent the night at the Shepardson's home before leaving the next morning for a honeymoon in Boston over the weekend.

※ ※ ※

There was a marked difference between work performed by slaves in the North and those in the South. In the more industrial northern states, enslaved people often performed as house servants, including butlers, maids, valets, cooks, artisans, laborers, and craftsmen. For the most part, northern farms were built on subsistence agriculture. The South had developed an agricultural economy dependent on labor-intensive commodity crops, and the vast majority of slaves worked in the fields cultivating indigo, rice, tobacco, and cotton.

The U.S. Constitution, adopted in 1787, prevented Congress from completely banning the importation of slaves until 1808. However, Congress regulated it in the Slave Trade Act of 1794 and subsequent Acts in 1800 and 1803.

During and for two decades following the Revolutionary War, every state in the North abolished slavery, ending with New Jersey in 1804. This did not necessarily mean that all slaves were set free immediately. The abolition movement was underway. By 1790,

Massachusetts, Vermont, and Maine possessed no slave population.

It did not take long before an "unseen highway" began running into and out of Boston, a noted rendezvous for refugees. Many traveled from southern ports; some came from Baltimore through Philadelphia; others arrived from underground stations developing primarily throughout eastern Massachusetts.

During the 1830s, most northern abolitionists were white Christians and their clergy. As the American Anti-Slavery Society grew throughout the decade, it aligned closely with various church denominations. At the same time, female anti-slavery societies attracted the most notable women abolitionists of the time.

Methodists, who viewed slavery as a moral issue, founded their first anti-slavery association in 1834. Three years later, Presbyterians fractured into two groups, the "Old School" and the "New School." They later allowed some Arminianism into the churches. This movement included a plea for the freedom of all God's human creatures, especially the Southern slaves. In 1840, the American Baptist Anti-Slavery Society was formed. Unitarian and Congregational denominations included many churches which supported abolition. Quakers were the only religious sect that had always decried slavery.

In the 1840s and 1850s, runaway slaves poured into Boston. By 1851, hundreds of fugitives were sheltered in the city and its environs.

As part of the Compromise of 1850 between the Northern Free-Soil Party (opposed the extension of slavery into the western territories) interests and those of southern slave-holding states, the U.S. Congress passed the Fugitive Slave Act in September of that year. It required law enforcement and citizens of free states to cooperate in the capture and return of slaves to their masters. This act exacerbated northern fears of what some called a "slave power conspiracy." It met with considerable resistance in free cities and states and galvanized those who previously sat on the fence.

Abolitionists faced a dilemma. They could either defy what they believed to be an unjust law or break with their own consciences and beliefs. Officials also wrestled with hard choices. Those who chose not to arrest an alleged runaway slave could be fined $1,000. All it took was a claimant's sworn testimony of ownership. The suspected fugitive had no rights. He or she could not ask for a jury trial or testify on his or her behalf. If caught in the process of running away, slaves could be killed.

A month after the Fugitive Slave Act was passed, a vigilance committee was formed in Boston by fifty men to organize passage through the underground railroad. Its membership quickly rose to more than 200, including those from outlying cities and towns. For ten and a half years, these people performed a variety of activities to ensure that more than 300 freedom seekers traveling through the Boston area arrived safely at their destinations.

Many more fugitives were sheltered and transitioned by other abolitionists and free Negroes not affiliated with the vigilance committee. Most assistance came from fellow slaves and free blacks. The majority of shelter, financial support, and directions came from their free brothers and sisters. Slave insurrection, Negro writers, speakers, and abolitionists combined to help lay a foundation for underground railroad activities.

Within a year of their marriage, John and Mary Shepardson found a sixty-acre tract of land on the edge of Norton, almost halfway between their two families in Wrentham and Taunton. The property included a four-bedroom house, a four-room cabin, and a good-sized barn. John planned to start growing a variety of vegetables on ten acres and tobacco on twenty acres. Woodland covered about another twenty acres.

Mary would begin teaching children that fall. Classes for the lower grades had grown so large that the current teacher, Miss

Audrey Buehler, requested an additional teacher and class space from the Norton City Council. Mary agreed to assume the position if Negro children were accepted as students. After a month of discussions with the town's two church congregations, members returned with an affirmative answer, much to Mary's delight.

The Shepardsons located a free black couple with two young sons to live in the cabin. George Davis gained his freedom papers at the age of eighteen from his white father, who owned a plantation in Frederick County, Maryland. The land sat on the Monocacy River, a tributary to the Potomac River. He went to Baltimore, then found his way to Philadelphia, where he met and married nineteen-year-old Sally Greene two years later. Sally's parents were both born free. Her father, Nate, was a cobbler. Her mother, Sarah, whose father was white, worked as a seamstress, as did her mother. Sally cooked for three years in the Reynold's beautiful home on South 8th Street before it was purchased by the Morris family. She then cooked for a women's boarding house on Chestnut Street.

George and Sally knew the reputation of eastern Massachusetts as a major center for abolitionist activity. Their first son, Cato, came along in March 1814, followed by Abram in January 1816. As soon as the family accumulated funds to travel and the children had grown a bit, they would head north, where there was more safety for their people.

In the meantime, Nate's Greene's leather supplier referred him to a harness maker in the city, a Mr. Hewitt. George had taken care of horses on the plantation and learned to repair harnesses as a youth. When Nate took his son-in-law to Mr. Hewitt's shop, which was five blocks from his small shop, the older Irishman agreed to hire George on a contingency basis. He did not disappoint. For the next six years, Mr. Hewitt, George, and another assistant, Devin Hurley (a more recent Irish immigrant from Antrim), worked steadily to make or repair mainly harnesses and bridles but occasionally other leather items, including specialty saddles.

In June 1822, George and Sally looked to the ocean as the route to New England. Roads were notoriously rough. Slave catchers rode ships and patrolled land for runaways. Both routes were potentially hazardous to free Negroes. But it was a long distance by land to reach their destination, which was New Bedford, on the southern coast of Massachusetts. A coasting vessel would be quicker and easier on little boys. They would see far fewer people.

Mercifully, the family arrived without incident. They headed west just past Fall River to the Taunton River, then north to Taunton, which became an underground railroad route. Once there, they found shelter with a family from the Congregationalist Church and learned there were many abolitionists in the area. They connected with Dier and Zilphia Pratt, who suspected this young family might be able to provide assistance that daughter Mary and her husband, John, needed now that they had started their family.

George looked forward to working in the country again since that was all he had ever known before moving to Philadelphia. He had not worked in the fields at the plantation, which covered 600 acres, most of which was planted in tobacco. He could probably write a book on the plant's production through osmosis. He had periodically helped with vegetable production for consumption in the big house. Forty acres seemed quite manageable. Also, the growing season would be shorter in New England.

Sally had always lived in the city. She loved the salt air sailing up the coast and the open spaces since their arrival. She wanted to raise her children in this environment. Mistress Shepardson, who insisted she calls her Mary, would be taking them to her classroom, undoubtedly giving them more individual attention than they would have received in the city. Cooking for this small number of people would be a pleasure. She did not think she'd mind keeping up the house.

Ruth Pratt Shepardson became the second child of John and Mary when she arrived in April 1823. Four siblings followed for a total of five daughters and a son. She took after her mother spelling and reading at an early age. She also inherited her spunk and sense of humor.

All the children loved being outdoors and assisting with the farm. Having Cato and Abram around was like growing up with older brothers. The children looked after chickens and goats from an early age. They also learned to help tend the family garden near the house. They enjoyed harvesting Concord grapes from trellises, which their mother and Sally turned into jelly. They foraged the woods for wild edibles from spring into early winter, starting with tender young dandelion leaves. A little later in the spring, wild leeks could be harvested. By July and August, the children loved picking blueberries, huckleberries, Northern blackberries, and red raspberries. In September, they gathered American hazelnuts from the trees. In October and November, cranberries grew in a small pond on the property.

Playmates were never far away. Aunt Sarah Pratt married Amasa Presbrey, who they called Mace, in 1827. He was born and raised in Norton, as was his mother, Anna Newland, and both of her parents. Although they married in Norton, Sarah and Mace settled in Taunton, where they had their first child, Esther, in 1829. However, Presbrey's cousins lived in Norton and now shared their lives with the growing Shepardson family.

The Presbreys had been in the Taunton area since William Presbrey arrived from London in 1711. Young William's family placed him on board a British man-of-war when he was only ten years old. He was bound to serve in the Navy until he came of age. Eleven years later, his ship anchored in Boston Harbor. He received permission to go ashore. He felt as if he had rendered his service, and he slipped away, probably with high hopes for a future in this new country. He headed south and received employment with a farmer, miller, and shoemaker in Taunton. A few years later, he bought land and built a house. He reportedly built one of the first properly rigged sloops to navigate the Taunton River. He married, fathered three children, and lived to be eighty-one years old.

The Shepardson children wanted to be on the water as often as their parents would take the time to get them there. Fortunately, two of John's sisters, Sally, who married John Wood, a brass craftsman, and Lucy, who wed Charles Bartlett, an accountant, had located to the Providence, Rhode Island area. Also, Abigail Pratt, a sister of Mary and Sarah, married Joshua Turner, and they lived in the village of Lime Rock in Providence County, where Joshua worked as a stone mason.

John was the fourth generation of Woods to have grown up in Swansea, located just west of Fall River at the mouth of the Taunton River. The entire town is part of the Narragansett Bay watershed area, twelve miles southeast of Providence. Many residents made their living from the sea.

As a very young man, John's father, Seth Wood, realized the potential of creating nautical products with brass. He convinced his father, John Wood Jr., of the profit potential by presenting him with a business plan. The elder Wood knew his son had a good head on his shoulders, and Seth had demonstrated that he was not afraid to work. His father gave Seth a loan at a low-interest rate and helped him clear out storage space on their property for a shop. In five years, the younger Wood had trouble keeping up with orders coming in. Soon after, he hired an assistant, Ian Burke, and moved to a shop closer to the waterfront.

Even as a boy, John, Seth's oldest son, demonstrated talent with his hands. He was fascinated by what his father could do with brass. As soon as he became old enough, he started working in the shop beside his father, who needed help. They made brass parts for ships and boats of all sizes, such as fog horns, passageway lights, bells, a few ship's wheels, port holes, cleats, and oar locks, among other items.

In 1805, when Seth Wood turned seventy-five and could no longer work, John moved the business to Cedar Grove, the southern section of East Providence. (The Narragansett Bay lies to the west and the Rummins River to the east.) John took Ian Burke, also a bachelor, with him. They attracted so much business that he hired talented, young Ethan Wilkerson.

In 1820, at the age of fifty-six, John Wood married Sally Shepardson from Wrentham. She was twenty years younger. It was the first marriage for both. In 1823, they produced a son, Calvin. Two years later, their daughter, Lucy, joined the family.

It was not all work and no play. The Woods owned a fishing schooner and a smaller fishing boat to take them up the rivers. When Sally's family came down for a few days in the spring, the men took off hoping to catch river herring or American shad, returning from the sea and running up the rivers and streams of the Narragansett Bay watershed. In the summer, they might be gone two or three days fishing for flounder, black sea bass, striped bass, mackerel, butterfish, scup, tautog, or their favorite bluefish.

In the meantime, the women took children to shorelines to dig for clams and quahogs. There were so many bi-valves in the area that people in the town of Cedar Grove became known as "Clam-diggers."

"Mother, I'm not waiting on those two," Ruth, age ten, yelled back toward her mother and aunt as she carried her bucket and tried not to drag her shovel and rake through the reeds.

"Me either," echoed sister Betsy, twelve, who stopped to watch their younger sisters, ages five and four, doddle along as if they had no place to be.

Mary Shepardson knew there would be no reining in her older girls. She was not even going to try. She wanted everybody to have a good time today.

"You two don't worry about us. But I don't want you to get out of sight. You hear me?"

"No, we won't do that," replied Betsy.

Calvin had already run a couple of hundred yards ahead. His sister, Lucy, who was now eight, hung back with her cousins.

They timed it perfectly. It was just now low tide, and the girls started walking out to where the water had been. In minutes, they saw coin-sized depressions in the sand where they knew clams were buried. Ruth dropped her bucket and tools. She pounded the ground around one of the holes. After a few seconds, water spurted up.

"I have one," she announced.

She put her shovel in the sand, stepped on it hard, and scooped out the sand. She then raked through it to see if she had dug deep enough. And there it was: her first clam of the day. She brushed off as much sand as she could and carefully placed it in the bucket. Then she refilled the hole.

"Look at this nice big one," shouted Betsy. "Seems like we're in a good place. Mother, Aunt Sally, come on down. We may be in luck today."

A neighbor dropped them off and said he would be back by noon. Three hours in a constant wind proved to be plenty for the girls. But even little Lucy and Mary held up well since they had the important job of toting two of the rakes. All four buckets were well over half full of clams. A good haul!

When they got back to the house, Grandmother Shepardson, who had come down from Taunton for the month, had a simple dinner ready. Then, it was time to prepare the clams.

Everybody agreed on clam chowder. Even though they had rinsed the clams in water at the shore, they were washed and scrubbed again. The clams were steamed until they opened, the black caps removed, the liquor strained and reserved, and the clams chopped. Salt pork was diced and fried. Onion slices were then sauteed in the fat, and thinly sliced potatoes were added, along with salt and pepper. Chopped clams and reserved clam liquor were added to this. After cooking for twenty minutes, the fried pork was added. Milk was heated and added to the chowder, along with butter and additional salt and pepper. It made a hearty, traditional dish for supper, one the men would be happy to dig into when they returned from the water.

"Calvin, run this little pot of chowder over to Mr. Lewis and thank him again for carrying us to the river this morning," said Sally.

"Why me? Can't one of the girls do it?"

"Because I asked you to do it, please.

"That boy is full of contrariety, I'm afraid. It's gotten him in trouble with his father."

"We have one like that," Mary Sr. said. "Likes to argue about everything,"

"And I wonder which one that might be?" replied Sally, smiling.

"Ha! That apple certainly does not fall far from the tree," said the children's grandmother. "Young Ruth is just like you, Mary. Can already hold her part of a conversation with anybody."

By 1819, runaway slaves were arriving at New Bedford by water. This influx continued and increased for the better part of the next three decades as staunch abolitionists provided a safe haven for those seeking safety. A number of these families were Quakers.

A strong anti-slavery sentiment prevailed in southern Massachusetts and neighboring Rhode Island. The Shepardsons, Pratts, Woods, and Rounds, who were the family of John Wood's mother, Roby Rounds Wood, constantly kept their ears to the ground for developments of the underground railroad in their neck of the woods.

In late 1838, a young man named Frederick Bailey and his new bride, Anna Murray, arrived in New Bedford after escaping from Maryland and moving through Baltimore, Philadelphia, and New York. They would change their married name to Douglass. Frederick Douglass became a social reformer, abolitionist, orator, writer, and statesman in his seventy-seven years. As a twenty-year-old in New Bedford, Douglass subscribed to William Lloyd Garrison's weekly journal, *The Liberator*. The abolitionist newspaper, which appealed to the moral conscience of its readers, profoundly influenced young Douglass. In 1841, he first heard Mr. Garrison speak in a meeting of the Bristol Anti-Slavery Society. At Mr. Garrison's invitation, Frederick Douglass addressed the Massachusetts Anti-Slavery Society's annual convention on Nantucket Island a few days later. He astonished the gathering with his eloquent speech.

John and Mary Shepardson sat in the audience with their oldest daughters, Betsy, now twenty, and Ruth, eighteen. They had traveled down from Norton with their neighbors, Peter and Arabella Anker, who were stationmasters on the underground railroad. In Taunton, they had picked up sister Sarah and her husband, Mace Presbrey.

The ship ferrying passengers from New Bedford to Nantucket was abuzz with the news that Maria Weston Chapman and her sisters would be attending. With Maria leading, the Weston sisters were stalwart supporters of Mr. Garrison's radical call for immediate abolition of slavery. Deborah Weston was well-known in New Bedford because she had taught school there. The sisters were talented, articulate, witty, energetic individually, and formidable as a group.

In 1834, Maria, Caroline, Anne, Deborah Weston, and eight other women formed the Boston Anti-Slavery Society. They circulated petitions, raised money, wrote and edited numerous publications, and left behind remarkable correspondence.

The Shepardsons all remembered that week as a turning point in their commitment. First in Bristol County, then on Nantucket Island, they listened to speeches by some of the most passionate New Englanders dedicated to human justice and talked with fellow abolitionists and anti-slavery activists.

Ruth agreed with Maria Chapman when the Weymouth, Massachusetts, Native claimed that slavery was a direct violation of the laws of God. Ruth kept going back to what the disciple said in Matthew 25:30: "And the King shall answer, 'Verily I say unto you, inasmuch as ye have done it unto one of the least of these my brothers, ye have done it unto me.'" She realized there was much work to do. And the place to connect was Boston.

Slave catchers traveling through New England soon realized they faced "stout fellows and hard liars" who didn't suffer fools. Local solidarity and loyalties greatly inhibited the flow of information. These hunters of humans on the run found their foes to be descendants with the intellect and fierceness of their recent ancestors, who had beaten back Indians and Redcoats. More than one southern slave searcher was alleged to have disappeared along the coast of Rhode Island and Massachusetts or perhaps in the bays, estuaries, rivers, marshes, or many area ponds. Of course, if you asked the local populace, people claimed ignorance of such a notion.

When the Shepardsons returned home, they created a hideaway under the floor of George's leather shop in the barn, which they had helped him build in the late 20s. It was small, just big enough to hide two people. But they felt it was comfortable and secure. Thus, the family became an underground station. Sometimes they welcomed a single person, or a couple sent their way. Other times, they accommodated an overflow from their neighbor, the Ankers.

Ruth already kept journals. Now, she began sharing her writing with abolitionist publications. It would be a couple of years before any publication accepted one of her submissions. The process, however, heightened her awareness and extended her contacts.

The Shepardson sisters and their mother also started cooking in quantity and sharing the food with those in the area who provided hiding places for freedom seekers. Four to eight women would come to the Shepardson's house once a week with big baskets of supposed sewing materials. They stayed for at least a couple of hours, and a few did, in fact, sew while they were there. Mary's younger girls, Lucy and Mary, who were teenagers by now, looked after any children who came with their mothers. The baskets were loaded with food prior to their leaving. Depending on the season, sometimes there would be potato rolls, sometimes pumpkin biscuits; maybe cauliflower soup one week, cabbage soup another; green beans in casserole, succotash, Harvard beets, white beans, carrots with fresh mint, braised parsnips, baked sweet potatoes with apples; blueberry pies one week, and strawberry crunch another. Every week differed as to need. They never knew how many "guests" to expect. But somehow, the food always seemed to work out.

One summer day in 1845, Ruth went to the barn and noticed Cyrus White in George's shop. She had not seen him in at least two years. She thought he must be about eighteen now. He sure looked different. She stopped to say hello. She had gone to school with his sister, Sarah, who was a year younger than her. He said his father sent him to pick up a new harness George had made. She invited him into the house for lemonade.

"Is it safe for me to come in here with all you Shepardson girls?" joked Cyrus.

Ruth asked, "And just how many of us do you think there are?"

"Well, I've heard there's a houseful."

"I think you're safe. Sister Betsy up and unexpectedly got married last year so she is no longer around. That leaves four of us girls. Catherine is two. Joe is nine now and always happy to have another male in the house."

"Cyrus White, is that you?" asked Lucy. "That blond hair looks even blonder against your dark skin. I believe you've been out in the fields."

"Sure have. Father and I wore out an old harness, getting the ground ready for planting. We've got everything seeded now, though. Elbridge is about to be thirteen, and he's more helpful than he was last season."

"Why, hello, Cyrus. Here's something to drink. Do sit down." said Mary.

"Thank you, ma'am."

"I haven't seen your father in a while. How is he getting along since you lost your sweet mother? I know it hasn't been easy," Mary said.

"My sister, Sarah, was just thirteen when Mother died. It was very rough on her. When Mother started getting sick, we moved down here to Norton since this is where the Blandins are from. When we lost her seven years later, Aunt Susanna and her daughter, my cousin Sarah, who was sixteen at the time, came over nearly every day with dinner for us despite having those younguns at their house. They did that for nearly three years until Sarah learned to cook. Thank goodness Uncle Jesse is a patient husband.

"I don't think Father will remarry. He says that when he took his marriage vows, he meant it when he said, 'forever.' He fully expects to be reunited with my mother in Heaven. He truly loved her."

As Ruth listened, it struck her that Cyrus had grown into a compassionate man. She sensed he had a good heart. Some woman would be lucky to attract such a man.

Before Cyrus left, Mary invited him and his father to supper later in the week. The Whites were not involved in the abolition movement. They belonged to the Unitarian Church and kept up with developments through church members. They had heard there were area families who sheltered fugitives on the underground railroad, but they did not know who they were.

Within a few months, Ruth and Cyrus started spending time together. Ruth found him to have an easy disposition. He was a good conversationalist, intelligent, and witty.

Cyrus went with the Shepardsons to an abolitionist society meeting in Fall River in the fall of 1846. It was the year after Frederick Douglass published his best-selling first autobiography, *Narrative of the Life of Frederick Douglass, an American Slave*. Attendees could purchase copies at the meeting. The book caused a flurry of excitement.

On the last day of the meeting, during a discussion on how evangelicalism factored into religion's increased denouncement of slavery, Cyrus declared, "If God's grace can individually free us from slavery to sin, guilt, and shame, He will surely provide a solution to human bondage which threatens to tear this country apart. I have to do what I can to help."

At this point, Ruth felt compelled to share her family's involvement. She trusted Cyrus. She wanted to become his wife. She sensed a strength in him that would help solidify her potential usefulness.

In September 1850, they were married in Norton, days before the Fugitive Slave Act was passed by the U.S. Congress. Ruth explained that she had to live in the Boston area to take advantage of all the contacts. They had postponed the wedding until Cyrus's younger brother, Elbridge, turned eighteen and could step into his shoes on their father's farm. Finding a farm around Boston became their focus.

They found more than they were looking for at 266 Albion Street in Wakefield, twelve miles north of Boston. The nearly forty-acre property included a forested portion extending to Crystal Lake, where the town received its drinking water. It also included a two-story late 1700s farmhouse with a hidden space behind receding paneling above the kitchen (where the previous couple hid runaway slaves), a large barn, and a second, smaller house. Peggy Webb Coates had recently died unexpectedly. The widower, Douglas Coates, who was childless, agreed to sell the property for a reasonable price when he discovered that the Whites were searching for farm property that they could continue using as a station on the underground railroad.

It did not take long for word to get out that Mr. Coates sold to a young abolitionist couple from Bristol County, who planned little service disruption. The recently passed Fugitive Slave Act had stirred up a hornet's nest in the North. Between 1850 and into the 1860s, a black wave was to sweep north across the landscape as escaped slaves tried to reach freedom in Canaan, as many of them called it. Therefore, conductors were relieved that the Whites would maintain this station on the railroad, as everyone was needed.

Jesse and Susanna Blandin's oldest son, Henry, and his wife, Chloe, had married in 1834. By 1850, when their cousin, Ruth, decided to move to the Boston area to become more involved in abolitionist activities, they, too, felt the need to commit their time and energy to protecting fugitives from pursuit and capture. They considered slavery to be archaic and unjust.

When they heard that the Whites had purchased property in Wakefield, Henry and Chloe arranged with her sister to keep their two youngest children since Sarah Ann was now two years old and weaned. Their oldest child, George, fifteen, begged to go along with his parents, and they relented. He was as big as a man and mature beyond his years. He had always been good with horses and could drive a four-horse team. Therefore, he drove the carriage up to Middlesex County on the late April ride. Henry and Chloe sat in the back. The ride lifted their spirits as spring green popped from trees along the way.

Ruth and Cyrus were surprised to see family so soon and glad for the company and help. It did not take more than a day to decide that it would benefit everybody if the Blandins relocated and moved into the smaller house on the property.

Cyrus would certainly need help on the farm. He gave the family room and board in exchange for Jesse's labor. He told him there was extra land for him to pursue another agricultural operation on his own if he so chose. They walked the property on the day after their arrival. Jesse noticed the back of the moderate hill in the back of the house sloped off slightly in bright sunlight. He thought if the trees on the little incline were removed, it would be a perfect location for a vineyard of Concord grapes.

Chloe made beautiful jewelry out of metals, including silver, copper and pewter. Ruth offered to let her set up a shop in a little end room with an outside door in the bigger house. She looked forward to the selling advantage of living near the large area surrounding Boston.

Considering the secret nature of the underground railroad network, it seemed word traveled fast to those who needed to know. In early June, Cyrus heard about Poor's Wagon Shop in Andover. William Poor became an expert wagon maker under the tutelage of his maternal grandfather, George Bradley, of the North Parish in Andover, when William became his apprentice in 1826 at age twenty-one. In 1833, he opened his own blacksmith shop. His brother, Jonathan, joined him as a wheelwright. Thirteen years later, William's sixteen-year-old son, Joseph, joined the business. He developed a "rare genius" for mechanics. By 1850, the Poors were known as the best wagon builders in the state. The business included a wheelwright shop, a blacksmith shop, a lumber shop, and a carriage house.

The Poor family were abolitionists. Their home and business had been linked to the underground railroad as safe stations for fugitives on the run to Canada. They constructed wagons with false bottoms to secretly transport human cargo.

Henry and George talked about becoming conductors. They discussed the possibility with Cyrus, who called in Mr. Coates since he knew people operating as conductors and stationmasters. They talked with a Mr. and Mistress Lincoln. The Lincolns had escorted slaves between safe houses for the past four years. They discussed time demands, possible problems encountered, potential dangers, and the many rewards.

In the end, all agreed. It was not an opportunity they could pass up. One day in late June, Cyrus, Henry, and George took a carriage over to Reading, then up to Andover, about a fifteen-mile ride. Poor's Wagon Shop was located in Frye Village.

Every part of the business held young George's attention. He was especially impressed that Joseph was just five years older and had started the business at sixteen, which George would be the next month. The young men talked, and Joseph explained the blacksmithing end of the operation. He demonstrated his ingenuity when working through the details.

Cyrus and Henry handed Mr. Poor a referral. They said they needed a wagon to carry fugitives from station to station and one that would provide many years of service on the farm. They left after giving Mr. Poor a down payment. Unfortunately, the wagon would not be available until late fall because they could not build them fast enough to keep up with orders.

The Whites soon heard about the heavy underground traffic along the nearby coast. Simeon and Betsy Dodge operated a long-time station in Marblehead. The Dodges had assisted numerous runaway slaves over the years by providing shelter, clothes, and food and making arrangements for them in other safe houses in town. Coastal homes made ideal stations because hiding places already existed to conceal smuggled goods. Escaping slaves could be hidden in attic rooms, cellar storage spaces, secret staircases, or closets with fake walls.

Those providing a station on the underground railroad communicated with stationmasters, conductors, and runaways using a variety of means, including secret words, codes, signals, and signs. Mr. Coates had run a line of gourds from the end of his driveway up to the house. This marked the residence as a safe station. Slaves traveled in the dark. Many followed a group of stars that looked like a cup with a very long handle, known as the Drinking Gourd. They often used gourds to dip and drink water. Two stars on the cup's edge always point to the North Star, which directs them toward freedom.

One night, the first week of their first July in Wakefield in 1851, Cyrus and Ruth were awakened by a man's deep voice singing outside their window.

"Follow the drinking gourd!
Follow the drinking gourd.
For the old man is a-waiting for to carry you to freedom
If you follow the drinking gourd.
When the sun comes back and the first quail calls,
Follow the drinking gourd.
For the old man is a-waiting for to carry you to freedom
If you follow the drinking gourd.
The riverbank makes a very good road,
The dead trees will show you the way.
Left foot, peg foot, traveling on,
Follow the drinking gourd."

Cyrus rushed out of bed and stumbled into his trousers. He dashed down the stairs and threw open the door.

A coal-black man stood on the stoop with his hat in his hands. Behind him at the bottom of the steps stood a woman, and a couple of feet to her left side, a boy and girl, maybe just about to reach their teen years, although it was hard to tell with a half moon overhead.

"Sur, a friend of a friend sent us," said the man.

"You've come to the right place," replied Cyrus as he introduced himself.

By that time, Ruth was by his side. "Welcome to our home," she said. "I am Mistress White. Cyrus, bring them back to the kitchen door, and we'll take them up to their room. Then, I'll get you something to eat. I know you must be hungry."

"Yes, 'um," said the woman. "Thank ya, kindly."

Cyrus took bags from the woman and the girl. He walked the family along the porch, which intersected with a breezeway to the barn. It was not visible from the road. Two steps led into the big corner kitchen. Then they climbed a lower flight of stairs into a guest bedroom over the kitchen. Here, Ruth lit a lantern and led the way. A door revealed a narrow set of stairs into the attic. Ruth pushed a spot on the wall, and a panel opened. Small steps dropped into a good-sized space that might accommodate up to ten people if crowded. It lay between the guest bedroom and Cyrus and Ruth's bedroom. It held mattresses, many quilts, pillows, six chairs, and a table. There was no window, of course, although air vents matching those in the bedrooms to either side had been added. Ruth left the lantern and pointed out the privacy curtain and the location of the chamber pot. Said she would return with food.

Ruth realized they needed extra airflow. She left the panel open at the top of the stairs leading into their hidden space and opened the four windows in the corner guest bedroom for ventilation.

As they went through the kitchen, Ruth started boiling water. She made a pot of coffee and a pot of oatmeal, found honey and cream to go with it, and grabbed a loaf of brown bread with butter she had made the day before.

When she returned with breakfast, the man apologized for not introducing his family right away. "I be Cletus. This here my wife, Sade; our girl, Patsy, who be fourteen, our boy, Chester, twelve. We believe the Lord protects us through good folks such as yoselves. Bless ya'll, ma'am."

"We're happy to have you and your family, Cletus. You sleep as long as you want tomorrow. Ring the bell on the table when you're awake, and I'll bring you something else to eat. We will get you baths tomorrow. We'll check and make sure the area is safe for your travels and where you can stay next. But now, eat before it gets cold. Rest well."

Perhaps once a month, fugitives walked up to the White's house during the night. But nearly always, they came in wagons driven by a conductor. Sometimes, Cyrus and Ruth knew they were coming, but not always. The wagons would come into the barn, and the much-relieved passengers, after stretching their legs, went directly into the house. They might stay one or several nights. One time, they sheltered eight people for four weeks because there was a large slave patrol roaming the coast and coming inland from Gloucester over to Andover, down to Medford, and back up to Lynn.

New Englanders are nothing if not ingenious. Lives depended on secrecy to efficiently run the underground network to freedom. One humble house in eastern Massachusetts had a deep cellar that could be entered by a hidden broadside door in a woodshed. Another had a deep wide hidden cellar beneath a shallow, innocuous storage place for potato and apple bins and cider barrels.

The Whites added two new members to their household in quick succession. Selim was born in December 1855, followed eleven months later by Edson.

The following April, Chloe Blandin died at the age of forty-three of sepsis shock while combating an infection that developed after one of the horses stomped on her foot, breaking the skin and bone. Her youngest, Sarah, had just turned eight. After losing her mother, she stayed with the Whites much of the time, doing what she could to help Ruth look after her young sons.

In 1858, Abraham Lincoln said, "American republicanism can be purified by restricting the further expansion of slavery as the first step to putting it on the road to 'ultimate extinction.'" When he assumed the office of the presidency in March 1861, seven Southern states seceded from the Union.

Southern forces attacked the U.S. Army installation at Fort Sumter, South Carolina, on April 12, 1861. Four additional slave states seceded. The action officially ignited the American Civil War. Northern leaders viewed the situation as unacceptable since the Confederate States of America now controlled the Mississippi River and parts of the West.

In the early summer of 1861, George Blandin drove his Aunt Ruth White and his sister, Elizabeth, twenty-three, who went by Nellie, into Boston to meet Aunt Mary Putnam, Aunt Ruth's sister. Her husband, George Putnam, and his father, Tom, operated a cotton manufacturing and brokerage business near the waterfront. They hired a young man from Michigan, who came to Boston hoping to acquire funding to sail to England. His name was Henry Dunbar. He now worked as a runner for the Putnams.

When Henry saw Nellie and realized she was among Mrs. Putnam's family, he boldly asked if they might not want another man to accompany them when he heard Mr. Putnam say he could not join them for supper. The proposition startled both Georges. But then they saw Nellie smiling at Henry.

"That's acceptable with me," said Mary's husband. "You know a place or two they might enjoy. But I will defer the question to Mrs. White."

"It might be nice to have a young man along who can guide us," Ruth said, "We drove a three-seater because I did not know how many would end up going."

Henry married Nellie on the Boston waterfront a year later, and that is where they had enjoyed their first day together. Nellie married a man whose adventurous spirit matched her own. She saw gold in her future. Henry was smart enough not to argue with his new bride. They immediately made plans to head west in the spring. The couple settled in Placerville, California, where gold mining operations thrived.

Congress passed the Confiscation Act in August of 1861. It barred slaveholders from re-enslaving captured runaways, which the Union now considered contraband of war if they came into Union possession.

Late in 1861, when the war was getting underway, George Blandin got a job delivering mail and parcels in Wakefield. On the night of July 15, 1864, he went to a co-worker's house with a couple of other friends for supper and cards. He left shortly after dark to walk the mile home. About halfway there, someone pushed him into a field. There was a scuffle; the left side of his face was badly cut and bruised, and there were scratches on his knuckles. George was not a small man, nor was he weak. His father believed at least two men attacked him. The knife went into the left side of his neck.

Henry rode to the post office the next morning because his son did not return all night. When told George had not come in, he asked his friend, Joel, if he had made it to his house the previous evening. Joel said, "Yes, and he left a little after 9:00 p.m." From there, Henry hurried to the sheriff's office. Searchers quickly discovered George's body. They ruled out robbery as a motive. No witness came forward. No evidence was found. The killing forever remained a mystery. George Blandin would have turned twenty-nine in two days.

Shortly after that, Henry and his fifteen-year-old daughter, Sarah, moved to Holliston, located west of Boston. The postmaster in Wakefield said that his brother operated the Post Office in Holliston, where they needed another mail deliverer. Said he would be happy to refer Henry to his brother. Henry realized he needed a change in scenery.

On January 1, 1863, President Lincoln issued the Emancipation Proclamation by executive order. Approximately three million slaves became legally free as soon as they escaped the control of the Confederate government by running away or through the advance of federal troops. The proclamation did not apply to border states. That came on April 9, 1865, following the surrender of General Robert E. Lee at Appomattox.

The Fugitive Slave Act had been formally repealed in 1864.

The Whites and Blandins rejoiced with their abolitionist neighbors as all of New England let out a collective sigh of relief now that the terrible war had ended. Nearly 14,000 Massachusetts soldiers and sailors died in the war. The only close White family member to have enlisted was Granville Morse, husband of Catherine Shepardson, Ruth's youngest sister. He enlisted in the Massachusetts 18th Regiment in August 1861 and mustered out in October 1864. Then, he volunteered for the Massachusetts 32nd Infantry Regiment in October 1864 before coming home the following June. In February 1863, he obtained leave, returned to Norton, and married Catherine. He survived sickness and several of the deadliest battles of the war.

All slaves did not become officially free until December 6, 1865, when three-fourths of the states ratified the Thirteenth Amendment, abolishing slavery. William Lloyd Garrison, then president of the American Anti-Slavery Society, moved at its convention months later for its disbanding.

Cyrus and Ruth found a young couple to live in their smaller house. Alex and Lilly Morgan, both in their mid-twenties, grew up on farms. Alex needed no instruction in the fields. Lilly helped Ruth harvest a thriving Concord grape vineyard on the far side of the hill, planted and nurtured by Henry Blandin. In late summer, the women enjoyed making jams and jellies. They sold all they made at a weekly farmers market, along with bread baked by Lilly for a full day before each market day. She made her soda bread with flour, baking soda, salt, and buttermilk, just like her mother and grandmother did.

Lillie's mother, Cassidy, married Thomas O'Toole, a fisherman whose father had captained a vessel out of Gloucester, which Thomas now ran. She came from a long line of Wards in County Donegal. Cass Ward came from Ireland in 1836 with her parents and five siblings, who settled on the first point of land they saw. The Wards bought a small farm on the edge of town. As they grew, Daideó Eamon and his grandsons kept corn, sweet peas, and potatoes planted in the rocky soil. When they arrived, Cass's mother, Maeve, insisted they bake for their new neighbors. Two years later, they opened a small bakery. The next year, Cass married. The three Ward granddaughters spent time in the shop learning recipes from their Mamó and Mum over the years.

Corn grew and sold well, as did all vegetables, since the Whites lived outside a major population center. Most of their corn was converted into meal at a Wakefield grist mill owned by David MacLaren and operated by his sons, James and John. The majority ended up in large sacks to be sold wholesale. Some went into small flour sacks, which Ruth and Lilly sold at the farmers market.

Two blond-headed, almost teenage boys helped with chores, ran the woods ragged, and aggravated their father to take the time to go to the lake with them at the far end of the property so they could swim, which they were not supposed to do by themselves. Selim White demonstrated an affinity for numbers. He possessed natural mechanical skills. His younger brother, Edson, took after his mother and grandmother. He wrote in a journal every day, and he would have had his nose stuck in a book every minute if he could have gotten away with it. Edson spent fifty-one years at the Boston Globe, most of those on the editorial staff. He revered the Wakefield Library, where he became a trustee later in life.

By 1875, Cyrus started exhibiting adverse physical symptoms, including fatigue, headaches, abdominal pain, breathing difficulty, hypertension, reduced urination, and blood in the urine. By the time he passed away on April 26, 1880, at age fifty-three, doctors had diagnosed Bright's disease. Although there was no confirmation of the disease that claimed his mother at age forty-six, her seven-year decline was suspected to have been Bright's disease.

In 1884, Henry and Nellie Dunbar relocated to Philipsburg, Montana. Mining peaked there from 1881 to 1893. The area became Granite County in 1893, named after the mountain that contained the Granite Mountain Silver Mine. Most of the lode gold was extracted from silver ores found in district creeks.

Elizabeth "Nellie" Blandin Dunbar inherited the same disease that killed her aunt, Sarah Blandin White, and great-uncle Cyrus White. She died on July 22, 1898, of Bright's disease in the mountains of Montana at the age of sixty.

Ruth White lived another twenty-three years after the loss of her husband, Cyrus. She inherited the Shepardson and Pratt longevity. Son, Edson, lived in the Albion Street house until he died in 1933.

Son, Donald, his wife, Ruth Haseltine White, and their five children moved into the house upon Edson's death to look after Grandma Alice Currier White until she passed on five years later. They were the last Whites to live there.

Ice King of Lowell

Gage (White)

Daniel thought people must have heard the cracking all the way to Broadway as he lay in bed with little hope of going back to sleep in the predawn hours of this night in April of 1872. Giant ice blocks on the Merrimack River fronted his house and finally began breaking up in response to rain and unexpected warmer temperatures over the past week.

Residents of Lowell, Massachusetts, prepared themselves each year for the possibility of spring floods attributable to ice jams. The preceding month set a record for cold temperatures with heavy snowfall. The ominous weather served as a warning.

His wife, Abiah, rolled over and touched his arm, "I know you're awake," she said.

"It's started," Daniel responded. "There is going to be a lot of ice coming down through here. Let's pray it does not get too blocked up so the water can flow."

"Thank goodness you have harvested your ice, your ice houses are already full, and your workers have their pay. That is a lot to be grateful for, my love," said Abiah.

"So it is. Now, I must dress and check on things outside. It would not surprise me if a couple of the men didn't wander over to the office or the ice house to make sure everything was alright. You stay in bed."

This was Daniel's second year as proprietor of the Daniel Gage Ice Company. Even though his businesses' buildings, just like his house, sat high enough to prevent serious damage from anything but calamitous flooding, his family has not been on Merrimack Street long enough for him to feel completely secure under present conditions. He knew Mother Nature could have a mind of her own.

Daniel stepped outside. The rain had stopped, and the sky was dark under a new moon. Still, ice outlined the river, which appeared to undulate. It growled and rumbled as water levels rose and pushed on ice blocks covering the top of the river, breaking them apart. The sound reverberated through him.

He carried an armload of wood into the office, just yards from the Gage house, and stoked the fire in his stove. He then lit a lantern above his desk before settling into his chair.

Prospects for a profitable year looked good. Workers had filled his ice house along the south bank of the Merrimack River. He was negotiating for another large ice house above Pawtucket Falls in the Pawtucketville section of Lowell. He intended to purchase most of the ponds and lakes in the Greater Lowell area. There was also a pond in nearby Chelmsford he had his eye on. Proceeds from this year's harvest should speed the process along.

People had to have ice. Every two to three days, families purchased a block of ice for their cooler at home; farmers needed it to keep their milk, butter, eggs, and other perishables from spoiling; meat packers, brewers, and other industries bought ice; railroads used it to keep food products from spoiling while being transported; hotels, restaurants, and dining cars made up a huge market.

Daniel Gage recognized ice as an indispensable commodity by 1853, when he was twenty-five years old and working on his family's farm in Pelham, New Hampshire, located over the state line. He did not want to farm, but every winter, he joined his brothers and other men in the community in harvesting ice from several ponds in the area. He understood that a man could create wealth from ice if he knew what he was doing. He vowed that he would somehow learn all there was to know.

"Good morning, Mr. Gage," said Henry Dawkins, one of Daniel's delivery drivers. Henry Dawkins worked as a delivery driver for the company. He came from good stock, and Daniel felt blessed to have him. Only two out of twenty-five employees failed to work out in two years.

Daniel asked, "Dawkins, what are you doing here so early?"

"I figured this was your first time living down here since the river acted up. Thought you might be up and want some company. Here, Lizzy made biscuits with ham and coffee. Hungry?"

"As a matter of fact, that sounds good. I told Mrs. Gage not to bother getting up. But I was wishing I had a good cup of coffee. Set that pot on the stove for a few minutes. Thank you."

"You know, the Dawkins family goes back several generations in Lowell. I've grown up hearing all about the flood of 1836. It just about drowned a good part of New England. I was born right in the middle of all that. It started raining on March 11 and did not stop until the 23rd. I arrived on March 18th that year."

"I'm certain that's something your parents never forgot," Daniel replied.

"At least we were safe. Our house was still standing, which was more than a lot of people could say. The Merrimack in Lowell rose sixty-eight feet. Can you imagine? Many of the mills were heavily damaged.

Dawkins continued, "Up your way in New Hampshire, they say it rained twenty-two inches in fourteen days. I guess you remember your family talking about it."

"Well, I was just a boy, but yes, I do remember people being upset about so much loss of life," said Daniel.

"I think there were 200 killed and about 14,000 left homeless over New England," Dawkins added. "Grandma said ladies at the church kept the doors open for weeks feeding people who needed a meal."

Daniel had moved to Lowell, or what was then still part of the town of Dracut, in 1854 to learn the lay of the land and integrate himself into the community. He used his natural business acumen, along with recommendations from a handful of Hillsborough

County farmers, to start a business in the city's wholesale beef trade. In the fifteen years that followed, he had learned the names and the needs of most farmers in the northeastern Massachusetts counties.

With quick railroad service from Lowell to Boston, he found a ready market for beef in Eastern seaboard cities. The meat canning business originated in Massachusetts and Maine early in the century. It was greatly boosted by the start of the Civil War since armies needed nonperishable food. Daniel was in a perfect position to provide fresh products to canning factories. He also discovered that ice was needed to ship beef long distances without using excess salt and smoking procedures as preservatives.

"I believe I'll stroll down to the bridge and see what's going on," said Dawkins. "If there's going to be any backup, it's liable to happen there first."

Just then, the door opened, and Daniel's ten-year-old daughter walked in.

"Good morning, Miss Martina," Dawkins said.

"Oh, Mr. Dawkins, I didn't know anybody else would be here. Good morning to you."

"Daughter, is your mother up?" asked Daniel.

"Yes, Father. How is anybody supposed to sleep with all that cracking going on? She said to tell you breakfast would be ready in about ten minutes. She doesn't think we will have to go to school today because it might flood, but she wanted me to ask you."

"No, no school today. Mr. Dawkins is just now going down to check on the bridge, but we don't know how the day is going to progress. It would be safer if you and your sister stayed here. Tell your mother I'll be right there."

The first light of dawn broke as Daniel walked back into the house. He realized his wife must have been up for at least an hour because the stoves were blazing, and their heat had knocked the early morning chill out of the house.

Alice, the Gage's seven-year-old, stopped setting the table long enough to run over and give her father a kiss.

"No school today, Father!"

"You don't say," Daniel responded as he hung up his coat.

"I think I'll go to the bridge and watch huge chunks of ice come down the river," his young daughter announced.

"No, that is definitely not what you are going to do. There'll be big crowds at the bridge all day, probably already are. Ice will be knocking against the supports. It may very well get hung up there, which could create a dangerous situation. Not a good place for curious little girls to be. Je suis désolé, petit chéri."

The smell of coffee lured him into the kitchen just as Abiah poured two cups. Despite the earlier ham and biscuits, Daniel found himself hungry again when he smelled what was frying on the stove.

Yesterday, Abiah had made a couple of loaves of her delicious cracked wheat bread. This morning, they ate Scotch eggs with the toasted bread and fried potatoes with onions. There were just six jars of blueberry jam left from the canning session last summer, a precious commodity since all four family members loved it.

✸ ✸ ✸

The families of both Daniel and Abiah had been long-time, prominent residents of Pelham, New Hampshire. Their hometown lay about eight miles north of Lowell.

Abiah's parents, Moses and Pamela Eaton Haseltine, were both born in Haverhill, Massachusetts, then moved to Cheshire County, New Hampshire, after they married in 1777. She grew up hearing about the family's connection to Hannah Duston, although the Haverhill woman's exploits would not become famous until the early 1800s.

Much to Daniel's surprise, when his sister, Mary Gage, married Amos Currier in 1857, he discovered that Mary's new family were direct line descendants of Hannah Duston, who, by now, was practically a household name. Daniel's relation to this brave pioneer meant something to him. His great-great-great-grandfather, Daniel Gage I, lived in Bradford across the Merrimack River from Haverhill. He was fifty-eight at the time of the devastating Indian attack in March 1697, during which twenty-seven residents were killed. His youngest of ten children was seven years old. His wife, Sarah, had been dead for five years. The people of Bradford might just as easily have been the victims, and Daniel's long Gage line could have been considerably shortened.

Abenaki Indians from Quebec raided Haverhill one day in early March 1697 during King William's War. Hannah Duston Emerson, thirty-nine, had given birth to Martha, her ninth child, six days previously. Her nurse, Mary Neff, assisted her bedside.

Hannah's husband, Thomas Emerson, directed the older children toward the fort from horseback while he stayed within sight of his house, firing on the enemy in the yard. A neighbor ushered him away when it became obvious he could do nothing about his family in the house.

The Abenaki captured Hannah, her infant daughter, and Mary Neff. Before getting out of town, one of the Indians snatched the baby and bashed her head against an apple tree, knowing she would impede their progress. The tree sat on the property of Jonathan Eaton, who was the great-great-grandfather of Abiah Gage. Jonathan's wife, Sarah, who had given birth to a son on the same day that tiny Martha Duston was born, hid in a nearby swamp during the raid. She became sick from exposure and soon died from lingering complications.

Hannah and Mary were marched nearly one hundred miles and transferred to a smaller band of Abenaki. The group included two adult males, two adult females, six children, and fourteen-year-old

Samuel Lennardson, captured the previous year in Worcester, Massachusetts. Two weeks into the journey, on Sugar Ball Island, at the confluence of the Merrimack and Contoocook rivers, north of Concord, New Hampshire, Hannah, Mary, and Samuel killed the two men, one woman and five children with tomahawks and knives while they slept one night. The other woman and a child, although badly injured, got away.

The escapees then sunk all the birch bark canoes, except one, which had been left at the site.` Before leaving, Hannah and Samuel scalped all of the dead as proof of what happened and as a bounty to collect a reward offered by the governor of Massachusetts. Traveling at night, terrified of another attack, they braved the cold, black, treacherous water of the Merrimack River, dodging sheets of ice and uprooted trees. Half starved, their woolen garments wet in weather ideal for hypothermia, they miraculously returned to Haverhill.

❦ ❦ ❦

Sometime in the 1730s, four Gage families moved from Bradford to the new settlement of Pelham, just over the New Hampshire state line. Daniel III, Josiah, and Amos Gage were sons of Daniel and Martha Burbank Gage. All Gages from Daniel's seven-generation family line in this country originated from John Gage and Amee Wilford, who immigrated from Suffolk, England, in 1630 and settled in Bradford.

James Gage, a nephew of Daniel and Martha Gage, also moved to Pelham with his cousins. The four families settled on what became known as Gage Hill.

Although much of Bradford in the early- to mid-1700s was dedicated to farming, the four ancestors who moved to Pelham wanted to settle in an area more open, less hemmed in by other small towns.

James scouted the area, which featured a river where numerous streams fed into it containing brook trout. Ponds with good, clear water dotted the area. Ample forest sheltered a bounty of wildlife. This accessible food supply attracted the Gages to the area. Turkey, deer, bears, rabbits, squirrels, and other wildlife provided much of their diet.

The families ended up farming, as did most settlers in the mid-state area of New Hampshire. New England soil never proved favorable to profitable farming; this land was no exception. They found the rocky soil good for subsistence purposes only. Corn continued to be their staple crop. Pumpkins, squash, and beans also grew fairly well. In their home gardens, herbs, leaf lettuces, spinach, and root vegetables provided food.

They gathered sorrel and watercress from the wild to make soups, among other dishes, as well as dandelion greens and fiddlehead ferns, both of which make good eating. Chestnuts went into stuffing and desserts. Favorite dishes from crops included corn chowder, greens soup, Brunswick stew (which called for squirrel meat), venison stew, roast duckling, quail pies, creamed carrots, braised parsnips, stuffed acorn squash, glazed turnips, and baked Indian pudding. They used cranberries, rhubarb, and apples in desserts.

One of the first orders of business was to hire a preacher for the new town. Abiah's great-grandfather, the Reverend James Hobbs, accepted the call in November 1751.

James received his education at Harvard College. He was ordained on November 13, 1751. A highly respected, intelligent young man, James's gospel ministry laid the foundation for the town's long-term support for the church. The church in Pelham was organized through a council of area churches. An initial membership of ten expanded to thirty-seven in two years.

For thirteen years, parishioners repeatedly expressed their gratitude for having the Hobbs in their community.

James married Elizabeth Batchelder about the same time he came to Pelham. The Hobbs and the Batchelder families were among the early immigrants who settled in Rockingham County on the New Hampshire coast. At the time, both families resided in Hampton.

An appreciable difference existed between coastal towns and the fledgling interior towns of Hillsborough County, where Pelham was located. Elizabeth's parents cautioned her about moving into a wilderness area with a myriad of challenges for a twenty-two-year-old new wife accustomed to more comforts than she might ever have in the place where she was headed. Then, there was the danger of ongoing mayhem created by continued assaults from Indians.

The town of Pelham immediately purchased a tract of land for Reverend Hobbs and his wife. Relatively quickly, they moved into a parsonage.

Elizabeth found a surprisingly thriving new town to make her lifetime home. She relished the various ministries associated with the church. Community members requested her presence in sickness, she was available when a death occurred, and she even assisted the midwife with births. She led an assortment of charity efforts through the church.

Reverend James Hobbs suddenly died in June 1765 at age forty. The doctor said he suffered from apoplexy.

The Hobbs family joined the Gages shortly after that when the oldest child of James and Elizabeth, James II, married Rebecca Gage in 1778. They would become Abiah's grandparents. Captain Josiah Gage II was Rebecca's grandfather, and his brother, Daniel Gage II, was Daniel's great-grandfather.

❧ ❧ ❧

On a Wednesday evening, July 12, 1883, Daniel opened the door to Dr. Meacham and his wife. His heart plummeted.

The Meachams left with the Gage's daughter, Alice, fifteen, for a two-week vacation over the 4th of July holiday at their Rockport cottage on the coast. They were scheduled to return that coming weekend.

The previous day, Alice and the Meacham girls, Kate, seventeen, and Emily, also fifteen, went for a swim, as they did every morning. About twenty yards from shore, Alice swam right into a red jellyfish. There had been a few scattered jellyfish in the water all week but no sighting of the dreaded red ones.

Alice screamed and backpeddled to get away from it. Her friends rushed to her aid and quickly got her to shore. She had dark red whelps on her arms, neck, and face. She panicked, and her breath became irregular. Dr. Meacham said her condition rapidly deteriorated. She was one of the very few people who suffered a severe allergic reaction to the poison. She died shortly after noon on July 11.

Daniel and Abiah remained stunned for weeks over the unexpected loss of their precious, precocious daughter. Her near-constant laugh, which was no longer there, seemed to ring throughout the large house. Daniel often found himself walking along the river to commune with nature, where he knew he would find her spirit.

All he had to do was look at his sister, Mary Gage Currier, to be reminded of his daughter. Mary was eleven years younger than Daniel, so he remembered his youngest sibling well as a child and teenager. Alice had always looked just like her aunt. Mary even had a daughter named Alice, who was seven years younger than his daughter Alice. She only slightly resembled her mother.

Daniel was now known as the "Ice King of Lowell." By the late 1780s, he was the largest taxpayer in his hometown of Pelham because he owned all the property around the major lakes and ponds.

With the proceeds, he thought he could start selling some of his land within the next decade. He would buy a large parcel of land for a park dedicated to children. And that is exactly what he did. The Gages donated a twenty-six-acre park to the city in the Centerville section of Lowell. It was called Gage Field.

Abiah and Martina, then twenty, handled their grief by responding to a cause their daughter and sister wanted to support. It had bothered Alice that there were so many orphans in Lowell. Not only did the Gages start committing financial resources to the Lowell Home for Young Women & Children in her memory, but Abiah and her older daughter started volunteering at the Home one day a week.

Abiah had never relied more strongly on her faith. When she was a teenager, her grandfather, James Hobbs, shared stories about his mother, Elizabeth, who lived another fifty-four years after his preacher father died so young. She endured plenty of hardship in the sixty-eight years she lived in Pelham while never ceasing to offer her services to others in a spirit of faith and grace.

Abiah's ancestors were strong people who overcame adversity. She and hers would be no different even though this Gage line would end with her husband.

Through Benjamin Batchelder, the brother of Elizabeth Hobbs's maternal grandfather, Nathaniel Batchelder, the family became related to statesman Daniel Webster. Benjamin's daughter, Susanna, married Ebenezer Webster, Daniel Webster's grandfather. Daniel Webster was born in 1782 on a small farm with nine siblings in Salisbury, New Hampshire. A quiet, reserved child, he becomes an accomplished orator. He served as U.S.

Secretary of State under three presidents and sought the Whig party nomination for president in 1836, 1840, and 1852.

Elizabeth Hobbs's mother, Mary Tilton Batchelder, brought a line of distinguished Tiltons into the family. They began in this country when William Tilton brought his wife, Susanna, from Warwickshire, England, to the coast of Massachusetts in 1640. Their son, Peter, had four sons: Peter, Samuel, Abraham, and Daniel. All settled in coastal towns.

Daniel Tilton, Abiah's ancestor, served as an officer in the colonial army during King Philip's War. He then became Hampton's representative in New Hampshire's Assembly from 1690 to 1713, serving as Speaker in 1702. His brother, Samuel, was the original European settler of Martha's Vineyard Island, Massachusetts.

The year after his daughter's death, Daniel became a partner in establishing the Lowell Co-operative Milk Association. Since he worked with many farmers in the area, he recognized the need to organize milk distribution between dairies and milkmen who bought directly from the farm. Dairies needed ice, and his company provided the product to most of them around the Middlesex County area. Of course, he saw the co-operative's capital stock purchase as a money-maker.

Within a few years, Daniel stuck to his propensity to deal in goods vitally important to people's standard of living. He elected to go into the coal and lumber businesses.

The *New England Gazetteer* in 1839 identified four coal areas in Massachusetts: three in Norfolk County and one in Bristol County. But by the later part of the century, when coal use spiked, it became necessary to import coal. Most of the coal coming into the state came by railroad from the relatively new mines in West Virginia and Pennsylvania.

The increased population called for more wood. Lumber all over New England had long since disappeared, and much of what

Daniel and his partners imported now came from Michigan and New York.

Charities toward the turn of the century did not generally receive state aid. They depended mainly on donations from wealthy individuals. Daniel donated ice to many of Lowell's charitable organizations.

#

Daniel felt restless on this Friday in February 1901. He could not stay in the office today. He needed to get out in the air.

"Martina, will you go over and tell Shepard to hold up the crew for a few minutes if he needs to? I'm going out with them to Fletcher Pond today. I may be old, but I'm not dead, and I need to get outdoors and observe what's going on with our workers," he said.

"Oh, Daniel, it was below twenty degrees all day yesterday and probably will be again today. Do you really want to be out and away from the office and house for an extended period when it's this cold?" asked his wife.

"Go on, Martina. Tell them I'll be there in less than thirty minutes."

Martina looked at her mother and rolled her eyes. Arguing, she knew, was useless. "Okay, Father, but only if they will have someone there who can bring you back by noon at the latest," his daughter replied.

"Aagot, why don't you make a sandwich and coffee that I can take with me?"

"Yes, Mr. Gage," replied Aagot Larson, their 31-year-old Norwegian housekeeper.

"Finish your cream of wheat," said Abiah, "I'll gather the clothes you'll need to start putting on."

Martina walked outside into the dawn of a new day. It was clear and very cold. Smoke rose from the chimney of the office, so she knew workers were soaking up the last bit of warmth before heading out to finish harvesting ice from Fletcher Pond beyond town. The ice would be stored in their ice house above Pawtucket Falls.

About a dozen men gathered inside the office, all familiar faces.

"Good morning, ma'am," Peter Shepard, the foreman, said.

"Good morning to all of you. Father is going to come out with you on the job this morning. Mother and I are leery about his being in these freezing temperatures. However, he's made up his mind. Honestly, he needs to be back by noon. I don't mean to sound overbearing, but it would not be good if he got sick at his age. Shepard, will you see that he gets back to the house by dinner time?"

"Of course. I'll have a couple of the men hitch the small buggy now. I'll take him over in that and have Jacob bring him back."

"I have half a mind to come get him myself," said Martina, "in case he gets obstinate. Which, as you know, he is capable of doing."

"Don't worry, Miss Martina. By then, I think he'll be ready to come back," said Shepard.

"Thank you. Hope you men get this job about finished today. Keep moving and try not to get too cold."

Shepard proved true to his word. A little before noon, Daniel walked back in his door a bit stiffer than when he left. The women already had a comfortable chair pulled up to the fireplace in the kitchen and a hot mug of coffee at hand. Abiah helped her husband peel off layers of clothes before he eased into his chair.

"They really did some work out there this week," he said when he caught his breath. "They have it broken down into cakes, and, with luck, they'll have most of it moved by the end of the day tomorrow."

"How did you do, Father? Honestly?"

"Well, as cold as it is, I knew I had to keep moving, and that's what I did. Of course, I did not get out on the ice. I walked around the perimeter of the lake and used my field glasses when I needed them. Occasionally, I'd walk over to the fire they'd built, which helped."

"I am glad you're back," Abiah said. "Fire or no fire, when it's in the teens, three hours, which I'd say is at least how long you were out there, is plenty long enough to get very chilled.

"When you get hungry, Aagot bought a fillet of sole, so we'll have sole in sherry with cornbread stuffing for dinner now. Tonight, she'll use the extra batter to make cornbread to go along with oyster bisque."

"In that case, I believe I'm hungry now," Daniel exclaimed.

The next day, Daniel woke up feeling achy. He did not get out over the weekend; the temperature only warmed slightly.

By Monday, a cough was accompanied by a fever. Abiah called Dr. Bellamy to come in Tuesday morning. He said to notify him by Thursday if there was no improvement or if he started chilling and/or had difficulty breathing, to let him know immediately.

Wednesday night, Daniel started chilling, and his breathing seemed slightly labored. The doctor returned around midnight. He said it appeared as though pneumonia had set into Daniel's lungs. The diagnosis could not have been worse. The prognosis was dismal, and treatment was virtually nonexistent.

The next morning, Abiah sent word to his sister, Mary, who lived in Wakefield, just north of Boston.

Thursday and Friday, Daniel suffered from progressively worse breathing difficulty. Friday afternoon, Mary and her husband, Amos Currier, arrived. Saturday afternoon at 4:10,

Daniel died of the leading cause of death due to infectious disease and the third leading cause of death overall in the United States.

Martina assumed ownership and leadership of the Daniel Gage Ice Company at age thirty-nine upon her father's death. Her business instincts proved more than worthy of the Gage name, as she kept the company profitable years past the time when refrigeration became available to homeowners.

Abiah passed away in her sleep on July 4th, 1908, at the age of eighty-two. The timing gave Martina two good reasons not to want to celebrate when the 4th of July rolled around since they lost sister Alice while she vacationed July 4th week.

Martina never married. She failed to see the point in committing herself to a man for life. She figured she had more to lose than to gain. After all, a wife's property became the husband's property, and she did not know any man worth giving up what her father and she had worked so hard to acquire. It just did not make any sense. She was perfectly content to go through life without the responsibility of raising children. Keeping the business competitive in the face of emerging technologies would give her plenty to do.

If her parents were disappointed about not having grandchildren, they never voiced their concerns. Martina had always been independent, intelligent, and goal-oriented. She was also happy. Daniel and Abiah left well enough alone. The result was a strong, self-assured woman more than capable of taking care of herself and those for whom she was responsible.

Martina retained control of the company for twenty-eight years after her father's death. She then passed the day-to-day responsibilities to a board of directors. In 1929, she sold the business to a Lowell-based company, relinquishing her role in active management.

Although Martina had moved out of the big house into a more manageable apartment around 1920, she retained a live-in housekeeper. She became a well-known figure in the Highlands neighborhood of Lowell. She maintained her health and lived a good life.

In the early morning hours of February 7, 1935, Martina Abiah Gage, seventy-three, suffered a stroke, just as her great-great-grandfather, Reverend James Hobbs, had. She died just before midnight.

Thus, Daniel Gage's direct lineage in Lowell, Massachusetts, ended. However, his niece, Alice, the only child of sister Mary Currier, married Edson White, who was raised in Wakefield. They had two sons, Cyrus and Donald, whose families extended the White name into the twenty-first century.

BYRNE families

Responded with Outrage

Allen (Byrne)

A bullet ripped through the powder horn hanging around the neck of Captain John Gorham, fifty-four. It did not pierce his body, but the powder exploded, blasting through his buckskin shirt, searing and tearing skin, cracking ribs. He wavered in and out of consciousness throughout the night.

On the morning of December 20, 1675, Captain Josiah Standish of Plymouth, Massachusetts, forty-two, helped Lieutenant Robert Barker of Pembroke carry their fellow militiamen and friend, Captain Gorham of Barnstable. He survived the wound a month and a half before dying of an associated fever.

The men were part of a slow procession walking the fifteen miles from South Kingstown, Rhode Island, east to Narragansett Bay, with nearly 150 colonists wounded in battle the previous day. They also transported seventy bodies of those killed for burial on Aquidneck Island.

Snow started swirling again in the sub-freezing temperatures. Josiah's hands hardly had feeling enough for him to hang onto his heavy load. He knew they were no more than halfway to the bay. This nightmare was not over.

Captain Benjamin Church, the principal military aide to Governor Josiah Winslow of Plymouth Colony, had taught Josiah Standish frontier skills and developed him into one of his rangers. Yesterday Captain Church received a wound while fighting. Maj. William Bradford Jr., commander of their Plymouth Colony regiment, did too. Captains Isaac Johnson, Nathan Davenport, and

Joseph Gardener, all friends of Josiah and members of the Massachusetts Bay Colony regiment, died in the battle. Josiah tried to focus on anything other than what took place in and around the fort on the big swamp. But scenes kept flashing in his head. He prayed to God that what he visualized hadn't actually happened.

He did not know when he'd been able to sleep. He suffered from exhaustion, the cold, hunger, pain, and the effects of fear. Maybe his mind was playing tricks on him. He could not shed tears because they would freeze on his eyelashes and add another layer of ice to his mustache and beard.

Suddenly, Josiah felt sick. His knees buckled. Lieutenant Barker eased Captain Gorham to the ground. He helped Josiah sit up and offered him sips of the little water in his canteen that had not turned to ice already.

"Robert, what happened back there? What in the bloody hell are we doing?"

"Trying to get control of this Indian situation."

"My father was known to exhibit brutality against the Natives on more than one occasion," said Josiah. "But he never slaughtered women and children. Nor would he ever have condoned it."

"We call them savages. Now, I know for a fact that white men are no different. No better."

What became known as The Great Swamp Fight in south-central Rhode Island on Thursday, December 19, 1675, between the New England Confederation, comprised of the Massachusetts Bay Colony, Plymouth Colony, New Haven Colony, and Connecticut Colony, and the Narragansett people, was, by many estimates, the single greatest calamity to occur in seventeenth-century New England. It turned into a massacre. When the large fort was taken by the militia and set afire, many elder Indians, women, and children were burned alive. About one hundred of their warriors died, while an estimated 600 non-combatants were killed.

The tribe had retreated to the five-acre fort in the center of the great swamp near Kingstown the previous month after Governor Winslow led a force of more than 1,000 colonial militia, along with about 150 Pequot and Mohegan Indians, against the Narragansett living around the Narragansett Bay. Although they were not known to participate in ongoing attacks against the settlers, they did shelter those involved in raiding parties.

The attack at the big swamp was precipitated by a strike by Narraganset warriors against the Jireh Bull Blockhouse in South Kingstown on December 15. The house was torched, and fifteen occupants died. A fifteen-year-old boy escaped, survived pursuit, and warned area residents.

Four days later, in the snow and bitter cold, two of Governor Winslow's three regiments attacked the Narragansett's fort early and sustained heavy losses. Captain Church then led his forces, which included Josiah Standish, in a coordinated assault that broke through the log palisade. They encountered fierce fighting, much of it hand-to-hand. The bloodbath lasted for hours.

Metacomet, otherwise known as King Philip, was sachem of the Wampanoag, a confederation of several New England tribes. He escaped the battle with some of his warriors and their families through the swamp, although many died from exposure. He headed south to New York to establish a winter camp.

Metacomet's father, Massasoit, chief of the Wampanoag, had made overtures of friendship with the colonists since the arrival of the *Mayflower* in 1620 and the subsequent establishment of Plymouth Colony. Relations had generally been peaceful for decades despite the continuing arrival of white settlers. Massasoit died in 1661. His oldest son, Wamsutta, took the English name Alexander and assumed his father's role as Sachem, passing away within the year. The second son, Metacomet, then became head of the Wampanoag people.

Philip, as he was known to the English, did not trust the colonists. In 1671, Plymouth Colony leaders forced major concessions from him. The rapid expansion of the European population and encroachment onto what area tribes considered to be their land set the stage for hostilities that broke out in King Philip's War. Between 1675 and 1678, thousands of people on both sides of the conflict would die in southern and northern New England.

After the Great Swamp Fight, many settlers living in Rhode Island moved to the relative safety of the fort on Aquidneck Island. Other residents in nearby towns cared for wounded members of the militia who did not make it to the island. Other surviving militia members returned to their homes because they lacked supplies for an extended military campaign.

Over the winter of 1675 and into 1676, Indians continued to attack settlements and destroy dozens of homes, torturing and killing inhabitants as they went. The captured invaders were either hanged or shipped to the Caribbean as slaves.

Finally, on August 12, 1676, Captain Benjamin Church, with Captain Josiah Standish, by his side, tracked Metacomet to Mount Hope in Bristol, Rhode Island, while on a punitive mission. He was shot dead by John Alderman, a Wampanoag praying Indian. Sixteen days later, Captain Churches' unit found Anawan, a chief captain of Metacomet, in Rehoboth, Massachusetts. He, too, was executed and beheaded.

In a little less than a year and a half, more than half of New England's 110 towns had been attacked by Indians. Twelve of the region's towns were destroyed. The economies of the Plymouth and Rhode Island colonies were severely crippled. They lost one-tenth of the 16,000 men available for military service. More than 1,000 colonists died.

The Native population was decimated as a result of King Philip's War. It is estimated that Plymouth Colony sustained a loss of about 6,000 among the tribes due to deaths in battle, sickness, and starvation, and those sold into slavery. In southern New England, the population was reduced by forty to eighty percent.

Fighting continued in northern New England until the Treaty of Casco was signed in 1678. Many English settlers refused to obey the terms of the agreement.

Captain Myles Standish agreed to be the military advisor for the *Mayflower* based on his experience as an English military officer in the coastal lowland region in northwestern Europe. The *Mayflower* sailed from Plymouth, England, on September 16, 1620, and dropped anchor near the tip of Cape Cod on November 21. There were 102 passengers and a crew of twenty-eight aboard. By vote, Captain Standish became military commander of Plymouth Colony for life. He regularly drilled men in military procedure. He advocated intimidation to deter his rivals. The man was short in stature but exhibited a fiery temper.

Josiah Standish was the fifth child born to Captain Standish and his second wife, Barbara Mullins, in Duxbury, Plymouth Colony. In 1656, Josiah married Sarah Allen of Braintree, just south of Boston, daughter of Samuel Sr. and Ann Whitmore Allen.

After the August 1676 mission with Captain Church that eliminated Metacomet and virtually shut down the war in southern New England, Josiah returned home to Duxbury, where Sarah waited with a one-year-old Israel and their four older children. He then assumed responsibility for the governorship of Plymouth Colony, which he held until 1680.

ƒ ƒ ƒ

Samuel and Ann Allen, both born in Essex, England, ventured to Massachusetts on the *Mary and John* in 1632, along with their two-year-old son Samuel Jr. They settled in Braintree, where Samuel worked as a sawmill operator. He was granted twenty-eight acres in 1640 after becoming a freeman. Over the years, he served as town clerk, selectman, surveyor of highways, constable, and deputy.

The progenitor of this Allen family in America was George Allen, the father of Samuel Sr., born in 1568 in Saltford, Somerset, England, in 1624. The village of Saltford sits on the River Avon in northeast Somersetshire, which is bounded in the north and west by the Bristol Channel. Its coastline faces Wales. George first married sixteen-year-old Katherine Davis in 1592. They produced ten children before Katherine passed away in 1619.

Somersetshire was a hotbed of religious dissent as King Charles I began his reign in 1625. He made an unfortunate alliance with William Laud, who became Archbishop of Canterbury in 1633. He enforced the king's religious reforms with a heavy hand. He designed liturgical practices meant to bring uniformity within the Church of England. He strongly believed in Episcopalianism or rule by bishops.

Religious Dissenters and Separatists in Somersetshire met together and worshiped as they believed. Many paid the price. More than a few were Anabaptists, including the Allens. Most Anabaptists embraced a literal interpretation of the Sermon on the Mount in Matthew 5-7, which teaches against hate, killing, violence, taking oaths, participating in the use of force or any military actions, and participating in civil government. The Amish are direct descendants of the early Anabaptist movement.

George took nineteen-year-old Katherine Starkes to be his second bride within months of the death of his children's mother. She was born in Woking, Surrey County, twenty-three miles southeast of central London.

Many of their neighbors were moving to Holland or America to escape the heavy penalties imposed in the Episcopal courts. People wanted to worship as they pleased without fear of repercussions.

Three of George's oldest sons had already immigrated. In addition to Samuel and his wife, Ann, his younger brothers, William Jr. and Ralph Allen, sailed to Boston in the early 1630s. Samuel and Ann ended up in Norfolk County. William, a house carpenter, and Ralph, a wheelwright, remained in Boston for a few years.

In 1635, a group of 106 people, under the leadership of Reverend Joseph Hull of Somerset, left Weymouth, England, on March 20 aboard the *Assurance* and arrived in Boston Harbor on May 6. Among the passengers were George Allen, fifty-six, his wife, Katherine, thirty-one, sons, George III, sixteen, William, eight, Mathew, six, and a servant, Edward Poole, twenty-six.

Joseph Hull was born in Crewkerne, Somerset, in 1595. He graduated from Oxford University in 1612. In 1619, he was ordained a deacon, and two years later, he became a priest. In 1621, he accepted the priesthood at St. Giles Rectory in Northleigh, Devon. By 1633, he had moved back to Crewkerne after gaining enemies in the church, who called him contentious.

King Charles I ascended the throne four years after Reverend Hull assumed his duties as a priest. The king and William Laud made life difficult for him and his fellow Calvinists. The High Church started persecuting Puritan clerics and laymen.

In Glastonbury, Reverend Hull was quoted from a sermon as saying that "judgment hung over the land and that first it would fall on the clergy and then the laity." Known to avoid confrontation, he was expelled from the Church of England on February 17, 1635, for "failing to respond to the court's citation."

Forty-one days later, Reverend Hull and his family, the Allen family, and twenty other families departed from Weymouth, a seaside town in Dorset on the English Channel, for the shores of America.

Two months after arriving in Boston on the *Assurance*, the Dorsetshire families were granted leave to settle at Wessaguscus

Plantation by the General Court of Boston. In September, the settlement was given municipal rights and renamed Weymouth. The people acquired one representative in the General Court in Boston, about twenty miles north by land. From its inception, residents of Weymouth governed themselves in town meetings rather than having a governor.

This inlet of Massachusetts Bay attracted the second oldest settlement in Massachusetts by white men in 1622, two years after the Pilgrims founded Plymouth. Its proximity to Boston, a deep harbor protected from storms by barrier islands, and the peninsula of Hull and the Fore and Back rivers, both deep enough to anchor sailing ships and other boats, meant pine and cedar could be harvested from the forest and transported. The rivers flowed rapidly in places where mills could be built. Fish and shellfish would remain major components of the New England diet. Settlers raised grains, vegetables, and animals. Salt came from the marshes. They dried marsh grass to thatch the roofs of their huts. They packed dense seaweed along the base of their houses to keep out the winter cold.

Reverend Hull became the first authorized minister in Weymouth under the rule of Massachusetts Bay Colony. He was confronted with a mix of religious persuasions and almost immediately found himself in trouble again. Those still supporting the Church of England, Separatists, Puritans, Episcopalians, and other Christian sects did not bring tolerance with them to the new country.

"George, I feel almost as torn here as I did back home," said Katherine Allen one late winter day. "I know Reverend Hull is an educated, religious man who seeks God's word for solutions to conflict, but I think his argumentative approach is detrimental to our well-being."

"I don't like this pressure coming from the outside," George responded. "The Pilgrims and the Puritans are at each other's throats. And, no, Joseph Hull is not acting as a conciliator."

George Allen and his son, Ralph, became landowners in Weymouth after landing in Boston in 1635 and reuniting with their twenty-year-old son. However, the Allens relocated to Saugus, which would become Lynn, situated on Massachusetts Bay, the following year.

In April 1637, ten Saugus pioneers sought permission from Plymouth Colony to establish the first plantation on Cape Cod, to be named Sandwich. These leading townspeople, including George Allen, arranged with Joan Swift, widow of William Swift, a loan to be paid to Edmund Freeman, a confirmed Anabaptist, for founding the town of Sandwich. The Swift's daughter, Susanna, would marry Ralph Allen in 1645.

Fifty other families from Lynn, Duxbury, and Plymouth moved to Sandwich in 1641. Most were farmers. The court asked Captain Myles Standish to go to the new plantation to define and allot land for the newcomers.

The Cape Cod Bay borders Sandwich to the north. Like the rest of the Cape, the landscape in and around the town featured many small hills and small ponds. The trees were mostly pine or oak. Old Harbor Creek, with several small creeks feeding it, provided a safe harbor for smaller ships, although not a lot of shipping took place. Residents farmed large crops of cranberries. Orchards, including apple, pear, peach, plum, cherry, and fig trees, provided a source of profit. Fish and other seafood, of course, were plentiful, but little was shipped.

The year after the first group from Saugus settled Sandwich, the town of Barnstable was established to the east. It was incorporated in 1639. It fronts what would be named Barnstable Harbor, which sits behind Sandy Neck and separates it from Cape Cod Bay. To the south is Nantucket Sound.

In 1636, Reverend Joseph Hull left Weymouth with his family amid bickering among various religious groups, both within the community and from those outside, attempting to influence their behavior. The family briefly went to Hingham, just north of Massachusetts Bay, where he received a land grant. Joseph became involved in the civic affairs of the town.

That fall, Joseph led a group of people to Cape Cod, where they founded Barnstable. He preached from a big rock located beside the road in what would become the middle of town. Although he had been a member of the General Court of Massachusetts Bay Colony in Hingham and a magistrate and a minister in Weymouth, he quickly fell from grace. Because he retained his attachment to the old establishment, he became a thorn in the side of the Boston Puritanical Party and Governor Winthrop.

The Hull family made three more moves in the next nine years before Joseph returned to England with his second wife, Agnes, and a few of their youngest children. In 1662, he sailed to Maine. Reverend Hull died on the Isles of Shoals in November 1665.

In 1638, Reverend William Leverich came to Sandwich to pastor the first church formed there. He arrived in Salem from Gravesend, England, on the *James* in 1633 and two years later was admitted to the First Church in Boston. In 1637, he relocated to Duxbury, where he became an assistant to Reverend Ralph Partridge, grandfather of Sarah Allen and the daughter-in-law of Samuel Allen Sr.

Reverend Leverich's compliance with Puritan principles did not sit well with many settlers in Sandwich, who brought their liberal Anabaptist beliefs with them. Colonial authorities enacted laws that denied residents town rights without the consent of Reverend Leverich. Freedom of religion became a wedge that drove the pastor out of town by 1654.

Katherine Allen, fifty-one, drowned in June of that same year trying to rescue a granddaughter from one of the ponds. Her husband, George, had died in his sleep six years earlier. He provided religious thought which propelled his children to the forefront of Quakerism in this country.

In early 1656, Nicholas Upsall, at sixty, was banished from Boston to Sandwich as punishment for befriending and then joining persecuted Quakers. Puritan-run Boston exhibited extreme antagonism toward dissenting religious viewpoints and immediately began a vicious campaign against the first known Quakers to arrive in the Massachusetts Bay Colony that year.

After arriving in Sandwich, Mr. Upsall helped found the first Monthly Meeting of Friends in America. On April 13, 1657, that historical meeting was hosted by Priscilla Browne Allen and her husband, William Allen, a son of George Allen, at Spring Hill in East Sandwich. Priscilla's father, Peter Browne, was one of the original Plymouth colonists who came over on the *Mayflower* in 1620.

It wasn't long before the official notice of this meeting by the small group of Quakers got out. As a result, Mr. Upsall was expelled from the town.

In August, Christopher Holder and John Copeland, young Quaker immigrants from Gloucestershire, England, found their way to Sandwich. They immediately connected with William Newland, husband of Rose Allen. Another early leader of the Society of Friends in Sandwich was Richard Kirby, father of Sarah Allen, wife of Mathew Allen, and brother of Rose, William, and Ralph.

Ralph Allen and his friend William Newland were jailed in October for refusing to post bond for good behavior after becoming the first men charged for Quaker activities in Sandwich. They spent five months in jail. Mr. Holder and Mr. Copeland were also soon jailed for their activities on the Cape. At that point, the group knew they had to find a secret location for their meetings.

They called the new place "Christopher's Hollow," a dingle with a brook running through it surrounded by high hills.

In April 1658, Mr. Holder and Mr. Copeland returned to Sandwich. Each man was given thirty-three lashes as punishment for their various offenses and to discourage their preaching. On June 3, the pair went to Boston, where they were immediately arrested. Mr. Holder's right ear was cut off to punish him for his "heretical" preaching.

The nemesis for Quaker families in Sandwich was Marshal George Barlow, "a hard-hearted, intolerant, tyrannical man, abusing power entrusted to him, and seemingly taking delight in confiscating the property of innocent men and women or dragging them to prison, to the stocks or the whipping post."

Authorities in Boston sent Marshal Barlow to Cape Cod to suppress the spread of Quakerism. When he hauled people into court and levied fines for holding or attending unauthorized meetings, he took commodities that affected their day-to-day living because people held little cash. Livestock, farm implements, and household furnishings, including cooking utensils, were maliciously confiscated.

The Allen family, in particular, suffered as Barlow tyrannized the growing community of Friends. They were fined, lost property, jailed, put into pillory stocks, and whipped. Yet they survived to carry religious freedom forward through many generations.

King Charles II returned from exile in Europe in 1660 to mark the Restoration of the Stuart monarchy in the kingdoms of England, Scotland, and Ireland. His coronation initiated a reversal of repressive Puritan morality.

New England had supported the English Commonwealth and the Protectorate governed by Oliver Cromwell. In August 1661, Massachusetts became the last New England state to accept the Restoration. Authorities there assumed that while Cromwell was Lord Protector, he would ignore their persecution, torture, and hanging of Quakers, which went against English law. With King Charles II back on the throne, they became concerned that they might become targets. Therefore, twenty-seven Quakers who were imprisoned in Boston, including brothers Ralph and William Allen, were released.

♦ ♦ ♦

"No taxation without representation." This rallying cry from rebelling colonists in the streets of Boston in 1770 reverberated throughout the rest of Massachusetts and beyond.

The Allen family of Bridgewater in Plymouth was among Patriots sick and tired of British interference in their lives. Their ancestors fought Natives who tried to deny them the right to establish homes on this new land. Then, they suffered at the hands of fellow Englishmen who sought to prohibit them from worshiping as they believed. One hundred years later, the British government taxed people in the thirteen American colonies because of its huge war debt.

In 1765, the British Parliament levied The Stamp Act directly on American colonists. It imposed a tax on all paper documents in the colonies. The Americans countered that only their representatives could tax them, declaring the act unconstitutional.

Two years later, the British Parliament passed a series of measures taxing goods imported to the American colonies, known as the Townshend Acts. Colonists saw this as an additional abuse of power, which added kindling to a rapidly growing fire.

Frustration and anger boiled over when the British attempted to enforce their repressive tax laws. Skirmishes broke out between colonists and soldiers, colonists with Patriot alliances, and those with Loyalist leanings.

Five colonists were killed and six wounded on a cold, snowy evening in March 1770 in front of the Boston Custom House on

King Street when violence erupted between the King's soldiers and townspeople. The deadly riot became known as the Boston Massacre. It set the stage for what was to come.

Britain repealed its tax on imported goods except for tea. Massachusetts colonists were incensed that they were still required to pay the British a tax on imported tea. On the night of December 16, 1773, at Griffin's Wharf, Bostonians dressed as Native Americans, including a group of revolutionists known as the Sons of Liberty, boarded three British East India Company ships loaded with tea from China. They first split open 342 chests of tea with tomahawks, then threw them into the harbor.

The British swiftly retaliated against what became known as the Boston Tea Party. The Coercive Acts, known in the American colonies as the Intolerable Acts, included four punitive laws passed by the British Parliament in early 1774. Although targeted toward Boston, these Acts were meant to warn all the other British American colonies of the consequences of rebellious behavior. Each Act caused serious damage to a crucial aspect of colonial life.

New Englanders, in particular, responded with outrage. As a result, delegates from twelve of the thirteen colonies met in Philadelphia on September 5. Opinions among the attendees differed as to their ultimate goal. Some wanted to develop "a reasonable solution to the difficulties and bring about reconciliation" between the colonies and their Mother Country. Others wanted to develop a decisive statement of the rights and liberties of the colonies.

When the delegates disbanded on October 26, they asked the colonies to stop importing goods from the British Isles beginning December 1 if the Coercive Acts were not repealed. If Britain failed to respond, they agreed to meet again on May 10, 1775,

The British army destroyed powder stores held by colonial Patriots in mid-April. Afterward, a brief skirmish ensued in Lexington with a greatly outnumbered group of armed

Minutemen. Eight Americans died, and ten others lay injured. British soldiers then moved to Concord, where they were ambushed. They quickly decided to retreat to Lexington. Along the way, a rapidly growing colonial militia used guerrilla tactics to pick off their enemy. By the time the British reached Boston, they had sustained about 300 casualties.

The Revolutionary War was underway.

When the Second Continental Congress convened on May 10, again in Philadelphia, it began putting a new government in place. The most urgent task was directing the war effort. Patriots quickly besieged Boston to prevent British troops from moving onto land from that point. On June 14, Congress appointed George Washington of Virginia as commanding general of the newly created Continental Army. Delegates signed the Declaration of Independence on July 4. Two days later, Congress approved a Declaration of Causes which justified armed resistance by the thirteen colonies.

John Adams, Samuel Adams, Thomas Cushing, and Robert Treat Paine served as Massachusetts delegates at both sessions of the Continental Congress.

Colonel Jonathan Warner gathered with three regiments of militia in Brookfield, located in Worcester County, Massachusetts, on April 17 when he received word that the British had imminent plans to seize a Patriot arsenal in Concord. The following day, he planned to move his troops from mid-state toward Boston, suspecting a pending need for trained, armed Minutemen.

Nathan Allen Sr., his wife, Rebecca, and their youngest child, Phil, thirteen, lived in Bridgewater. But they had traveled to Brookfield on April 13 for the first time to visit with their son, Nathan Jr., his wife of two years, Persis, and their one-year-old grandson, Thomas. They helped to celebrate the younger Nathan's 26th birthday on Wednesday the 16th.

Nathan Jr., who had trained with the militia in Worcester County in response to rising tensions with the British, brought along his firearms, clothing, and other pieces of equipment needed for military engagement. He stayed prepared. When his son and his father-in-law, Captain Thomas Gilbert, who trained with the militia in Plymouth County, received the call for deployment; he did not hesitate to join their 13th Massachusetts Regiment's march east.

Sarah Gilbert, Thomas's wife, said she would be glad to have Rebecca Allen and her younger son in their home for an extended stay while the men were gone. Nathan figured young Phil could get his mother back home if necessary.

Back in Bridgewater, Rebecca Jr., twenty-three, the Allen's second oldest daughter, worked on her plans. She had long had an interest in easing the suffering of the sick. With the country on the precipice of war, there would be a great need for medical attention in the field. She also wanted to head south–maybe the Carolinas, where there were big ports and major agriculture, and Lord only knows what else the Brits might want to stalk.

Rebecca knew exactly where she would start. The Adams family lived practically right down the road from the Allens in Bridgewater. She knew John Adams would be getting ready for the upcoming Second Continental Congress. His wife, Abigail, remained in Braintree to manage the farm and educate their children. She was equally intelligent and almost as well connected as her influential husband.

A note requesting an audience with Mrs. Adams resulted in an invitation to tea later in the week.

Mrs. Adams, who was seven years older, asked Rebecca to call her Abigail. When Rebecca outlined her plan, her hostess asked, "Have you prayed about this?"

"Oh, yes, I do pray over it. Every day."

"You know, I grew up in Weymouth, and my mother spent a lot of her time visiting the sick and bringing food, clothing, and firewood to those families who needed help. I often went with her. I do understand the need to help others," said Mrs. Adams.

"I'm not sure you or I can imagine the brutality of war. Our conflict with the Natives may not be over, but it has not personally touched us. We have not had to witness the consequences.

"Helping the sick and working with surgeons are two different things. Working on a battlefield, receiving wounded soldiers, and assisting doctors trying to piece those men back together will present unfathomable horrors. You have to have a very tough constitution to survive that environment.

"And then there is this trip through the Appalachian Mountains in a covered wagon with men you do not know under unpredictable circumstances. I presume you would not want to take the coast highway because of the likelihood that Redcoats would be everywhere. Potentially dangerous circumstances in a time of war. That's a lot to consider."

"Yes, it is," Rebecca acknowledged. "I have thought about every point you make. My family will be horrified."

"I am certain they would be. No parent wants their daughter exposed to those kinds of dangers."

"I've thought about going into the Southern frontier for years," said Rebecca. "I don't know why. I can not explain it in a way that makes sense. Something about it calls to me. And honestly, I wish I could become a doctor. We know women can not go to medical school. It's not a possibility. That doesn't mean I cannot be around doctors and learn what they know. Does it?"

Abigail Adams sat back and smiled. "I think you are a pioneer, Rebecca Allen. We women can learn anything we want. Yes, I will help you.

"As you know, Dr. Joseph Warren serves as president of our state's Provincial Congress and is a close associate with my husband. He has a younger brother, John Warren, who is probably about your age. He graduated from Harvard College, and he has been studying medicine under his brother. He is also an ardent Patriot. When this situation with the British spills over into war, he will probably serve as a surgeon on the battlefield. The Warrens might be best able to advise you on how to proceed."

Rebecca could not communicate with Dr. Warren, who served as a leader in the Patriot organizations in Boston. He enlisted Paul Revere and William Dawes to ride from Boston to Lexington on April 18 to warn Samuel Adams and John Hancock of movements by the British Army. Paul Revere assisted the revolution as a courier of the Boston Committee of Correspondence and the Massachusetts Committee of Safety and rode express to the Continental Congress in Philadelphia.

Their nighttime warning resulted in perhaps as many as forty other riders throughout Middlesex County alerting citizens of the British Army's advancement. Mr. Adams and his family escaped their home in Lexington, and the people in Concord, where the arsenal was located, had time to mount a defense.

Dr. Warren participated in the battles at Lexington and Concord the following day. His brother, John Warren, chose not to go the route of a soldier.

Mrs. Adams wrote John Warren saying her young neighbor, Rebecca Allen, had a business proposition she wanted to discuss with him. When could he come down to Bridgewater to visit?

John was too happy to leave Boston and would do anything to accommodate John and Abigail Adams. Much to his dismay, his brother, a commissioned member of the military, was seemingly engaged in this inevitable war, leaving him in a bit of a quandary.

John met Rebecca and her cousin, Barnabus Edson, seventeen, at the Adams's house on May 5. They knew big things would be happening in Philadelphia in the coming days. John Adams had already left to meet with other Patriot delegates before the Second Continental Congress officially got under Wednesday, May 10.

The prospect of finally breaking the bonds of British rule created an electricity amongst many of the populace. That was certainly true in the Adams household. Mrs. Adams not only campaigned for independence, but she believed in equal rights for all people.

Mrs. Adams took John Warren, Rebecca, and Barnabus into her husband's office and shut the doors to get away from neighbors in a celebratory mood. When Rebecca explained what she had in mind to John, he sat back and thought, "This is a brave young woman with an admirable mission in her heart."

A part of him wished he could take off and go with her. He knew that was not possible. His brother would need him. New Englanders did not fly the coop. They generally didn't move south of Connecticut or west of the line bordering Connecticut, Massachusetts, and Vermont. Maybe a few ventured over into New York. But for the most part, they stayed put.

"I have three friends who graduated a couple of years ahead of me at Harvard who have since become doctors. Two, in particular, are adventurous souls. Neither is yet tied down. Both Patriots. I'm guessing they will want to contribute to the war effort as surgeons in the field. Charles Hanson practices in Cambridge, and David Quincy in Braintree. Dr. Quincy has a feisty, unmarried twin sister, Dinah, who helps him in his practice. Who knows, maybe she'd be interested in this too?

"There is no question that nurses will be needed to assist in what I'm afraid will be rather gruesome emergency field hospitals. It will not be easy work, and certainly, it won't be pleasant. I'm not sure how capable medical help will be down there. I do not doubt that this war will also be fought on Southern soil."

"Oh, my, that sounds promising, Mr. Warren."

"No, no, I'm John to all of you, please."

"Okay, John. If we could recruit a couple of competent doctors to teach me as we went and another experienced nurse, we could take a couple of wagons down with what few supplies we had room for. Barnabus has volunteered to drive a wagon and carry a gun. I'm sure we could find another armed driver. Some Southern regiment would undoubtedly be thrilled to have us."

"Undoubtedly. And you need to get on a shooting range yourself, Rebecca. You'll probably be going into hostile territory, and your accuracy with a gun could save your life."

John stopped for the night in Braintree on his way back to Boston to visit with his friend David Quincy. The next morning, he swung through Cambridge to see Charles Hanson at his office. When he outlined the intent of Rebecca Allen and her pending adventure, both men said the same thing. They realized the war would interfere with their medical practices, and they both looked to serve the Patriot cause as surgeons in the field. Yes, they were up for a journey into the south. David thought his sister would also jump at the opportunity.

Participants agreed to meet at the Quincy's home in Braintree on Saturday, May 27. Many pieces to their plans needed to be pulled together.

Both doctors consented to locate and purchase two large, well-constructed covered wagons and eight healthy, driving horses. David had talked to a man who was experienced in handling teams of horses and was looking to avoid recruitment as a soldier. Nick Carter, forty-six, agreed to drive a wagon, mentor young Barnabus on the other wagon, and take care of the animals in exchange for food. A thirty-year-old light mulatto woman, Eadie, who escaped from a North Carolina plantation ten years previously, worked as a cook for the senior Hansons. She used to help her mama skin animals that the men brought in. Reluctantly, she agreed to go along as a cook for the group. She had watched Charles grow from a youth into a man, liked him, and trusted him. Charles swore to keep her with him in the Southern military camps where she could work as a cook. He promised to bring her back home with him. Dinah Quincy had begun collecting items needed in field hospitals, such as blankets, muslin, and linen, that could be ripped into bandages.

By June 1st, the party rolled out of Boston and headed to Philadelphia to pick up the Great Wagon Road. Before leaving Pennsylvania, they passed through Lancaster and York. From there, the road turned southwest, crossed the Potomac River, and entered the beautiful Shenandoah Valley in Virginia, bounded by the easternmost part of the Appalachian Mountain range. This was Rebecca's first glimpse of the Southern mountains she had heard so much about.

Once they made it through the Shenandoah Valley, they reached the Roanoke River, flowing through the town of Big Lick, which would become Roanoke. They took a southwest fork in the road leading into the upper New River Valley at that point. Then on toward the Holston River in the trans-Appalachian region, North Carolina, later to become the upper Tennessee valley.

On the road, they heard that a group of families from North Carolina, led by James Robertson, had recently settled on the Watauga River, part of the watershed of the Holston River. A fort had just been built at the Sycamore Shoals of the Watauga River to help defend against attacks from the Native Cherokee. With the start of the Revolutionary War, tribes were being encouraged by the British to increase their assaults against settlers in the mountains.

The Massachusetts travelers decided to follow the river and meet the pioneers who had formed the Watauga Association. In its three years of existence, this semi-autonomous government has gained acclaim throughout the Appalachians. It was administered by John Sevier, James Robertson, Charles Robertson, Zachariah Isbell, and John Carter.

They arrived in Sycamore Shoals the second week of August. It had been a long, hard trip for inexperienced travelers. Nick Carter proved to be their salvation. The other six people and the horses were exhausted.

Residents warmly welcomed the group. A tavern offered food, drink, and beds. They received surprisingly current war news. Eadie thanked God there were no slaves among the population, nor did she hear any discussion about slavery. Barnabas met a pair of sisters he thought were prettier than any girls he had ever seen back home. He believed he could get used to a little dirt.

When they sat down with community leaders and explained the intent of their journey, John Sevier, who, at thirty, was just five years older than Drs. Hanson and Quincy assured them that there would be ample opportunity for them to assist in upcoming battles as surgeons.

"Unfortunately, the British have further riled up Indian tribes here west of the mountains," explained Mr. Sevier. "They'll be more warrin'. And, for certain, as the British move South and attack from the coast, we'll need every Patriot we have to beat 'em back."

"Experienced doctors and nurses will be in short supply. Your skills are and will be desperately needed.

"The first week of September, men 'il be comin' here to talk military strategy for the coming year against the Cherokee and Creeks, who are hostile. We have spies out. Our fort is now constructed. We need to make sure we stay one step ahead."

Francis Hughes, twenty-six, lived in a part of Rowan County that would soon become Burke County just east of the mountains. A neighbor, Griffith Rutherford, who settled in Rowan County in the 1750s, had served as captain of a local British colonial militia during the French and Indian War. He now planned to fight the British as a Patriot. He took Francis and a couple of other county Patriots to Sycamore Shoals to meet with the Watauga group.

The meeting lasted for the better part of the week. Eadie volunteered to help cook for the nearly two dozen visitors. In the evening, after supper, people gathered. A couple of fiddles, a three-stringed dulcimer, and a jaw harp appeared. Singing commenced, and then dancing started. The New Englanders had never seen or heard anything quite like it. Many were Scotch-Irish, and the tunes followed their grandparents and parents across the ocean.

Francis and Rebecca had eyes on each other from the first day he arrived. She thought he was nothing if not handsome. He loved her laugh, beautiful green eyes, and a magnetism that drew almost everyone to her.

On the third day of the gathering, Francis asked Rebecca if she would like to take a walk by the river with him after supper. The skies were clear. The moon came up almost completely full and reflected off the slower-moving late summer west-flowing Watauga River. Crickets chirped. Distant wolves howled. They heard the sing-song whistle of a whippoorwill.

Francis shared that his great-grandfather, Charles Hughes, a Quaker, came over to Philadelphia from Denbighshire, Wales, on the *Vine* in 1684 after being enticed by William Penn. He married a young woman, Rebecca, who sailed on the same ship.

Their son, Francis, married Christina Jonasson in 1730, daughter of Swedish immigrants. Her parents first settled their family with a group of their countrymen along the Delaware River. Then, thanks to William Penn, they received a grant of land for settlement just west of Philadelphia. It was known as the Swede's Tract. The settlement would first be called Morlatton, then Douglassville, in what became Berks County.

After Rebecca died in 1747, Francis moved to Augusta County, Virginia, with their children.

"John Sevier and I had a conversation last night. We figured out that his father, Valentine Sevier, and my grandfather, Francis, whom we call Teida, were neighbors on Smith's Creek in Augusta

County. How 'bout that! He moved to the Watauga settlement two years ago along with five sons and three daughters."

"My parents, John and Sarah, came down the year before that and settled on the banks of the Nolichuckey River southwest of where we are now."

"What made you go over to Rowan County and stay," asked Rebecca.

"I don't know. Guess I wanted to go over the mountains and see what was on the other side. Went by myself. Probably not a good idea considering that Indians have been in such an agitated state."

By the end of the week, Francis had asked Rebecca to be his wife. To her utter disbelief, she said, "Yes." Never had she imagined finding a husband in the Southern wilderness and agreeing to marry a man she'd known for a week seemed slightly insane.

Barnabus confirmed that she had taken total leave of her senses. "Dear God, Rebecca, you want to stay down here? You can't live like this. You'll raise little heathens."

"Oh, stop it, cousin. It probably does not make sense. I know it's right, that's all. This man makes my soul sing.

"And besides, he knows colonels and generals over in Rowan County that you, the doctors, Dinah, and Eadie can follow into battles in the east. You can find another driver to replace Nick. I know he doesn't want to go anywhere near the fighting."

"Why do you think that is," Barnabus asked.

"He saw his little brother accidentally get shot when they were young. Blown to kingdom come. I guess that's not the way Nick wants to go. Although he can sure use a gun, as we saw coming down."

When Francis started living along Canoe Creek, a tributary of the Catawba River in the wilderness of Rowan County's Catawba Valley, he became good friends with the Penland brothers. Robert,

George, and William Penland had arrived from Pennsylvania about five miles outside of what would become Morgantown in the late 60s.

When the Revolutionary War started, all three brothers became captains in the Rowan County militia under Colonel Charles McDowell. Francis volunteered in June 1776 as a ranger and spent two and a half months under Colonel McDowell and Captain Robert Penland as they sought out hostile Cherokee and Creek Indians.

These troops became known as part of the famous Overmountain Men.

In mid-July 1776, Griffith Rutherford, now a colonel, started gathering militia forces on the headwaters of the Catawba River in preparation for an invasion into Cherokee country. On September 1, he led a force of 1,700 officers and men west toward Cherokee land.

Colonel McDowell's forces met Colonel Rutherford's troops, and Frances Hughes volunteered to join the venture. They proceeded west across the mountains to the Cherokee Nation's Overhill Towns on the lower Little Tennessee, lower Tellico, and lower Hiwassee rivers in what would become the state of Tennessee. By the end of September, thirty-six towns had been burned, and crops and storehouses destroyed, thus effectively reducing the Cherokee threat.

Colonel John Sevier recognized the need to build a fort to retake the western settlement on the Watauga River. In January 1778, Francis volunteered to assist in the effort since the location at Gallagher's on the Nolichuckey River in Carter's Valley was near his home now. He and Rebecca had moved to the Nolichuckey soon after they married to be near the extended Hughes family. Work on the fort took twelve months.

Colonel Sevier again recruited Francis in September 1780 for an expedition against Loyalist Major Patrick Ferguson, who had been recruited to protect Lieutenant General Charles Cornwallis's main flank. They met up with the Patriot militia led by Colonel Joseph McDowell, who had settled at Quaker Meadows in Burke County, a brother of Colonel Charles McDowell.

On Saturday, October 7, around noon, 910 American soldiers, directed by Colonel William Campbell, met about one hundred troops under Major Ferguson's command in what became known as the Battle of King's Mountain, practically on the border of South Carolina and North Carolina. The stunning Patriot victory proved to be a pivotal moment in the Southern campaign of the war.

Colonel Sevier and Colonel McDowell led Francis and 108 other men in a column around the southern flank of the high ridge, which was 600 yards long. Colonel Campbell's column was ahead of them, moving around the southwest base when they began drawing fire from above. They then decided to assault the ridge. Colonel Sevier and Colonel McDowell's men became intermingled with them. As they neared the crest, the British started a bayonet charge.

"Damn, they're going to slice us up," yelled Francis to Joe Greer, crouched just to his left. "What do we do?"

"Pick out one of the febs and squeeze the trigger. Then, turn around and run like hell. That tall, blond one coming this way is mine." Under his breath, he muttered, "He's already dead." In the next couple of seconds, Joe's rifle belched fire and smoke.

Francis then fired off a round that hit a charging Redcoat square in the upper chest. He then skedaddled along with other members of his column back down the ridge.

For the next twenty minutes or so, they were reinforced by Colonel Issac Shelby's column. Hand-to-hand fighting ensued. Francis had never seen such brawling. The Overmountain Men pulled their knives out of belts and taught the Brits a lesson in backwoods savagery.

Major Ferguson was shot out of his saddle and died after about an hour of fighting. His second in command raised the white flag.

Perhaps miraculously, only twenty-eight Americans lost their lives, while sixty-two received wounds. The British ended up with 290 dead, 163 wounded, and 668 captured.

That winter, Francis again volunteered to march with Colonel Sevier against the Cherokee, who remained a threat to white settlers. When they reached the border of the Cherokee Nation, they discovered that the instigators had disappeared into the interior.

Rowan County proved to be the entryway to service during the war for the Massachusetts cousin and friends of Rebecca Allen Hughes. By 1776, Colonel Griffith Rutherford and the McDowell brothers liked the idea of having their own hospital unit available to follow them into battles. Doctors Hanson and Quincy, Dinah Quincy, and Eadie all survived some of the major battles of the war, most of which were fought in South Carolina.

On November 15, 1781, days before the British evacuated Wilmington, Brigadier General Rutherford and his 1,500-man army marched toward the port city in southern North Carolina. They moved upon a brick house and abatis comprising a British fort opposite the city. About fifty soldiers declined to surrender. During a brief skirmish, several of the Patriot fighters were wounded. Barnabus Edson was gut shot and died within the hour of his wound.

Francis and Rebecca Allen found themselves with five children at the close of the war. Instead of nursing wounded soldiers, she nursed newborn babies, ran after toddlers, sewed, tended a garden, raised chickens and sheep, learned to cook under what seemed to her primitive conditions, learned to make butter, jellies, jams, and canned vegetables. Even skinned animals. She ordered a spinning wheel from Boston, which actually found its way to her, and learned to spin cotton and weave. The whole process seemed magical, and she loved it. Her sisters-in-law taught her virtually everything she needed to know. And the women grew close.

In 1783, Greene County was developed from the Nolichuckey settlement, which had been part of North Carolina's Washington District, along with the Watauga settlement.

The oldest child of Francis and Rebecca, Christiana, married Nathan Cooper in Greene County in 1791. By the 1820s, they had moved to White County in Middle Tennessee. Their grandson, John Cannady Cooper, located from Spring Creek in Overton County, where he was raised, one county west of Granville in Jackson County. His granddaughter, Annie Carter, married William J. Byrne in Gainsborough in 1885.

Called to a Spirit-Filled Life

Woodson (Byrne)

They arrived in small boats shortly after the daily summer afternoon showers over the James River stopped. The occupants were young adults, fourteen males and six females. All exhausted, famished, scared. And ebony black.

Dr. John Woodson chinked between logs in the outer walls of the kitchen in his new home at Flowerdew Hundred when he spied the four boats coming upriver in late August 1619. Since he shared an investment in the cargo, he dropped his tools and headed for the docks to assist George Yeardley, governor of Jamestown and owner of the plantation. Also present was Abraham Piersey, Virginia's cape merchant. The two men were the largest individual landowners in the fledgling colony. Both had traveled to Point Comfort, at the extreme tip of the Virginia Peninsula, almost sixty miles downriver, to meet two English ships that had accompanied a pirated Portuguese slave ship across the Atlantic. Those contracted for departure in Virginia were traded for food provided by Governor Yeardley and Mr. Piersey.

Although the twenty new arrivals were listed as indentured servants, chains binding their wrists and ankles told a different story. They became the first recorded slaves in the Colony of Virginia.

The following day, Mr. Piersey and two assistants took seven newcomers. They headed to his plantation called Pierseys Toile, located on the upper side of the Appomattox River, a tributary of the James River. Governor Yeardley kept another seven. Dr. John and wife, Sarah Winston Woodson, collected one of the older women, Aja, twenty-six, and five males aged fifteen to twenty-five.

The Africans came from the Ndongo kingdom inland in what would become Angola on the continent's west coast.

Just before the turn of the 17th century, Portuguese slave traders recruited a band of African marauders, known as Imbangala, to start what turned into brutal warfare against the people of Kabasa, the capital of the Ndongo kingdom, as well as those in the rural inland areas. Thousands were killed with European guns, and thousands more were herded to the coast to be sold as unpaid labor on plantations in Portugal and Spanish South America.

In 1619 alone, thirty-six shiploads of captives were processed by Portuguese slave traders operating in Luanda on the northern Atlantic coast, State of West Africa.

One of those Portuguese merchant-slave ships, the *San Juan Bautista,* left the port of Luanda on August 1 with around one hundred Ndongan prisoners en route to Vera Cruz, Mexico. Two English ships owned by Robert Rich, 2nd Earl of Warwick, consorted to capture the Spanish galleon. The *Treasurer,* sailing as a heavily armed privateer, joined the English warship *White Lion* under Captain Jope. The ship was fully capable of attacking any Spanish or Portuguese ship. By flying the Dutch flag, the *White Lion* managed to deflect blame for its piracy of a loaded slave ship. The prize was then escorted to the east coast of North America with its human cargo.

John Woodson, born in 1586, was the fourth child of Sir Alexander Woodson and Alice Hammon of Bristol, Devonshire. Young John became a doctor after finishing his studies at St. John's College, part of Cambridge University. He moved to Dorset, one county to the East, to start practicing medicine.

Early in 1619, Dr. Woodson married Sarah Winston, a Native of Dorset. Sarah, thirty, agreed to start life with her new husband in the wilds of America.

Sir George Yeardley, born in Southwark, Surrey, England, had assumed charge of colonial affairs in Jamestown. He gathered about one hundred passengers and on January 29, 1619, the *George* sailed for Virginia at what turned out to be a rough crossing. They did not arrive until April 16.

Temperance Flowerdew Yeardley, twenty-nine, the wife of Sir George, suffered severe seasickness on their passage. Sarah Woodson served as her nursemaid, and the two women became close friends, as did their husbands.

Governor Yeardley offered Dr. Woodson land on Flowerdew Hundred in return for his agreement to serve as the ship's doctor and future doctor for the plantation's growing population.

The Woodsons were joined on the journey by John Harvey, an acquaintance from Dorset. Eight years later, Sir Harvey would be knighted by King Charles I and appointed a member of Governor Yeardley's Council in Jamestown. From 1628-1639, Sir Harvey was appointed governor during a contentious time for the still struggling colony.

Since English settlers, financed by the Virginia Company of London, made their way up what was then known as the Powhatan River in May 1607, survival had been tenuous at best for those attempting to establish Jamestown. Starvation and disease wiped out most of those early arrivals. Threats by the many Natives living along Coastal Plain rivers started early.

In 1609, King James I sent a third supply mission of nine ships carrying around 500 passengers, including women and children, to the Virginia coast to provide much-needed support. Heading the fleet was the new *Sea Venture*, commanded by Adm. Sir George Somers and Vice Adm. Christopher Newport. Tragedy struck early. Yellow fever broke out on two of the ships.

After eight weeks at sea and only seven days from their expected arrival, when the fleet was an estimated 450 nautical miles northeast of the Bahama Islands, a ferocious hurricane scattered eight of the ships and sent the *Catch*, commanded by Master Matthew Fitch, to the bottom of the sea. The *Sea Venture* took on several feet of water in her hull. Men desperately worked at pumping and bailing. They were blown southeast. They were driven onto stunning coral reefs at Discovery Bay in eastern Bermuda three days later. Miraculously, all of the passengers and crew survived the ordeal.

George Yeardley, twenty-one years old, had been invited to join this voyage to America. Sir Thomas Gates, newly appointed governor of the Colony in Virginia, asked Captain Yeardley to serve as a personal bodyguard. George was among the 152 people stranded on the island for ten months as they salvaged hardware from their wrecked vessel and collected enough Bermuda cedar to construct two light sailing ships to take them to Virginia.

They arrived at Fort James on May 23, 1610. Horrified at the condition of the few surviving colonists, Governor Gates decided to abandon the fort and return everybody to England. Instead, they met three mission ships coming up the James River to their rescue. Leaders decided to give it another go.

Both Yeardleys were intimately familiar with the early struggles of Jamestown when they sailed on the *George* in 1619. George had married Temperance Flowerdew in 1613 in England. Temperance first found her way to the wilderness from Norfolk, England, with her first husband, Richard Barrow. They accompanied Captain Christopher Newport on the *Susan Constant*, his flagship sailing to America. It left with the *Godspeed* and the *Discovery* in late December 1606 and arrived on the coast of Virginia in May.

Unlike most of their fellow countrymen, the Barrows survived sickness, disease, and hunger for over two years. But in November 1609, the Powhatans laid siege to the fort at Jamestown. Indians prevented the settlers from leaving the fort for six months, which would become known as the Starving Time.

Richard Barrow perished. Temperance was among sixty out of 240 people confined within the walls of the fort to survive. Passengers from the first seven ships in the Virginia Company of London's third supply mission stared at skeletal figures. The sight became seared in their memories in upcoming battles as they helped to fight these Native people who would deny them entry to a land offering opportunity and riches.

Incidents of violence with the Natives were sporadic under Opechancanough, or Chief Powhatan, leader of the Pamunkey tribes in the Tidewater Region of Virginia from the south side of the James River north to the Potomac River and parts of the Eastern Shore. He died in 1618, and his succession was passed to his younger brother, Opitchapam, and, soon afterward, to his next younger brother, Opechancanough.

Opechancanough hated the presence of white settlers encroaching onto Powhatan territory. Early in 1622, he executed a coordinated series of surprise attacks on outlying settlements, mainly along both sides of the James River.

On Friday, March 22, the "Massacre of 1622" destroyed about one-fourth of the population of the Colony of Virginia — 347 Europeans died. Twenty women were taken captive. Thirty-one separate settlements and plantations suffered loss. Flowerdew Hundred considered itself relatively lucky, with six killed. Jamestown was severely damaged.

During the next two decades, colonists regrouped, and the population grew after their stunning losses. The Natives, too, recovered as the result of harsh repercussions that followed their butchery and destruction of property.

But on April 18, 1644, Opechancanough and his forces struck hard again along the James River. About 300 settlers lost their lives in the attacks.

The next day, on Tuesday, April 19, Dr. John Woodson visited a patient on Curles Plantation, where his family had recently relocated. The patient lay in the sharp curl on the north side of the James River in Henrico County on a narrow neck of land about thirty miles upriver from Jamestown.

Spring planting had taken the slaves into the fields. Sarah's sons, John, twelve, and Robert, ten, were in the house with her because Lieutenant Colonel Thomas Ligon, an acquaintance of the Woodsons and a soldier in Governor William Berkeley's militia, stopped by needing the doctor's services. When Sarah told him he was out tending to a patient, the colonel said he would wait for his return. Just out the back door, Aja, who had worked in the Woodson household for twenty-five years, was skinning rabbits.

Shortly after his arrival, Lieutenant Colonel Ligon saw Indians approaching the house. He told Sarah to hide the children, then grabbed his 8-foot long, 12-gauge rifle, powder horn, and shot pouch and slid out the door.

Sarah told Aja to "quick, get in the house." They bolted the doors and latched the shutters. Then, they put Robert in the root cellar where potatoes were kept during the winter. They turned up a big wash tub and hid John under it, telling them not to move or make a sound.

"John Woodson, I don't want you to budge until somebody comes to get you out of there. You understand me?"

"I do, Mother"

"I mean, no matter what you hear out of me or Aja or anybody else, you do not make a sound or move. If you do, you could be killed. Is that plain enough for you?"

"Yes, ma'am," John answered.

The women always kept a big iron pot of water heating over a fire that never went out. Sarah quickly added more wood to the fire. She automatically scanned the large living area for potential weapons. There was not another gun in the house. Her eyes immediately fell on the wrought iron poker by the fireplace. She set it in the hot coals. A small hatchet for chopping kindling sat by the stone mantel. Aja went to the kitchen and pulled out her favorite butcher knife. It felt like a second hand to her. She knew she could carve a man up with it, just as well as an animal if she had to. She also pulled down a cast iron skillet small enough to wield as a weapon if needed.

Sarah peeked out of a crack in a shuttered window and counted nine hostiles. Suddenly, she saw her husband ride out of the forest with his gun ready to fire. Lieutenant Colonel Ligon had found a perfect notch in a tree just outside the door to support his long weapon. Before he could fire, an arrow pierced John in his breast. Immediately, he fell from his horse. His assailants rushed at him with raised tomahawks.

About the same time, much to Sarah's distress, she heard footsteps on the roof around the chimney.

"Aja, you hear that? Surely, they are not going to come down this chimney with a fire burning."

"Pick up dat ax. We haf ter be ready, Mistress. For the chiluns sake!"

The Indian dropped straight into the large pot of scalding water, screamed, and fell onto the floor. After just witnessing her husband's murder, Sarah's rage spilled out. Aja stopped her from swinging the hatchet again after the man's face became pulp and his skull split open.

Not a minute later, a second one fell down the chimney. Aja had grabbed the iron poker out of the fire and killed him with one stroke to the back of the head.

Meanwhile, outside, Lieutenant Colonel Ligon had felled three men with his first shot. His second took out two. He then killed two more. He looked stunned when he walked into the house.

"You two can fight with me any day," he said. "I'm so very sorry about John. He would be mighty proud of you, Sarah."

"And Aja," Sarah replied. "She killed the second one all by herself. Saved my boys and me."

"Let me drag this mess out of here, and you can retrieve those fine lads. But stay vigilant," the colonel advised

⁂

On an already sticky August morning in 1678, Robert Woodson made his regular rounds into his tobacco fields on his stallion, Blazer. His wife, Elizabeth, was about a month away from giving birth to their last child, Mary Ann, and had spent a miserable night sweating and cursing the heat. She'd threatened him within an inch of his life if he made her with child again. He thought it safer out in the fields. Sallie, Elizabeth's maid, would handle any crisis at the house.

Robert and his brother, John, owned 531 acres on Curles Plantation. They also partnered with Robert's father-in-law, Richard Ferris, and his son, William, in a land grant covering 1,637 acres.

When the Woodsons moved to Curles Plantation in 1644, Richard Ferris, his wife, Sarah, and their five young children already lived there. They brought along Aja (who became indispensable to the household), five of the original six field hands, plus four more, and four wives and their offspring for a total of seventeen available to work the fields.

This was the third year these 400 acres had been planted in tobacco. Some farmers would undoubtedly push and plant a fourth year, but not Robert. He went for quality over quantity. Competition for the best leaf remained fierce in the late fall European markets. Those who cut corners in production practices suffered when prices were assigned to their allotment as the bidding started.

The tobacco plants stood about eight feet tall. The yellowish-green leaves were thick, rough, and downy looking. When Robert slid off Blazer, he tore a leaf and folded it between his fingers. It broke, showing good elasticity. Temperatures had rarely risen into the 90s over the summer. Rainfall was above average. They suffered no bad wind storms. All worked in the crop's favor. He thought if everything continued on track, it should be ready to cut with sharp knives between the bottom leaves and the ground in early September. After harvest, the plants would be hung on sticks and put in large sheds to cure for four to six weeks. It would be struck from the sticks and laid on floors to sweat for a week or two. Then, it would be sorted if it had absorbed just the right amount of moisture. Workers would separate it into units of equal quality, then tie them together in bunches of five to fourteen. Again, it would be laid on the platforms to sweat.

Finally, the dried, pressed tobacco leaf went into a large wooden barrel called a "hogshead." Merchant vessels moved from one plantation dock to another on the major rivers in the Tidewater area, loading up barrels of tobacco and heading for ports to be shipped across the Atlantic. Virginia collected a two shillings per hogshead export tax on tobacco, providing more revenue to England than any of its colonies.

Natives to the area had long grown and smoked Nicotiana rustica, a dark, bitter-tasting plant. When John Rolfe arrived on the James River in the early 1600s, he immediately recognized an opportunity to grow a less harsh variety of tobacco in what looked to be an ideal climate along rich bottomland. They would be exported to Europe, which could not get enough of this product already supplied by Spain.

Mr. Rolfe brought Spanish seeds from Trinidad with him, which were a milder, sweeter tobacco with a dark leaf, Nicotiana tabacum. In 1612, he established Varina Plantation in Henrico County, about twenty-seven miles upriver from Jamestown. In March 1614, he exported four barrels of what he called Orinoco tobacco from Virginia to England, which put Virginia on the map.

Profitable tobacco production required large tracts of fertile land. The plant depleted the minerals and nutrients in the soil. Once a field was depleted, it had to lay fallow for twenty years before the soil would yield healthy crops again. Farmers in the 17th century knew virtually nothing about crop rotation. The learning curve was steep.

Tobacco production is labor-intensive. Colonists desperate for work tried to carve out fields for agriculture from the wilderness. Pressing leaves into barrels took at least one-third of the year, and the rest of the year was spent clearing land.

Labor required for such work was not available in colonial Virginia. In 1618, the headright system began in Jamestown in response to labor shortages. The economy and growth of the area had already become greatly influenced by John Rolfe's tobacco experiments. When someone paid the transportation costs for a laborer or indentured servant to come to the American colonies, they qualified for one of these land grants.

The stream of indentured servants from England declined after the decade-long English Civil War ended in 1651 and the restoration of King Charles II in 1660. Scottish settlers in Ireland had started immigrating as indentured servants by the 1650s, and this rapidly increased by the end of the century.

The primary source of labor on Virginia tobacco plantations from early on was slaves from Africa. How much tobacco could be planted depended on available labor. Clearing land and the repetitive tasks in the production process did not require skilled labor. The return on slave labor was great. They helped to keep costs down, and profits surged.

Robert felt lucky to have secured an experienced planter to supervise their slaves and help walk John and him through critical production decisions. Although the brothers had been around tobacco since they were boys living on Flowerdew Hundred, they absorbed a wealth of information from Mr. Farris, his planter, other area plantation owners who visited, and the slaves themselves. When their mother remarried in 1650, she made it clear that her sons, then eighteen and sixteen, would have dominion over the plantation.

The Woodsons moved to Curles Plantation in 1644, and Robert immediately found his first and last love in Elizabeth Ferris, who was the same age. Her sense of adventure nearly matched her brother, Richard Jr., a year older. Brother John joined in the fun, and the four soon-to-be teenagers started on a series of escapades that lasted nearly into their twenties.

Although the boys were expected to work, they found time to explore this waterway paradise, including the big river and tributaries, creeks, branches, and freshwater marshes. Some of their favorite places included the swamp on Turkey Island, Four Mile Creek, which ran into the James River right beside Curles, and the Chickahominey Swamp. In the fall, they ventured up to Bear Forest on a branch of the Pamunkey River to hunt with adults.

Robert and Elizabeth married in April 1656, to no one's surprise. By then, they knew what they were getting into, and neither could imagine being apart. Their first child, John, came along on December 10, 1658.

A week after January 1, 1661, Sarah Woodson, seventy, bundled up and went outside to play with her six-year-old grandson, John III, son of John and his wife, Mary Pleasants, in snow that had fallen overnight. She always loved snow. Much to the concern of the boy's mother, the older woman even lay down and showed the youngster how to make snow angels. On January 17, the family's matriarch died of pneumonia.

In September 1677, Richard Ferris Jr. and his brother William, along with six slaves, were hauling tobacco ready for sale on a barge around the warehouse at Varina. They barely got out into the channel when they hit a big submerged tree so hard that it knocked one of their workers into the water. He did not immediately resurface. Richard pulled off his jacket and boots and jumped in after him. After almost a minute, William told the other slaves to break open one of the barrels because the barge surged nearly one hundred yards past where the men had disappeared. He needed a float to help rescue them. He flung off his jacket and boots and swam to the point where he thought they went down. He saw Richard's white shirt about 15 feet below and to the right behind a net entangled in tree branches. Immediately, William dove down and pulled out his knife. Richard blinked his eyes, but there was little struggle left. His brother frantically started cutting the tightly woven net from around him. It took the longest minute of William's life before he finally pulled Richard free. With every ounce of strength he had left, he carried Richard to the surface and swam with him about twenty yards to the broken barrel.

The Ferris slaves pulled their masters onto the barge. One lay exhausted. The other had no heartbeat.

Curles Plantation went into mourning. The Ferris family heir was gone. And they lost a valuable piece of human property. Richard Jr. left behind a wife and a five-year-old son, Richard III. No death had impacted the Woodson brothers more since they lost their father in the Indian attack thirty-three years earlier.

Even though tobacco prices fell in the 1680s and 1690s as the market became less stable, the Woodson brothers continued to buy land primarily in Henrico County to help secure the future for their combined twenty children. In October 1687, Robert partnered with Giles Carter and Roger Cumins to purchase 1,780 acres on the north side of the James River at White Oak Swamp. At the same time, he joined William Lewis, a brother-in-law, and Thomas Charles in buying another 470 acres on the north side of the James River.

John Woodson died at age fifty-two in October 1684 while out quail hunting with his two oldest sons, John III and Richard. The cause was a suspected ruptured appendix.

✳ ✳ ✳

Many people fled Great Britain to worship as they pleased. Yet, after arriving in the New World, the religious intolerance of their forefathers gripped their hearts and minds quickly.

Several Quakers arrived in colonial Virginia in the early years. Most settled on the Eastern Shore. This so-called Society of Friends almost immediately clashed with the ruling authorities.

By the mid-1600s, the courts began their harassment. In 1658, Quakers were banned from the Colony of Virginia by the General Assembly. Anyone receiving a Quaker into their home would be fined one hundred pounds. In 1661, the General Assembly decided to fine anyone who failed to attend services of the established church, sanctioned by the Church of England, for one month. Fines were levied against those who defied militia regulations, another way to attack the Quaker population. Despite the sanctions and threats, Quaker numbers continued to grow.

The General Assembly described The Quakers as: ". . . an unreasonable and turbulent people, who daily gather together unlawful assemblies of people, teaching lies, miracles, false visions, prophecies, and doctrines tending to disturb the peace, disorganize Society and destroy the peace, destroy all laws, and government, and religion."

Few suffered more than the Pleasants from the lack of justice directed toward Quakers by the courts and laws in Virginia. The family owned many acres on the Curles Plantation. They developed a thriving tobacco operation that somehow attracted unwanted attention.

John Pleasants and his wife were fined 240 pounds for "illicit cohabitation" because they were living together unlawfully according to the rules of the Anglican church. They were fined 2,000 pounds of tobacco for not having their children baptized in the Anglican church and another 500 pounds of tobacco for hosting

Quaker meetings in their home. Although John was elected to the House of Burgesses from Henrico County in 1692, he became ineligible to serve after he refused to take the oath prescribed by the act of Parliament. Quakers took issue with swearing oaths.

The Woodson family first connected with the faith when John Woodson, at twenty-two, married Mary Pleasants, twenty-one, on Curles Plantation in 1654. Mary was one of nine children of John and Katherine Munford Pleasants of Norwich, Norfolk, England. Six immigrated and found their way up the James River.

John Pleasants Jr., a brother of Mary, arrived in the mid-60s and started acquiring large acreage in Henrico County. He quickly agreed with the tenets of Quakerism and became an active and prominent participant in the church. At first, he held Quaker meetings in his home. Then, he donated land to construct a meeting house and space for a cemetery.

John Pleasants married Jane Larcombe Tucker in December 1680. Her first husband, Captain Samuel Tucker, son of a London merchant and a pioneer of the Colony of Virginia, was master of the ship *Vine Tree*. He transported Virginia tobacco to England. He sometimes carried English Quakers who wanted to start a new life in America on return trips. In September 1680, Captain Tucker went down with his ship and an early load of tobacco headed to London.

In 1670, Mary Tucker, daughter of Samuel and Jane Tucker and then step-daughter of John Pleasants, married John Woodson III, son of John and Mary Pleasants Woodson. Both spent many years growing up on Curles Plantation.

Sarah Woodson, the third out of four daughters of Robert Woodson, John's brother, married Edward Mosby in 1682. Sarah had become devout in her beliefs, and her new husband soon followed her lead.

The Mosby family lived comfortably, but they were not wealthy. Edd farmed and became a skilled carpenter. He built a steady supply of coffins for the Quaker community. He helped construct the meeting house on Curles Plantation in 1701 and supervised workers in 1722 when another meeting house was built for congregants on White Oak Swamp.

Benjamin Woodson was a year younger than his sister, Sarah, and he was Robert and Elizabeth Woodson's youngest of six sons. He married Sarah Porter on June 9, 1700, in the Curles Meeting House.

William Porter Jr. left Norfolk, England as an infant with his parents, William Sr. and Mary Copeland, and sailed for Virginia. First, they settled in newly founded Gloucester County on the Chesapeake Bay, where they met other Quakers. They then moved up the James River and made Henrico County their home.

The first child born to William Jr. when he married Margaret Amos was Sarah in 1668. When Sarah Porter wed Benjamin Woodson thirty-two years later, they survived off of the life-giving water of the James River for their entire lives while living on Curles Plantation.

Robert Woodson was the fifth son born to the couple. He left Henrico County at an early age and acquired property on the south side of the James River in Goochland County above the falls. He wed Rebecca Pryor in 1720. Her parents, John and Mary New Pryor, lived nearby where the Tuckahoe Creek flows into the big river.

Thomas Mims II was among the first Mims known to have sailed from England to America. He and his wife, Anne Stanford Mims, arrived on the Virginia coast in 1657. They headed up the York River and settled on the Chickahominy River, which flows in Henrico County and along the southwest border of the new county of New Kent.

King William III had officially created the villages of Manakin and Sabot in Henrico County with a grant of 10,000 acres. Hundreds of French Huguenots, Protestant refugees, emigrated via

London to this land northwest of Richmond, previously occupied by the Monacan Indian Nation. Thomas III and Mellyann Martin Mims started a family with a son, David, on the first day of 1701 in Manakin, about twenty miles above the falls of the James River.

David Mims took Agnes Weldy as his wife in 1721. Thirteen years later, their son, Shadrack, was born. He planned to marry Eliza Woodson, the granddaughter of Benjamin and Sarah Woodson, in 1760. On November 17, 1777, both Shadrack and Eliza were killed when a wheel came off their wagon on a narrow bridge that went over the side into Dover Creek.

Robert Mims was thirteen when his parents were killed, and his younger sister, Betty, was just eight. They were among eight Mims' children left orphaned. He married Lucy Poor eleven years later, and they moved to Russellville in Logan County, Kentucky. Early on, his mother had, "because of love and affection for my son Robert Mims," given him a slave named Lucinda and her children, Eady, Elizabeth, and Fleming, "with the increase from the females."

Robert Mims' sister, Betty, married Robert Poor, brother of Lucy Poor. Robert Poor was a cornet in the Revolutionary War. The Poor children were raised by Lieutenant Abraham and Judith Gardner Poor on Lil Byrd Creek, which flows into the James River in Goochland County. The Poor's land was near Elk Island.

Mary, who they called Polly, was born in 1790 to Robert and Betty Poor. As a seventeen-year-old, Polly married Reverend John James, thirty-two, who grew up on Lickinghole Creek, Goochland County. They moved to Lickskillet on Whippoorwill Creek in Logan County, Kentucky, 1807 near the Middle Tennessee border.

Young John James felt called to a spirit-filled life from an early age. He shared a sense of accountability to God with his parents, William and Nancy Hines James, because he saw the consequences of wrongdoing among people. The minute he understood the concept of redemption, he knew he had to reach those who needed help.

When John was thirteen, he and his father went to a general meeting of the Baptist General Committee at Williams Meeting House in Goochland County on March 7, 1788. Six months earlier, the U.S. Constitution had been adopted in Philadelphia. Baptists contended for religious liberty as well as political. Attendees at the meeting discussed the principle of personal liberty as it pertained to slaves.

Participating was Reverend John Leland, a leading proponent of the full separation of church and state. After over a decade of tensions in Virginia between the established Anglican Church and Baptists, he opposed any form of state support of religion. Fellow Baptist preachers had been imprisoned, and Leland himself was threatened with a gun.

The following resolution was offered by Reverend Leland at the 1788 meeting and adopted:

"Resolved, That slavery is a violent deprivation of the rights of nature, and inconsistent with a republican government, and therefore recommend it to our brethren to make use of every legal measure to extirpate this horrid evil from the land, and pray Almighty God that our honorable legislature may have it in their power to proclaim the great jubilee, consistent with the principles of good policy."

Kentucky was admitted to the Union on June 1, 1792. After the end of the Revolutionary War in 1783, the territory experienced a great influx of population. The Baptist Church served more of these early pioneers in Kentucky than any other denomination. The Anglican Church, particularly in the South, was weakened after the war because of its association with Great Britain.

John James, twenty-five, heard about the Revival of 1800 at Red River in Logan County, Kentucky. He knew he had to travel west to see what all the excitement was about. The following spring, he took his brother, Samuel, and brother-in-law, David Hodges (who had married their sister, Nancy James), to the camp meeting at the Gasper River Meeting House in Logan County to meet Reverend James McGready.

The emotional outpouring at the gathering clearly demonstrated to John the desire among common people for a moral compass to direct them away from a host of corruptions in a fairly lawless society. He found Reverend McGready to be full of divine grace and unfeigned piety.

Reverend McGready arrived in Logan County from North Carolina in 1797. He observed that church attendance was sparse, even in the more populated areas of the state.

In his 1856 autobiography, Peter Cartwright described Logan County as "Rogue's Harbor," a destination for criminals fleeing justice in the East. The Cartwright house was three miles from the Red River Meeting House.

Several other Presbyterian, Methodist, and Baptist ministers assisted Reverend McGready in hosting a series of multi-day outdoor camp meetings that attracted large crowds in southwestern Kentucky and Middle Tennessee. Many traveled long distances to attend. Their generation of religious enthusiasm led to the conversion of hundreds of Protestants.

People in backcountry settlements, who tended to be fiercely independent, responded to evangelicalism throughout the nineteenth century. Reverend McGready carried a message of regeneration or new birth — restoring personal salvation.

Sister Nancy and her husband, David Hodges, joined John and Polly James in Logan County, Kentucky. Brother Samuel and his second wife, Pernina Dean James, settled in Pike County, Kentucky, on John's Creek. They were in a remote mountainous region on the West Virginia side of the river valley.

Sam and Pernina James did not know it, but when their daughter Sarah, whom they called Sally, married William McCoy in 1836, they took a front-row seat in the later decades of the century to backwoods lawlessness that quickly became legend.

The Hatfield-McCoy feud, described by journalists as the Hatfield-McCoy war, involved families of Randolph "Old Ran'l" McCoy, of Pike County, Kentucky, William McCoy's first cousin, and William Anderson "Devil Anse" Hatfield of Logan County, West Virginia between 1863 and 1891. Both Sally and William lived long enough to see most of it play out, as more than a dozen on both sides were killed in battles between the families.

On January 17, 1827, the day after her daughter Mary Elizabeth was born, Polly James died, leaving Reverend John with eight children. Within weeks, he, too, had passed away of undetermined causes.

Robert Sallee James, their third out of five sons, was nine years old at the time and went to live with his sister, Mary, who was about to marry John Mims, grandson of Shadrack and Lucy Mims.

Robert became a gifted orator even as a student at Georgetown College in Georgetown, Kentucky. Chartered in 1829, it became the first Baptist college west of the Appalachian Mountains.

Zerelda Cole met Robert at a religious gathering a year before he was to graduate. The Cole family came from Pennsylvania and went through Virginia to Kentucky outside Lexington. Her grandfather, Richard Cole Jr., developed courage as a lieutenant in the Woodford County Light Infantry Company during the Revolutionary War. Young Zee, as she was called, inherited his strong personality and fanatical loyalty to his family.

Robert married Zee in December 1841. He was twenty-three; she seventeen. The following August, the newlyweds went to Clay County, Missouri, to visit her mother, Sarah. She had married Robert Thomason after James Cole died when thrown from a horse. Zerelda was two years old.

Robert returned to Georgetown College to finish his degree after studying theology. He could not return to Zee and their new son, Alexander Franklin James, until the following January. In 1848, he again returned to Georgetown, where he completed a Master's Degree.

The couple decided to settle in Missouri near Centerville, soon to be renamed Kearney. Migrants from Virginia, Kentucky, and Tennessee populated the county, as did others north and south of the Missouri River, which ran along the southern edge of Clay County. These Southern families brought their slaves and started cultivating considerable tobacco and hemp.

Robert James bought land from Asa Thomason, brother of Zee's step-father, and built a cabin in the spring of 1849 with the help of two slaves he brought back with him. The three of them started producing hemp. He also developed Baptist churches at New Hope, Lincoln County, and Providence, Boone County.

At the same time, he was approached by a group of Baptists, who had received a charter from the Missouri legislature to found a college. They discovered this educated young minister in their midst whose skills in the pulpit generated excitement. He agreed to become a co-founder of William Jewell College, a private Baptist college in Liberty, the seat of Clay County, located six miles north of the Missouri River.

🪶🪶🪶

The California Gold Rush caused a virtual human stampede west in 1849. Many traveling overland to the Sierra Nevada foothills trekked through Kansas City/Independence or St. Joseph, Missouri, to access the California Trail or the South Pass through the Rocky Mountains. The network of wagon roads presented a daunting journey under the best of circumstances.

Robert woke up in the middle of the night on February 18, 1851, with a sense of destiny. He did not have a vision exactly. Maybe God's voice was in his ear - undeniably a Divine nudge.

Two nights after a full moon, he got out of bed, unlatched the front door, and walked outside. The sky was clear and still bright two nights after a full moon. He heard what he thought was probably a snowy owl he'd seen twice in the last few days.

Surely, he could stay home, tend to his obligations, and serve those in the immediate community. Did he receive communications from on High, or was he crazy?

After two days, Robert sat down at the table with Zee and said he needed to talk.

"I believe I'm 'spose to go California, live amongst the miners, and preach the Gospel," he said. "I see hit as a mission. I don't know t'other way to interpret hit."

His wife was silent for almost a minute. Then she said, "Yore a good man, Robert.

A gifted teacher. Wise as a counselor. Much to give. What makes ye think yore a needin' ter go 2,000 miles to do God's work? The need is great right here."

"The Lord come ter me a couple nights ago in my sleep," he replied. "Men ere working in rivers out there with little spiritual direction, no doubt. Single fellers ere probably a lookin' fer trouble. Married men have left their wives behind to prospect fer gold. I would hope most of 'um ere a tryin' to avoid trouble."

"Trouble is what I see," said Zee. "All manner of trouble. Plenty of ne'er do wells, drunks, thieves, hustlers of all kinds. Even killers. Not to mention disease that surely follers the crowds. Jesus himself would be hard put ter handle all that."

"I'll keep a prayin' on hit," her husband responded.

On Saturday, April 19, Robert went up to St. Joseph with a couple of area men, and one of their older teenage sons wanting to prospect for gold. They had outfitted a wagon and secured oxen. Two days later, they started with a convoy headed west, who readily agreed to accept a minister. They arrived in Hangtown, El Dorado County, California, on Friday, August 1. Three years later, it would be renamed Placerville. Robert was immediately encouraged that the town's first church, a Methodist Episcopal, had just been constructed.

On August 18, Robert James, thirty-two, died of cholera, one disease among several that swept through wagon trains in the 1840s and 50s.

Feisty Zerelda, who stood six feet tall, was back home in Missouri with a one hundred-acre farm growing hemp and tending to sheep. In addition to her son, Frank, who was now eight years old, she had Jesse, four, and a daughter, Susan, two, to raise. There was also one female slave, Cinda, and five slave children.

Zee then married a well-known widower, Ben Sims, who had five children in September 1852. The union turned out to be short-lived due to problems with all the children. Mr. Sims died in an accident involving a horse right after the first of the year in 1854 before a divorce was finalized.

Three years later, Zee married an area doctor, Reuben Samuel, who handled her dominating personality well. They added six more children to the household. The second and third, John and Fannie Samuel, were born during the war Between the States, which greatly affected the border state of Missouri for its duration. Populated by both Union and Confederate sympathizers, the conflict led to neighbor-against-neighbor violence that often resulted in bloodshed.

Zerelda was an outspoken supporter of the South. Son, Frank, was almost twenty when he hooked up with Quantrill's Raiders, led by William Quantrill, a Confederate deserter. These partisan guerrilla bushwhackers resented state leaders for refusing to declare Missouri a secessionist state despite the support of Southern-leaning, mainly farming-dependent families. They were not the only group of pro-Southern guerrillas but the most notorious.

Allen Parmer, who also grew up in Kearney, was another member of Quantrill's Raiders. In 1870, he married Susie James, the younger sister of the James brothers, much to the dismay of Jesse. By the mid-70s, Allen and Susie had moved to Wichita Falls, Texas, with the first of their eight children. Susie died at age 39 in March 1889, right after the birth of a stillborn son.

Coming into northern Missouri counties from Kansas soon after the start of the war were bands of pro-secession bushwhackers creating havoc among communities. Henry Younger, a prosperous farmer in Jackson County, just north of Clay County, who was a Union sympathizer, was killed by a Union soldier from Kansas. As a result, his son, Cole Younger, and brothers, Bob, John, and Jim, would join the James brothers in retaliatory gang activity.

Jesse James joined his brother, Frank, in 1864 as a guerrilla when he was sixteen. At the time, the group operated under the leadership of William "Bloody Bill" Anderson and Archie 'Little Arch" Clement after William Quantrill lost control of the raiders. They targeted Union loyalists and federal soldiers in Missouri and Kansas.

Bloody Bill Anderson lost his life in a Union ambush in Lexington, Kentucky, in May 1865. Archie Clement then assumed responsibility for the gang, which started robbing banks. In December 1866, Arch Clement was shot to death by state militia on a street in Lexington, Missouri.

At that point, the James-Younger Gang sprang into existence. In addition to brothers Frank and Jesse James, the following were also members at various times: the Younger brothers, including Cole, Jim, John, and Bob; John Jarrett, who married Josie Younger, sister of the brothers; Arthur McCoy; brothers George Shepherd and Oliver "Oll" Shepherd; brothers William McDaniel and Tom McDaniel; Clell Miller; Charlie Pitts; and Bill Chadwell.

They robbed banks, trains, and stagecoaches and murdered until 1876. The gang operated over a geographic range that included the states of Missouri, Kentucky, Tennessee, Iowa, Kansas, Minnesota, Texas, Arkansas, Louisiana, Alabama, and West Virginia between 1868 and 1876.

In 1874, big railroads hired the Chicago-based Pinkerton Detective Agency to track down the James brothers. They received false information that Jesse and Frank were visiting their mother's house in Kearney. Agents surrounded the house on January 26, 1875. An incendiary device exploded after being thrown into the house. It killed eight-year-old Archie Samuel and injured his mother's arm so badly it had to be amputated at the elbow.

The James brothers moved their mother to Whites Creek on the outskirts of Nashville, Tennessee, to save her from potential further harassment.

Zerelda later located back to Kearney. She died of a heart attack on a train en route from Oklahoma to Missouri on February 10, 1911. She was eighty-six.

Both of the James brothers married in 1874. Annie Raulston became Frank's wife. She was the daughter of Colonel Samuel Raulston, an immigrant from Northern Ireland, a supporter of the Southern cause during the war, and a successful businessman in Independence, Missouri. Sons Robert and Jacob arrived in 1877 and 1893.

Jesse married his first cousin Zerelda Mims, daughter of John and Mary James Mims, who had moved from Logan County, Kentucky, to Kansas City, Missouri. Zerelda was named after her mother's sister-in-law, Zerelda James. They produced a son, Jesse, who they called Tim, in 1875 and a daughter, Mary, four years later.

No one questioned the validity of the James-Younger Gang's status as outlaws. Jesse James explained their crimes as "a means of exacting revenge on all things Yankee." The family had been persecuted and tortured at home by a local militia of Union supporters shortly after the start of the war in 1861 when Frank and Jesse were teenagers. They never forgot the experience. After the war, Jesse's hatred for the industrial north intensified, and, in his mind, his criminal activities extended the fight.

The gang generated support and sympathy, especially in the northwestern counties of Missouri, often called "Little Dixie" because of the number of families who moved there from the South. Some journalists also took up the banner romanticizing the gang's activities as tales of the Wild West.

In late 1881, Jesse's family moved to St. Joseph under an assumed name. He had a $10,000 reward on his head. He was planning one more robbery with Bob and Charles Ford, former gang members. The brothers met at the James home on April 3, 1882, to outline plans for a bank robbery in Platte County, Missouri. Bob shot Jesse below the right ear, killing him instantly. Jesse was thirty-four years old. His wife, Zee, was left with three children, ages three through eight. She suffered severe depression after his murder and never recovered. She died at age fifty-five in November 1900.

Frank James walked into Missouri Governor Thomas Crittendon's office five months after Jesse died and, at age thirty-nine, laid his gun belt on the desk. Said he was sick and tired of being hunted and knowing no peace. The public solidly supported his case. He was acquitted on all counts and returned home to the James Farm in Kearney, where he lived until the end of his life thirty-two years later. His wife, Annie James, stayed at the farm in Kearney and passed away at ninety-one.

Time For a Proper Toast

Briggs/McWhirter (Byrne)

"Remember the Raisin!" The battle rallied American troops to a game-changing victory, destroying the British-Canadian-Indian coalition after the War of 1812.

The men found themselves on the expansive marshlands at the confluence of the River Raisin and Lake Erie in the freezing early morning hours of January 22, 1813. Hundreds of cries pieced the air along the river and in the fields, as close to 600 British Regular soldiers and more than 800 Indians attacked. Because of their numbers and due to poor judgment by the American commanding officer, General James Winchester, sixty, the battle quickly turned into a rout.

Private Benjamin Briggs, twenty-nine, fought with several of the more than 700 militia volunteers from Kentucky. They rushed to enlist after Maj. Gen. William Henry Harrison, governor of the Indiana Territory and a future U.S. President, assumed command of militia armies in the Northwest theater of the war. Ben and his unit fought from behind the fence at Frenchtown on the River Raisin.

His high-spirited comrades held the enemy at bay even though they had marched through Ohio into Canada and what would become Michigan on the western edge of Lake Erie. They were ill-equipped for the fierce northern winter, cold, and half-starved. Plus, their ammunition was running low. They had no idea what was happening outside the small town limits until they saw the flag.

"Nate, you see that white flag comin' in from the Brit's line," Ben asked his friend, Pvt. Nathaniel Brown, fighting by his side.

"Yeah. That's a flag of truce, ain't it? You reckon they're backin' down?"

"Let's hope to hell they are," said Ben. "I don't have a good feeling about this. Looks like they's a whole lot more of them than us. And where is General Winchester? Not in sight."

A minute later, they saw that the flag bearer was an aide to General Winchester. That meant the American Regulars had surrendered. They then heard the first lie by British Gen. Henry Procter. He told them that if they surrendered, they would be protected from massacre by the Indians and that their property, except for their firearms and ammunition, would remain theirs.

Other Kentucky soldiers comprising the American right flank were in a poor defensive position in the fields. When the attack started, many immediately fell to British artillery and cannons, and others began to flee. Indians pursued them into the woods and massacred those caught. The eighty or so wounded and left behind died under Indian tomahawks, too. Of the 400 or so who ran, about 220 were killed, and 147, including General Winchester and his son, were captured.

The main body of British Regulars quickly departed, leaving a small detachment of soldiers and Indians to guard Americans in the homes of Frenchtown inhabitants. The next morning, Natives returned to the area, plundering and burning homes. They scalped many of the remaining U.S. soldiers too wounded to walk. They kidnapped others.

As Ben, Nate, and their other compatriots, who had escaped injury, walked out of the houses as prisoners, Indians took their coats, blankets, and boots despite promises made. They marched north in the snow to Fort Malden, very near Amherstburg. After three nights, Ben and a handful of others fled in the middle of the night and miraculously slipped away.

There would be no advancing by this group of riflemen to avenge the devastating loss at River Raisin. Few survivors made it back home.

"Remember the Raisin!" It rang through streets and house chambers as news of the slaughter reached Kentucky and beyond. Outraged legislators authorized Governor Isaac Shelby to detach 3,000 state militia for service to their country.

On September 27, Colonel Richard M. Johnson, who assumed command of 1,200 of Kentucky's volunteer soldiers, served as a member of the U.S. House of Representatives and became a U.S. Vice-President. He finally liberated Frenchtown. His cavalry then freed Fort Detroit on Lake Erie.

While General Harrison pursued British General Procter's troops withdrawing from Fort Malden, Colonel Johnson kept the Indians engaged, defeating Chief Tecumseh's main force on September 29. He then captured British supply trains on October 3. Two days later, Colonel Johnson's forces were the first to attack at the Battle of Thames, near Moraviantown in Upper Canada, Tecumseh's territory. Witnesses said that Colonel Johnson personally killed the renowned chief during the conflict. The American victory effectively ended the War of 1812.

That first night, when Ben and three other soldiers escaped from their captors outside of Fort Malden, they managed to strangle one of the Indians. They took his knife, tomahawk, a flint and stripped him. About a mile outside the camp, they quickly distributed his moccasins, leggings, buckskin shirt, woolen jacket, and gloves, which he had undoubtedly taken off of one of their dead.

Bright stars pointed them due south. The men needed shelter because daylight would be on them in about three hours. They holed up for days and traveled nights. Food was a priority. They scavenged rabbits and other small game even in eighteen inches of snow. They made and set traps at night and prayed that animals would walk into their traps. Once they found a well-ventilated cave, they could use their flint to build a fire to cook the meat. They used rabbit skins to make coverings for their feet. As it was, they used each other's bodies for warmth to keep from freezing.

Ben knew if he was going to live, every survival skill he had ever learned would now pay off. They were no different than any other animal in the woods trying to get through one more day. Except their number one enemy was a member of their own species. They did not talk during the day. They communicated by signal. They made every effort to proceed without sound and, when possible, hid evidence of having been there.

On the fourth evening, Nate found a cave with good covering along a rocky ledge and waved up Ben and Pvt. Abraham Wheatley, who were walking together. About thirty minutes later, Pvt. Jacob Tabler came along and saw Nate signing him in the woods by some bluffs. The two scooted into the relatively small entrance to a good-sized cave.

"By God, Jacob, what have you got there," asked Abe.

"I've got us three squirrels," Jacob replied.

"You'uns thought it was funny when I made a pouch out 'n that rabbit skin last night. I'd been seeing squirrels ever day and thought probably we ought ter add squirrel to the menu. Knew it was goin' ter be my turn to wear the gloves today so my hands would be warm enough ter grip. When I broke ice on that crick earlier to get a drink I noticed the perfect sized stones ter throw. Put 'um in my pouch. Dropped back so's it'd get real quiet. And I nailed three of the critters!"

"I knew you was a damn good shot. But who ever heard a killin' a squirrel with a rock?" laughed Nate.

"Goes to prove, when you're hungry enough, you'll do what ya have to," said Jacob.

Ten days out, the men hunkered down in a cave for three days and nights when a snowstorm dumped two additional feet on the area. Nearly a week later, they ran across their first occupied cabin, located on the Stillwater River, a tributary of the Great Miami River. A trapper by the name of Murphy provided welcomed hospitality. He said he hosted two other Kentucky men who escaped the River Raisin battle a few days ago. He wasn't sure they looked quite as bad as Ben, Nate, Jacob, and Abe. He offered lodging in his small barn, all the food they could eat, and blessed warmth in front of his fire. Since he worked as a trapper, he had animal skins and leather. Ben and Abe had worked with leather growing up. Jacob's mother taught him to sew. Murphy put all four to work, making clothes and boots to keep themselves warm in the elements.

When they left two weeks later, their host gave them another hunting knife and an older rifle, which he said could be ornery, shot, powder, a pouch, and food for the road. He told them the safest way to go. The friends departed feeling grateful, stronger, and hopeful.

They thought they should be in Cincinnati on the Ohio River in eight days if the weather cooperated. On the other side of the river lies Kentucky. They hoped somebody would pity them after hearing their story and offer room, board, baths, and maybe even haircuts before they traveled home from there.

The men walked into the growing town of Cincinnati on March 14. A few inquiries led them to an establishment sheltering soldiers seeking refuge from the war against the British and Indians in Canada. Again, they received a bed, decent food, and their first hot bath in they did not know when.

After resting for a full day, they proceeded to the docks and asked about the passage on the Ohio River to Louisville, about fifty miles southwest. Their luck held. A Captain said he just had two deckhands jump to another company. He said if they would help him load early in the morning, he would be glad to transport all four of them. He said he had a younger brother fighting with

Colonel Johnson's cavalry and had not heard from him in over a month.

The next afternoon, when they docked at Louisville, they helped to unload, and the captain allowed them to bunk on the boat that night. Waking up to light rain, the friends sincerely thanked each other, knowing everyone's cooperation and assistance had been life-saving. Then, each headed off to his hometown.

Ben's wife, Susan, whom he married in August 1810, and his nineteen-month-old son, Thomas, and his mother, Judith Briggs, anxiously waited about fifteen miles south of Louisville in Bardstown, Kentucky. They lost his father, William, in 1801. Everybody knew that General Winchester's militia suffered the consequences of the River Raisin massacre.

A covered wagon stopped two miles from Louisville to inquire about Ben's destination. Of all people, it was Jud Cravens and his son, Ray, neighbors of the Briggs. They excitedly told Ben to hop in. Ray, who had just turned twenty, got in the back with him, glad to escape the rain, which had picked up in intensity. They were happy for a conversation with someone who most folks thought was probably dead.

After about an hour, Mr. Cravens turned around and told his son to break out lunch. Said their guest was probably hungry, and so was he.

"Good idea," said Ray. "We have a store we always stop in right before we leave Louisville. Ever had beef tongue?"

"Ha! Can't say I have. But in January, and especially in February, I was so hungry fer days on end, I would a eaten anything," Ben said.

"Well, hit's marinated in pickling brine, then smoked. And it is delicious! Then we have a quarter wheel a cheddar cheese, 'cause mama and the girls all like that too, and about four loaves of fresh out-of-the-oven bread."

"You Cravens know how to do lunch up right!"

"Ray, while yore at it, son, grab one of them bottles a wine," Mr. Cravens said. "Let me pull the team over by the side of the road so we can pop a cork. If ever there war a time fer a proper toast, I'd say this tis hit. Not ever day a man gets to return from a battle that wipes out 'bout all the men on his side."

The wagon soon pulled up the Briggs's driveway and Ben jumped out onto the walk leading up to his house. They heard a high-pitched scream from within the house when thanking the Cravens for their hospitality.

"Guess that would be my wife," Ben grinned.

"I know your family tis mighty proud to have ye back," said Mr. Cravens. "God bless ye, Ben Briggs."

Ben turned and took half a dozen steps up the walkway before the front door suddenly opened. Just as Susan dashed out, he heard his mama say behind her, in a loud voice, "Honey, watch them wet steps."

Ben stood transfixed. He did not move as Susan ran straight into his arms despite knowing how he must look and smell in those clothes. He let out a long sigh of relief for the first time since he left.

After about a minute, he held her at arm's length and looked down at her stomach. Then he looked into her beautiful, tear-filled green eyes.

She smiled. "It's goin' to be a summer baby. Most prob'ly June."

"What day is this?" Ben asked.

"Hit's Wednesday, March 17."

"Just so's ya know, my precious, this is undoubtedly the happiest day of my life. I did not think I'd live to see hit. Here ye be. We got another young'un on the way. My belly's full. I did not have to walk from Louisville. Spring 'tis on the way. And the rain has stopped. God is merciful, after all."

In 1754, twenty-eight-year-old William Briggs came over the ocean with two of his brothers, David and Thomas, from Leslie, Scotland. Luck pointed the red-headed young man to Westmoreland County, Virginia, located on the Northern Neck area of the coast.

He soon met Original Wroe, a successful planter and large landowner. In 1760, William married Judith Wroe, 19, the third daughter of Original and his second wife, Jane Lyne, in Westmoreland. The couple soon moved to nearby Culpeper County, where Judith's father also owned land. By the early 80s, the growing Briggs family had headed west across the mountains to Bardstown in the north-central part of Kentucky. It was about to become Nelson County.

Even though there was a seven-year age difference, Ben always felt closest to brother George, his youngest sibling, growing up. The oldest three Briggs sons were grown men when George came along, so Ben took him to raise. There were no sisters even close to their ages.

When the family received the stunning news about what happened to Ben's troops at the Battle of Frenchtown, his mother wrote to George. He and his wife, Sarah McWhirter Briggs, lived in Logan County, Kentucky, on the line above Middle Tennessee.

George replied, saying he and Sarah would leave for Bardstown as soon as possible. They had a four-year-old and two-year-old twins, which Sarah's brother, George McWhirter, and his wife, Judith, of Nashville, Tennessee, agreed to take until the Briggs returned home. George and their unmarried sister, Liz, brought a wagon to Russellville to retrieve the little ones.

Almost two weeks after Ben arrived home, his brother, Ebenezer, rode into Bardstown. The family was at the supper table. Ben got up and looked out the window when they heard wagon wheels in the driveway.

"Oh, my Lord! Mama, it's George, and he's got Sarah with him. Did you know about this?"

Judith Briggs put her hand to her mouth but could not stifle a delighted squeal.

Ben flung open the door, and he and his older brother hurried down the walkway. George had already leaped to the ground. When he saw Ben, he froze, his mouth gaping open. By the time his brothers reached him, tears flowed.

"My prayers are answered. Thank you, God! I came up here a thinkin' . . . they would be no answers as to whether . . . you was alive or dead," George managed to say.

"Well, as you can feel, I ain't no ghost, brother. And I'm putting weight back on ever day."

"Sarah, it's so good to see you, little mama," said Ebenezer as he squeezed her. "I know Susan must be starvin' for female company."

"She sure is. And wait 'til you see our Thomas. The boy will be two come August," Ben said. "We're in there at the table. Can you eat before you tend the horses? Can they do with just water right now?"

"Yeah, I got buckets in the wagon for 'um," said George. "Reckon, they can wait long enough for us to eat a bite."

"You two go in the house. Ben and me will git the water," offered Ebenezer.

The matriarch of the Briggs clan died two years later in April at age seventy-four, while visiting a friend in New Haven on the southern edge of Nelson County. The diagnosis was apoplexy. Judith's death initiated the end of the family in Bardstown.

Mary Briggs, daughter of William and Judith, married James Latham, a fellow Native Virginian, in June 1792 after they both moved to Kentucky. They raised their ten children in Union County, which bordered the Illinois Territory.

James kept hearing about the great fertility of the Sangamon River Country in the central part of the territory. In late 1818, James and brother-in-law Ebenezer Briggs followed a couple of Latham offspring to the Sangamon River bottom. It overflowed. The party headed north to find more suitable land. They discovered the wooded hill of Elkhart with a free-flowing spring. They built the first cabin ever constructed north of the Sangamon River in Illinois. They cultivated their first crop and built a large double log cabin on the edge of the grove. In late summer, they returned to Kentucky. James brought back his family. Ebenezer collected his brood and persuaded Ben and Susan to make the move with their four children. Susan questioned her sanity because they arrived at their new home on Elkhart Hill in mid-September, and she gave birth to William, their fourth son, on October 4 with the assistance of three other mothers and no midwife.

None of the families ever returned east to live.

# # #

By 1820, George and Sarah Briggs had left Russellville, Kentucky, and moved to Wilson County, just east of Nashville, with their first five children. Middle Tennessee, especially around what would become Nashville, was moving from frontier status to an established place as more and more settlers arrived and commerce, industry, and agriculture began to thrive. It felt like a safer place to raise a family.

Many families from the Spartanburg, South Carolina area and around Mecklenburg County, North Carolina, rolled over the Appalachian Mountains and the Cumberland Plateau into the Nashville Basin with its growing grasses and profusion of flora. Sarah McWhirter, who married George Briggs in 1809, was a third-generation McWhirter who now had lived near what was first called Nashborough.

Sarah's grandparents lived in Mecklenburg County on the southwestern border of North Carolina after moving south from Lancaster County, Pennsylvania. Like many of their neighbors in the western part of the state, they grew frustrated with the provincial rule of Governor William Tryon. These independent-minded people wanted more freedom from the government. They heard that a like-minded man named James Robertson had established a community and fort west of the Appalachian Mountains just to the northeast in the upper Holston Valley near the Watauga River. It would one day be located in the state of Tennessee.

William McWhirter, of Scotch-Irish descent, possessed the heart of a frontiersman. He married Elizabeth Ferrier at her home in Middle Octararo, Pennsylvania, in 1767 after he became a doctor, shortly before they left for North Carolina. She relished the idea of adventures in untamed territory.

By the end of 1775, word spread that Richard Henderson, a lawyer and businessman from Granville County, North Carolina, worked with others, including the renowned explorer Daniel Boone, to form the Transylvania Land Company. Somehow, on March 17 of that year, they met in Sycamore Shoals, a historic strategic military location for the Cherokee near the Watauga settlement, along with four chiefs and 1,200 Cherokees to sign a land contract. The purchase covered a small corner of Virginia and territory in Kentucky and Tennessee, amounting to about twenty million acres.

The McWhirters understood that purchasing land from the Cherokees did not clear a safe trail for passage west. But they wanted to convince their three children, who ranged in age from twenty-five to seventeen, to accompany them or follow them over the mountains to Middle Tennessee at the first good opportunity. Their two sons-in-law seemed willing.

Richard Henderson selected James Robertson and Colonel John Donelson, a land speculator and surveyor, to lead settlers into this newly acquired Cumberland River region of Middle Tennessee. The men agreed that Mr. Robertson would lead an overland venture. Colonel Donelson said he would take another group along a water route.

In the spring of 1779, Mr. Robertson took off with a nine-man exploration party to an area known as French Lick along the banks of the Cumberland River. Just before they arrived, John Buchanan Sr. and his family arrived after traveling through the unusual cold from Harrisburg, Pennsylvania. Both men would play important roles in the historic years ahead.

Mr. Roberson's group returned to North Carolina. On November 1, he led a group of 200, mostly men and boys, including William McWhirter, then fifty-nine, overland with pack horses and livestock from Watauga toward the future Fort Nashborough. A difficult trek by way of southern Kentucky, they passed along the well-beaten trace through the mountains at Cumberland Gap, then through the Kentucky Gap to Whitley's Station on Dick's River, on to a location in Simpson County called Maple Swamp. Onward west, they crossed into Robertson County, Tennessee, and traveled along Red River to Cross Plains, heading south through Goodlettsville and passing over the frozen solid Cumberland River at the bluff where Nashville would one day stand. It was Christmas Day. They settled at French Lick in the worst winter in anyone's memory to await the arrival of their women and children.

More than one hundred people belonging to thirty of these families spent the winter of 1779-80 on what turned out to be not just a perilous but a tortuous water journey west led by Colonel Donelson. The flotilla included thirty or so flat boats, dugouts, and canoes on an expedition negotiating the Holston, Tennessee, Ohio, and Cumberland rivers. Thirty African slaves also accompanied the group. During the unexpectedly long four-month trip, the tough occupants of the boats suffered hunger, exhaustion, extreme cold, swift currents, treacherous shoals, a smallpox outbreak, and Indian attacks.

"Through the grace of God," as one of the women was overheard saying, on April 24, 1780, Colonel Donelson's party found their families and friends at Big Salt Lick. It had been close to a 1,000-mile paddle. Crude cabins awaited them, and a log stockade had been built along the top of a bluff overlooking the river, which the men named Fort Nashborough.

Several in the Donelson party said they were almost certain that Elizabeth McWhirter was a passenger in the last flatboat in the flotilla. When yellow fever broke out, women and children who had the fever were isolated in one boat. Elizabeth was among them. Indians captured the boat, killing most of the occupants. Someone said they heard screams way up the river after the boat was seized. William McWhirter's wife was never seen or heard from again.

On May 13, 1780, 256 colonists, including William McWhirter, signed the Cumberland Compact. It was adopted on May 30. The compact established a contract and relationship between the settlers and the Cumberland region. It marked the beginning of government in the West. Each signer was awarded 640 acres of land. It was based on the Articles of the Watauga Association, directed by James Robertson. This compact became a foundation document of the Tennessee State Constitution.

They explored fields, woods, and streams full of buffalo, black bears, wild turkeys, white-tail deer, beaver, raccoon, fox, elk, wolf, cougar, mink, and otter. They also discovered they were at peril hunting, cutting trees, planting, cultivating crops, or doing anything that exposed them to the wilds. Mainly, the Cherokee raged against their presence, and attacks remained imminent. Therefore, other forts were immediately constructed in the vicinity.

One of those forts, known as Mansker's Station, near Goodlettsville, was built by Kasper Mansker, another signer of the Cumberland Compact. Mr. Mansker, from Virginia, hunted and explored extensively in the Cumberland area. He built the fort in 1780 to protect travelers from Indian attacks. Indians burned it down, and two years later, he built a larger and more secure fort a mile from the original site.

William McWhirter settled on Mansker's Creek near Mansker's Station. His children soon followed him to Middle Tennessee.

Son, George Marlin McWhirter, thrived as a student back in Mecklenburg. The young man was a protégé of Reverend Hezekiah Balch, a Princeton College graduate and accomplished scholar, who quickly became a respected teacher when he returned to his hometown in North Carolina. He was also an ordained minister of the Presbyterian Church. Young Reverend Balch was probably best known as a co-writer, signer, and eloquent speaker before the assembled delegates who approved the Mecklenburg Declaration of Independence on May 20, 1775.

In the summer of 1776, Reverend Balch died at thirty years old. That January, he and his wife, the former Martha McCandless, born in Philadelphia, Pennsylvania, sold two pieces of property, perhaps in anticipation of his death. Mistress Balch was also an educated person who taught school. She knew George McWhirter as a former pupil of her husband. Soon, he assisted her in teaching.

Six years later, George and Martha became man and wife. The following March, the newlyweds accepted the challenge of moving to the new settlement in Middle Tennessee to start providing quality education for the Cumberland region's children.

That same year, 1783, George's pregnant sister, Elizabeth, and husband, George Pirtle, came with them. George Pirtle survived the Battle of Kings Mountain in South Carolina. He received a 640-acre land grant in what would become Davidson County,

Tennessee, for his service in the Revolutionary War. Elizabeth's twin sister, Prudence, her Scottish husband, Tom Ferrier, and their five children had come over with three other families from Mecklenburg two years earlier.

George and Martha settled on Mansker's Creek near his father's place, where sister Prudence and family had located. George Pirtle's land grant was located east of Fort Nashborough along Mill Creek, a tributary of the Cumberland River. The Pirtle's property lay less than a half mile from Buchanan's Station.

After John Buchanan's family arrived in the area in time to meet Mr. Robertson's initial exploratory party in 1779, they built Fort Nashborough and lived in it for four years. They then moved almost six miles east and constructed Buchanan's Station, a few buildings surrounded by a picket stockade and a blockhouse at the front gate overlooking Mill Creek.

Within a year of his family's arrival, William McWhirter took his son, George, and new daughter-in-law, as well as daughter Prudence and her family, up to Logan County, Kentucky, for about a year. Indian attacks and subsequent killings were on the rise. Daughter Elizabeth and husband George Pirtle felt they were close enough to the safety of the Buchanans to stay.

At midnight on September 30, 1792, ten-year-old Prudie Ferrier saw first-hand the bravery of her seventy-two-year-old grandfather during an Indian raid on Buchanan's Station. The family had been in the fort for a couple of nights because increased Indian movement was reported, and people were nervous. William McWhirter accompanied them because he had come up three days earlier to visit.

An estimated 900 combined Cherokee, Chickasaw, and Creek warriors attacked so suddenly that people had no time to dress. Twenty-one men inside the fort pulled off what many consider a miracle. Ammunition grew so low that the women, led by nineteen-year-old Sally Buchanan, John's wife, who was nine months pregnant with their first child, resupplied them with bullets, powder, and liquor. The young Mistress Buchanan melted down her pewter dishes to make those bullets.

At seventy-two, William McWhirter could no longer see well enough to fire a rifle. Still, he continuously reloaded powder and shot into the hot guns, and quickly handed them back to another man to be fired again. When the enemy retreated, the older man's hands were blistered.

# # #

George McWhirter began buying property in the area. In 1794, Colonel Robert Hays sold a section of land on the east bank of the Cumberland River to George and Thomas Hudson. When Colonel Hays moved to the area from Salisbury, North Carolina, in 1784, he erected a station called Fort Union.

Colonel Hays met and married Jane Donelson, the ninth child of Colonel John Donelson when he came to Middle Tennessee. Jane's sister, Rachel, married Andrew Jackson, who became a close friend of Colonel Hays. On March 4, 1823, Andrew Jackson would be named the 7th U.S. President.

The colonel commanded the Coldwater Expedition with James Robertson in 1787, attempting to stop Indian raids. After a war party attacked an outlying settlement and killed Mr. Robertson's brother, Mark, 150 volunteers, guided by two Chickasaw, hit the Indian town of Coldwater on the Lower Cumberland River. They killed half the defenders, wounded many others, burned the town, and departed.

George McWhirter and Thomas Hudson divided 160 acres, each purchased from Colonel Hays, into seventy-two one-half acre lots, intent on establishing a town named Haysborough in honor of Colonel Robert Hays. The Tennessee legislature granted a charter for the town in 1799. Lots sold quickly to established members of the community.

William McWhirter died in September 1802 at his home on Mansker's Creek at age eighty-two from "natural causes." Many of his family members, including his son, George, first considered moving outside the newly incorporated town of Lebanon in Wilson County, named a county in 1799. It was almost a thirty-mile ride into Nashville, which would not be incorporated until 1806.

In 1794, the territorial legislature authorized Colonel Hays to start raising funds for cutting and clearing a wagon road from a point west of Knoxville, near what would become Kingston, to Nashville. It would then climb the Cumberland Plateau, run through Crab Orchard to Monterey on the western edge of the Plateau, down through what would be known as Cookeville, then west through Smith County, and just northwest of Lebanon before arriving in Nashville. The following year, Colonel Hays surveyed and started construction of the road. By 1796, over 300 wagons had rolled over it.

The McWhirters predicted that what some called The Walton Road, but many referred to simply as "the turnpike," would attract settlers along the way, provide a market for agricultural products, and, hopefully, offer a buffer to Indian aggression. George and Martha thought it might offer more security and a better place to finally get their school started.

George Pirtle took his four children and their Briggs cousins to Wilson County. Their mother, Elizabeth, died in late spring 1799 when she and her daughter, Lizzie, then eleven, went out in the woods gathering poke greens to prepare sallet for supper. Elizabeth sat on a log, and within seconds, yellow jackets swarmed over her. She ran, then rolled on the ground while Lizzie beat them off of her with a sack. She helped her mother to the nearby creek and submerged her. Then she got her home and made compresses of tobacco to put over all her stings. However, Elizabeth had a severe allergic reaction and did not survive.

The families had found property below and up one side of Hickory Ridge, five miles west of Lebanon, in early spring 1806. George McWhirter hired another man to oversee the building of two cabins for two slave families he bought to help build two two-story houses, a barn, a corn crib, and a smokehouse. He would need the help to manage a farm on which he planned to grow cotton, corn, and hogs. On the ridge, in March 1809, George started constructing a large, three-room schoolhouse. His son, George Ferrier McWhirter, who turned twenty-one that month, George Pirtle, and his son, George Merritt Pirtle, who would turn twenty-four in April, worked with a third man who specialized in large logs.

Martha McWhirter planned to teach girls in one room, and George would teach boys in the other. The third room was to be used as an office, meeting room, and storage space, as needed. It became the first high school in the county. Elizabeth McWhirter, who turned sixteen in 1809, immediately started assisting her parents with their teaching when classes started the next year. Four years later, her sister, Patsy, turned sixteen, and she, too, began helping out in the classrooms.

In 1816, the McWhirters moved the school to Lebanon due to the number of students wanting to attend. The ground was donated by David and Catherine Bowen Campbell, parents of future Tennessee Governor William B. Campbell. The McWhirters then named the school Campbell Academy after their benefactors. A new building was constructed in 1840, and classes continued until late in the Civil War. At that time, Cumberland University assumed control of the academy.

One early April afternoon in 1818, three visitors drove up to the school in a carriage behind a fine-looking team of horses. The older man introduced himself as William McKnight, his wife as

Mistress Isabella McKnight, and the younger man as his son, Dr. William McKnight. They had heard about the excellent instruction at Campbell's Academy and wondered if they might stop for a visit.

"I'm so glad you did," said George, who came out to greet them. "My wife, Martha, and I are assisted by two of our daughters, Elizabeth and Patsy, so you certainly won't be an interruption to class time. Here, step down. Come into our office, please."

They poked their heads into each classroom before seating themselves in chairs Martha had arranged for them. After greeting each one, she handed them glasses of water.

The son, whom George figured to be no more than thirty, said, "We live Northeast of Murfreesboro, in Milton. I try to get around and visit with other area doctors. I heard there was a fairly new, young doctor in Lebanon, and we came up early today to make his acquaintance."

"Yes, Dr. Leary. Everybody is glad to have him here, too. He's been in Lebanon less than two years," George said.

"Good medical care and good teachers are hard to find," said Mr. McKnight. "There's such concern about the school situation in Rutherford County that a group of us are talking about building a new school and trying to recruit educated, experienced teachers. These folks are very lucky to have you, McWhirters. We thought perhaps you'd be available for consultation."

"We would be happy to share all we know with you," Martha said. "We were both educated in Mecklenburg."

"That is what we heard," said Mistress McKnight, who talked with a rather thick Irish brogue. "We came from Statesville in Iredell County, not so far from Mecklenburg that we did not know about the reputation of Reverend Balch. Somehow, you were related?"

"Yes, he was my first husband," said Martha.

"And he was my teacher for the last four years of his life. He died at age thirty when I was twelve," George explained.

The McKnights said their group would meet the first Saturday in May at noon in Murfreesboro. They invited the McWhirters to come and talk about their eight-year success in operating the high school in Wilson County. Almost all their children were married, so they had a couple of extra bedrooms.

On an overcast Friday, May 1, all four McWhirters traveled the twenty-five miles south to Milton. They enjoyed the late blooming white and pink dogwoods, crabapple, white serviceberry, or, as the mountain people say, "Sarvis," trees in bloom along the way.

They walked into a buzz of activity late afternoon as they discovered many McKnights in and around the house, much to the delight of Elizabeth and Patsy McWhirter. William's brother, Captain James McKnight and his wife, Eleanor, lived close by. They came for supper to meet George and Martha. They brought their three youngest adult sons and their youngest daughter, Susannah, who, at twenty-two, was a year younger than Patsy.

The next morning, after a huge breakfast served by Rosa, the McKnights' cook, George, and Martha rode to Murfreesboro with their hosts, along with a daughter, Jane, and her husband, Sam McDaniel. The younger William, whom the family called Will, insisted that the McWhirter daughters ride with him and his cousin, David, in a carriage with David's parents, James and Eleanor McKnight.

Neither family was the same after all that transpired that day. A surprisingly large group of parents and other community members met to discuss solutions to the lack of quality education in the county. The McWhirters fielded non-stop questions about their school. On the way back to Milton, the McKnights wasted no time suggesting that Elizabeth and Patsy would be a tremendous asset if they might consider offering their already developed teaching skills in Rutherford County.

When the McWhirters returned home, Patsy started in almost immediately, thinking about how she could not wait to see David again. When his letter arrived two weeks after they got back asking to call, she lost her focus. He said cousin Will was coming up in late June to make rounds for a week with his new doctor acquaintance in Lebanon, who he had been quite impressed with on his first visit. Both were bachelors, and the young men got along well. David had been invited to stay at Dr. Leary's house while the two doctors went to see patients for a few days.

Patsy was always the impetuous child in the family. When it came to love, it turned out she recognized it right away. Martha Patsy McWhirter, twenty-two, and Maj. David McKnight, thirty-seven, enjoyed a pre-Christmas wedding at George and Martha's Wilson County home the following year on Friday, December 10. Martha was glad she talked her husband into adding ten feet in length and eight feet in width to the original plan for their home's great room as friends and family from both sides poured in to help celebrate.

Pretty Elizabeth caught Will's eye the first time he walked into her classroom. The more reserved of the two sisters, he did not want to do anything to appear as if he was in any hurry, but by the end of that first summer, he, too, was calling at the McWhirter's home. Sometimes, Elizabeth went quail hunting with him, and it was immediately obvious that her father had taught his daughters how to handle a gun. She shot well. The two married at the McWhirter's place on Thursday, February 24, 1820, less than two months after Patsy and David. They opted for a smaller, quieter ceremony.

George Pirtle heard about good acreage southeast of Lebanon at Smith's Fork, especially for planting cotton, which George Briggs primarily wanted to harvest when he moved his family down to Wilson County from Kentucky. When George made a preliminary trip to the Pirtle's farm outside of Lebanon late in

1819, his wife's Uncle George Pirtle took him to visit the farmer who advised him on the available property. He liked the water source, the flatness of the land, and the good roads. George made a large down payment, and the owner agreed to hold it until the Briggs family moved in early spring.

In August 1826, Mary Ann Briggs, George and Sarah's seventh child out of nine, was born. With McWhirter, Pirtle, and Ferrier cousins scattered around Wilson, Rutherford, and Davidson counties, Mary Ann grew up educated and interested in teaching. She accepted an assistant teaching position early in 1850 in Liberty, located in DeKalb County, east of where she was raised.

One summer weekend, she found company at the house when she went home to Statesville, formerly Smith's Fork. Old man Reason Byrne owned property next to the Briggs, which his son, Hugh, now farmed. He had become a good friend and neighbor. They were distantly related to Byrnes in Jackson County, located to the northeast on the Cumberland River. Hugh was with him when Mary Ann and Alex Holleman visited that weekend.

The Holleman's farm bordered that of Terrell Byrne in Granville. Reason Byrne's sons still ventured over to Granville occasionally and had long known the Holleman sons. They had always had a close relationship with the Byrne siblings growing up. Reason Byrne was close to the age of Alex's father, Jim Holleman, who died in 1835.

Mary Ann's brother, Ben, who then handled most operations on the Briggs's farm, and his wife, Nancy, were also at the home that day. Nancy was helping mother-in-law Sarah prepare supper for the five men, so Mary Ann alternately helped in the kitchen and sat on the porch listening to much chit-chat.

She discovered that Alex Holleman would head to Williamson County just south of Nashville the next morning. His brother, Clint, married Susan Woodruff from Nashville in 1836. Her family operated a lumber company. They relocated to Franklin in 1840 and brought Clint into the business then.

After supper, the Byrnes returned to their place. Alex asked Mary Ann if he might stay for a spell longer so they could talk. They moved into the yard to sit in chairs under a big red oak tree. A light breeze made for a pleasant evening, and before they knew it, dusk fell. Alex said he would walk the ten minutes to the Byrne house. Then he asked if he might write Mary Ann. Delighted, she replied, "Of course."

Sarah Briggs died at age sixty in December of that year after a cold settled into her lungs and progressed into pneumonia. The following October, the Briggs family lost their father and grandfather when George, sixty-one, failed to recover from head trauma after being thrown from his favorite horse. It was suspected the animal became spooked by a snake or perhaps another animal darting from the brush.

Mary Ann received a letter from Alex Holleman less than a month after his visit. A correspondence began that lasted for four years. He would stop at Liberty several times a year en route to visit his brother, Clint. At least once a year, they met in Lebanon when she visited her cousins. Christmas week of 1853, he picked her up and took her to Granville to meet his family. They married Thursday, September 7, 1854, in a private ceremony on the Caney Fork River in DeKalb County, Northeast of Liberty. They honeymooned in a hunting cabin owned by a friend of the Hollemans from Jackson County.

The couple lived in Granville. Alex delivered the U.S. mail and was appointed Postmaster in 1885, four years before his death. In the early years of their marriage, Mary Ann taught school until their children started coming.

The Hollemans would become directly linked to the Byrnes through their granddaughter, Esther Neeley; in 1916, she married Arthur D. Byrne in Granville. He was a grandson of Terrell Byrne.

Looked Like Quite a Procession

Quarles (Byrne)

Few, if any, could say their transition as immigrants into the fledgling American colonies in the 1600s went smoothly. Some suffered more than others.

Captain Richard Quarles experienced a rough start. In 1623, the merchant from London arrived in Jamestown, Virginia, as captain of the ship *Ann.* There, he was granted rights to fish and transport passengers. But on March 23, the general court terminated his commission as captain, broke his sword, and sent him out of the port of James City with an axe on his shoulder. They brought him back into the settlement and nailed his ears to a pillory. He was presented with a choice. Either he agreed to pay a fine of one hundred shillings in sterling, or his captors would cut off his ears for speaking what was considered treason against the authorities. Jamestown leaders enforced a straightforward martial law that emphasized order and discipline.

A couple of years later, the Quarles family moved to the northern Tidewater region of Virginia along the Rappahannock River. Richard and his wife, Ellen James, who sailed with him from London, could not abide by the strict Puritan law of Jamestown's leaders. They sought freedom from English law when they immigrated; they certainly did not expect to have their means of income stripped upon arrival. Two like-minded families from the colony accompanied them as they relocated across from the Northern Neck area.

The Tidewater comprises a low-lying alluvial plain on the western shore of the Chesapeake Bay between the Atlantic Ocean and the fall line. It marks the junction between the hard rocks of the Appalachian Highlands and the softer deposits of the coastal plain. The Rappahannock River is one of four major rivers crossing the Coastal Plains. Others include the Potomac, York, and James rivers and their estuaries.

Algonquian-speaking Natives, primarily Powhatan tribes, inhabited the fertile river valleys, providing food and transportation. When Europeans started arriving in the early 1600s, there were an estimated 14,000 Natives with some 200 settlements in the region.

The Quarles family knew the potential dangers of striking out on their own. The year before they arrived in Jamestown, the warriors of Opechancanough Mangopeesomon Powhatan, who had recently become chief of the Powhatan Confederation, attacked small settlements throughout Virginia and killed hundreds of new settlers. However, they decided to take the risk. They brought a good quantity of woolen cloth to the new country for the explicit purpose of trading with the Indians. They hoped this highly desirable exchange commodity might pave the way toward peaceful relations for the family.

The strategy helped ease the way. Their first child, James, was born shortly after their arrival. For over fifteen years, the Quarles family lived peacefully near the Powhatans. They scratched out a small farm, growing corn, peas, beans, squash, and potatoes, and raised a few cattle and hogs while subsisting on fish from the rivers and plentiful game from the forests.

In the fall of 1640, Richard, one his neighbors, Mark Byron, and his nineteen-year-old son, Hollis, headed southwest for a week of hunting. Somehow, on their third day out, Richard disappeared. The Byrons spent the next two days searching for him before returning home with the distressing news.

Nothing indicated Indians had accosted him. No gunshot was heard. If a wild animal attack proved fatal, the Byrons felt fairly certain their search would have turned up evidence. They speculated that he could have badly injured himself and crawled into a cave or under a rock overhang for protection and not been able to get out to seek help. But no trace was ever found.

Richard's wife, Ellen, was left to raise their one-year-old son, John, who had been born the previous summer. Son, James, fifteen, could work unassisted in the fields. This stalwart woman not only survived her unfortunate early ordeals but faced every challenge with a determination that set an example for other females. Eventually, she went to live with her grandson, Captain John Quarles II, who married Jane Mallory in 1685. She outlived her husband by sixty-three years and both of their sons. Ellen was one hundred years old when she died.

Jane was the daughter of Captain Roger Mallory, Esq., and Jane Holland, who came from Cheshire, England, in 1668 after Roger obtained a grant of land in Virginia. His uncle, Reverend Philip Mallory, also willed him all his plantations in Virginia, which amounted to 2,514 acres situated on the south side of the Mattaponi River, a tributary of the York River, in New Kent County.

John Quarles helped construct a home for his new wife in the summer of 1685 on property adjacent to the Mallory's. Jane's parents had given it to them as a wedding gift. He found himself in the midst of the Mallorys' large-scale agricultural operation.

Captain Mallory continually cleared his rich bottomland so he could plant Spanish tobacco. He owned the land, acquired the necessary slave labor, and attracted an experienced overseer with excellent judgment since this was a new venture for him. He prayed for a certain amount of plain good luck since tobacco was a finicky crop.

The market for the product in Britain had been robust. No other colonial crop made such efficient use of cleared lands, providing a great labor return and could be as easily marketed. The product traveled well on ships in hogsheads (barrels) filled with about a thousand pounds of dried, pressed tobacco leaf.

Captain Mallory had a good feeling about his new son-in-law. Even though John had never lived on the water or worked on ships, Roger knew the history of his grandfather, who owned and served as captain of the *Ann* upon his arrival in Jamestown. He knew the grandson possessed intelligence and suspected some of those mariner genes had been inherited. Therefore, he sent John, along with his son, Will Mallory, with a direct shipment of their tobacco to England late in 1686. There, consignment agents sold it in exchange for a cut of the profits. They talked with various merchants and sellers since the market had become less stable. The two men debated whether it would be more economical to ship at their own risk to England, where a commission agent would, for a fee of two and one-half percent, store the tobacco, pay all duties and fees, sell it, and use the profits as they directed.

In April 1695, Roger Quarles became the fourth of five sons born to John and Jane Quarles. Twenty-three years later, when he married Jane Powhatan Hughes Tunstall, he knew his children's heritage would be forever linked to the Powhatan people.

Jane's father was Marshall Tunstall, who came to the Colony of Virginia from Cornwall, England. He sailed into the Chesapeake Bay and debarked at Jamestown in the early spring of 1691 with the idea of heading west toward the Blue Ridge Mountains. He talked to those who came before him about blending in with his surroundings. He wanted to know what frontiersmen wore. Marshall left with a buffalo coat he would use as a bed in warm months, a long, homespun hunting shirt and belt, open leather leggings, moccasins, a good leather hat with a brim to keep the rain out of his eyes, and a handkerchief to bind around his head. He purchased a good horse and saddle, a wool blanket, water bag, rifle, shot, powder, and pouch, knife and sheath, a small cooking pot, deer jerky and corn meal, and a decent-sized pouch of quality tobacco in case he needed to generate goodwill with

Indians. He then headed west along the north bank of the big James River.

On the fourth day, Marshall reached the Falls of the James River, where an important village of the Powhatan Confederacy had been situated earlier in the century. Now, more and more white settlers decided to build houses in what would become the port city of Richmond almost fifty years later, as ships could navigate the deep water of the James River. He spent the night in order to collect information about his projected destination.

Marshall learned of a connection of Indian trails in Henrico County, sitting in the shadow of the Blue Ridge Mountains. The Monacan Indian Nation originally controlled the Piedmont area through which he would travel west. It lay between the fall line and the Appalachian Mountain range. Until recently, these Natives had been hostile competitors with the Powhatan tribes. Now, they were moving mainly north, away from European encroachment.

A hunter passing through the settlement told Marshall about an old white trader with an Indian wife. He operated close to an Indian path that followed the James River through the Blue Ridge to what was known as the Warrior's Path. The man said the trading post with a tall stone chimney was in Henrico County on the upper banks of Harris Creek, near Otter Creek, not far from Tobacco Row Mountain. The man drew a rough map of the area as a guide.

"Reckon he'd be a good 'un to point ye in the right direction," the man said.

"I am much obliged to you, good sir," replied Marshall. "Daiawn."

Late morning of his tenth day out after leaving the settlement, Marshall rode along, marveling at the beauty of his surroundings. An hour earlier, he'd come to a rare opening in the budding trees, watched twin fawns scamper after their startled mother into the forest, and saw layers of blue-tinted mountains in the near distance. Obviously, if he continued to ride west, he would be climbing soon. He stopped to watch the sun glittering on the river and listened to birds welcoming warmer weather.

Suddenly, he thought he heard female laughter. Yes, there it was again. He dismounted, took hold of the reins, and walked Shone, his horse, toward the sound. It came from his left.

Not one hundred yards ahead and maybe twenty feet on the bank of the river were two Indian women. Or at least he thought they were both Indian. They were certainly both beautiful. He found himself standing and staring. He quickly regained his composure and walked Shone to the water for a drink.

He turned toward the women, removed his hat, and said, "Hello, I am Marshall Tunstall. Do ye speak English?"

At that, they both relaxed their surprised expressions mixed with concern. The older one replied, "Yes, we speak English."

"Ah, good. I look for a man named Trader Hughes, who I hear has a trading post somewhere in this area. Do ye know where I might find him?"

The younger one smiled and nodded.

The older one said, "We are his family. I am wife, Nicketti. This is daughter, Jane. When your horse drinks, we will walk you up."

✦✦✦

Captain John Rice Hughes had immigrated from Anglesey, Wales, to Virginia in 1682 as a sixty-seven-year-old man who had spent most of his life on the seas shipping goods manufactured in the British Isles to the Caribbean and the east coast of America. He was still strong and healthy. He figured great potential existed for establishing trade with the Natives in the wilds of this new country. He planned to find both white and Indian contacts at the Falls of the James River settlement, then head toward the mountains to locate a good place for a trading post.

His fortunes immediately got off on the right foot when he met and married Princess Nicketti Mangopeesomon, She-Sweeps-the-Dew-From-the-Flowers Powhatan, daughter of Princess Cleopatra Shawano Powhatan. Nicketti's aunt and Cleopatra's sister, was the famous Princess Pocahontas. She was a granddaughter of Wahunsenacawh (Chief Powhatan), former chief of the Virginia Powhatan Confederation and Chief Running Stream.

Of course, the marriage was not recognized. Unions between whites and Indians were against the law despite the fact that they occurred often enough.

Fortunately, John Hughes hired a trustworthy half-breed guide that led him to the confluence of Indian trails just off the James River in the foothills of the Blue Ridge Mountains. He thought it was the ideal spot for his proposed business. He became the first white settler in the area. It was widely assumed that the Monacan tribes gave him safe passage between his new home and the settlement to the east, where he picked up his supplies because of his wife's heritage. Everyone knew him as "Trader."

He mainly traded with the Natives for animal furs. In exchange, he provided European manufactured goods, including metal cooking utensils and pans, scissors, razors, mirrors, guns, shot, powder, knives, tools (such as axes, hoes, and hatchets), blankets, and woolen, cotton, and linen items (including broadcloth and thread), and glass beads and trinkets.

An immediate attraction existed between Marshall and Jane Hughes. Her father liked this young fellow Welshman and thought he had spirit venturing into the wilderness on his own. He told Marshall he needed help and offered him room and board for assistance around the property. He said he might also accompany him to the Falls of the James River settlement for supplies periodically when he hired men to bring in pack horses.

In the spring of 1695, Marshall and Jane wed. Jane wanted to return to King William County to live near the Powhatans, her mother's people. She was born there, and the family would welcome her back. Marshall wanted to be where his wife was happy. He liked the mountains, but he also loved the water, so they headed to the Pamunkey River, one of the two main divisions of the York River.

Marshall Jr. arrived in December of that year, shortly after the Tunstalls moved into their cabin within sight of the river. Three cousins and a neighbor pitched in to help build the four-room structure, which had a stone fireplace and a broad front and back porch.

After six days of lying sick in bed in February 1699, Marshall died of a fever at the age of twenty-six. Their daughter, Jane Powhatan Hughes Tunstall, was born five months later. Two cousins traveled to the Piedmont to notify John and Nicketti Hughes about the death of their son-in-law and the birth of their granddaughter. Nicketti returned with them to King William County and stayed with her daughter and grandchildren until the onset of winter. She then returned to her husband in the Piedmont, Trader Hughes, who lived to be 103 years old.

🍃 🍃 🍃

God and the soldier we like adore,
In time of trouble not before,
When troubles ended and all things righted,
God is forgotten and the soldier slighted.
Francis Quarles (1592-1644), London, Poet Laureate

When British Gen. Charles Cornwallis's army invaded Virginia in October 1777, Roger Quarles II joined the Continental Army. The Revolutionary War had rumbled for two years in the North, but bringing it to the South made it personal. The Quarles family sought refuge from the King's control when they came to these shores, and now was the time to help put an end to it for future generations.

Captain Quarles resigned in 1779 at fifty-nine years of age. His son-in-law, Francis Tompkins, assumed his position. He married Frances Quarles, whom they called Fran, in 1772, the eldest child of Roger and his wife, the former Mary Goodloe. Her father, George Goodloe, had been appointed sheriff, or chief executive officer of Caroline County, in 1737.

The Goodloe ancestry includes Richard Goodlaw, Equerry, and Commander of Horse to King Henry VIII. In about 1540, Henry VIII gave Sir Richard his Manor of Garsden ". . .because he rescued his King in Braydon Forest when he was thrown from his horse with his 'hedde in the mudde,' and the King, being 'fatte and heavie,' had been suffocated to dethe had he not been rescued by his faithful Commander of Horse." From that point forward, Sir Richard became a favorite with the king.

Francis Tompkins's father, Christopher, and Daniel Tompkins were brothers. They grew up on the North River, a tidal river that is an arm of Mobjack Bay, part of the Chesapeake Bay bordering Gloucester County. Daniel Tompkins daughter, Tabitha Tompkins Hawes, had a daughter, Ann Hawes, who became the wife of William Pennington Quarles.

The Tompkins trace their family line to Nathaniel Tomkins of London, a British Parliament member representing Carlisle and Christchurch. He was implicated in "Waller's Plot," an attempt to force an armed rising against Parliament during the English Civil War. Oliver Cromwell, Lord Protector of England, Scotland, and Wales, had him arrested. On July 5, 1643, he was hanged outside his home.

The British captured Charleston, South Carolina, on May 12, 1780, and William Pennington Quarles, twenty-eight, the Quarles's oldest son, took it as an ominous sign. In his mind, southern Patriots were now obligated to fight with the Continental

Army. He enlisted as an ensign with the 1st Virginia Regiment in Williamsburg, which became known as the "Shirtmen." The British captured most of the regiment in Charleston and desperately needed to shore up its ranks.

At the time, William was engaged to Nancy Ann Hawes, daughter of William and Tabitha Hawes of Gloucester. She had purchased her trousseau in England and was in the midst of elaborate preparations for their wedding when William unexpectedly took off to war.

William sustained a non-life-threatening injury late in the year. A vacancy occurred upon the resignation of Lieutenant Philip Courtney in early February 1781. On February 11, William returned to the line with a promotion to lieutenant.

The 1st Virginia Regiment disbanded on November 15, 1783, and William headed home. When they married days before Christmas, Ann wore a simple, white home-spun dress. The couple nurtured a love that produced ten children.

After their marriage, the Quarles lived in Caroline County. As a grant for his service in the war, William received 1,050 acres in Bedford County. They then moved to the new village of Liberty with their three daughters, Tabitha, Mary, who they called Polly, and Nancy, in 1789. Elizabeth was born in November of the following year.

The farm acreage lay about ten miles southeast from their house in town on the head branches of Little Otter River and Goose Creek. William grew tobacco on his plantation with the help of an overseer and a couple dozen slaves.

He served as an officer in the 91st Regiment of Bedford County's militia. When he resigned from his commission in 1809, he moved up through the ranks to become a major.

Bedford County boasted more than its share of Patriots who served during the Revolutionary War. William became friends with Sergeant John Buford, as well as his uncle, Captain Henry

Buford, who had served as county sheriff from 1790 to 1795. John Buford was the grandson of Gen. John Thomas Buford: his father, Captain Thomas Buford fought and died in October 1774 on the banks of the Ohio River in the Battle of Point Pleasant. Many believe this bloody one-day fight that forced the retreat of Shawnees and Mingos, who hoped to halt the advance of Colonel Andrew Lewis's troops into the Ohio Valley, served as the first real battle of the Revolutionary War.

Everybody knew the details of the vicious Point Pleasant battle. Earlier that year, increasing Indian attacks on British colonists moving onto land along the Ohio River caused the Governor of Virginia, John Murray, Lord Dunmore, to declare a state of war on hostile Indian nations. He ordered an elite volunteer militia force for the campaign. Captain Buford raised a company of fifty men from Bedford County and joined Colonel Lewis beyond the Blue Ridge, then marched with him to Point Pleasant. Attacking Natives surprised the troops on the morning of October 10 before they could cross the river. Seventy-five Virginians perished in the combat, and 140 were wounded.

Five more sons of Colonel Buford became soldiers during the ensuing Revolutionary War, including Captain James Buford, Captain William Buford, Colonel Abraham Buford, Captain Henry Buford, and the youngest, Ensign Simeon Buford. All survived.

William Quarles became a member of the exclusive Order of Cincinnati, an organization pledged to the care and protection of the widows and orphans of its members, all leading officers in the American army during the war. Between 1795 and December 1809, he served as an attorney at law and a "gentleman" justice, often presiding over the Bedford County court. At various times, he accepted the role of prosecutor, commissioner of the peace, and commissioner of revenue for the county's northern district.

William and Ann readied themselves for the wedding of one of their neighbors in Liberty one afternoon in the spring of 1808.

Molly Turner, a widow who lost her husband during the war, had four children. She was remarrying into the Watts family, which was related to the Bufords.

At the reception, the Quarles met Prudie Alexander, Molly's sister, and her husband, Dan, who traveled up from just west of the Cumberland Plateau in middle Tennessee. Dan had served as postmaster in Overton County. They operated an inn they constructed four years earlier on what was called the "New" Walton Road. Dan was looking to sell the inn and several hundred acres he had decided not to cultivate.

The Alexander's description of the eastern Highland Rim piqued William's interest. He always wondered what lay through the Tennessee Valley and west through the forested rolling hills. With Ann's nod of approval, he decided to find out. The Alexanders made the trip on horseback with one of their sons. They welcomed the addition of William on the ride back south.

∥ ∥ ∥

The Quarles looked like quite a procession pulling out of Liberty on November 20. Safe to say, nobody in town failed to notice their departure. William and Ann led all ten children and four sons-in-law after Tabitha married Will Hawes in 1801, and Nancy wed William A. Burton Jr. three years later. In 1808, Polly and Eliza married: Polly to Harrison Hughes and Eliza to Charles Burton, William's older brother. Eight-month-old Letitia Burton, the first child of Nancy and William and the first grandchild of William and Ann, made the trip. Thirty slaves accompanied the family over the mountains.

By mid-November 1809, William finally had all his business wrapped up when he signed the *Bedford County Order Book* as presiding justice. He had resigned his commission in the Bedford County militia in November. He sold the plantation a year earlier.

The new owner, a man William knew and trusted, contracted to lease William's slaves for a year. William continued to pay his overseer, Matthew Duggins, to stay on as a guardian of his valuable human property since the new owner needed his services. They were a good bunch. William treated them fairly and knew Mr. Duggins would do the same. In return, they worked hard and remained dedicated.

William expressed thanks for his initial journey to Tennessee the previous year. He would not want to travel blind with this many people under his care. In addition, of course, there were livestock, covered wagons, farm equipment, tools, and many household and personal items to transport, although they went through everything several times, paring down.

At daybreak on the 20th of November, under partly cloudy skies, they rolled west toward a valley in the Blue Ridge Mountains where the Roanoke River flows east at the salt licks. The Great Wagon Road ran out of Pennsylvania south through the small settlement in the mountains, which would one day be named Big Lick and then, toward the end of the century, Roanoke.

William hoped they could average at least ten miles a day. They pulled up to the Roanoke River by the salt licks in the early evening of the third day, which made him happy. The weather cooperated. There was no precipitation, and temperatures were only around fifty degrees during the days. Everybody seemed in good spirits despite having to climb their first real mountain.

The next morning, after breakfast, they turned south along The Great Wagon Road, called the Valley Turnpike by some. They headed toward a town developed seventeen years earlier from a concentration of taverns and rest stops. In another couple of decades, it will be incorporated as Christiansburg. Next, they ran into people on the New River in a small village that would be called Radford. In colder temperatures, they rolled through Evansham, which became Wytheville thirty years later. Following the foothills of the Appalachian Mountains in a southwest direction, the Quarles reached the northern border of the Cherokee nation when they arrived in Abington, founded in 1778. Soon, they found themselves at the Virginia/Tennessee state line when they discovered Shelby's Station, a combination trading post, way station, and stockade on a hill overlooking what would be named Bristol in 1853.

Once in Tennessee, the mountains thickened, and the hollows became more pronounced. They were slowed somewhat, but William was still pleased with the group's progression. Snow spit on them one day at higher elevations, but they experienced no accumulation and no below-freezing temperatures at night, although it was cold. Prior to departure, he provided winter clothing and footwear to all the slaves to keep them healthy.

Once in Upper East Tennessee, they followed the Holston River into Knoxville. Because of William's trip down with the Alexanders, he knew about The Walton Road opening September 1789 from Campbell's Station in west Knox County to Nashville. In 1801, the state legislature required the governor to incorporate an association of citizens with authority to collect tolls from the traveling public to open and keep this road in repair.

They passed near the junction of the Tennessee, Clinch, and Emory rivers from South West Point near Kingston, then Post Oak Springs, also in Roane County. Immediately afterward, they began the laborious process of climbing the east side of the Cumberland Plateau over Walden Ridge. They got a break arriving in Crab Orchard, named for its abundance of wild crab apple trees, in a gap in the Crab Apple Mountains. In a day and a half, they came to Lambeth's Crossroads, where they sheltered for the night. The small community sat atop the Cumberland Plateau amidst the headwaters of the Obed River. In the 1830s, it would be named Crossville. A blacksmith repaired one of their wagon wheels the next morning.

The Quarles finally walked off the higher Cumberland Plateau onto the Highland Rim, which sits between where they had been and the lower Nashville Basin to the west. Around noon, they all paused on an overlook before descending the last few miles to their new home. Sunshine lit the plains before them.

"Oh, Daddy, look how ever'thing sparkles," exclaimed daughter, Sallie, 11. "Hit's beautiful! I see a few hills out there, but the mountains are behind us, aren't they?"

"Yes, daughter. We're done with climbing." Cheers erupted all around him.

He turned to face his family and his slaves. "Anybody know what day it 'tis?" Ann, who stood at his side, smiled up at him.

Daughter Nancy, who sat in a wagon seat holding baby Latitia, said, "Oh, my, hit's not, is it?"

Her mother looked up at her, laughed, and said, "Yes, it assuredly is. Merry Christmas, everybody!"

William Burton, Nancy's husband, spoke up and said, "Wonder if'n we might perform Christmas magic and get all of us indoors with a fire and something warm in our bellies?"

"Let's go find out," his father-in-law replied.

Their property sat right along Walton Road just southeast of Algood. What would become known as White Plains, with development by William Quarles, had been part of Cherokee land ceded to the United States with the signing of the Third Treaty of Tellico in 1805. The plantation would lie in both White and Jackson counties.

William did not waste time getting the slave cabins built. He supervised the construction of a two-story log house with detached kitchen and office for his children who remained unmarried and at home, including twins Frances and William Jr., fifteen, James thirteen, Sarah, whom they called Sallie, John, eight, and Catherine, seven.

As soon as they no longer needed to use the inn as their residence, William obtained a license to operate it as an "ordinary," where they entertained travelers. It became one of the most popular stage stops on Walton Road. The Kentucky Stock Road also ran through White Plains and intersected with it. This free road connected Danville, Kentucky, and Huntsville, Alabama. Stockmen drove cattle, hogs, and sheep to northern markets over it and freight wagons and peddlers used it extensively.

The Quarles family established a blacksmith shop, a general store, and the post office for White Plains on their property. William became the postmaster for White County. He joined the White County militia as a major. He also served as county coroner, was admitted to the bar, and became the first judge in the Upper Cumberland. The first court ever held for miles around convened on the lawn at White Plains, with Judge Quarles presiding. Court for White, Overton, Jackson, and Fentress counties was held there until a more permanent site was established.

On April 2, 1814, barely over four years after the family arrived at their new home, William was returning from a militia meeting in nearby Sparta. It was thought he might have been walking his horse since it had been a brilliant early spring evening. For some reason that will never be known, William Phillips of Sparta allegedly bludgeoned William to death and dumped his body in a ditch by the side of the road. His horse returned to the house riderless.

Authorities quickly accused Phillips, who they later apprehended. He managed to escape from the White County Jail.

Reese Porter, a bounty hunter who fought alongside Andrew Jackson in the war, captured Phillips. First, he went to White County's jail again and then proceeded to Nashville. Once more, Phillips escaped. Governor William Blount offered a $100 reward for his capture, but he was never apprehended.

Ann Quarles had a good head for business. She continued to run the plantation community with assistance from her children and, soon enough, from grandchildren.

Daughter Eliza slid into a depression when her second child, Stephen Decatur Burton, was born on October 8, 1813. Six months later, she had the baby and two-year-old Frances Ann to care for as she tried to come to terms with the death of her beloved father. She struggled. Husband Charles, who now spent most of his time working in the family's store, Quarles & Hawes, assumed extra responsibilities at home to help out. The first week of October, Eliza caught a cold. Respiratory problems developed. On October 21, she died of pneumonia, a month shy of her twenty-fifth birthday. Charles turned over their children to Grandmother Quarles to raise.

In 1837, the Quarles family log cabin home caught fire and burned. Grandson Stephen Burton, although just twenty-five, had already started assuming responsibility for much of the day-to-day operations of the plantation. He set about designing a beautiful antebellum house that was constructed a quarter mile down the road from the original one, which put it in Jackson County. Completed in the mid-1840s, the home featured a full-height entry porch, fireplaces in every room, with each mantel being a different style, and gun cabinets located on either side of the front door. Outbuildings included a smokehouse, corn crib, and horse barn.

Shortly after, Stephen built a two-story schoolhouse for the community's children. Because of his inheritance, he became one of the Upper Cumberland's largest slaveholders, owning around one hundred slaves by the outbreak of the War Between the States in 1861. He lost his fortune in cotton when Union forces burned several warehouses in Chattanooga.

In 1843, the Court of Record was held at White Plains to determine the seat of justice of the new county called Putnam. White Plains became the county seat. The Quarles/Burton home served as the courthouse; therefore, the county commission convened there. Located three miles west of White Plains, Cookeville was established in 1854 and became the new county seat.

Ann Hawes Quarles died in her sleep January 4, 1844, at age seventy-nine. At the time, she had forty-one living grandchildren, twenty-two boys and nineteen girls. In October of that year, a grandson, John Knox Polk Quarles, would be born to her youngest son, John and wife, Patsy, in Missouri.

***

John and Patsy Quarles traveled due north to Columbia, Kentucky, in 1823 when Patsy's younger sister, Jane Lampton, married John Marshall Clemens. John liked his new sister-in-law. She was outgoing and witty, while her husband seemed more reserved and serious, although friendly. Two years later, Jane Clemens wrote that they wanted to move to Middle Tennessee, primarily for the sake of John's health. She asked Patsy to keep an eye out for an available house.

Joe Jared, who had lost his wife, Dorcas Byrne Jared, thirty, during childbirth the previous year, farmed a few miles west of White Plains. William and Ann Quarles knew his parents, Captain William Jared Sr. and Betsy Raulston Jared from Bedford County, Virginia, before they moved down to Buffalo Valley, which became Jackson County at the turn of the century. Captain Jared received almost a 1,000-acre land grant from the U.S. government for his service in the Revolutionary War.

Joe's older sister, Martha, or Patsy, as she was known, married Lawrence Byrne. As a two-year-old, Lawrence came east to Tennessee with his Irish immigrant father, William Byrne, and mother, Rhoda England, from Burke County, North Carolina. They settled just over the Highland Rim in Jasper.

When Joe heard that John Quarles's new in-laws were looking to move to the area from Adair County, Kentucky, he thought of his sister and her husband's small vacant house on a corner of their ample property outside Gainesboro. That Sunday morning, Joe rode to the Byrne's to share what little he knew about the Clemon's. Larry, as his family called him, and Patsy Byrne then took a carriage to the Quarleses to let them know about their extra house.

When the Clemens family arrived in Jackson County about six weeks later, to everyone's surprise, Jane was well along in her first pregnancy. The couple happily settled into the house on the Byrne's property. John, who became licensed to practice law in 1822, looked for work. On July 17, son Orion Clemens entered their world.

Byrne descendants would link back to the Quarles family through marriage one day. Lawrence Byrne's great-grandson, Arthur D. Byrne Sr. of Granville in Jackson County, married Esther Neeley in 1916. Her great-aunt Emma Neeley became the wife of Dr. Edward Burton of Putnam County in 1870. His great-grandfather was William Pennington Quarles.

Two years after the Clemens family landed in Gainesboro, they moved northwest to Jamestown, the county seat of Fentress County. There, John served as attorney general, became the first circuit court clerk of the county, and was appointed one of the county commissioners who drew up specifications for the courthouse and jail.

In 1835, John and Patsy Quarles decided to take their five children and relocate to Monroe County, Missouri. A handful of families they knew from their Upper Cumberland region of Middle Tennessee (as well as others from the area and Kentucky) were migrating to this northeast Missouri area that benefited from soil nurtured by the myriad of rivers. They brought their slaves and slave-holding traditions with them. They figured on their tobacco and cotton thriving there.

Ten years in Fentress County had been enough for Jane Clemens. When she discovered her sister and husband were moving to Missouri, she convinced her husband to move with them. He'd failed to reap enough financial incentives in Fentress County to stay.

Both families headed northwest and ended up in tiny Florida, Missouri, located where the north, south, and middle forks of the Salt River converged in Monroe County, about forty miles southwest of Hannibal, which sits on the big Mississippi River. The Salt River empties upstream into the Mississippi River in Louisiana.

The Clemens family came with four young'uns in tow ages three to ten. On November 30, Jane delivered her fourth son, Samuel Langhorne Clemens, two months early. Henry, the last addition to the family, followed in June 1838.

Jane and Patsy's father, Ben Lampton, became widowed in Kentucky when their mother, Peggy, died in 1818. The following year, he married Polly Hays. By 1830, they had moved to Tennessee to be close to his daughters' families. When everybody loaded up and took off, the older Lamptons gladly went along. Unfortunately, Grandpa Lampton passed away in March 1837 after bouts of angina. His nine-year-old granddaughter, Margaret Clemens, dealt the family another blow when she died in August 1839 as a result of whooping cough.

After five years, when it became obvious that the town of Florida represented no growth opportunities, John Clemens moved his family to Hannibal. He opened a dry goods store and eventually became a justice of the peace.

Hannibal's growth had recently been fueled by railroad transportation, the westernmost line before the Transcontinental Railroad was constructed. By 1845, Hannibal gained "city" status.

Steamboats arrived mid-century, too. They carried livestock, cotton bales, barrels, other freight, and any passengers who could be accommodated. Trips on the rivers were crowded, sweaty, dirty, smelly, and dangerous, as the Clemenses would discover soon enough.

When the Quarles family arrived in sparsely populated Florida, John immediately purchased a small general store, where his brother-in-law offered to work. He set about establishing a farm near the Salt River with twenty or so slaves they brought with them from Tennessee, along with Matthew Duggins, who agreed to relocate. Cabins for slaves already existed on the property. Cotton had been planted on most of the land. He decided to leave that land fallow for the first growing season. Tobacco went into about one hundred acres.

The family's large two-story log house with a wide hallway sat on a knoll by a small creek and faced north. The fireplaces were made of stone, and the chimneys were made of brick. The second-story rooms contained no fireplaces, and the outer walls at the front and back of these rooms were only about four feet high. This created low, slanted ceilings and low windows upstairs—a kitchen wing connected to a roofed-in porch with a spacious floor. Summertime meals were served in the middle of the shady, breezy porch floor, which lay to the southeast. Beyond the kitchen sat the smokehouse, cellar, and slave cabins. To the west of those was the orchard. To the north and east flowed a creek where most of the cropland was located.

Four healthy children were born to John and Patsy after they moved to Missouri, starting with Tabitha the following year. Then, on July 9, 1850, after a difficult pregnancy, Patsy suffered through a breached birth before delivering Jane Clemens Quarles. She failed to recover from the trauma. Martha "Patsy" Lampton Quarles passed away fourteen days later. The baby lived for another month.

In the mid-1840s, the Quarles had a special visitor for the summer. Sam Clemens looked up to his Uncle John, and apparently, the feeling was mutual. These summer-long visits to the farm in Monroe County had a profound impact on Sam's lifelong memories. It was there he broke out of his shell of poor health that had surrounded him for his first ten years since he had been born two months prematurely.

Most often, his brother, Henry, came with him. They played with their cousins, picnicked, fished, and swam in the river. He became well-acquainted with the slaves, especially "old Uncle Dan'l," who used to mesmerize the children with yarns every night in front of the kitchen fire, their only light. Uncle Dan'l became the prototype for the slave, Jim, in *Adventures of Huckleberry Finn*, when Sam used the pen name of Mark Twain, who was the celebrated author the world came to know.

As a lad, Sam pulled mischievous tricks as a matter of course. He developed this behavior quite young. After his early birth and slow physical development, his mother coddled him, yet he tested her patience.

In the final of Jane Clemens' eighty-seven years, Sam asked his mother about those early years when he was frail. "I suppose that during that whole time, you were uneasy about me?"

"Yes, the whole time," she answered.

"Afraid I wouldn't live?"

His mother responded, "No, afraid you would."

This exchange could have taken place anytime in the mid-to late 1880s when Mark Twain's popularity was perhaps at its highest. *The Adventures of Huckleberry Finn* was published in 1885. It suggests from whom Sam Clemens probably inherited his sense of humor.

When Sam recalled Uncle John's farm in his later years, he described it as ". . . a heavenly place for a boy. It is the part of my education which I look back upon with the most satisfaction."

Remembering Uncle Dan'l, he said, "It was on the farm that I got my strong liking for his race and my appreciation of certain of its fine qualities."

In 1847, John Clemens died of pneumonia. His oldest son, Orion, returned to Hannibal from St. Louis, where he was studying law, and bought *The Hannibal Journal*. This is where Sam got his first journalism experience. Six years later, Orion moved to Iowa and, first, ran a small newspaper, then, a book and job printing office. Sam followed his brother north and gained additional experience.

As a boy, Sam admired riverboat captains dreaming one day he might join them. In 1857, at the age of twenty-one, on his way to South America, he met notable Captain Horace Bixby in New Orleans and asked for an apprenticeship. Sam spent time on the Lower Mississippi River with Captain Bixby for the next two years, who occasionally placed him with other pilots.

The experience served Sam well in spinning his tales up the road. Captain Bixby's character is part of Sam's *Life on the Mississippi* memoir. Years later, he said that the profession of riverboat pilot was the most congenial one he ever followed.

"A pilot, in those days, was the only unfettered and entirely independent human being that lived in the earth," he wrote.

In June 1858, Sam sometimes worked with another captain on the *Pennsylvania*. His brother, Henry, had come down and was hired as a crew member for the boat. On the 13th, Sam was not assigned to go out on the *Pennsylvania*. That day, on Henry's twentieth birthday, one of the double boilers exploded. Henry died one week later as a result of injuries sustained in the explosion. A few days before, Sam had a terrifying dream in which he saw the body of his brother lying in a casket. He forever blamed himself for the death of his closest sibling.

Sam came off the river when the war started in 1861, which greatly curtailed traffic. He feared he might be impressed as a

Union gunboat pilot. He returned to Hannibal and tried to keep his head down. That summer, he accompanied Orion to Nevada. After the election of President Lincoln, Orion Clemens was appointed secretary to the new government of the Territory of Nevada.

In 1862, Sam worked as city editor of the *Enterprise* in Virginia City. Three years earlier, Virginia City developed into a boom town with the discovery of the Comstock Lode, the first major lode of silver in the U.S. Nearby Carson City had been newly established as the territorial capital.

Sam started signing his letters, "Mark Twain," when he went to Carson City to report on legislative proceedings. It was perhaps the first of many things collected from the river, which would follow him into his world as a writer. The name was suggested by the technical phraseology of Mississippi navigation, where, in sounding the depth of two fathoms, the leadsman calls out to, "Mark twain!"

Some of Sam's stories had appeared in New York papers by then. In 1864, he moved to San Francisco and became a full-time reporter for *The Call*. For a time, he went to the Tuolumne foothills to mine. While there, he heard the widely known story of a jumping frog. He wrote *The Celebrated Jumping Frog of Calaveras County*, published in the *New York Saturday Press* in November 1865 and subsequently reprinted throughout the country.

Celebrity came quickly. Sam began traveling throughout the country and overseas, lecturing, meeting people, and collecting story ideas. He met Charlie Langdon on a ship returning from abroad. The young man invited him to dine with his family in Elmira, New York, where he introduced Sam to his older sister, Olivia (who went by the name Louise). Their father, Jervis Langdon, was a prosperous businessman who helped Sam buy into a newspaper in Buffalo, New York, after he and Louise married in 1870.

The 1870's and 1880's were prolific decades for Sam as novels unfolded. Tom Sawyer and Huck Finn jumped off Mark Twain's pages and into the hearts of millions of readers around the world.

The Clemens's first child, Samuel Langdon Jr., born November 1870, died less than two years later of diphtheria. While they lived in Buffalo when the toddler was sick, his father worked on the book *Roughing It,* which was about his experiences in the Wild West. Their second child, Susy, died of spinal meningitis in August 1896 at the age of twenty-four. Sam was in London when he was notified of his daughter's death. To help counteract his grief, Sam wrote *Following the Equator: A Journey Around the World,* published in 1897, an account of his world lecture tour. The same year they lost Susy, daughter Jean was diagnosed with epilepsy. The family went through Europe to see different doctors, searching for a cure.

In 1901, Louise Clemens's health took a serious turn for the worse. She moved to Italy, which seemed to temporarily improve her condition. But on June 4, 1904, she passed away in Florence.

Daughter Jean, twenty-nine, followed her mother to the grave five years later on Christmas Eve. Beside her deathbed, her father wrote *The Death of Jean,* published in 1911.

Grief-stricken over Jean's death, Sam traveled to Bermuda in January 1910. He started to experience chest pains in early April. On April 21, he died at Stormfield, his mansion in Redding, Connecticut, where he lived the last two years of his life.

Mark Twain will be remembered, first, as a humorist. But he was also a public moralist, a popular entertainer, a political philosopher, a travel writer, and a novelist. He cinched his place in American literacy culture with characters he developed from the various places he knew firsthand and jobs he experienced over the years.

By far, the most valuable well of inspiration for his writing came from his family and home territory on the farm and along the rivers in Missouri — dialect heard around the table on their porch summers while eating Aunt Patsy Quarles's sumptuous meals with Uncle John and his cousins, as well as among the slaves; Aunt Hanner, and particularly Old Uncle Dan'l and his endless folktales; people in the towns, and on the wharves. All appear as characters in more than one of his books. The pranks he often pulled with his cousins resurfaced when he sat down to write.

Samuel Clemens knew what a story was. He sought adventure, identified characters, and through Mark Twain, he surely could tell a tale.

He brought country living into the hearts and minds of untold boys and girls, who shared his stories with their children and carried those images to their graves.

No Hills to Get in the Way

Byrne/Longmire

Fanny never wanted to relocate. Now that she was suddenly gone, her husband's world had shifted, his future just got closer.

A depression hit the U.S. in what became known as the Panic of 1893. Area farmers were already hurting. Outside markets virtually shut down. Gold reserves dropped, wheat prices crashed, and because of the state of the economy, there was a run on the banks. Hundreds of banks closed, thousands of businesses failed, and many farmers were forced to call it quits.

Lawrence Byrne held the reins driving back from the Methodist church on this breezy late March day after burying his wife of fourteen years. Their only child, Augustus, twelve, sat beside him on the buckboard, silent and withdrawn, as he had been since the accident three days ago.

Francis, or Fanny, as everybody knew her, had gone out to their smokehouse fifty yards behind their house despite gusty afternoon winds. Just after stepping outside with a slab of cured bacon, the top half of a dead tree broke off and struck her. She died of head trauma. Gus, as they called the boy, discovered his mother's body.

Lawrence sensed that now was the time for him to pursue his dreams. At thirty-six, he was in his prime, and opportunity beckoned as the twentieth century approached. But not in Jackson County. As a farmer, he realized this hilly, rocky land with marginal soil offered little future. Like his grandfather, father, brothers, and uncles, he struggled to grow corn and tobacco and raise cattle on this same Middle Tennessee land. That is not the life he wanted for himself or his son.

Lawrence longed to go to the great Northwest. As a youth, he became enthralled by learning about pioneer families journeying along the Oregon Trail to settle in Oregon and Washington. He'd heard about the fertility of the soil and the variety of crops being produced in those states. He correctly assumed that farming would greatly expand since railroads now offered transcontinental service.

Since his teenage years, he dreamed of seeing the Pacific Ocean, the majestic mountains of the Cascade Range, and farming the plains that lay between. He was so sure it would happen from the first time he received pay for a job he put a small percentage of it into what he called his "travel fund." It had been twenty years since he established his fund toward his dream. No one knew about the account, which, he thought, was secure in the Gainesboro Bank, where he went once a month or so to make a deposit while picking up supplies. It was now safely buried on his property. He never even told his wife.

Two years ago, Lawrence's youngest brother, Lemuel, a practicing attorney in Jackson County, ventured out to Washington at age of twenty-six. They received word that last March, he married Anna Callow of the pioneering Callow family, who live in the upper Kamilche Valley northwest of Olympia. The couple settled in nearby Shelton.

"Gus, how would you like a new life?" Lawrence asked his son as they rode toward home.

"What? What on earth are you talkin' about?"

Lawrence leaned back, transferred the reins to one hand, put an arm around the boy, and looked him square in the eye.

"Is there anything here in Granville you couldn't walk away from tomorrow if you had an opportunity for a better life?"

"Well . . . no . . . not really. I mean, we have a whole mess of family here. But . . . I kind of like the idea of making new friends. Why are you asking me this?"

Lawrence pulled to the side of the hard-packed dirt road and reined in the two horses. For the first time in days, a hint of a smile crossed young Gus's face, which looked more every day like Lawrence's younger brother, Fayette, who they lost four years ago at the age of twenty-four to consumption.

"Because you and I are going to take the Sunset Limited, a Southern Pacific passenger train, from New Orleans to Los Angeles. Then we'll make our way to Tacoma, Washington, on the Puget Sound. That is very close to where we want to be. It's supposed to be an agricultural paradise out there. And it is someplace I've wanted to go since I was just a little older than you are."

"Papa, who else knows about this?"

"Nobody," Lawrence replied.

"What about the farm and the animals? The house and everything in it?"

"You leave all that to me. Don't worry about the details. All of that will be worked out."

"We're going all the way to the Pacific Ocean?" Gus asked.

"Yes, son, we are."

In a completely unexpected gesture, the boy knocked his father's hat into the dirt and just about shoved him out of the wagon when he lunged and put him in a bear hug.

"Yippee," yelled Gus as he stood and threw his hat into the air. He then jumped down, causing the horses to skitter, as he whirled around to retrieve the hats.

"When we get to the house, I want you to just keep your britches on because there surely will be family there with food," Lawrence said. "We can't go disrespectin' your Mama, and that's liable to be the way some folks take it if we tell them right away that we're leaving. Everybody's already upset. You understand?"

"Yes, sir."

"Good. Right now, this is between you and me. The first one I'll tell is Grandpa."

✦ ✦ ✦

The Jackson County Byrnes had, for the most part, not ventured far from the homestead. It was not a restless spirit driving Lawrence but an opportunity to discover conditions that would allow him to thrive doing what he loved to do. That's probably exactly what his great-grandfather, William Byrne, hoped for in 1792 when he left County Wicklow, Ireland, as a twenty-seven-year-old and arrived on the coast of North Carolina.

Serendipity played its hand in William's voyage across the Atlantic. He spied pretty Rhoda England on board, who was traveling with her parents, John and Anne England, from Burke County, North Carolina. John farmed outside of Morgansborough, the county seat. Both had been born in Ireland and scraped up enough money to bring their nineteen-year-old daughter to meet her Irish family. John and Anne knew this would be the last time they saw their parents.

A casual acquaintance between William and Rhoda quickly sparked. When they debarked in Wilmington, the Englands invited William to travel with them to Burke County since he, too, farmed, and his destination was generally west. He stayed in Morgansborough for nearly two years before he and Rhoda wed. They aimed to cross the Blue Ridge Mountains and look for property somewhere west of the Cumberland Mountains in Middle Tennessee.

Two of Rhoda's brothers decided to accompany their youngest sister and her new husband into the frontier. They knew extra protection might become necessary due to periodic hostile Indian activity. Rhoda remained forever grateful to the wives of her brothers, Aaron and Ezekiel, when they consented to their husbands making the journey, which lasted nearly three months. Unknowingly, Ezekiel's wife, Charlotte, discovered shortly after his departure that she was in the early stages of pregnancy with what would turn out to be twins.

When the foursome rolled down off the west end of the Cumberland Plateau without major incident, they found land to William's liking on Indian Creek with ready access to the Cumberland River in what would soon be named the state of Tennessee. William thanked God for a safe passage, a kind, loving wife, and the prospects of producing a decent living from this soil.

Lawrence's grandmother, Martha Jared Byrne, came from a father who was also a true pioneer. The family always called her Patsy. As an infant in 1796, she journeyed with her parents, William Jared, his wife, Elizabeth Raulstone Jared, and older brother, Moses, from Bedford County, Virginia, through the Cumberland Gap, into Kentucky, and down into what became Tennessee. They settled on a tract of land patented to Will for his service in the Revolutionary War. Buffalo Valley became their home.

When he was a young lad, Will Jared's family moved to Londoun County, on the northern edge of Virginia. It was an untamed, mountainous, physically demanding territory with unpredictable Indians and wild animals.

Out of necessity, the backwoods people became proficient with wood. Sawmills provided a means of making furniture. Will became an excellent carpenter. He also learned to make tools necessary for farming. Because they depended on horses, he gained blacksmithing skills as well.

Like most people venturing away from the East Coast, the Jareds favored a government independent from the English. When the war for independence came, Will was in his early twenties. He, his father, John, and brother, Joseph, were torn between his mother's Quaker faith, which forbade participation in war, and a fierce desire to fight for the cause of freedom. The three enrolled in the Continental Army. All returned home intact.

The Byrnes and the Jareds arrived in Tennessee about the same time and became neighbors and friends. But, soon enough, they became much more than that. One son and two daughters of William and Rhoda Byrne married children of Will and Anne Jared. Lawrence Byrne, born 1798, married Patsy Jared, born 1795. Malinda Byrne, born 1800, and Moses Jared, born 1794 wed. Then, Dorcas Byrne, born in 1803, married Joseph Jared, who was born 1800.

"Thus," Lawrence had explained to Gus when he was younger and loved hearing the stories about how their kin got here — crossing oceans, fighting wolves and Indians, battling the Redcoats in the War of Independence — "that is how I got both of my names.

"Also, that's how I came to marry your mother. My Grandpa Lawrence and Grandma Patsy's oldest child was Alexander Byrne. As you know, he was your mother's father. And Terrell, his brother, is my father."

"Well, how did I get my name?" asked Gus.

"You are named after your Uncle Michael. His middle name is Augustus, and so far as I know, he's the only one in the family with that name. I like it. It's a strong, dignified name."

"How about my middle name?"

"Bailey was a free black man who lived just up the road from us growin' up. You knew Bailey; he died just two years ago. We think he was seventy-two. At one time, he was a slave to the Spurlocks, your grandma's family. Bailey's mother, Ruth, worked in the house for my grandparents, Josiah and Leah Spurlock. Ruth's mother, Chloe, born around 1767, the same time as old man Drury Spurlock, was also a house slave. Chloe lived well into her seventiess and never worked for anybody but the Spurlocks. Neither did Ruth. But Ruth died unexpectedly when she was in her thirties. Bailey was a very young man, then about fifteen or sixteen. Out of loyalty, Josiah drew up papers sayin' that when he passed on, Bailey was to be set free. And that came to pass in July

1854. Bailey was seven years old when your grandma's brother, Drury, was born. There were, I think, three young Spurlocks even closer in age to Bailey, and all those boys ended up playin' together as children.

"When Bailey was legally emancipated, Drury, whose property butts against your grandpa's, gave Bailey ten acres, and he found help in buildin' his two-room house. To everybody's surprise, he planted most of that land in sugar cane each year in early May. Then, in September or October, we'd all get together and help him cut those cane stalks close to the ground, put them on a sled, and haul them to his cane mill, which he ingeniously built. Us kids loved to feed the stalks between the rollers and watch the sweet juice being crushed into a tub while the mule walked 'round and 'round the mill. He built a furnace of rock and mud where the juice was boiled down to thick, sweet, golden molasses. It was then strained through a cloth into jars. Bailey would sell every jar he produced right out beside the road. People loved Bailey's pure molasses.

"The man never married, so he had no children. He worked for Papa often or for anyone who needed him, who would treat him fairly. He is skilled with his hands. A good man. Despite the terrible things his people suffered, he believed his reward would be in Heaven one day. Everybody kind of looked after Bailey, and I believe he looked after us. In gratitude and respect, I passed his name along to you, son."

✔ ✔ ✔

Gus Byrne reeled from all his new experiences. No matter what lay ahead, he thought he would forever be grateful to his father for having the foresight to leave Tennessee and bring him into this big, beautiful country, offering so much promise.

The train from New Orleans provided first-class luxury, all Pullman sleeping cars whisking them across Texas through Houston, San Antonio, and El Paso, then through Tucson, Arizona, where he'd never seen so many cowboys, and through Palm Springs before rolling into Los Angles. Gus loved every second of it. This is what he wanted to spend his life doing: working for the railroad.

It was July 2, 1894, when Lawrence clutched the starboard rail of the freighter on which he luckily booked passage for himself and his son in San Francisco. They now stood side by side, watching as the ship slid past Cape Flattery into the Strait of Juan de Fuca, which divides the United States from Canada. Within the hour, they saw the San Juan Islands directly to the North and snow-covered Mount Baker looming to the east past the islands. Then they passed Whidbey Island on their left, easing down through the Puget Sound to Seattle, where they spent a night while much of the ship's cargo was unloaded before continuing the short distance to Tacoma, their destination by water.

Mother Nature welcomed the pair to the West Coast with favorable weather. San Francisco had seemed pleasantly cool for late June compared to Tennessee temperatures. The northern Washington sky was virtually cloudless as the afternoon advanced.

There had been strong winds or a Category 6 on the Beaufort Wind Scale the evening the ship passed the confluence of the Columbia River and the Pacific Ocean at Cape Disappointment. The captain swung out a bit further than he normally would have under calmer conditions. The area is known as the "Graveyard of the Pacific." Gus learned all he could about the Beaufort Wind Scale and everything else he could absorb since this was the first time he or his father had ventured on an ocean vessel.

Lawrence quickly found a room when they disembarked in Tacoma the next day. All they packed was a large trunk each and a satchel they carried over a shoulder to hold a change of clothes, toiletries, and a book. Lawrence needed to purchase a sturdy wagon, two horses or mules broken to pull a wagon, which could be used for work, and a rifle. It would be the 4th of July the next day, and he thought, after all their travels, it would be fun to take a day and celebrate on the water.

Neither had ever eaten seafood, but that's how people who lived on Puget Sound celebrated their July 4th. The locals offered grilled salmon, tuna, bluefish, king crab, Dungeness crab, shrimp, muscles, and scallops — a feast from the depths. That night, fireworks exploded over the water as if to welcome the Byrnes to Washington.

It took three days before Lawrence agreed to purchase a wagon, harnesses, and a pair of Belgian draft horses. The owner guaranteed their health and temperament in the field. Lawrence did not like doing business without a referral, but that was the position in which he found himself. He paid half again what he was thinking about paying for a horse. However, he had no idea such strong, beautiful animals would be available. He could only hope he would get a good return on his investment.

Finally, they loaded up the wagon and headed south. Lawrence knew pioneer families coming through the Naches Pass on the Oregon Trail settled in Pierce and Thurston counties. His idea was to drive through the plains of nearby Thurston County, see what struck him as good agricultural land, and talk to some folks.

On the third day out, they crossed the Nisqually River. Gus exclaimed, "Papa, this really is unbelievable land. It's flat. No hills to get in the way. This river flows right through it. And that huge mountain we've been seeing way over yonder to our left is like the protector of it all."

"Yep, Mount Rainier. It probably has snow year-round because it's so high and so cold up there it never completely melts.

"Tell you what, let's go on to Yelm. It's a small town. We'll stay there and talk to some people. How about it?" Lawrence asked.

About an hour later, they spotted a grocery in Yelm and pulled the team up outside. They were more than ready to eat but they were also looking for information. Lawrence asked his son to find water for the horses while he went inside.

Gus grabbed two of the four buckets out of the wagon. He walked around the side of the building, where he found a trough of water fed by rain that had fallen off the roof. After filling the buckets, he stood watering Molly with Polly, as he had named them, patiently waiting for her turn, when he heard a woman's voice behind him.

"Hello, young man. Do these fine-looking animals belong to you?"

Gus set the almost empty bucket down and turned to face two women who were a bit younger than his father.

"Afternoon, ladies," Gus responded as he swiped his hat from his head. "Yes, they do. My Papa and I were right pleased with how they handled drivin' the wagon down from Tacoma."

Polly nudged him in the back. "Excuse me," he said as he turned and held the other water bucket in front of the horse.

"I must say, that's the best-looking horse flesh I've seen in a while," said the one who spoke before.

"Thank you, ma'am. We're hoping they perform as well in the field."

Gus set the bucket down, took a couple of steps forward, extended his hand, then drew it back and laughed. "My name is Augustus Byrne. Gus is what they call me. My Papa's name is Lawrence Byrne. I was goin' to shake your hand, but you don't want me to do that. I'm right dirty."

Both women smiled warmly. "I'm May Bell Longmire," said the one who had spoken, "and this is my sister, Anna Lee Longmire. Our Uncle Frank operates this store.

"I assume your father is inside? We'll go in and see if we can't help answer his questions."

"Ma'am, can you ask him to hurry along with the lunch makings? I am starving."

The women walked into the store and observed their uncle behind the counter, amicably chatting with a man who looked to be nearly six feet tall. He had his back to the door. Anna waved, and Frank said, "Hello, sisters. I'm talking to Mr. Byrne here, who just rolled in. He's looking to settle in these parts."

The stranger then turned around, and May, almost inaudibly, gasped, "Oh, my!"

"What was that?" her sister softly asked.

"What you better do," Anna said to her uncle, "is make some lunch for Mr. Byrne and his son because the boy is famished."

"Better yet, let me go ahead and get a few things together that the Byrnes need, and how about you two going back and slicing a loaf of the wheat berry bread?" Frank said. "The Janssens from Skagit County came down yesterday with some of their fine cheese. Cut a couple of pounds off that. And another two pounds from the bologna. And go ahead and fix a couple of sandwiches for them. Throw in a dozen apples."

Before Lawrence knew it, he and Gus had been well-fed while sitting on the store's front porch benches. To his amazement, he discovered through an hour-long conversation with May and Anna that they were among siblings belonging to Sophrona and John Longmire, son of the famous explorer and settler, James Longmire. The patriarch of the large Longmire clan was now seventy-four years old and lived with his wife, Virinda, on the family farm located on the eastern edge of the Yelm community. To his further astonishment, the women invited father and son to follow them home. If Lawrence wanted to learn about farming opportunities in the area, May said, there were none better to talk to than their family members. They offered a guest house for lodging and meals.

As they got up to leave, Frank walked out on the porch. May said, "Uncle if Clarence is not tied up in the morning, why don't you send him out to the ranch early? I'd say he and Gus are about the same age, and it might be good company for them both. I'm thinking we will take the big carriage out for a tour in the morning after breakfast."

"I think you're right. Clarence would enjoy that. I'll have him up and out," said Frank.

Hot baths felt good, and Lawrence appreciated a shave. It was nice getting into clean clothes. Supper at the Longmire's large table consisted of delicious lamb stew and cornbread. Afterward, they walked around part of the farm and talked with their host, John, his brother, Elcaine, and two of his sons, Ben, eighteen, and Washington, whom they called Wash, sixteen. They had come from their ranch on the Lacamas Prairie in the Bald Hills further east to bring a wagon load of sheep.

Lawrence discovered that the Panic affected farms in western Washington, too. Mines had shut down, and the lumber industry slowed. Farmers were not planting as much wheat, oats, and flax for export but were planting more vegetables because people still had to eat.

When they said goodnight and returned to their room, Gus said, "Papa, Elcaine Longmire sure 'nough looks like a mountain man."

Lawrence laughed. "He looks like the pioneer he is, son. I think he was about your age when the family came over the Oregon Trail in 1853. His brother, John, was just a toddler. So Elcaine well remembers those days. He has cleared land, built houses, and started farms. I think he worked under the shadow of Mount Rainier. Some day, you can talk to him about all that."

"Does that mean we're stayin' here?" Gus asked.

"I don't think we'll find better people to have as neighbors, do you? We'll go on a tour tomorrow, but I feel very comfortable here. How 'bout you?"

"Yeah, even those older boys was nice to me. And you know what? When you're not lookin', Miss May stares at you a lot and smiles. I think she'd like for you to stay," Gus snickered.

"Is that right? Well, I'm hittin' the hay. We'll get an early morning knock on our door in time for breakfast."

"I can't wait. I'm ready to eat again now."

"Son, you're always ready to eat," said his father.

In the morning, sitting around the breakfast table piled with blueberry pancakes, sausage patties, and fresh coffee were James and Virinda, John and Sophrona, May, Clarence Longmire, eleven (son of Frank), Martha (sister of Frank), and her husband, Joseph Conine, a Yelm farmer, and their son, Herbert, nineteen, as well as Elcaine and his sons, who were preparing to return home. Most of the Longmire's eleven children, except for seven-month-old Neva, who demanded an early feeding, would eat in a second shift. Conversations shifted from the Byrnes' experience riding the transcontinental passenger train to speculation about fruit and vegetable processors forming in Seattle, to Herbert's desire to attend Washington State Agricultural College (which had been established in Pullman four years earlier), to labor needed for the fall harvest, to town gossip young Clarence had heard in his father's store.

Walter Longmire, John, and Sophrona's twenty-year-old son, brought their three-seater carriage to the front door after breakfast. May was the first one out the door. Walter jumped down off the seat, but his sister caught him and said, "Git back up there and drive. I want our guest to sit back here with me. I'll tell Papa."

When the others came out, May said, "Clarence, you and Gus get in the back with Herbert. Uncle Joe can sit here with me and

Mr. Byrne. Papa, you can be our guide from up front, if that's okay?"

John stopped and looked at his daughter. Then he looked up at his son, who held the reins and was grinning like a Cheshire cat. He nodded at May and climbed into the shotgun position.

Lawrence stepped in and closed the door. "May," he said, giving her his best smile. "I'm afraid I'm going to have to insist on one thing."

"Oh, and what might that be?"

"From here on out, you call me Lawrence."

On the ride, John explained that the Nisqually River provided the boundary between white settlers and the Nisqually Indian Reservation. He said crop diversity would be possible with an enhanced irrigation system, but he did not foresee such a development until at least the early 1900s. He said that the Northern Pacific Railway finally came through in 1873, which greatly boosted the ability of area farmers to move their products. It was a two-day drive to Olympia, located on the Puget Sound, the avenue to large markets. With the train, Tacoma and Seattle became accessible.

An amazing diversity of crops grew in western Washington, including wheat, oats, flax, hops, spinach, cabbage, lettuce, celery, sugar beets, potatoes, various berries, and tree fruit. Lawrence immediately saw that with the economy in a slump, the smartest thing he could do would be to read everything he could find regarding plant science, range management, and farm economics in the state of Washington.

There was land at a good price right now, but the timing wasn't right. It made sense to rent a place, enroll Gus in school for the fall, and see if he couldn't make a little money when the harvest started, using his horses and wagon to transport crops.

John's youngest brother, George, who also farmed in Yelm, experienced his third setback over the past year when one of his mules died. He and his wife, Louisa, had a decent-sized barn and an old, smaller, vacant house on their property. Lawrence drove John over in his wagon with Molly and Polly to meet the younger Longmire. George admitted that he was barely hanging on to the farm. He could no longer afford to pay for labor and was now down to one mule. He had wanted to get the smaller of his two fields planted in fall vegetables.

Lawrence said that if George would accommodate Gus and him in the small house on his property and agree to stable and feed his horses, he and the boy when Gus wasn't in school, would work by his side in cultivating a new crop. The men agreed with a handshake.

May persuaded sisters Eva and Mabel to join her in helping their Aunt Louisa clean the old three-room house from top to bottom in preparation for Lawrence and Gus moving in. They stocked the kitchen and found a small table and a couple of chairs, a couch, two beds, which they made up with sheets, quilts, pillows, a couple of bedside tables, a bureau, a mirror, and even a couple of big hooked rugs.

Lawrence and Gus found themselves among those regularly invited to the Longmire's. Different family members showed up on different Sundays, but there were always two shifts for dinner at the big table. Lawrence discovered that his seat was reserved for the first shift next to May. It didn't take long before his heart lurched when she scooched her chair next to his and gave him that grin.

At first, he argued with himself over her age. She was, after all, nearly nineteen years younger, closer to Gus's age than his. But, seriously, what negative held sway?

Lawrence recognized a gift when one came his way. May was a healthy, strong, smart young woman who had been raised on the frontier. She helped to rear a passel of younger siblings so motherhood would be innate. She could handle anything inside the house or out in the field because she was a Longmire. She inherited her grandmother's eyes, and God knows there was a world of wisdom in those. If she carried old Virinda's longevity in her genes, May could be around to help with their grandchildren and maybe even their great-grandchildren.

It was the first of October. Lawrence thought George's farm should have the onions, cabbage, carrots, broccoli, pole beans, lettuce, kale, and spinach harvested by the end of the month at. A professor from Washington State Agricultural College would be available in Tacoma in mid-November for discussion and consultation, and Lawrence planned to be there.

First, he would ask John's permission to marry his daughter. Then, he'd ask May to become his wife. He wished for a simple wedding before the end of the year.

The proposal came to absolutely no one's surprise, nor did May's enthusiastic acceptance. The wedding took place on Saturday, December 7, in the Yelm schoolhouse, which also served as the non-denominational and only church in town. Afterward, all the Longmires returned to the main Longmire farm for a post-wedding feast. Sophrona agreed on the date, even on the heels of Thanksgiving because she knew all her girls would pull together to make a special meal for her May Bell. A fattened calf had been slaughtered, and an assortment of fresh fall vegetables lined the table, along with yeast rolls. Aunt Martha specialized in desserts, and made several huckleberry cakes with boiled icing. Gus stayed with those who were now his cousins that night while the newlyweds went to the little house on George's farm to begin their life together.

There, they spent their first Christmas Eve as a family, which was also Lawrence's thirty-seventh birthday. May baked a cake, and Aunt Louisa brought a supper of baked chicken, roasted Brussels sprouts and boiled potatoes, as she and Uncle George shared in the celebration. Gus had taken the wagon with one of the horses up near the river and found a beautiful little tree. May, Aunt Louisa and a couple of cousins decorated it with homemade ornaments, and that night, it twinkled with little candles. The next day, everybody went to the ranch to spend Christmas day with extended family.

§ § §

Who was this family who now claimed Lawrence as one of their own? The more he learned, the more honored he felt to be on the fringe of their story. The children May hoped to bear him would carry a legacy of determination, strength, and leadership.

Lawrence wrote the details of the elder Longmire's cross-country journey along the Oregon Trail into Washington in a letter to his family back in Tennessee. He used James's written account of coming west, supplemented by conversations with his wife and other Longmires, as necessary.

Terrell and Mary Jane Byrne, Granville, Tennessee

Thurston County, Washington, December 18, 1895

"Greetings, Papa and Mama and all Jackson County Byrnes,

I'd wish you a Merry Christmas, but by the time you receive this, I suspect we will already be into 1896. I hope this finds you in good health and weathering the financial storm as well as possible.

I am faring better than I could have possibly expected. On Dec. 7, I married young May Bell Longmire, so I now have a wife who adds joy to my life, and Gus has a mother he is quite fond of. This is the family I told you about in the letter I sent soon after our arrival in Yelm, who immediately treated us with such kindness and generosity. As it happens, they are also one of the most well-known and respected families in the state. May's grandfather, James Longmire, was an explorer, settler, guide, a Puget Sound Ranger during the Yakima Indian War of 1855-56, a legislator, and capitalist. His exploits will go down in history. I want to share their story with you since your future grandchildren will share this heritage.

Virinda Longmire, James's second wife, was twenty-three and toting eight-month-old John, along with their other three children, when the couple left their eighty-acre farm on Shuwme Prairie, Fountain County, Indiana, on March 6, 1853. They viewed the move as a safety valve in response to societal and financial pressures building in the nation. They spent over 1,000 miles on steamers traveling through Evansville, St. Louis, and then up the Mississippi River to St. Joseph on the Missouri River. In James's words: 'There I bought eight yoke of oxen and a large quantity of supplies, and proceeded in wagons along the river to Cainsville, now Council Bluffs, and camped. As it was yet too early to start on our long journey, the grass not grown sufficiently to feed our oxen along the routes, we decided to remain for several weeks and make some preparation for another start.'

It was May 10 before their party crossed the Missouri River and headed toward Fort Kearny on the Platt River. They killed a few antelope along the road, jackrabbits, and even a stray buffalo or two rolling through Kansas and south Nebraska. Once they reached the Platt River, for more than 400 miles, they found clear navigation, abundant fresh game, and wood for cooking fires. They also discovered the beginning of hundreds of graves along the trail. They received advance warning that mud holes through this warm, arid environment simmered with organic waste ripe for the spread of cholera. They filled every container they had at Fort Kearney and even purchased as much ale as they felt they could carry because they knew the water from here to Fort Laramie in Wyoming posed a potentially fatal risk.

God had been merciful to their entire party as they crossed the Rocky Mountains at South Pass in western Wyoming. When they reached the Snake River for the first time and crossed a quarter mile above Salmon Falls, they learned two things about western Indians inhabiting territory around the trail. One, they were indispensable crossing the treacherous rivers. Two, they could not be trusted.

Another 200 miles brought the Longmire party to Fort Boise in Idaho, a Hudson Bay trading post operated by an Englishman and his Indian wife. James Longmire nearly lost his life attempting to swim his cattle over the Snake River at this post. James's description of the incident is as follows: 'I tried to get an Indian to swim our cattle over, but failing, Watt proposed to go with them, if I would, which seemed a fair proposition, and as they would not go without someone to drive them, we started across. Watt carried a long stick in one hand, holding by the other to the tail of old Lube, a great rawboned ox who had done faithful service on our long, toilsome journey. I threw my stick away and went in a little below Watt but found the current very strong, which drifted me downstream. I thought I should be drowned and shouted to Watt, "I'm gone." With great presence of mind, he reached his stick toward me, which I grasped with a last hope of saving my life, and by this means bore up 'till I swam to Watt, who caught on the tail of the nearest ox. Thus, it gave me a welcome hold on old Lube's tail, which carried me safely to the shore. Only for Watt's coolness and bravery, I should have lost my life at the same spot where one of Mr. Melville's men was drowned on the previous evening.'

At the Grand Ronde River, a tributary of the Snake River, the party connected with two advance men with much welcomed news. Workers had started from Olympia and Steilacoom to make a road for the Longmire travelers through the Naches Pass on the Cascade Mountain range. They would become the first wagon train party to attempt a crossing north of the Dalles on the Columbia River. They rolled another fifty miles to the Umatilla River, where a trade center was at its junction with the Columbia River. After resting for two days and purchasing additional supplies, thirty-one wagons left what was part of the established Oregon Trail. Fort Walla Walla became their next destination.

After becoming lost and correcting their mistake, the weary travelers endured the sometimes necessary but unwelcome presence of Indians. On September 18, they crossed a canyon and then experienced rough going east of Selah Valley on the upper Yakima. They crossed the Naches River fifty-two times before starting for the summit of the Cascades north of Mount Tacoma. In three days, they found plentiful grass and good water. They stopped for two days rest to let their exhausted animals eat and drink.

Three days later, they came to Summit Hill, where they experienced one of the toughest challenges of the trip. Again, I'll use James Longmire's words to describe their task: 'We spliced ropes and prepared for the steep descent, which we saw before us. One end of the rope was fastened to the axles of the wagon, the other thrown around a large tree and held by several men, and thus, one at a time, the wagons were lowered gradually a distance of 300 yards. Then, the ropes were loosened, and the wagons were drawn a quarter of a mile further with locked wheels before we reached Greenwater. All the wagons were lowered safely, but the one belonging to Mr. Lane was crushed to pieces by the breaking of one of our ropes, causing him and his family to finish the trip on horseback.'

They commenced to cross the Greenwater River sixteen times and the White River seven times before reaching first Porter's prairie, then Connell's prairie, then on to the Puyallup River. They finally reached the Nisqually plains and camped at Clover Creek. There, they were met by locals, who invited them into their homes.

On October 10, James and two of his companions searched for homes. They received notice from the Hudson Bay Company not to settle on lands north of the Nisqually River due to that being Nisqually Indian territory. James wrote: 'We crossed the river and went to the Yelm prairie, a beautiful spot. I thought it was a scene fit for an artist as it lay before us covered with tall waving grass, a pretty stream bordered with shrubs and tall trees flowing through it, and the majestic mountain standing guard over all in its snowy coat.

They found it not only beautiful but also fertile soil. The third generation of Longmires is making a good living off this land. I hope to start doing the same soon. I will keep you advised as events develop. Please write and let me know what is going on back home.

Your loving son, Lawrence."

Due to several bankrupt farms in the Yelm community over that past year, Lawrence and May found an available fifty-acre farm with a three-bedroom house. The owners had moved to Olympia in late summer. They quickly came to reasonable terms, and by the 1st of February, 1895, the Byrnes settled into their own house.

With help from Gus and May, Lawrence started repairing fences, securing the chicken coop, cleaning out the barn, inventorying equipment, making lists of what needed replacing, and determining how much acreage would need to be readied for spring planting. They counseled with the Longmires and other farmers about what, conservatively, should be planted. The first animals to acquire would be chickens, sheep, a bull, and a handful of cows. At least they'd have meat and eggs later in the year.

The state of the economy proved stressful for everyone. Having just made a cross-country move, entered a new marriage, and acquired a new farm, Lawrence knew he needed to assess his finances seriously. He must tighten his belt, not spend his cash. He thought he should not plant crops with spring upon them until this panic ended. The two Belgian horses were his most valuable resource. Maybe he should use them to generate income since everyone in the county had expressed admiration. May and Gus could plant and tend a garden for the family's use, care for their few animals, and hang on until farm commodities started moving again. This situation had to end eventually.

In the summer of 1897, lots of gold was discovered around the Klondike River region of the Yukon in Alaska which turned the economic tide for the Pacific Northwest. Thousands of prospectors poured into Seattle, which became the outfitting capital for those venturing into the wilds to seek their fortune. Miners needed food to last them for months as they advanced north. Suddenly, farmers in Washington had a ready market for their crops. The influx of people needing supplies impacted every corner of the market, and cash started flowing again.

Grandpa James Longmire barely lived to hear the good news. He died that September in Tacoma at the age of seventy-seven while visiting his son, Robert, and his wife, Amy.

For the first time, on August 1, Lawrence planted thirty of his fifty acres in wheat Ten acres were planted in fall vegetables because he figured there would be a market in Tacoma or Seattle. When the wheat was harvested in the spring, he would use Polly, Molly and his wagon to haul his wheat and that of his neighbors, who needed help, to storehouses in the community to await rail transportation.

Two years later, it proved to be a milestone for the Byrne family. On February 5, 1899, May gave birth to Norman Terrell, making Lawrence a father again, seventeen years after Gus was born.

Gus graduated from high school in early May. He never forgot the thrill of riding cross-country on the train. He knew the Northern Pacific Railroad ran across the northern United States and learned that it had a division in Tacoma. He wrote the manager, Mr. Gilbert, explaining his background, what piqued his interest, and why he'd like to spend his career with the railroad. To his delight, he received a response inviting him to Tacoma for an interview.

His Papa handed him a list of items he needed from Tacoma. The previous week was May's birthday, and Lawrence asked his son to buy a new dress for a late present. Gus immediately went to his grandmother's house for advice on size. Also, where should he go for women's and men's clothes in Tacoma? He wanted to get himself a new suit for his job interview.

"Now, why do you need to spend money on a new suit just for an interview?" Aunt Mabel asked.

"Because I just have one suit, and the sleeves come halfway up to my elbows I've grown so much," Gus laughed.

"I'm sure the boy has a point there," said his grandmother, Sophrona.

"Besides, I need a nice suit to come to your wedding, Aunt Mabel."

"Ha! I'm not going to marry, Boy. When you get married, you have babies. And Lord knows I've helped raise more than enough babies right here under this roof. No, I'm perfectly content to live my life without a man and without young'uns of my own hanging all over me, wanting to be fed all the time, asking questions, and making all manner of demands," Mabel declared.

Grandpa John, who'd come in and sat down in his rocker, laughed and said, "Gus, you stepped right into that one. When are you going to Tacoma?"

"I'll leave on the twenty-first. I'm taking the wagon because Papa needs supplies."

John asked, "Mind if I add a couple of things to the supply list?"

"Of course not."

"Who is going with you?"

"Far as I know, I'm going by myself," said Gus.

"Probably not a good idea for a young man with a wagon of supplies to be driving alone on that road from Tacoma back down here," Grandpa John explained. "Robbers have been known to operate along there. You need somebody riding shotgun with a shotgun handy. I don't know why Walter couldn't ride up there with you or maybe George or one of Elcaine's boys."

Two weeks later, on a Monday, Uncle Walter spent a day in Tacoma rounding up supplies for the family. Meanwhile, Gus entered a menswear store and found a nice-looking business suit. They agreed to alter it by the next afternoon when he explained his circumstances. Unexpectedly, he purchased his first pair of black dress boots with socks. He then found a women's clothing store, described his mother, where they lived, and described her lifestyle. The saleslady helped him choose a pretty dress he thought May could wear when she went to events off the farm.

They found a blacksmith the next day and left the horses to get shod. He took Walter by the women's store, and he decided he had better go ahead and get his wife, Mamie, her Christmas present. He bought a blouse and skirt, as worn by the saleslady. Something simple but comfortably elegant looking, unlike anything she had. Mamie would love it. While he was at it, he bought nightgowns for his mother and grandmother for Christmas. The pair then meandered up to the waterfront and ate seafood for lunch, a rare treat. They spent time on the docks watching a flurry of activity before heading back late afternoon to retrieve the horses. When Gus tried on his suit and looked in the mirror, he found it perfectly tailored.

"Damn! Brother, I'd say on looks alone, you've got this interview in the bag," Walter said. "Very sharp. What time did you say it's scheduled?"

"Eleven o'clock in the morning."

"That's perfect. You can eat breakfast, then run over to that barber shop up the street from our room for a haircut and a shave. Come back and get dressed. And easily be on time."

The next day, Gus found himself sitting across a desk from a man not much older than his father. He told him he would be willing to seek additional education if necessary, but he'd like a job on a train. Someday, he said, perhaps he could be a general freight and passenger agent or even an engineer.

Mr. Gilbert sat back and smiled as if sizing him up. He said, "Augustus, someday that might be possible. But for now, how would you like to be a server on our Columbia and Puget Sound Railroad? Since it's a relatively short route, the dining car offers drinks and light fare. You'd learn a lot in there about life on a train."

"Yes, sir. That sounds wonderful."

"Good. Be here at the office on June 12. We'll have a couple of other new hires. That day you'll go through an orientation. Then we will get you started."

"Thank you so much, Mr. Gilbert. I'll see you then."

Lawrence knew this day would come, but he did not expect it to be so soon. It seemed that almost overnight, God blessed him with a new son, and then took one away. He was simultaneously thrilled and wounded. His best help on the farm disappeared. Being born with two sets of Byrne genes, the boy was already two inches taller than Lawrence, six feet even, and strong from working on the farm.

Lawrence bought another twenty acres for the animals from his neighbors to the west. For the next twelve years, he would sometimes substitute oats or flax for part of his wheat acreage. And he started dedicating five acres to Irish potatoes. May took care of the chickens and tended a herd of sheep, which they tried to limit to about twenty. Every March, the two of them sheared sheep, bundled the wool, labeled it, and handed it off to Elcaine or one of his sons, who picked up sheep's wool from other Longmire families to add to their own before hauling a wagon load up to Tacoma. He sold it to a shop owner there, whose family spun and wove it.

May also started tending a second son when James Gordon Byrne arrived June 24, 1901. One or the other of her two sisters, , Eva and Mabel, who remained spinsters, came during the days to help with the baby, toddler Norman, and the house, to free up their mother for her chores around the farm. Of course, she didn't get too far from the house because baby James wanted to be fed on a regular schedule.

For a while now, Lawrence has studied the profitability of fruit crops relative to production expenses. Through continuing consultation with Washington State Agricultural College specialists, he determined the potential for increased profits with fruit crops. However, production, marketing, and financial analysis showed western Washington to be a marginal location for such an operation. For one thing, berry plants are susceptible to spring frost.

In 1910, Lawrence heard about the organization of the Wyandotte Land Company in Butte County, California. Managed by Timothy Hornung, the company's objective was to buy, sell, improve, and develop orchards in the Wyandotte and Bangor sections of the county. Butte County lay in the state's Central Valley, known as the thermal belt. Olive production flourished there.

The Wyandotte Land Company owned 3,985 acres. About 500 acres had already been developed into orange, lemon, and olive groves.

What attracted Mr. Hornung to the area in 1909 was the potential for expansion of water rights of the old South Feather Water and Union Mining Company, which he reorganized into the South Feather Land and Water Company. The company started acquiring the rights and titles to numerous small streams. It also secured about seventy-five miles of pipelines, flumes, and canals from the former company. Ranchers in the area became the beneficiaries of this water.

Lawrence decided the opportunity to become a fruit farmer in California was now. He headed down to Butte County to investigate the opportunity. He considered negotiating for acreage already planted with three-year-old olive trees. He thought almond trees would be a nice compliment. But he wanted to sit across from Mr. Hornung and evaluate what lay ahead long-term.

At fifty-two, Lawrence experienced pain, especially in his joints and back. It had not bothered him in previous years. He knew he should, perhaps, slow down a bit. His boys were eleven and nine. It would be another five or six years before they could contribute substantial help. He figured he could go another ten years without serious consequences.

When Lawrence arrived at the Wyandotte Land Company, he was shocked to be greeted by a man who looked to be Gus's age. In fact, Timothy Hornung was three years older. The son of German immigrants who came west from his parents' farm in Illinois, Mr. Hornung was smart, college-educated, opportunistic, insightful, honest, and, as it turned out, trustworthy.

When Lawrence was seated and began talking about his life, Mr. Hornung immediately thought that Mr. Byrne reminded him of his oldest brother, who he missed. However, none of his seven living brothers and sisters followed him to California. He could use family intimacy and trust with personnel in his business, but he had to operate on gut instinct.

After talking, the men got in one of the company's two new Mack trucks and toured the properties. Mr. Hornung explained inputs, the expected time for trees to bear fruit, the needed output in order to make a profit, survey results of their reservoir sites and canals, sources of outside help, and more.

Tim Hornung needed someone he could trust to serve as a liaison between the company and farmers in the area. He liked Lawrence's personality and temperament. It was obvious he understood general agriculture. He asked intelligent questions in response to information received in the field. He decided he would ask Lawrence to accompany him for the next couple of days and take notes on everything he observed, including conversations that would take place.

Lawrence went into the office on the third day, which was a Friday.

"Have a seat, Mr. Byrne. I have a proposition for you. I understand you came here with the idea of buying property and farming. Let me run an alternative by you. Honestly, it would take five to ten years for you to get up and running to build a profitable business. At your age, I am not certain that's what you truly want to do. With children still in the house, I'm guessing you need income for your family. I am also guessing that, physically, your body doesn't want to do the work it once did.

"Now, I would like to hire you into the business. I need someone with your intelligence, your knowledge of agriculture, and your personality to function as a link between me and our farmers. That's why I had you ride with me these couple of days and take notes. I wanted to see your powers of observation. Your notes are impressive. Exactly the feedback I need to have every day. What is going on with who, where, when?"

Lawrence didn't know how to feel. Give up farming? But wait. Was this a blessing in disguise? He realized that Mr. Hornung had quit talking and was sitting there smiling at him.

"You'll be amply rewarded for your efforts. And, of course, you will be provided with a vehicle to drive."

"That, sir, is a proposition I will seriously consider," Lawrence replied.

"You take the weekend to think about it."

Lawrence knew the answer even as he debated it back and forth with himself over the next two days. He met with Mr. Hornung Monday morning and accepted his offer. It was now mid-September. They agreed on November 5 as a start date.

Before he headed back home, Lawrence wanted to let Mr. Hornung know what he had in mind for housing. He told him that his wife would want to continue raising chickens and probably a few sheep. He wanted his boys to stay active on the land. He asked him to keep an eye out for around ten acres of grass with a three-bedroom house.

May seemed oddly relieved when Lawrence explained his unexpected job situation in California. They would have more money coming in than they ever had. She realized her husband no longer had the pep in his step he used to, and, on occasion, saw him grimace, so she knew he was in pain, although he denied it.

Fortunately, the Byrnes sold their property in Yelm to their neighbors and their animals to family members. They shipped their belongings by Southern Pacific rail from Tacoma to Sacramento. On October 23, they arrived in Wyandotte. The house they closed on earlier in the month sat back from the road on fifteen acres of grassland. There was a small stream on the back side, a tributary of the North Fork of the Feather River.

A couple of weeks after Lawrence started his new job, he met James Seadler, vice president of Wyandotte Land Company. The conversation turned to duck hunting. Butte County is a vital winter site for waterfowl, geese, ducks, and swans, migrating through the Pacific Flyway. Lawrence had primarily hunted small game but he was interested in learning to hunt birds. He knew he needed a good dog. Mr. Seadler advised him to visit his brother in nearby Chico, who bred, trained, and sold German Shorthaired Pointers.

There was a more immediate reason he wanted a couple of good dogs. The terrain in Butte County crawled with rattlesnakes. He talked to his boys about paying close attention to where they stepped and where they put their hands every time they went outside. But a Pointer to accompany them would scout the area ahead, stop, and point to anything in the grass. If a snake should strike, the dogs were more than capable of killing one. Lawrence also wanted one of the dogs to accompany him as he visited and walked over the territory.

A huge surprise came to the family in a little bundle in 1914. California Bell Byrne arrived on September 7, much to her mother's relief. They called her Callie. Lawrence and May long surrendered the thought of ever having another child. May suffered through the hot, dry summers that started in early June and lasted through September. Carrying this baby for the final three months in ninety-degree temperatures put a stop to activities that even hinted at exertion. Luckily, the boys were old enough to assume responsibility for the animals when school ended.

Baby Callie did not like the heat any more than her mother. She came out squalling, and her presence would forever be felt. She remained vocal. Her father said later that she was his little whirlwind.

※ ※ ※

Four years later, it was time for the Byrnes to move back north. Norman had been out of high school for a year already. He had been accepted to the University of Oregon in Eugene. May had tolerated the heat in Wyandotte longer than she wanted to.

Eugene lies in the heart of the Willamette Valley. Known for its highly fertile soil, it became an early destination for pioneers heading west. The Willamette River, which flows the entire 150-mile length of the valley, flows right through the middle of Lane County and Eugene. It is known for exceptional berry production. Lawrence and May agreed that a small acreage close to Eugene and the river, where they could grow blueberries, strawberries, and raspberries, would be doable. No farm animals. Just fruit. And, hopefully, no rattlesnakes for a rambunctious four-year-old girl to encounter.

The family landed in the Glenwood community between Eugene and Springfield in mid-June 1918. It was an agricultural area with established fruit trees. Their six-acre property is nestled between a farmer growing cherry and plum trees and another with a significant acreage of filbert or hazelnut trees. The Willamette River flowed within sight of their house, which had been the old homestead of their neighbor's family, the Robinettes, who had farmed this land for three generations. The younger Robinette, David, had long since built his own home down the road and decided to sell the property when his father, Henry, died in the spring. They had not planted the small, long, narrow acreage in order to give the old man privacy and quiet.

A call for help went out, and apparently, the family considered Eugene to be within striking distance. May's letters let it be known that Lawrence's arthritis restricted his ability to farm full-time. May's sister, Mabel, said she'd be coming to Oregon "with bells on."

Sister Eva would undoubtedly have come with her, but they tragically lost her in the winter of 1914. She had spent the night in town with Uncle Frank and Aunt Louisa. Snow fell overnight. That morning, she cut through a field and her horse stepped in a hole, and came up lame. She slowly walked him back to the farm. Within days, a cold turned into pneumonia, and they were not able to draw it out of her.

Six months earlier, their mother, Sophrona, suffered an appendicitis attack. There was no surgeon in Yelm. Just one doctor and an Indian midwife, which many mothers preferred to go to. They tried to get Sophrona to the hospital in Tacoma, but her appendix burst after they reached town, and she died an agonizing death at the hospital.

When May's sister, Anna Lee, who lived with her family in Olympia, received notice that the Byrnes were moving up to Eugene in June and needed help, she was beside herself with excitement. She wanted so badly to see May after an eight-year absence. In February, Anna Lee gave birth to little Winston after thinking that Ginny, born in 1910, was her last child. Her eldest daughter, Ethel, was eighteen and volunteered to look after the infant while her mother was gone. Even though Ethel would be married in December, she had been ten when Ginny was born and, thus, had no experience with babies as an adult. Therefore, Anna Lee arranged to keep Winston with Maggie, her youngest brother Bud's wife. Maggie and Bud had a six-year-old son of their own and readily agreed.

Also promising to assist Lawrence's family in settling onto their Eugene farm was his brother Lemuel's wife, Anna, and their older son, Thad. The lad had just finished high school and thought he would enjoy getting back to his Callow family's farming roots for a month or so in Oregon. Besides, he and his brother had only gotten to spend time with his Byrne cousins twice when his family visited Yelm, and all the boys were children then. He told his mother it would be good to leave Seattle and see a new country.

Anna and Thad arrived on the last day of June amid a swirl of activity in and around the house. Sisters Mabel and Anna Lee arrived two days later. Lawrence and May found a two-story farmhouse inhabited for two decades by a widower who paid little attention to details. Not only was intense cleaning first on the agenda but carpentry skills were also needed inside. The outside could wait. The kitchen needed immediate help to be functional. A new stove and refrigerator came from Eugene within a week of their arrival.

The Robinette family invited their new neighbors, along with every other farm family in Glenwood, it seemed, to their 4th of July party. It felt good for all ten of the Byrnes and visiting family to bathe, dress up, and socialize for the day. May took a bowl of marinated olives they brought from California, a welcomed and unique contribution to an immense food table. For nearly a decade, two brothers and their families from Mexico had worked for the Robinettes. Manuel and Leticia Flores, as well as Javier and Araceli Flores, lived on the property. A couple of years earlier, their younger cousins, Eduardo and Gloria Flores and Jorge and Silvia Martinez, came up and joined them. Every year on this holiday, Manuel and Javier slow-roasted pigs in a pit the Yucateca way called Cochinita Pibil. It was the most delicious pork any of the Byrnes had ever tasted. The wives made black beans, pickled red onions, habanero salsa, and hot corn tortillas to serve with it.

Lawrence informed the congregated neighbors that he wanted to plant berries and welcomed suggestions or assistance. He said seedlings for a vegetable garden were needed right away. He let it be known that they had to find a couple of carpenters and wanted to buy a used tractor and plow.

Lawrence and May soon discovered just how accommodating their new neighbors were. Norman, nineteen, James, seventeen, and cousin Thad, seventeen, were the first to meet a member of the Davidson family at the Robinette's party. Ben Davidson, also nineteen, introduced them to other teenagers. When Ben realized that this was the family who had bought old man Robinette's property, he introduced the boys to his parents since their property sat practically right behind the Byrnes'. Norman then walked Mr. and Mrs. Davidson over and introduced them to his parents. A rather lengthy conversation ensued.

The next day, Robert Davidson and his two sons, Ben and Leland, fourteen, showed up after breakfast with two tractors, one attached to a mower, the other to a plow. It felt like a godsend. While they had help, everything needed to be sped up, and this would do it. First, Leland mowed the area where they wanted a vegetable garden, then proceeded around the rest of the acreage. Ben had the garden area plowed in no time. The two men walked to the far end of the property, where Lawrence considered planting the berries. The house and barn sat in the middle of the six acres.

Therefore, Robert suggested planting blueberries in the front because it was closer to the river. He thought blackberries and strawberries would grow well on the back property.

The unfortunate but not completely unexpected news was this: despite the cooler-than-usual weather this year, it was too late to plant blackberries or strawberries. Those require spring planting. However, blueberries could be planted in the fall. Robert suggested Lawrence go ahead and plow the front acreage and work the soil in preparation for planting blueberries around the first of October or earlier.

Lawrence immediately knew that if it would be two years before their berries started bearing fruit, vegetables would need to be planted. Robert agreed with this resolution for income. He generously agreed to leave the one tractor until Lawrence plowed what ground he needed for production.

The boys were available to plant an acre of cabbage, cauliflower, and carrots. Next month, collards, Swiss chard, and leeks would go in the ground on a second acre. In September, broccoli, onions, and leaf lettuces should flourish on another acre. By then, school threatened to put a kink in the operation. Without the help of Norman and James through the week, temporary help loomed as a necessity until the blueberry bushes were planted.

The day after the Davidsons brought their tractors, another neighbor stopped by to tell the Byrnes about a woman in town who owned a good-sized greenhouse. She was certain this woman, Cheryl Milner, would still have vegetable seedlings and transplants available.

Then, David Robinette brought Jorge Martinez by on Saturday. "Lawrence, I understand you need carpenters," said David.

"I do. You know the state of this house, and I want to get it shored up before we get all our furniture moved in. It needs repairs inside and out, but right now, I'm concerned with what needs to be done inside."

"Jorge here, and his wife, came up from Mexico two years ago with his sister, Gloria, and brother-in-law, Eduardo. I believe you remember them from the 4th. "

"I sure do. They were helping their cousins with some mighty tasty cooking."

"Well, Jorge is a pretty fine wood worker. He has built me a couple of sheds since he's been here and completed several other smaller carpentry jobs. Eduardo helped him with most of those. I've offered them a couple of weeks off from my place to come over here and help with whatever you need. They have agreed."

"You are a good man, David, and a very good neighbor. That's an offer I'm going to take you up on. I absolutely need the help," Lawrence said. "I'll pay them at least what you do."

"I'll send them over here early Monday morning. ¿Hablas Español? Well, their English is still barely passable. I'll have Manuel come with them so you can explain exactly what you want them to do. He'll interpret in case there's a question. Then Manuel will leave. I do not anticipate a problem."

"Jorge, you speak English good enough to get along okay here, don't you?"

"Sí, Señor Robinette. We do alright," said Jorge.

Anna loved being in this Oregon farming community. She'd grown up in rural western Washington and didn't realize how much she missed getting her hands in the soil and starting the process of new growth.

One day, Norman took Chad to the university, where he attended an orientation session. Chad, who thought he wanted to enroll in the University of Washington, came back highly impressed, thinking he might consider coming to Eugene instead.

When Anna and her son returned home to Seattle, she burst into her husband's study with a plea: "Oh, Lem, let's get out of the city. I want to move to Eugene where the people are so friendly, there are fruit trees everywhere, I could play in that rich soil with May, the winters would be milder . . ."

Lemuel couldn't help but laugh. "Sweetie, I'm thinking you had a good visit. And surely, you're going to come over here and give me a kiss."

Anna rushed to her husband and gave him a long hug.

"I have missed you. I wish you had been there with us. It was a wonderful, long family reunion. May and I truly bonded. It was good having Anna Lee and Mabel there, too. Chad can tell you all about it. He enjoyed his work on the farm, but he plans to send his transcripts to the University of Oregon."

"Lawrence suffers from his arthritis. The pain in his knees and back prevents him from doing everything he needs to do. He's stubborn, though. He's consulting medical specialists affiliated with the university.

"I am serious about relocating to Eugene. It would mean the world to Lawrence if he could have his brother back in his life again. And I believe you'd benefit equally. He's your blood, Lem. You have been in such close proximity yet seen so little of each other since coming out here," said Anna.

"You're right, of course," Lemuel responded. "Thad is ready to enter college, and Leon will be right behind him. Since I practice inheritance law, I can establish clientele anywhere. We can start wrapping up things here if you truly want to go. We'll talk to the boys."

It was in January 1921 before Lemuel and Anna moved to Eugene. They found a house on the edge of downtown with a second-side entrance. Lemuel set up his law office in a couple of rooms there. Thad had enrolled at the University of Oregon in the spring of 1919 to pursue a degree in education. Leon stayed in Seattle, starting studies at the University of Washington in the English Department in the fall of 1920. He then studied journalism at the University of Oregon before becoming a reporter for the Oregonian.

Lawrence and May were thrilled to have their family in Lane County. Their berries would fruit for the first time this season. Anna looked forward to helping with the harvest. She was amazed at the progress made on the farm in the two and a half years since Thad and she came down. The house looked so clean now that it was repaired and painted. A small greenhouse allowed May to grow her own starter vegetable plants.

Norman worked on his undergraduate degree in anthropology at the university. James always demonstrated an aptitude for tools. He liked taking things apart and putting them back together. He could repair anything. Now he was repairing people's machinery and making a business out of it. He would not start college until after his brother graduated. When the berries were expected to ripen, James, Norman, and Thad would be in the fields, helping every minute they could spare.

That fall, much to everyone's joy, Gus visited on his way to Oakland, California, where he was being transferred by the railroad. For the first time, the family met his wife, Annie, who came from Hardin County in West Tennessee. They met in 1902 when Annie, then twenty-four, was staying in Seattle with her father, George Harrison, and brother, Albert, twenty, while traveling through the Pacific Northwest. Gus and Annie were immediately smitten with each other. To her father's consternation, she refused to continue the trip with her family, staying in Seattle. Four months later, she married this tall, handsome Westerner with Tennessee roots. The couple remained childless.

Mid-morning on October 27, 1922, young Callie, who had turned eight the previous month, was met by her ever-present dog whining and spinning in circles around her. The dog wanted to run to the back property. Callie followed and found her father lying amongst the blackberry trellises. He was not moving. He did not respond to her pleas to wake up. She ran screaming back to the house. Her mother met her at the back door.

Lawrence Jared Byrne died of a heart attack that morning. He had two full seasons of successful berry production. Their little farm in Eugene made him a happy man.

May was more content there than she'd ever been. She claimed this as her home. She would proceed with their plans and see if she could make a go of it with seasonal hired help and assistance she knew would come from her wonderfully generous neighbors, who were now friends.

Norman had just married Elizabeth de Gomree that September. They then left for Los Angeles, where he pursued a graduate degree in anthropology at UCLA. Lemuel and Anna stayed in Eugene until 1925, when they moved back to Seattle, although Anna returned every spring for a month to help May get her vegetable transplants in the ground and start pruning the berries. James married Catherine Stuplere from Portland two years later. Their daughter and May's only grandchild, Barbara, was born in May 1931 in Berkeley, California, where they were then living.

May traveled to Yelm in February to see her father and those siblings still there. At sixty-nine, John Longmire was just six years older than her husband would have been. He still looked amazingly strong and rugged. The old house felt warm. She needed this love to enfold her.

May talked Mabel into coming to Eugene. The sisters had always been close. Now that they were both single and into middle age, there was no good reason why they should not live together. Elcaine's youngest daughter, Mattie, lived in the house with her grandfather. Martha "Mattie" L. Longmire Stute would live to be 109 years old.

The Byrnes offered a "pick your own" operation for their strawberries and blackberries to save on labor costs. However, they continued harvesting blueberries and selling them on what remained a strong market. The year after Mabel moved in, May decided to buy a flock of chickens to teach her daughter the responsibility of maintaining the animals. Callie was thrilled with their egg production. She put a sign up on the road and sold eggs on the farm. However, the first bird to get its neck wrung to go into the pot caused the girl trauma. Soon enough, though, she realized that farm animals were destined for the dinner table.

Mabel passed away in June 1940 from uterine cancer. In March 1944, Lemuel died of heart failure at the Byrne's vacation cottage in Grays Harbor, an estuarine bay on the southwest coast of Washington. Five months later, Anna followed him. The housekeeper found her one morning after she had slipped away in her sleep.

May Longmire Byrne lived on her farm in Eugene until a stroke killed her in June 1953. She was seventy-six. Surprisingly, Callie, then thirty-eight, stayed with her mother and helped with the farm. She would not marry until 1964. At the time of their mother's death, Norman was a professor of anthropology at Los Angeles City College. James worked for the Pacific Telephone and Telegraph Company as a technician in Salem, Oregon's capital.

Lawrence lay in his field that late October morning, thirty-one years before his wife would leave this earth, after being brought down with sudden and intense pain on the left side of his chest. It felt crushing. Dizziness prevented all thoughts from rising. He looked up in the crystal blue Oregon sky and thought for a split second about the seasonal rains coming soon.

Nowhere would he rather be. He dug his fingers into the earth. He closed his eyes, and his entire life flashed before him. He came West in search of an opportunity to become more than if he had stayed put. Never could he have imagined that he would find a wife and a different family that was so loving and supportive. The fertile soils of western Washington and the Willamette Valley in Oregon made farming a pleasure. The people God put in his path enriched him and his family. All his children brought him joy. He faded away a blessed man.

A True Sense of Gratitude

Goodner (Byrne)

Excerpt of a letter from George W. (G.W.) Goodner to brother William J. Goodner, St. Clair County, IL. March 28, 1861

> "The political sky is very dark. Every corner of the union seems to be in a perpetual commotion. The devil is in the people, and it is beyond comprehension where it will all end or how. I wonder what the good Lord is going to do with us all anyhow. Some are for Paul, some for Apollis and some for Jeff Davis. My mind is that the devil has pretty well run his course. That the time will soon be that he will be chained. As that time nears, he will be more malicious in the hearts of the people."

September 1863, Adams County, Illinois

The timing darn sure could have been better. Just goes to show what little control we have, he thought. If God, in His infinite wisdom, knows what He is doing amongst the turmoil this country finds itself in, He surely must be the only one who does.

Reverend Benjamin Goodner stood on a ladder perched against branches of an apple tree amid one of his eldest son's orchards, staring into a brilliant blue mid-September sky and pondering the dichotomy of life. On a beautiful, idyllic morning such as this, a body might think fear would grant a man a reprieve. Part of him wanted to question the strength of his faith. The rational part of his brain, however, understood that the outcome of war is heavily contingent upon mortal men with diverse agendas.

He heard workers occasionally yell back and forth to each other, dogs barking, and children laughing. Horse hooves clomped on the driveway, announcing a new arrival. "Grandpa, you alright?"

Benjamin shifted his gaze down into clear, blue ten-year-old eyes that mirrored his own.

"Yes, Daniel. But I'm coming down to empty this load and get a drink of that water you're hauling there."

"Then you might as well come to the house because Aunt Jeanetta will have dinner on pretty quick. I think she has been doing most of the cooking today because Aunt Salinda is plumb-tuckered carrying that baby."

"You are right about that, son. Traveling up here so close to when she is supposed to birth that child probably did not do her a lick of good, but she wanted to be close to your mother and Aunt Jeanetta. Of course, your mama just had baby Florence, so she shouldn't be doing much right now. Even though your Uncle John is a doctor, he's away from the house tending to patients, and your Aunt Salinda did not want to be by herself so much. She's sure not alone around here."

Benjamin reached the ground, picked up the dipper from the water bucket, and took a long drink.

"I'd say Doc Lacey would rather be up here in Payson with his wife, but he knows Dr. Mueller has years of experience birthing babies, and he's on call for another one here. He delivered all of you, and you turned out alright."

"Well, yes, I did, but what about Lewis?"

"Ha! Now, Daniel, I'd suggest you not voice that opinion aloud. Your Papa, and I know your Mama, would take exception. There's a what, a five-year difference between you and your brother? You want to be big and strong enough to defend yourself if you offend another man. And you better be right quick, too. If I was in your shoes, I would not be scrapping with Lewis just yet."

Benjamin turned away from his grandson to watch other workers in the trees so the boy could not see his big smile. The youngster was, in fact, smart, with a sense of humor. His grandfather liked his chances in life.

As the pair strolled toward the house, they saw bushels full of apples lining the sloped rows between trees. It was Saturday, so extra help showed up early this morning, including young teenagers normally in school throughout the week.

The summer months were characterized by relatively moderate temperatures and sunny days. Trees responded to these ideal conditions with a banner crop.

The ongoing war resulted in men continuing to enroll as soldiers. Farmers in this heavily agricultural mid-state area worried whether the necessary labor for planting and harvesting would be available since no one knew how long the military struggle would last.

Thus far, the Lord has bestowed His blessings on fruit producers. Thousands of bushels of apples were being transported in Quincy, located adjacent to Adams County. Situated on bluffs overlooking a nearly one-mile expanse of the Mississippi River, Quincy featured a transportation center second to none in the state. Riverboats and rail service carried agricultural products, among others, to destinations west, and into Chicago.

The Goodners and their neighbors received thirty to thirty-five cents per bushel and $4 per barrel from apple cider with the barrels furnished. Benjamin's son, William, purchased part of another orchard in Adams County earlier in the year.

William's wife, Jeanetta, along with family and friends, canned and dried apples for their winter diet. There would be plenty of apples to turn into cider, pies, and, of course, apple butter.

Just as Benjamin and young Daniel reached the two-story clapboard farmhouse, one of the girls rang the dinner bell. To their left, several wooden tables with slat seats were pushed together under a pair of large, old oak trees. Soon, women would bring dishes out to set on the tables, which had been simply decorated with various flowers picked from the gardens.

"Daniel, how come you're loafin'," teased his cousin, Laura, two years younger.

"I've come down to refill my water bucket and I brought Grandpa to dinner. You think you need to be checkin' up on me?"

Benjamin walked up three steps and into the house. He recognized the visitor as Horatio Eyman. His heart skipped a beat for a second, but there were smiles all around and no apparent tension in the air.

Realizing he had not bothered going behind the house to wash in galvanized tubs set up for that purpose, he rubbed his hands hard over his work pants and, apologetically, extended his hand toward his old friend.

A buzz of activity flew between the front door and the kitchen. He thought the predominant smell was roasted chicken, which suited him just fine.

"Amy, find something to get that cornbread out of the skillets in the outside oven and into serving baskets. Then cover them with towels and get them on the tables out there, please," said Salinda Lacy, Benjamin's youngest daughter, who was about to give him another grandchild.

"Horatio, come outside. I assume you've already washed up. Let me do the same and we'll sit down and eat. Then we can talk," Benjamin said as the men ambled onto the porch.

The family patriarch walked around to the back of the house and, once again, he thought about Nancy, his beloved wife, who they lost eighteen years ago to a bout of cholera. She did not live to see her grandchildren. Not one.

Benjamin's father, Conrad Goodner, immigrated from Germany with his parents about 1765. His mother, Elizabeth Scherer, was born five years after her German parents settled in east Guilford County, North Carolina, in the mid-1700s with other Reformed German and Lutherans. Hardscrabble North Carolina soil proved resistant to farming. Conrad knew that good soil awaited them somewhere in a country the size that this one was supposed to be,.

In the late 1780s, many families moved out of the area and headed west, primarily due to a faltering economy. The Goodner, Scherer, Jackson, and Goddard families were among a group that settled over the mountains in Sullivan County, North Carolina, known as the State of Franklin when they arrived.

Eight out of the twelve Goodner children, including Benjamin were born in Sullivan County. They lived in the mountainous area for sixteen years. However, it became the first of four stops on the way west before the family arrived in St. Clair County, Illinois, a section called the "Land of Goshen" and the "Land of Promise." This is good land, Conrad decided, begging to be farmed.

When the family arrived in 1815, Benjamin was twenty years old. He harbored no doubts about who he wanted for his wife.

In 1801, William Jackson drowned in the Watauga River when he fell and hit his head on a rock during a hunting trip. Two years later, his wife, Catherine Goodner Jackson, died from pneumonia. The Goodners immediately took in Mary, eight, and Nancy, five, suddenly orphaned since Catherine had been Conrad's sister.

Little Nancy adored Benjamin as a child, and he loved her mischievous nature and laugh. Their closeness grew through the years, and even though they were first cousins, by the time their teenage years stretched out, it became clear to everyone that a lasting love had developed.

They married in 1816 among old friends who had arrived in Illinois before the Goodners. Present were new friends, many of whom were Germans in a surprisingly large historic belt of German settlement along the Mississippi River in Illinois counties extending into the Missouri Rhineland.

Benjamin found local Irishmen to provide music at the wedding as a surprise for Nancy. Ian McCracken played "Madame Cole" on his Celtic harp for the processional. O'Carolan composed the piece in 1719 for Madame Cole on her wedding day. Ian and his cronies willingly agreed to come and play gratis, with perhaps a dram or two thrown in, when they discovered their music was to honor William Jackson (who immigrated to these shores from Antrim, Ireland), his parents, Samuel Jackson and Martha Vateau of Antrim, and all of their ancestors whose lives together made it possible for Nancy Jackson to be in this time and place.

Temperatures were in the sixties on that magnificent sunny April afternoon. Trees showed shades of increasing green. Dozens of species of ducks continued to migrate north and were joined by loons, which created a consonance of sounds all their own.

Benjamin's bride radiated beauty, wonder, and love for all that God had bestowed on her. They had already spent thirteen years together as best friends and now they would have twenty-nine more to raise their family. Not a day went by that Benjamin failed to thank God for such a miraculous gift.

"Reverend Goodner, it's good to see you," said a young, lanky teenager with cropped dark red hair and the start of a scraggly beard.

"Why, hello, Thomas. Thanks for taking a day off to give us a hand getting this apple harvest in. We've about got more work than we have help to get it done."

"Yes, sir, I'd say that's right."

"I hear your father and James both left out with the 116th Regiment in late summer."

'They did, and Ma is none too happy about it. She told Pa before he left that when he married her and started laying us young'uns on her, his job was to support us, not to run off trying to get himself kilt in a war that oughtn't be happening in the first place."

"I will include you and your family in my prayers, son. When you leave today, find a poke and fill it with apples to carry to your ma."

"Thank ya kindly, but she won't want any charity, Reverend Goodner."

"Then tell her we have so many; those apples would have just ended up rotting on the ground, and you know that's the truth."

"You're a good man, sir. A good neighbor."

"Let's go eat, boy."

When Benjamin got to the tables, more than two dozen people were seated. He stood at one end, removed his hat, looked down the length of the table at his family and neighbors with a true sense of gratitude, bowed his head, gave thanks for all present, and asked for the safe return of those who were not.

"My friend, I know good news is a little hard to come by these days, but I hope you have some to share," Benjamin said as the two fathers settled into wicker chairs on the front porch of the house after the meal.

All three of Horatio Eyman's sons enlisted in the Union Army in Harristown, Macon County, in July 1862. The following month, George Goodner, one of Benjamin's sons, was sworn into service with the 116th Regiment in Decatur, as hundreds of men, including many other Germans, stepped up to fight the Confederacy. Few secessionists stuck their necks out in this part of the country, which was heavily Democratic. George's brother, Benton, mustered in as an orderly sergeant with the 9th Regiment Missouri Calvary Volunteers in November 1861.

On January 10, Captain Lewis Eyman was shot through the heart with a minié ball in the Battle of Arkansas Post, part of the Vicksburg campaign in Mississippi. The Union Army easily captured a strategically located fort at Arkansas Post with the victory. Captain Eyman carried one of his men off the field and returned to retrieve another when he was killed. Then, on June 7, Edward Eyman died fighting at Milliken's Bend, a decisive victory for the Union Army in another important battle of the Vicksburg campaign. News came to their parents that same month that their other son, John, lay very sick in a St. Louis hospital.

"Well, Benjamin, I went to St. Louis, and I'm not sure but what John may have some brain damage from being so sick. You know he came down with malaria, I guess from being exposed to all those blasted mosquitoes in Mississippi and, mercifully, they did not just let him die down there. They got him up to the hospital in St. Louis. But he slid into a coma that lasted nigh on to a month. Didn't think he was goin' to make it. By some miracle, he woke up the first of August and a couple a weeks ago the doc told me to bring him on home."

"Good news, Horatio," said Benjamin. "I had not heard."

"You remember we nearly lost his mother last year to typhoid fever, and I do not know whether she's strong enough to look after him. She's still heartbroken over losing our Marthey to typhoid this spring, as we all are. I don't know if she is going to survive all this. Three children in the ground this year and a fourth come mighty close to it," Horatio continued.

"If there is a silver lining, it's that, God willing, we will not be losing our homes. I cannot see the Rebs advancing north. On the other hand, if rumors prove true, General Sherman may be on a major offensive south once he's done burning Mississippi."

1863, Mississippi and Tennessee battles

George Goodner's stint as an infantry soldier took a long time to unfold. When it did, his three-year commitment seemed interminable.

The 116th Illinois Infantry was attached to the 4th Brigade, 5th Division, District of Memphis, XIII Corps, Department of the Tennessee. Little did George or any of his comrades know that his regiment would fight in several of the most notorious battles of the Civil War under the command of a general whose name would provoke anger in the hearts of Southerners for decades after the conclusion of the war.

George suffered an illness by January, and his regiment departed without him. In the interim, he married a neighbor, Mary Huff, on January 7.

Finally, on March 30, he reported at Springfield, Sangamon County, the capital of Illinois, for transportation to his regiment. He arrived at Youngs Point, a Union supply depot on the Louisiana side of the Mississippi River just above Vicksburg, on April 10, having been "very unwell" the two previous days.

Excerpt of the letter from G.W. Goodner to William J. Goodner, Youngs Point, Louisiana, April 13, 1863

> "The regiment is reduced greatly. I guess that there is about 340 men in the regiment that is fit for duty. There has been about one hundred died with sickness and a few by gunshot. They have nearly all be troubled with camp diarrhea and most of the deaths have been caused by that complaint."

The 116th Regiment dug what would become a historic canal in the ensuing days. Many struggled with the task of being sick for so long. Surely their leaders realized this group could not be able to mount a sustained march.

So many troops had gathered that the area smelled like a pig sty, especially with the amount of sickness among the men. George's appetite had improved somewhat since his arrival, but he still had diarrhea and, at times, severe abdominal pain. Seemed every other soldier suffered from the same symptoms. What good were the doctors if they could not diagnose and treat diseases that were killing men every day, he wondered. Having to live with the constant stench certainly did not make it any easier.

While he dug, George had a thought.

"Captain Windsor, a moment of your time, please, sir. This entire place reeks to high Heaven. I know you are as sick of smelling it as anybody. It occurred to me that if we dug a long, deep ditch away from our quarters, the men could shit in a hole instead of on the ground for all to smell and step in. That way, it could be buried.

"My mum always said, 'Cleanliness is next to Godliness,' and, for the first time, I think perhaps there's more to that than we even know."

"What's your name, Private?"

"George Washington Goodner, sir."

"I have no argument with anything you say, Private Goodner. The situation certainly merits attention. I'll take it to my superiors. With the number of recruits continuing to arrive, perhaps they would spare a few to dig such a ditch. There's so much diarrhea going around, we do need a solution."

"Thank you, Captain," replied George.

Excerpt of a letter from G.W. Goodner to brother Joseph Benson Goodner, Vicksburg, Mississippi, June 6, 1863

"We moved from Youngs Point to Millikens Bend on the 3rd of May, and on the 5th, we had orders to march up the river, which we did and was ordered back. Got to camp the 8th at 10 a.m. and started for Grand Gulf at 1 p.m. and reached that place on the 11th and crossed the river. On the 12th, we took the Jackson Road and reached a little town east of here called Raymond on the 15th and from there took the Vicksburg Road. On the 16th we came to the enemy's line, and only missed a battle by the enemy moving to our right to out flank us when they came in conflict with (Brig. Gen. Peter J.) Osterhaus's division. A battle ensued that was hotly contested for three hours when (Maj. Gen. John A.) Logan came up, and the Rebs retreated in confusion leaving knapsacks, blankets, ammunition, wagons, etc. That evening, our men brought in a great many prisoners.

"On the 17th, they bothered us some on the Black River, but we finally crossed on a pontoon bridge and reached this place on the 18th without any more difficulty. On the 19th, we made a charge on their breastworks, but was repulsed with a smart slaughter. On the 22nd, the whole line charged but was repulsed with greater loss than before. In the two days, our regiment lost eighty killed or wounded, and our flag had twenty-one bullet holes put through it and one cannon shot. Since then, we've been digging rifle pits and building forts. We have a great deal of artillery operating with the picket every day, while the mortar and gun boats are pecking it to them on the other side.

"I suppose that we are two or three miles from the 'Burg. We are looking all the time for them to break out as they are manifesting uneasiness. The Reb General Joe Johnston is in our rear with a few thousand men trying to get in, but I don't think he can come in. We get our supplies up the Yazoo River by way of Haines Bluffs and have them to haul five or six miles; we got a plenty with what foraging we get. Our rear line reaches back to Black River, where they are entrenched, and I suppose our cavalry are considerable ways on the other side. I think it is about eighteen miles to Black River. We are in the 15th Army Corps with General Sherman commanding. The 2nd division commanded by Colonel (Morgan Lewis) Smith of the 8th Missouri. There are five regiments in our brigade, the 6th and 8th Missouri, the 113th and 116th Illinois and the 13th regulars."

After the two failed federal attacks on Vicksburg, Maj. Gen. Ulysses S. Grant decided to besiege the city beginning on May 25. It lasted forty days. The previous month, George speculated that the eventual goal might be to cut their supplies and starve them out.

Occasional deserters who came into camp said the people were worn out and willing to come to terms. If the Union held out a few months longer, they could likely have peace.

Excerpt of a letter from Joseph Benson Goodner to G.W. Goodner, Vicksburg, Mississippi, July 29, 1863

"After the surrender of Vicksburg, Grant started most all of the army after Joe Johnston under the command of Sherman. Johnston was the man who was going to raise the siege of Vicksburg. We found the Rebel pickets at Edwards Station, five miles from Black River and had skirmishing with them until we drove them into fortifications at Jackson. Johnston had a force of 25,000-30,000 and was well fortified but would not give us time to surround him. Jackson is on the west bank of Pearl River, a small stream. When Johnston saw that Sherman was trying to get a force in his rear, he pulled up stakes and burnt part of the town, thus destroying his supplies that he could not get away. He crossed the Pearl River, burning the bridge after him. There is not much of Jackson standing now.

"After the evacuation of Jackson, I went in a series of raids down the Jackson and New Orleans railroad to the sixth station, taking them in rotation as we went, destroying the railroad, burning the bridges and towns, plundering the stores, and stripping Dixie in general. Buckhaven was the last town we went to; it is considerable of a town and there were a great many of the secech prisoners from Port Hudson that had been paroled at that place. As soon as we opened the doors, they walked in and helped themselves to what suited them. So, you can imagine that we had a mixed-up mess: women, children, white, black, everyone helping himself. Southern pride is becoming humble fast."

Benson Goodner, two years older than his brother, George, had joined the Missouri 9th Regiment Calvary Volunteers months after spending time in California prospecting for gold in 1861. By the following year, the 9th Regiment merged with the 10th, under a division led by Brigadier General Osterhaus, who was known as a superior tactician.

Benson visited George several times while the two were in Mississippi since their camps frequently seemed to be in the same vicinity. Benson somehow managed to avoid all the illnesses being passed around. Reports home, however, said he looked "poor and slim."

After the devastation of Jackson in late July 1863, the troops finally got much needed rest at Camp Sherman near the Black River. Brigadier General Grant ordered Colonel Sherman, who would receive the same rank that month, to Chattanooga in late September.

Excerpt of letter from G.W. Goodner to William J. Goodner, Cherokee Station, Alabama, October 24, 1863

> "We left Camp Sherman the 27th of September, got aboard a packet at Vicksburg the 28th and arrived at Memphis October 4th. We lay at Memphis about a week. When we started by rail on the Memphis & Charleston R.R. and come to Corinth, stopping a few hours at Lagrange, where some fighting was going on, but we were not engaged in it. We camped about a week three or four miles south of Corinth on the Columbus & Mobile R.R. From Lagrange to Corinth, we done the fastest traveling that I ever done. The 116th and Company A, Chicago Battery were on the same train. The cars were loaded with camp equipment, horses, mules, etc., and the soldiers were piled up on top, every one of them and as thick, too, as we could sit. While going at about one mile every two minutes, or faster, the top of the car that I was on cracked and sprung like a buggy, but it made out to hold up until we got to a water tank where we stopped, and about half of us got back on flat cars with

the artillery. We marched from Corinth here, stopping a day in Inka.

"The railroad is in running order as far as Burnsville a few miles this side of Inka. We are now about 125 miles from Memphis. I suppose they intend repairing the railroad to the Tennessee River and perhaps to Chattanooga. There is a lot of Rebel cavalry prowling around, some say there is one regiment some say 8,000 strong, but many or few, they have been fighting some in front, and we don't know how soon it may become general. The 1st, 2nd, and 4th divisions are here, and I understand that the 3rd is coming and also the 16th corps. I guess that we will be prepared for any number that we may come in contact with. Sherman is in command, and he is very popular among the boys.

"I have just been to dinner. I had fresh pork, sweet potatoes, hard tack, and coffee. I haven't fared better for some time. Last evening, I and two others started to a sweet potato patch, and a little before we got to it, we saw a hog, which we pressed into service. That's the way we fare so long as such articles are in our reach, and when we can't reach them, we don't take them. Sometimes we fare pretty hard. Generally, when we are in camp, we have soft bread baked by a baker. I am in a Reb's house, have a good fire, and slept here last night. The woman says that her husband is a forage master in the Rebel army. Most of the women around here are very sour, but it makes the boys worse, and they take such as they want."

From Inka, just east of Corinth, Sherman's Corps commenced the long march toward Chattanooga, which they reached on November 21. Under Gen. Giles A. Smith, the 116 Illinois and the 6th Missouri regiments constructed pontoon boats to float down the Tennessee River to the mouth of Chickamauga Creek. This small tributary of the Tennessee River bordered the last strategic center of the whole Confederacy. The Indians had named it the River of Death. They captured Confederate pickets there, thus allowing the entire corps to cross the river.

Three days later, George found himself among 20,000 of Sherman's soldiers fighting to force Confederates to retreat into Georgia by claiming a victory in the Battle of Missionary Ridge. It was one of three battles of the Chattanooga campaign that collectively resulted in an estimated 13,824 casualties, making it the second bloodiest of the war.

Much to the distress of George's regiment, they were immediately sent to Knoxville without an opportunity to return to their camp on the other side of the Tennessee River for overcoats, blankets, and other winter provisions. Maj. Gen. Ambrose Burnside needed reinforcements after he outmaneuvered Confederate Gen. James Longstreet, who attempted to hold the city. When Brigadier General Sherman's troops arrived from Chattanooga, General Longstreet abandoned the siege of Knoxville on December 4, 1863.

The majority of Brigadier General Sherman's Army returned to Chattanooga with their leader. It was an especially cold winter, and the soldiers suffered at night from the weather. They hunkered down to close an eventful year in anticipation of a spring march into the Deep South.

1880s and 1890s, A Granddaughter's Musical Vision in Illinois

Lenna settled back into the comfortable leather seat about ten minutes after she boarded the Cincinnati Southern Railroad in Cincinnati and headed south. Solid clouds cut morning glare, but they shielded warmth from the sun that would have felt good on this chilly March day.

Accompanying her on the tour, which originated in Chicago, were her cousin, Henry French from St. Louis, who, at twenty, was seven years younger, Marshall Whitt, and Rebecca Royal, both of whom were musician friends she met in Chicago.

The older three of the quartet had played together with another cellist for almost three years. Since he could not arrange to go on the tour, Lenna invited Henry to come up and perform with them.

Despite his youth, Henry left home in Decatur, Illinois, when he graduated high school at seventeen and moved to St. Louis to live with the Etheridge family. The father, David, fought alongside his great-uncle Benson Goodner, a brother of his grandfather, John Goodner, during the war. The grandfather, Duncan Etheridge, knew someone associated with the St. Louis Symphony Orchestra, the oldest major symphony in the United States. One of the orchestra's cellists offered lessons and agreed to accept Henry as a student on a trial basis. The arrangement worked so well that the young man had realistic hopes of becoming a member of the symphony.

Lenna's Chicago friends thought Henry handled their musical repertoire very well and invited him to go along on their scheduled tour into the South. Rebecca, twenty-six, also unmarried, joined Lenna on the violin, and Marshall, twenty-nine, who, last year, auditioned for and was accepted as a member of the Chicago Symphony Orchestra, played the viola to make up the quartet.

Henry tried to get used to her companions calling her "Nellie." She was called Lenna by all her Goodner family, but once she moved to Chicago, she started using her middle name, Nellie.

Lenna, George Goodner's only daughter among five children, always loved music. At family and community gatherings, people invariably brought instruments, and little Lenna danced and paid closer attention to the musical instruments than most small children.

The Irish gravitated to such social occasions. Lenna noticed at least one fiddler always played. She immediately loved the sound of the strings. The movement of the bow mesmerized her. It was not long, of course, before she wanted one of her own. But a neighbor who played patiently showed her that she was not physically big enough to master the instrument yet. Her father promised that he would buy her one when she grew into her teens.

Young Lenna had a cousin, Laura Goodner, who grew up in Decatur. Laura was seventeen years older and had lost her mother when she was two years old. Lenna's mother died when she was seven. Having no maternal influence in her childhood caused Laura to gravitate toward her young cousin. Also, Laura loved to sing, and when she later recognized Lenna's inclination toward music, she was determined to encourage her interest and talent because girls rarely received male direction when it came to their future if it lay outside of marriage.

In May 1876, John Adams Clark Goodner unexpectedly died, leaving Laura, eighteen, and her sixteen-year-old brother, Stover, orphaned. Without hesitation, George Goodner moved his brother's two children into his home of six.

As often as she could, Laura traveled west to Adams County to visit her Uncle William and Aunt Jeanetta because she was close in age to most of their children, four of whom were girls. Compared to what she was used to, you never knew what to expect, and she loved all the activity.

Shortly after they buried their father, Stover drove the buggy west to Adams County with Laura. Almost two years earlier, she met A.H. McKnight, a friend of her cousin, Will. Her father said he wanted her to be at least 18 before she married. If her brother liked him, she was prepared to tell A.H., "Yes."

The couple did marry in July on the Goodner's ample property. They lived in a small house behind his parents' home on their farm about four miles down the road from Laura's cousins. Three months later, A.H. died when his horse tripped, threw him, and landed on top of him breaking his neck.

Hiram French, a Civil War veteran from New England, moved to Harristown in 1867, where two siblings lived. He farmed with his brother, Charles, near Warrensburg. Early in 1877, Hiram met pretty, young Laura Goodner McKnight at the Stookey's home after they invited him and a couple of other neighbors over to Sunday supper. He discovered she was newly widowed. And a niece of Caroline Goodner, who married Daniel Stookey.

Laura liked his quiet demeanor, the respect he showed for her opinions, a maturity that demonstrated self-assurance, and the fact that he and his brother operated a successful farm. Soon the pair spent what time they could together, considering it was planting season.

They married in April 1880 at the Stookey's home, where all manner of Goodners came to help them celebrate. It was the start of forty-nine years together. Laura was happy to be on her home turf, close to those who most supported her.

Clara French, Hiram's sister, brought her mother's piano from New Hampshire when she and brother, Charles, moved to Illinois. Much to Laura's delight, the Frenches inherited their parents' love of music. Upon arriving in the rich mid-state farmland, they did not know about their neighbors "fiddles," but they did know about violins. So, Clara spread the word that she wanted to meet people in the area who played string instruments, among others, which might be found in an orchestra.

Within a few months, she received a handful of responses. At first, for a couple of Sunday afternoons a month, they gathered in the French's parlor to play. Then, two or three more joined them. As the years passed, others joined in, and they found themselves gathering in a small church to play.

When Laura met Hiram, she went to their weekly sessions and took young Lenna Goodner, who was right there among them, listening to the conversations and soaking up the sounds.

Henry French was born in 1882. Seven-year-old Lenna ended up spending more time at Laura and Hiram's house because her Uncle George remarried in 1881 after losing Mary, his first wife, four years earlier. Lenna helped to look after the infant Henry and started learning how to maintain a household.

Laura's brother, Stover, never liked farming. He was sixteen when their Papa died. As the only boy, he was expected to help on the farm. His Papa would have said it was like pulling teeth trying to get his son out in the fields. Truth be told, the youngster did not mind working in the vegetable garden. People considered a garden to be women's work, though. However, their mama was long dead. Papa hired a woman to do chores in the house. He had a man helping with the farm. And they needed a garden, so he allowed twelve-year-old Stover to take over the task. His sister had her hands full, helping to cook and raise chickens and goats.

What the boy wanted to do was draw. He figured that if he expanded the garden, he could sell the extra produce and use the money to buy drawing paper. Maybe he could even sell hastily drawn portraits. He demonstrated much skill as an artist.

When Stover turned seventeen and graduated from high school, he moved to St. Louis to study drawing at Washington University, which offered industrial training outside normal working hours. He wanted to study architecture and design buildings.

Thanks to Uncle Benson Goodner, he received an opportunity he could not turn down. During the war, Uncle Benson fought beside David Etheridge of St. Louis. The two became inseparable during the murderous years they served the Union.

Stover's uncle had saved his friend's life at least twice on battlefields. The Etheridges never forgot his bravery or allegiance. When Benson moved his family to Washington state, David and his father promised to provide for his extended family in any way possible.

Stover heard his Papa talk about David Etheridge joining the architectural design business of his father when he and Uncle Benson returned from the war. He contacted the family, explained his intentions to study at the university at night, and asked if they might consider hiring him in some capacity during the day.

"Yes, Stover, come on down," David Etheridge responded. "I would love to see your drawings. And we'll be happy to put you up."

The turning point for Lenna's interest in music came in 1893.

Stover married Rowene Barnes in March of that year. Ronda, as she was called, cultivated a love of music from her English mother, Rebecca. When she was twelve, Ronda talked her dubious father into buying her a clarinet. "Why can't a girl play a horn?" she argued. Mother and daughter went to hear the St. Louis Symphony Orchestra as often as possible.

The wedding was held in the Etheridge home. Lenna was thrilled to see an eight-piece string octet entertaining at the reception. Two musicians were women, and three played for the St. Louis Symphony Orchestra. The harmonics exceeded anything she had ever heard live. She wanted to be able to play the violin like those people. And somehow, by golly, she would.

Since she turned eighteen that summer, her father decided to take her to the World's Columbian Exposition, a world's fair commemorating the 400th anniversary of Christopher Columbus's arrival in the New World. The festivities took place in Chicago's Hyde Park neighborhood. They went in early September. She loved the hustle and bustle of the city and the extraordinary buildings. She thought the various cultural ensembles and street musicians were spectacular.

One thing above the rest captivated Lenna's imagination. The Chicago Symphony Orchestra, formed in 1888, topped her list of "must-sees." It was performed outside on a perfect early evening. She could not have imagined anything more powerful or perfect.

She teared up at the sound. She did not see any women in the orchestra, but she badly wanted to be sitting among them.

She also got up her nerve and inquired if any orchestra members were available for violin lessons. To her amazement, she came away with a couple of names and addresses. Before she and her father left the city, he made good on his promise to buy her a violin.

Lenna returned home and wrote to Emanuel Knoll, a Chicago Symphony violinist who also gave lessons. She explained her lifetime passion for music. Then she considered the question she knew he would ask. Why did she want to learn to play the violin? She knew why. The instrument gave her joy. She wanted to express that joy to other people, to speak to them through her music. She believed orchestras would accept women into their ranks one day, and when that day arrived, she wanted to be first in line.

Mr. Knoll agreed to meet with her. Within six months, Lenna started a new life in Chicago.

Her soon-to-be violin instructor referred her to Chicago Symphony patron Judge Joseph Kratz and his wife, Margaret, who boarded two other young ladies looking to expand their musical horizons. The last of their three daughters had married two years prior, and they enjoyed filling their rooms with youthful energy. Lenna thankfully accepted the couple's offer to have her stay in their home.

Lenna needed to find employment as soon as possible although her father and cousin, Laura, advanced her enough cash to cover a couple of months while she searched.

After taking an afternoon to explore the eclectic Wicker Park neighborhood, where the Kratzes lived. Lenna decided she fit right in. The majority of the population were Germans, Norwegians, Polish and Irish.

On her third night, Judge Kratz invited Lenna into his study after supper.

"Come in, Lenna. I want to run a suggestion by you."

"Of course, sir."

"Mother and I have been talking, and we like to take care of our own. I'll bet that Goodner was perhaps a Guttene or a Guthier at one time" the judge surmised.

"That's a very good guess. My great-great-grandfather was Johannes Guttene from Bavaria, Germany. He and his wife immigrated to North Carolina in the mid-1700s."

"Young lady, I am quite impressed you know all that."

"Our family history is handed down through each generation," explained Lenna. "It's important we know how we get to where we are."

"Indeed, it is.

"Would you have any interest working in a court room as a stenographer? They take down every word of the proceedings, transcribe it, to document what happens in the courtroom. It would take a year or more of training. During that time, if you're interested, I can probably arrange for you to work some in the library at Kent College of Law. You completed high school, you appear to be well-read, and you obviously have goals and are willing to work toward those goals. I would not anticipate a problem."

Lenna was speechless.

"Well, you can consider what I've said and get back to me."

She opened her mouth, and slowly, words came. "Oh . . . no . . . sir. I really don't think I need more time. What a gracious offer. Yes, I accept. It . . . all sounds wonderful."

"Very well. I will let you know tomorrow who your contact at the law library will be and when you can meet with them. I'm certain they can help you register for stenographer coursework."

"Thank you, Judge Kratz. Thank you so very much."

Inspiration for a tour came from Helen May Butler and Her Ladies' Military Band. Young ladies did not go sashaying around the country performing in public. But that is exactly what this talented, brash woman from New England was doing.

Lenna saw Miss Butler's popular band perform in Chicago in 1899 and was thrilled at the prospect that she, too, might soon perform on a much smaller scale. Why not form a quartet with another woman and a couple of men to lend respectability? She had long wanted to go South into the land of her ancestors. This could be a perfect opportunity.

As the train climbed the Cumberland Mountains before its descent into Tennessee, Lenna looked over at Henry, now asleep in the seat next to her. She was glad it worked out so her cousin could join the quartet and accompany her on this tour. She expected the experience to enhance prospects for them both.

Goodners and other family members, who she had never met, remained in Knoxville, Maryville, Cleveland, and Chattanooga. Her father sent letters with a copy of Lenna's tour schedule to those he suspected of still living in the area , hoping that a few would show up for a performance or two.

She especially hoped to meet up with family members in Chattanooga. After their performance at U.S. Grant Memorial University, they planned to spend a couple of extra days touring the battlefields at Missionary Ridge and Lookout Mountain.

"Where's your mind right now, Nellie?" asked Marshall, seated across from her.

"Oh, I was wondering which of my Goodner family down here fought and where. What would it be like to have shooting going on so close to your home? Did any of your people fight in the war?"

"Thank goodness my father did not," Marshall said. "His right hand was mangled in an accident at our family's mill when he was thirteen doing something he should not have been doing. But his brother volunteered. He got winged, but he came back relatively unscathed. We were lucky.

"Grandfather lost seven out of his twelve workers at the mill to enlistment. Four of those never returned home."

Lenna wondered about the selective nature of war. Was there any rhyme or reason to it? Did divine providence have a hand in it? Or was it a crap shoot? A matter of luck if a soldier got to come back home? Or not, if he failed to return?

Uncle Hiram's introduction to the war was quick and brutal. One month after enrolling with the 9th New Hampshire Volunteer Infantry, his regiment fought in the Battle of Antietam in Maryland. September 22, 1862, was the bloodiest one-day battle ever fought in American military history.

He told stories about his regiment being ordered to charge across a plain, double-quick while attempting to reach the Rebel breastworks at Antietam. They ran right into a storm of cannon balls, shells, grapes, and canisters bursting over their heads (in some instances) and killing many of his comrades. They then had to climb over several fences in range of the enemy's cannon fire where he saw a head here, a leg or arm lying there, and piles of wounded and dead men. He said shells and minié balls passed within inches of him, but he remained unhurt. The next morning, he lay looking through a fence row with a boy so close he said he could have reached out and touched him. Suddenly, the boy took a shot to the head. He died instantly.

His regiment fought in an unexpected battle on December 11 around Fredericksburg, Virginia. The four-day battle turned into one of the most contentious of the war.

Miraculously, Uncle Hiram made it through the war without a serious injury or hardly a wound. Lenna's father had been just as fortunate, with no war wounds, which still puzzled him.

As the train headed down into the Tennessee Valley where Knoxville and Maryville sit, Lenna looked forward to these next four days. They had concert dates at Staub's Theatre in Knoxville and Maryville College. The cities are located at the edge of the Great Smoky Mountains. The group agreed they wanted to drive into the mountains one day to take in the scenery and fresh air.

She hoped that her papa had located an address for their Goddard family, who lived in the area.

The Goddards connected with the Scherer side of the family when Jacob Scherer's granddaughter, Betsy Jordan, married Joseph Goddard in 1802 in Sullivan County (which had become part of Tennessee in 1779). Sometime before 1812, after their first four children, Betsy and Joseph moved to the Stock Creek community in Knox County, almost adjacent to the Blount County line. The couple eventually had seven additional children. Almost all stayed close to home and raised their families in Knox and Blount counties.

They were Lenna's third cousins. All traced part of their lineage back to Jacob Daniel Scherer and his wife, Hannah Sophia Dick. Both were born in Rheinland-Pfalz, Germany, and the couple immigrated to North Carolina in 1760. Had they not, Lenna considered that none of them would be here. Their daughter, Elizabeth, married Conrad Goodner. They were Lenna's great-grandparents.

If she chose not to marry, Lenna wondered who would not get to be born. Life is so tenuous, she thought.

Everybody remained quite receptive to their music. Not a negative comment had been heard about the two young women showcasing their musical talents in a public venue. Quite the opposite, in fact, after four performances.

The next few days exceeded expectations. The weather was sunny and, although still somewhat brisk, certainly warmer than what they had left in Illinois. People were friendly and accommodating. They had been invited into a music class at the college in Knoxville. She loved the interaction with students.

What she perhaps loved the most was hiking along a pristine stream under giant hemlocks in the beauty of the mountains. It was as if you could feel them, hear them, and certainly smell them. She wished she could be here in another month when the wildflowers burst forth.

Lenna failed to connect with any of her Goddard family. She promised herself she would make it a priority when she returned to the area.

"Henry, this is going to be a short train ride today."

"I asked the man in the station if there are any mountains between Knoxville and Chattanooga," Henry said. "He explained there is one descent hill past Cleveland and that's it. Should be smooth sailing."

"A letter from Papa came in yesterday," said Lenna. "We might run into a nest of Goodners today."

"I hope so."

Archbishop of Sydney and author, wrote in the twentieth century about *Lex Rex*:

"Most of these in the Cleveland and Chattanooga area are brothers and sisters," Lenna explained. "Their grandfather, John Goodner, who was my grandfather's brother, settled in Bradley County, outside of Cleveland. And they spread out into Chattanooga, one county over. Both border Georgia.

"We don't perform until tomorrow, Thursday. Then we'll take a couple of days to visit and tour the battlefields."

After they all took their seats and the train lurched slightly as it started to roll out of the station, Lenna thought it would be good to sit still and gather her thoughts. She leaned her head back and closed her eyes so as not to be disturbed.

Mr. Knoll occupied her mind today. He brought Lenna from being a virtual beginner to a good violinist in eight years. Many, many hours went into her lessons with him, as well as time spent practicing. The Kratzes tolerated her progression with grace. They never failed to encourage her.

Lenna had met and practiced with Marshall, Rebecca, and Caleb Fischer, a cellist, since 1899. They decided what music they wanted from different eras, then settled on a repertoire that fit their talents and personalities. Henry amazed her, stepping in and playing his cello parts as well as he did. He received superior training in St. Louis.

Lenna opened her eyes after dozing as their train rolled into Cleveland. She got off at the thirty-minute break just to make sure no Goodners waited. They arrived in Chattanooga in little more than an hour later.

She heard them almost before she saw them grouped outside the station. The woman looked at Lenna as the four arrivals strolled down the platform.

"Laws a-mercy, just look at you. They grow pretty Goodners up north, don't they, Eliza?"

"Now, Tennie, don't scare her right off the bat."

"Ohhhh, and who is this fine young man? Lenna, your Papa said you had a younger first cousin with you."

"Hello, I'm Henry," he said as he stepped up to the solidly built woman, who looked to be in her fifties. "My mother was Laura Goodner before she married, and her father, John, was a brother of Uncle George, Lenna's father. My father is Hiram French. He came west from New Hampshire."

"And I'll just bet, Henry, you take after your daddy. Don't see a speck of Goodner in you," Tennie exclaimed.

George Taliaferro, Eliza's husband, said, "That's a whole lot of chit-chat, Tennie, when our visitors don't even know who anybody is. Don't ya think?"

George walked over to Marshall and Henry, shook their hands, and welcomed them. He then kissed Rebecca and Lenna's hands.

"Okay, from left to right are my wife, Eliza, and our two daughters, Mattie, who is now eighteen, and Anna, who is sixteen. And then, the one doing all the talking, Tennie, and her husband, James McDonald, who also lives in Chattanooga. Lenna, I don't believe you knew they were coming down, but this is your Uncle George Goodner and his wife, Callie, from Cleveland. Now Tennie and George are siblings. Eliza's father, John Jarius Goodner, is a brother of Tennie and George. Strange, I know, because the three of them are very close in age."

"It's like a family reunion," gushed Lenna as she threw her arms around each of them.

"It is," said Aunt Callie. "We're all going to be here for the next two or three days. It's an exciting occasion. And I can't hardly wait to hear the four of you play."

"For cryin' out loud, let's skedaddle. Go to the house and see if we can find anything fit to eat," Aunt Tennie said.

They all gathered at Aunt Eliza and Uncle George's house for breakfast Friday morning, including Mary, youngest sister of Tennie and George, her husband, George Hawk, and daughter, Gertie, twenty-two. They came the day before from their home in Cleveland for the concert at the university.

It turned out to be an eventful evening. The concert drew a surprisingly large crowd. Their family apparently invited everybody they knew. Plus, the university did a good job with publicity. They even held a reception afterward with punch and refreshments.

"I'm certain word's out that the Goodner's other half are highfalutin," said Tennie. "The music coming off them strings was purty near the most beautiful sounds I've ever heard. Truthfully."

"Absolutely professional," Uncle George Taliaferro added.

"As you heard, Marshall is now a member of the Chicago Symphony Orchestra. And I have complete faith that Cousin

Henry will soon be accepted as a member of the St. Louis Symphony," said Lenna.

"I hope that before too long, Lenna and Rebecca and other female musicians will be welcomed as members of orchestras. They can't keep talented women out forever," Marshall speculated.

"No," said Rebecca. "They cannot."

Plans for the day called for the group to take two carriages and head south of the city to Lookout Mountain and Missionary Ridge. The aunts opted to stay behind and prepare supper. All of the cousins went, including Grover Taliaferro, eighteen, and John Lee Goodner, fifteen, who assisted the help in harnessing and hitching eight horses. The boys rode their own horses.

Lenna had long felt compelled to see the ground where the Battle of Missionary Ridge took place. By the grace of God, both her Papa and Uncle Benson survived this horrible chapter of the war. The Union victory cleared the way for its invasion into Georgia. It came at a steep price in human sacrifice.

She rose from her chair.

"Before we leave, as a prelude to what we are about to see today, if I may, I want to read aloud to you part of a letter my Papa sent me earlier this year," Lenna said. "He talks briefly about what happened in battle here thirty-nine years ago. But perhaps more importantly, he describes what the victory allowed the Union army to do as they moved South. That was their objective. It puts it into perspective, I believe."

Lenna looked down at the paper in her hands. Then she looked up into the faces of family members she hardly knew. What she realized was that every one of them had been Confederates and had surely lost as a result of the conflict — lost property, lost their means of earning a living in some cases, lost loved ones, lost their pride.

Thank goodness she saw no animosity, only respectful attention. They lived under one flag now. Wounds ran deep, but time would heal. What better place to start than with family?

CURREY families

Flood of Newcomers Planned to Stay

Rutherford/Walker (Currey)

Every man by nature is a freeman born; by nature no man cometh out of the womb under any civil subjection to king, prince, or judge.
— Reverend Samuel Rutherford, Saint of the Scottish Covenant (1600-1661)

Battles raged throughout the British Isles in the mid-1600s. Heads rolled. Poverty and famine prevailed.

Reverend Samuel Rutherford worried about his brother, James Rutherford, a captain in the Scots Brigade of the Dutch Army, who lived in Ultrecht, Holland. He knew James was participating in the Franco-Spanish War. Late in 1644, he received word that James had lost a leg while fighting alongside the French in the Siege of Gravelines, located in the Spanish Netherlands, which would become the northern region of France.

At the time, Reverend Rutherford lived in London with his second wife of one year, widow Jean McMath.

He participated there as a commissioner on the famous Westminster Assembly from 1643 to 1647. The Assembly lost little time in re-establishing Presbyterianism.

In 1637, King Charles I made the mistake of trying to mold the Church of Scotland into an Episcopalian entity, much to the ire of the Scottish population. The following February, in opposition to the proposed reforms, the Scots committed themselves to the Kirk or National Church of Scotland.

The National Covenant re-asserted the spiritual independence of the church. At the same time, it urged loyalty to the king.

Samuel and James R. Rutherford were among four sons of William Rutherford and Margaret Jane Gibson of Nesbit, Roxburghshire, located in the Southern Uplands of Scotland along the border with England. Three of the grandparents were of the Rutherford Clan. All grew up in the low hills among the scattered lochs, the River Teviot, and its tributaries.

The Rutherford brothers' maternal grandfather was Thomas Rutherford, The Black Laird of Edgerston. He was born in 1550 as one of nine sons of Lord Richard Rutherford of Edgerston.

On July 7, 1575, Sir John Foster, warden of the middle marshes of England, and Sir John Carmichael, deputy warden of the middle marshes of Scotland, met on a hill near Jedburgh, Roxburgh, to iron out grievances. Clan members and townspeople assembled for the meeting. Negotiations went sideways. Fighting ensued. Thomas Rutherford led a force of Scots, including his father and eight brothers, in driving off the English. In the process, they captured John Foster and several other English officers, who were kept for a few days before being sent back home.

What became known as the Battle of the Reidswire inspired Sir Walter Scott later to write a ballad in remembrance called *The Raid O' the Reidswire*. Included in a verse was this:

> Bald Rutherford he was fou stout
> Wi' a' his nine sons him round about
> He led the town o' Jedburgh out
> All bravely fought that day"

The battle took place just three miles south of the village of Edgerston, which had been part of the Rutherford estate since at least 1448. It lay four miles from the Anglo-Scottish border.

Samuel and James R. Rutherford's maternal great-great-grandfather was Sir Walter Scott, 3rd Lord of Buccleuch, who married Lady Janet Kerr of Ferniehirst. The Scott and the Kerr clans became embroiled in a feud beginning in 1626 that culminated in Sir Walter's death on High Street in Edinburgh on October 4, 1652. He was killed with a sword when he encountered a group of Kerrs.

Both of Samuel and James R. Rutherford's parents were closely tied to the Kerr family. In addition to Sir Walter Scott marrying Lady Janet Kerr, William Rutherford's maternal grandfather, John Rutherford, wed her younger sister, Isabella Kerr a year later.

The Kerr siblings were fathered by Sir Andrew "Dand" Kerr of Ferniehirst. Their brother, Sir John Kerr, 8th Baron of Ferniehirst, rescued Queen Mary from incursions by the English against the Scots. His son, Sir Thomas Kerr, 9th Baron of Ferniehirst, also noted for his loyalty to Queen Mary, built her a fortified house in the center of Jedburgh.

Reverend Samuel Rutherford spent his four years in London with the Westminster Assembly wisely. He wrote five major books, which came to define him.

When his work, *Lex Rex*, came off the press, it caused a sensation. The basic premise was that the king is not above the law but is subject to it. Reverend Rutherford sought to demonstrate that "all civil power is immediately from God in its root."

Marcus Loane, Archbishop of Sydney and author, wrote in the twentieth century about *Lex Rex*:

"It provides us with a fine statement of the principles and policies of Puritan government. It was well-knit with a convincing argument and great dialectical ability, bound and clapped with the iron bands of proof from Scripture and a mass of syllogisms. The king is the highest servant of the state but is a servant always; absolute power would be both irrational and unnatural."

In 1651, parliament summoned Reverend Rutherford to appear before them to answer the charge of high treason. By that time, he was on his deathbed. He replied by saying that he had received a summons from a superior Judge. "I behove to answer my first summons; and, ere your day arrive, I will be where few kings and great folk come."

Reverend Samuel Rutherford, sixty-one, died March 20, 1661, with eleven-year-old daughter Agnes, his only surviving child, standing by his side. He acquired a "vast store of learning" in his lifetime and became highly respected as a teacher, writer, and preacher of the Gospel in pursuit of holiness and truth. He crusaded for religious liberty.

Lex Rex was burned in 1661 in Edinburgh by the hangman. Then again, at St. Andrews College, where Reverend Rutherford had been Professor of Divinity.

Captain James R. Rutherford remained in the Netherlands with wife, Margaret Gladstone, until he died in March 1668.

All four of Captain Rutherford's sons, James, John, Samuel, and Robert, fought in the Battle of the Boyne in 1690 between two rivals of the English, Scottish, and Irish thrones. In 1688, Protestant King William III, known as William of Orange, deposed Catholic King James II. They faced each other in battle across the River Boyne near Drogheda on the east coast of Ireland.

King William gathered about 36,000 troops from several different countries. Because he was Stadtholder of the Netherlands, he called in troops from Holland and Denmark, whose professional soldiers used the latest flintlock muskets. All of his troops were better equipped and trained than those of King James.

After the victory, Captain James Rutherford II returned to Utrecht. His brothers, John and Robert, stayed in Ireland and received land there for their military service. John settled in Newry, County Down. Robert ended up in Oratory, located in County Tyrone next to County Monaghan, where brother Samuel had located. Samuel, like his Uncle Samuel, became a Presbyterian minister. In 1689, he published a doctrine that angered the Church of England. As a result, he was banished from Scotland to Ireland. Thus, the three Rutherford brothers ended up in Ulster, Northern Ireland.

Reverend Samuel's older brother, John, was also called to go into the ministry. He met Isabella Alleine in 1669 when her Uncle William Alleine, and cousin, Helen, brought her with them from Bristol, England, on a tour of Protestant Ulster to minister to the Scottish people. Samuel and Isabella married the following year.

Those within the ministry on the British Isles knew about the Allienes. Isabella's father, Reverend Joseph Alleine, and wife, Theodoshia Alliene, were first cousins. Sir Alan Alleine, 1st Lord of Buckenhall, was the father of Tobias, Joseph's father, and Reverend Richard Alleine was Theo's father.

Joseph Alleine, born in Devizes, Wiltshire, England, in 1633, began his path as a non-conformist theologian at an early age. By eleven, he claimed to have been addicted to private prayer. His oldest brother, Edward, a clergyman, died unexpectedly in 1645 at age twenty-seven. This event profoundly impacted young Joseph.

Puritans placed a premium on a learned ministry. Joseph told his father he wanted to succeed his brother in the ministry and asked permission to begin the necessary education. Tobias Alleine consented to his twelve-year-old son starting his higher education. For the next eight years, Joseph studied in Oxford and at Corpus Christi College, where another student commented, "He could toil terribly."

Joseph declined offers to serve the state in 1654, a year after Oliver Cromwell became Lord Protector of the Commonwealth of England, Scotland, and Ireland. Instead, he gladly accepted an invitation by the Reverend George Newton to be his assistant at St. Mary Magdalene in Taunton. The two men adhered to preaching based on scripture and from everyday life experience.

After Joseph and Theo Alleine were married the following year, she opened a boarding school at Reverend Newton's house. She stayed busy hosting about twenty boarders.

Reverend Alleine spent his first few years in Taunton preaching, teaching in the church, and going out into the community to evangelize, much as he imaged Jesus must have done in Galilee. He attracted a group of people who welcomed his preaching of the Gospel. Others were not so receptive.

The Parliament of England passed the Act of Uniformity on May 19, 1662. It produced dire consequences for all ministers, deacons, priests, and bishops outside of the episcopal realm, specifically outside the established Church of England. The act prescribed the form of public prayers, administration of sacraments, and other rites and ceremonies as found in The Book of Common Prayer.

Reverend Alleine and Reverend Newton refused to take the required oath. So did about 2,000 other clergymen. They were expelled from the Church of England in what became known as the Great Ejection of 1662. All assumed the label of non-conformists.

Preachers preach, though, and an underground network immediately developed. Reverend Alleine ministered privately until the law caught up with him on May 26, 1663. He was committed to Ivelchester gaol, fined, and made to suffer. There, he shared one room with seven other ministers and fifty Quakers.

His letters written from prison demonstrate the spiritual concerns of a deeply devout Christian. They express a true spirit of piety despite his personal hardship.

A year later, Reverend Alleine was released from prison. He was unwell.

He chose to ignore the Five Mile Act of 1665, a penal law of the Parliament of England, which made it illegal for any clergyman to live in a parish within five miles from which he had been expelled. He continued preaching but was again imprisoned.

In 1667, distemper progressed to the point that he lost the use of his limbs. He died at the age of thirty-five in November 1668. His body was committed to the chancel of St. Mary Magdalen in Taunton.

Reverend John Rutherford and Isabella Alleine spent sixty-nine years together as man and wife in Newry, located in the beautiful southeastern part of Ulster, Northern Ireland, in County Down. Their home sat in a valley between the Mourne Mountains to the east and the Ring of Gullion to the southwest, very close to County Armagh.

Reverend Rutherford generated support as he ministered to his Scottish Presbyterian congregants in the face of resistance from English Protestants in Ulster, who were mostly Anglican. It did not hurt that he married into the Alleine family.

Isabella stayed in contact with her father, Reverend Joseph Alleine, and her uncles, Reverend William Alleine and Reverend Richard Alleine. They were non-conformists in Somersetshire, ejected from the ministry and forced to start preaching privately.

By the 1660s, Protestants made up roughly a third of the population in Ulster. Due to seven terrible years of famine in the 1690s, an estimated 20,000 more Protestant Scots poured mainly into the coastal Irish counties of Down, Antrim, and Londonderry. They now constituted a solid majority.

In 1662, language in the Act of Uniformity ended any aspirations by Scots of extending Presbyterianism into England. The Rutherfords and Alleines realized the danger lay in future attempts by England to control or invade Northern Ireland.

The so-called Glorious Revolution of 1688 resulted in James II, who had become king three years earlier, being forced into exile. His daughter, Mary II, and her husband, William III, assumed the English monarchy. The Declaration of Rights, a subsequent document produced by the English Parliament, dictated permanent Protestant rule over England and a shift to a parliamentary monarchy.

In Ireland, this revolution produced gloom and death. The result was 200 years of penal law, economic servitude, religious unrest, and abject poverty, particularly for Catholics but also for the Protestant population. Neither controlled their own destinies. The Protestants had been granted power over their own faith, yet they found themselves bound to the English for their nationality.

The revolution compounded tensions between Ulster Scottish Presbyterian migrants and their neighbors, who were English Protestant Anglicans. English penal laws discriminated against both Presbyterians and Catholics.

The Test Act of 1703 was an English penal law designed to force nonconformists and Catholics to take communion in the established Church of England if they wanted to hold public office. Penalties were pronounced against those who refused to comply.

Early in the eighteenth century, Scots-Irish immigration to America rapidly increased. Between 1717 and 1775, an estimated 200,000 Ulster Presbyterians found their way to the shores of what became the United States because of conditions that became increasingly intolerable in Ireland. Most of these people were poor, rugged, brave settlers who transformed the frontier through their determination and ended up bearing the brunt of unrelenting Indian attacks on the colonies.

Katherine Rutherford, the youngest daughter of Reverend John Rutherford and Isabella Alleine, married John Walker II in 1701 when both families still lived in Wigton to the south of Scotland in County Ayrshire. She was nineteen; he twenty-one.

In 1710, the couple moved with their eight children, along with his parents, from Wigton to Newry, Ireland, at the head of Carlingford Bay, where the senior Rutherfords had located.

♦ ♦ ♦

John Walker II and his family sailed from Strangford Bay on the Lecale Peninsula in County Down in May 1726 and arrived on the coast of Maryland three months later. They found Rising Sun situated in the southeast corner of Pennsylvania in Chester County. It would later become Cecil County, Maryland. The little town had been founded in 1702 by Quakers.

John Walker III married Ann Houston, whose mother was a Quaker, in March 1733 in Chester County. John II passed away there the following year and wife, Katherine, followed him in death four years later.

Shortly thereafter, the family moved, en masse — John and his brothers, James, Samuel, Alexander, and Joseph; plus sisters Elizabeth and husband, John Campbell, and Jane and husband, James Moore, along with two of Uncle Alexander Walker's sons, John "Gunstocker" and Alexander, called "Sawney" — southwest through Virginia to an area just below Jump Mountain east of Goshen. They named it Creek Settlement because they called the swift creek running through it Walker Creek. Along the way down, they picked up other families from Ulster, who would become relatives.

By the 1750s, there was hardly a family west of the mountains in Virginia who was not affected by the escalating Border Wars. Natives had been suspicious of the white man since his earliest arrival in North America. Once it became apparent that the flood of newcomers planned to stay and expand their infringement on territory, the fight was on.

Prior to the Revolutionary War, the Virginia frontier extended north as far as the Great Lakes and west to the Ohio River. Both Virginia and Pennsylvania claimed the land west of the Allegheny Mountains, including what would become western Pennsylvania. That large geographic territory, plus what was to be Kentucky, features mountainous ridges, fertile valleys, and many rivers, large and small. It was considered the gateway to westward expansion.

It had long been the hunting grounds for Natives from across the Ohio River. The Wyandottes lay claim to the valley of the Sandusky River; the Delawares occupied land along the Tuscarawas and Muskingum rivers; the powerful Shawnees lived along the Sciota, and the Great and Little Miami rivers; the Mingo tribe lived in the neighborhood of Steubenville; the Ottawas were situated in the valleys of the Sandusky and along the Maume River; and the Chippewas lived north along the southern shores of Lake Erie.

All fought ferociously to keep land they felt rightfully belonged to them. The forests of Virginia, and what would become West Virginia, were stained with blood for decades.

Living primarily just east of the Allegheny Mountains in Rockbridge and Augusta counties, all of the Walker men participated in the Border Wars. Moving into the wilderness, they realized that skills developed with weapons and those learned in the woods would sustain them. Or not. Reports mounted of isolated families being slain.

John Walker II brought his skills as a gunmaker from the British Isles with him. After arriving in Pennsylvania, he became known as "Gunmaker." He worked with metal and made the locks and barrels for rifles on an anvil in his blacksmith shop. His nephew, John, known as Jack, came with the family from Ireland and carved gun stocks from black walnut trees found in area forests. People began calling him "Gunstocker John."

Although the elder John lived just eight years after coming to America, the pair sold their guns as fast as they could make them. The family carried at least a dozen with them when they headed southwest toward the wilderness shortly after John II and Katherine died.

The Walkers set up a blacksmith shop after settling in Rockbridge County. Young John had also acquired blacksmithing skills, along with cousins Sawney and Jack.

People in the Walker Creek area and beyond began looking to the Walkers to repair and craft household items, such as gate hinges, horse shoes, fire dogs for their fireplaces, as well as fireplace racks and pot hooks, broadaxes, and other tools, including spades, shovels, and rakes, shields for their plows, brackets for shelves, candle holders. And gun barrels. Every mountain household needed more than one. Word soon got out that a rifle made by the Walkers was a finely crafted weapon.

By the mid-1750s, word circulated that hunters and families attempting to settle northwest over the mountains from where the Walkers lived were increasingly being massacred by marauding Natives. Those in the Piedmont and Shenandoah Valley were still having their own problems with northern raiding tribes.

There were few fixed fortifications on the frontier, primarily due to the unavailability of military troops, which were needed elsewhere. Some farmers built sturdy wooden houses that served as defensive structures.

In 1754, the French and Indian War broke out with a dispute over control of the confluence of the Allegheny and Monongahela rivers, called the Forks of the Ohio, at the site of the French Fort Duquesne. At the time, it was part of Virginia; later, it became Pittsburgh, Pennsylvania. The seven-year conflict involved the colonies of British America against those of New France to the north. Native tribes chose which side to support.

An alternative to fixed forts on the frontier was to hire rangers to scout the backwoods, report to officers in the few forts on movements and activities by Indians, and handle raiders directly when encountered. In 1755, John Walker III, at fifty-one, had become a proficient hunter and tracker. He knew the Piedmont area, the mountain trails and the passes. He realized he must help protect more than just his family.

Over the next six years, he earned the reputation as a fierce Indian fighter. He roamed the edges of the Shenandoah Valley west into the northern Shenandoah Mountains and into the Allegheny Mountains, south to the Greenbrier River, and further southeast over the Appalachian Mountains to the junction of the Great Trading Path and the Richmond Road near the New River.

Fort Chiswell was constructed on the site in 1758, the furthest south of five forts built during the French and Indian War in the area covered by John Walker. Next up the line was Fort Draper, in what would become Blacksburg. In July 1755, during a Shawnee attack, six settlers were killed and five captured in Draper Meadows. Three forts to the north were located in Bath County, including Young's Fort, Fort Lewis near Millboro, and Fort Dinwiddie outside of Warm Springs.

From the 1750s on, fifteen members of the Walker family were either killed or captured by Indians. The tragedies continued through the Revolutionary War years. Much grief ensued.

Two daughters of John III and Ann Houston Walker married Cowan brothers: Ann to Samuel, and her younger sister, Mary Jane, to Andrew.

Samuel Cowan served in the Augusta County militia during the French and Indian War. He married Ann in 1766, then took his new bride to North Carolina the next year to join brother Andrew. Settlers wanting more land were being forced to move south after King George III proclaimed in 1763 that none of the colonials could settle west of the Blue Ridge Mountains.

In 1772, the two Cowan families left North Carolina and moved up near brother, David, in southeast Virginia, along a long stretch of land in the Clinch River Valley called Castle's Woods. It then became Fincastle County. Later, it would be Washington County, then Russell and Scott counties. Castle's Woods lay on the Wilderness Road near Cumberland Gap, a natural passageway running through the Appalachian Mountains.

Ann's father, John Walker III, now lived on a 300-acre tract of land on Sinking Creek, a tributary of the Clinch River, which he named Broadmeadows. The land was surveyed and entered in Fincastle County records in April 1774 when he was seventy years old, four years before his death.

Ann and Samuel Cowan settled on a 284-acre tract of land in lower Castle's Woods, situated on both sides of McKinney's Run, a south branch of the Clinch River. By then, they had four children.

In late July 1776, families living along the Clinch River Valley received word that the Cherokee were planning to attack Fort Houston on Big Moccasin Creek, ten to fifteen miles north. Although the waters of the Big Moccasin Creek are a tributary of the Holston River, the stream flowed more in the Clinch River defensive area.

Samuel Cowan raced from Castle's Woods to Fort Houston to warn occupants sheltered at the fort. He arrived safely. Against the advice of those at the fort, he insisted on immediately returning to his family, knowing the imminent threat.

"We can provide a fresh mount, but surely ya won't ride back now with savages waiting for an exit out'n our gate," said Captain Daniel Smith. "They's not enough daylight to make it to the Clinch River, if a miracle allowed ya to get that far."

As tired as Samuel felt, he could not remain in the fort. "I must go," he said. "My family might be threatened as well. They need me."

"What good will you do 'um dead," asked Captain Smith. "You were a lucky man to make it here in one piece. For that, we most probably owe ya our lives. Why push fate?"

Samuel ate and departed for home. Within earshot of the fort, he was fired upon. Men within the fort rode to his assistance and found him shot and scalped. They carried him back to the fort, where he died that night.

Two miles separated David Cowan's Fort in Upper Castle's Woods from Moore's Fort on James Moore's property in Lower Castle's Woods. James Moore was John "Gunmaker" and Katherine Walker's grandson, who would be killed by Indians in July 1786 along with his wife and six of their children.

One day in May 1778, four people walked the road between the forts. Shawnee attacked. The now widowed Ann Walker Cowan watched her brother, Samuel, lose his life. Another man escaped and made it into Moore's Fort. Ann and her four-year-old daughter, Jane, were taken hostage and marched to a predetermined rendezvous point.

Meanwhile, William Walker, eleven, a grandson of John Walker III, was riding a plow horse in a field and was abducted by Delaware Indians. He, too, was taken to the rendezvous point where his aunt and cousin waited. Almost immediately upon arriving, young Jane was killed when she would not stop crying and screaming.

Ann's trials were far from over. Her tough Walker constitution helped her survive when she was forced to run through the Shawnee gauntlet, where she was beaten from one end to the other with sticks to determine her toughness. Afterward, Ann was taken west by her captors, and young William was taken east. It was the last time they saw each other.

Ann ended up in a Shawnee village in Ohio. She served as a slave for six years before escaping at age forty-one and finding her way back to the Ohio River, then down to the mouth of the Kentucky River. She wanted nothing more to do with the frontier. She moved back to Rockbridge County, where family members still lived.

Young William Walker went with his Delaware captors to their settlement on the Whetstone River. He was adopted into a family which treated him kindly. As a young teenager, William accompanied his Delaware family and friends to a council meeting in Detroit, where they met a large group of Wyandottes. Among them was a white man named Adam Brown, who had been captured in Dunmore's War four years earlier and then adopted into their tribe. He recognized William because he had known his family in Virginia. The man talked to William in English. He then negotiated with the Delaware for his release, and William was permitted to join the Wyandot tribe.

William lived with Adam Brown until he married Catherine Rankin when he was twenty-two. Catherine came from Quebec. Her father, James Rankin, was an immigrant from County Tyrone, Ireland. Her mother, Mary Montour, was three-quarters mixed Sacokie and Wyandot Indian and one-fourth French. Her maternal grandfather was Big Tree Eghohowin Wyandot, and her grandmother named Madame Montour, half Sacokie and half French, both of Quebec.

William and Catherine spent fifty-two years together and raised ten children, mainly in Upper Sandusky, the primary Wyandot town located on the headwaters of the Sandusky River in northwestern Ohio.

William Alexander Walker Jr., their fourth son, born in 1799, became a leader of the Wyandot people. He received his education in a Methodist school in Worthington, Ohio, and spoke English, French, and six Native languages. He developed a reputation as an articulate speaker. His writing on both political and literary subjects circulated and gathered acclaim.

Hannah Barrett was educated in a Christian mission school at Upper Sandusky. When William met her, she had begun serving as private secretary to Lewis Cass, governor of the Michigan Territory. Right away, William saw this pretty, intelligent woman, who was ten months younger, as someone he needed by his side as he began making his mark on the world.

Later Hannah would say that when William first walked through her door, she saw greatness etched on his strong yet kind young face. This turned out to be prophetic.

William and Hannah married in April 1824. Twins James and Nancy were born in December the following year in Wyandot. James died shortly after birth. Nancy lived sixty-one years, longer than any of their six children.

In 1835, William became chief of the Wyandot. Three years earlier, he led a small delegation of his tribe to explore land in what would become the state of Kansas due to increasing political pressure on the Wyandots to exchange their lands in Ohio for territory to the west. His subsequent report was uncomplimentary of both the land explored and the people encountered.

The U.S. government began negotiations for resettlement of Indian tribes in the 1820s. The Indian Removal Act of 1830 accelerated the process. Increasing violence persuaded an eventual move by the Wyandots. In 1843, after a treaty between the United States and Wyandots, 664 Wyandots left Ohio by steamboat and relocated to new land purchased from the Delaware tribe in Kansas. They are situated on the junction of the Kansas and Missouri rivers.

By the early 1850s, migrating whites began squatting on land set aside for Native tribes. William Walker was elected provisional governor of the territory of Nebraska on July 26, 1853, at a meeting at the Wyandot council house. Wyandot tribe members were joined by white traders and others who wanted to get a jump on the federal government's attempted organization of the territory due to infringement by white settlers.

Congress passed the Kansas-Nebraska Act in May 1854, establishing the Kansas Territory and the Nebraska Territory. A provision of the act stipulated that settlers in the Kansas Territory would vote on whether to allow slavery within its borders. Violence erupted in the territory between 1855 and 1858. Four state constitutions either endorsing or condemning slavery were presented, with Congress having the final say. The convention drafted and adopted the last constitution on July 20, 1859. Known as the Wyandotte (Nation) Constitution, it outlawed slavery. Kansas was admitted as the thirty-fourth state into the Union as a free state under this constitution on January 29, 1861.

William's political efforts prevented the Wyandot from being removed from their homes in Kansas as they had been in Ohio. He generated great respect as a member of the Wyandot elite and became an influential citizen of his state.

William E. Connelley, a Kansas historian who wrote about the Wyandot, said this: "When the Wyandots came to Kansas no member of the tribe was more than one-fourth Indian. The tribe was Indian; the people three-fourths white. They brought with them their church, their schools, their Masonic lodge, a code of laws for their government. They set up their institutions here. They enforced the law."

☷☷☷

Although Kentucky officially became a state in 1792, the territory remained unexplored by Europeans until the mid-1700s.

Dr. Thomas Walker organized and led the first known exploration of this territory in the early summer 1750. This group crossed a river just north of the Cumberland Gap and named it "Cumberland" after the Duke of Cumberland, son of King George II. They then traveled through a V-shaped passage in the Appalachian Mountains, which would be named after Dr. Walker's River.

Colonel Christopher Gist was chosen that same year by the Ohio Company to explore the Ohio River Country. The following year he explored western Pennsylvania and western Virginia south of the Ohio River and the area between the Monongahela and

Kanawha rivers. He traveled into the Kentucky territory and used the Cumberland Gap in his journeys.

On May 1, 1769, Daniel Boone, aged thirty-four, rode from his home on the Yadkin River in North Carolina with five other men, including brother-in-law John Stuart, to find the rumored passage into "Ken-te-ke." On June 7, they first saw the beautiful, virgin wilderness stretching into the distance from atop a ridge beside the Cumberland Gap that would open the western frontier. It soon became part of the Wilderness Road, running from Philadelphia, Pennsylvania, southwest to the Holston and Clinch Rivers and into East Tennessee.

Margaret Walker, a daughter of John "Gunmaker" and Katherine Walker, married James McCown IV, son of Scottish parents, born in County Antrim, Northern Ireland. Their daughter, Anne, married Robert McAfee in 1767, and his parents, James and Jane McGee McAfee, were both born in County Antrim.

James and his wife, who he called Jinny, first lived in Lancaster County, Pennsylvania, when they arrived in America with sons James Jr. and John. Infant son, Malcolm, died en route and was buried at sea.

They then took a circuitous route before settling on 300 acres in Augusta County, Virginia, on Catawba Creek by February 1748. Three more sons and three daughters had joined the family by then. William was born two years later.

The McAfee home was right on what would become known as the Wilderness Road. From childhood, the McAfee sons regularly met hunters, traders and early explorers, including Dr. Walker, Colonel Gist, and Daniel Boone. They listened to stories shared with their father about the vast territory of Virginia found up and down the Ohio River and the importance of opening Kentucky to travel and settlement.

In the fall of 1768, son John McAfee, thirty-one, was killed by Indians on Reed Creek close to where it empties into the New River in Wythe County, southwest of his home.

The McAfee brothers long talked about exploring the Kentucky wilderness to survey property for homesteading. They had been enamored by first-hand descriptions of the beauty and fertility of areas leading into this new territory. They were used to hardship, and the idea of being the first to cross the threshold to claim land held great appeal.

Besides, they were James McAfee's sons. Their father was a "large, square-built, raw-boned Scotch-Irishman" over six foot in height. He demonstrated passion and a well-defined character. His sons inherited his physical characteristics and a sense of adventure.

They knew well of the potential dangers. For years, they had listened to one tragic tale after another of journeys encountering violence or ending in grief.

Daniel Boone explained the Natives' attitude. They considered the mountains to be a spiritual realm.

"These southern mountains are their huntin' grounds," he said. "They's not of a mind to share. They see the invasion of whites as a threat. Ever time ah venture into the wilds, ah keep all my senses sharp. My life depends on hit. Had close calls and lost friends to their savagery," explained Mr. Boone when he visited the McAfee home in 1771.

"Last February John Stuart, my brother-in-law, and me was trappin' beaver along the Kentuck River with a couple others and John just disappeared. One amongst us was so unset he left and went back over the mountains to home."

On May 10, 1773, James McAfee Jr., thirty-seven, led a party of five men, known as the McAfee Company, into territory uninhabited by white people. The group included his brothers, George, thirty-three (who at six feet, four inches tall, they called Cornstalk); Robert, twenty-eight; James McCoun Jr., twenty-seven, (brother of Robert's wife, Anne); and nineteen-year-old Samuel Adams (whose second wife was James McCoun's sister, Jane). They took along John McCoun, brother of James and Anne, and James Pawling, a neighbor, for the first 165 miles to return their horses once they started traveling by canoes.

When they arrived at the Kanawha River around the middle of May, they selected trees and dug out two canoes. They then descended the New River to the mouth of the Ohio River. From there, they paddled south, reaching the mouth of the Little Sandy River on June 10, and the mouth of the Scioto River the next day.

They discovered Big Bone Lick on July 4 and marveled at the monstrous skeletons scattered around. A salt lick deposited around the sulfur springs attracted mammoth mastodons, sloths, and possibly tapirs at least 10,000 years ago. The date of the McAfee Company journal indicates they may have been the first white men to observe the site.

They saw numerous buffalo, elk, deer, bear, beaver, and wolves around the salt lick, where, until July 17, they camped nearby, hunted, and made their first surveys.

In the late afternoon of the 17th, they hit the Kentucky River. They camped on what would later become Kentucky's state capitol grounds. The family spent the rest of the month surveying and establishing claims on hundreds of acres of fertile land.

To return home, the men decided to go up the Kentucky River and through Powell's Valley rather than go back to the Ohio River. The decision made for perilous traveling. The river became crooked, and they had to cross it nearly twenty times a day. Finally, on August 11, they left the river.

Robert McAfee wrote in his journal:

"We traveled across the worst Laurel mountains that I ever saw about twenty-nine miles, and campt with little to eat, and on the 12th we traveled over the same kind of mountains which seemed to us that we should never get out out of them."

On August 13, they came to the head of Powell's Valley, where they met Daniel Boone, his family and a group of friends preparing to travel down to Kentucky. James Boone, seventeen, Daniels's oldest son, and his friend, Henry Russell, also seventeen, son of Captain William Russell was tortured and killed on Wallen's Creek in Kentucky on the morning of October 9 by a group of Delaware, Shawnee, and Cherokee Indians. They, along with several other young men and two slaves, had become separated for the night from their main party. All except two died in the assault.

The Boones again experienced trauma on July 14, 1776, when sixteen-year-old daughter Jemima, along with friends Betsey, sixteen, and Fanny Calloway, thirteen, (daughters of Colonel Richard Calloway, a future Revolutionary War officer), were kidnapped by five Indians while floating in a canoe on the Kentucky River outside of Boonesborough. When their boat was discovered, their fathers and others, immediately pursued and quickly retrieved the girls.

James Fenimore Cooper would publish his wildly popular novel, *The Last of the Mohicans*, part of his Leatherstocking Tales series, in 1826, based on the kidnapping.

It was a period of dramatic upheaval on the frontier.

John Murray, 4th Earl of Dunmore, governor of Virginia, knew action must be taken to staunch the raids and massacres of white settlers pouring into the Upper Ohio Valley and onto land south of the Ohio River since the Treaty of Fort Stanwix had been signed in 1788.

What became known as Lord Dunmore's War had a dual purpose: the governor aimed to subdue the Natives and, in the process, open central Kentucky to colonial settlement. In May 1774, he requested the Virginia legislature to authorize militia forces and fund a volunteer expedition into the Ohio River Valley.

Two forces assembled by early October. Governor Dunmore led 1,500 from Fort Pitt in southwest Pennsylvania. Colonel

Andrew Lewis expected around 800 men to join him at the head of the Kanawha River. More than 1,100 showed up. They marched to the Ohio River at what became known as Point Pleasant. Shawnee leader Cornstalk assembled what was estimated to be half that number from the west side of the river.

On the morning of October 10, the Shawnee attacked Colonel Lewis's forces as they started crossing the river. Bloody fighting lasted most of the day. A flanking maneuver by Captain George Mathews was credited with Cornstalk's retreat. Seventy-five Virginians died, and about 140 were wounded. Indian losses could not be determined.

Brothers James Jr., George, and Robert McAfee fought in the Battle of Point Pleasant were. Samuel Cowen, Ann Walker's husband, survived the battle only to be killed by Indians two summers later outside of Fort Houston. His brothers, William and David, fought beside him at Point Pleasant under Captain William Russell, father of Henry, James Boone's friend, who had been murdered beside him the previous year.

Lord Dunmore's gamble paid off. The outcome reduced Indian assaults. The Shawnee ceded all claims south of the Ohio River, which would become the states of Kentucky and West Virginia, and obliged tribes to return all white captives to Fort Pitt.

The following February 1775, all five of the McAfee brothers, along with Samuel's brother David Adams, James Pawling, who went on the initial trip, and friend John Higgins, all headed for Kentucky. After traveling nearly 400 miles, the group reached James Prawling's spring on the Salt River. They stayed a month, cleared land, and planted corn.

In September, they returned with John McCown IV and John McGee, son and son-in-law of John McCown III, and David McCown, twelve, nephew of James McCown III. They drove forty head of cattle with them, cleared more ground, and built cabins.

The start of the American Revolution postponed further trips south until August 1779. The McAfees, Adamses, Curreys, and other families arrived in late September and immediately began building McAfee's Station on the Salt River as fortification against Indian attacks.

The county became Mercer in 1785, seven years before Kentucky became the 15th state of the union. It was not until then that people in all parts of the state began to feel safe enough against Indian attacks to start moving away from the forts.

Mary Walker, born in 1723, the youngest child of John "Gunmaker" and Katherine Walker, had married William Adams by 1744, whose family also immigrated from County Down in Northern Ireland.

William and Mary Adams took most of their seven children from Rockbridge, Virginia, down to the Salt River with their large group of extended family and friends in 1777. They spent the last few years of their life in Harrodsburg.

Daughter Margaret, named for her mother's sister, married John H. Currey in Botetourt County, Virginia, in 1762. In the early 1790s, their son John B. found his way with his wife, Eleanor Walsh Currey, who they called Nellie, to Harrison County.

The Currey family multiplied and thrived in the mountainous northwest area of Virginia, what became West Virginia in 1863, well into the twentieth century.

Fourteen Point Their Bow West (Bennett)

Hill/Bennett (Currey)

Lady Judith Atkinson Hill feigned more bravery than she thought she possessed. In her mind, boarding a large ship and sailing west across the Atlantic Ocean to the New World equated with heading into the abyss.

No one pretended to assure her of safe passage. God only knew what awaited their arrival. She could stay behind with her three teenage sons, say goodbye to her husband, and chance a future meeting. But she chose to go and gamble that they would live through the voyage. Survive whatever lay ahead.

William Atkinson, sixty-one, would join his only child and her husband, Robert Hill, on this journey. He lost Judith's mother when his daughter was only two in 1570. Although he remarried in Yorkshire the following year, he never produced another child.

Judith's mother, Lady Margaret Langstroth, was the third generation in the family residing in Yorkshire to pass along Plantagenet blood. King Edward IV of England was Judith's third great-grandfather. With the exception of her grandfather, Thomas Langstroth, Judith's royal line had been maintained by females.

In 1609, King James I issued a new charter to the Virginia Company of London, a joint stock company, to allow for reorganization and additional capital for the floundering English settlement of Jamestown just off the coast of Virginia. This third supply mission was the largest fleet England had ever organized to the West. Nine ships carrying around 500 passengers, including women and children, transported livestock and enough provisions to last the year for the 200 or so colonists thought to have been living there since the previous summer.

William Atkinson paid eighty-seven pounds and ten shillings to the Virginia Company of London, and he, along with his daughter and son-in-law, boarded the *Diamond*, the second largest ship under Captain John Radcliffe and Captain William King. It sailed with the other eight ships from Plymouth, on the southwest coast of England, on Tuesday, June 9, 1609. It sailed with the other eight ships from Plymouth, on the southwest coast of England, on Tuesday, June 9, 1609.

The flagship of the fleet was the new *Sea Venture*, commanded by Vice Adm. Christopher Newport.

They skirted the shores of Europe, heading to the Canary Islands. From there, favorable winds would have taken them west straight toward North America. Mother Nature had different plans, though.

Yellow fever raged in London at the time of the fleet's departure. Tragically, the disease broke out on two of the ships, including the *Diamond*, and thirty-two people were buried at sea.

The fleet stayed together for seven weeks. Then, on Saint James Day, Saturday, July 25, they sailed into a severe West Indian hurricane, well past the Azores, about 450 nautical miles from the Bahama Islands. One survivor described it as "a terrible and vehement storm." The ships scattered as the tempest terrorized passengers and crew for three days. One, the *Catch*, commanded by Master Matthew Fitch, was lost at sea.

William Strachey purchased two shares of the Virginia Company of London stock and joined Adm. Sir George Somers and Sir Thomas Gates, governor of Virginia, aboard the *Sea Venture*. As the hurricane intensified, he wrote:

"The cloudes gathering thicke upon us, and the windes singing, and whistling most unusually, . . . a dreadful and hideous storme began to blow from out the North-east, which swelling and roaring as it were by fits, some houres with more violence then others, at length did beate all light from heaven; which like an hell of darkenesse turned blacke upon us, so much the more fuller of horror . . ."

Judith enjoyed their first couple of weeks at sea. She and her father had sailed across the English Channel to Boulogue-sur-Mer before she married. Then, she and Robert sailed to Saint-Malo before the children were born. They did not anticipate sea sickness being a problem.

Summer skies were clear, heading south along the western edge of Europe. Warm winds felt good on their faces. Judith took great pleasure watching and listening to puffins as they first took off, as well as guillemots, white pelicans, gray herons, osprey, gulls, and terns. She watched dolphins at play. They brought enough food and wine to hold them that first couple of weeks before they had to start depending on the ship's fare.

They liked Captain Ratcliffe and trusted his judgment. When sickness broke out, Judith immediately discussed her concern with him. Her father was in good health, but due to his older age, she did not want to risk putting him, or any of them, around those with the fever. She requested that separate quarters be set aside for individuals who became ill. The captain assured her the sick were being isolated.

During the early morning hours of Friday, July 24, passengers aboard the *Diamond* were being rocked more than usual in their berths. When Judith and Robert arose at dawn and walked up to the top deck, various shades of gray clouds blanketed the sky, and a brisk wind stretched the sails. Five-foot waves eliminated any prospect of a morning stroll. Robert retrieved tea and a light breakfast. Judith reported the situation to her father. Within thirty minutes, the rain arrived.

Captain Radcliffe came around about noon, advising everyone to secure their belongings.

"We are heading into a tropical geography vulnerable to increased storm intensity," he said. "These storms are unpredictable. Best be cautious. What does not get tied down could become projectiles should the ship get tossed to and fro.

"I do not need to tell you, Lady Hill and sirs, do stay away from the top deck. As you can hear, the wind is picking up and, with the rain, conditions are apt to become frightful up there."

Judith looked over to her father, who sat with his head bowed.

"Father, what are you contemplating?"

"I have spoken with a survivor of a southern cyclone. They are fierce, savage, and tempestuous. Hrēoh is the word the old English used for such weather.

"Robert, if this, indeed, comes upon us full bore, we will likely get knocked right out of our berths. As a precaution, go find leather straps we can somehow attach to our berths to secure us in. If any of us gets flung about, we might become badly injured."

That night, passengers on the *Diamond* experienced intermittent sleep, at best. Most suffered sea sickness. The ship rode ten to twelve-foot waves and the wind seemed as though it doubled in velocity from the daytime hours. Sails were trimmed.

By mid-afternoon the next day, winds came from all points on the compass. The ship rode huge walls of water up to one-half a mile long and an estimated twenty-five to thirty feet high. At times, it rolled a terrifying forty degrees. It was through sickness, tears, and fervent prayers that passengers and crew held on until the ferocious storm began to abate on the third day.

When the crew opened the hatches, they discovered the foremast had been swept overboard. It was their most significant loss. Not surprisingly, they also discovered themselves to be all alone. Not a single ship lay within sight. The captains did not know where they were. No land was spotted. Once the weather calmed, they would straighten the ship and point their bow west.

Captain Ratcliffe considered it a miracle they stayed afloat. Never had he been forced to batten down his hatches and leave his ship at the mercy of a storm. He had pleaded with Manannán Mac

Lir, Celtic sea god, a pre-Christian pantheon, for his mercy. Generations of sailors have called on the help of this ancient deity, and even though the captain was English to his core, he always assumed Manannán's protection extended over the people of all the British Isles.

Eighteen days later, the *Diamond* reached Comfort Point, at the extreme tip of the Virginia Peninsula, located at the mouth of what would be named the Hampton Roads. This is where the Powhatan River, called the James by the English, meets the Atlanta Ocean. Jamestown had been established forty miles inland on the northeast bank of this river by the Virginia Company of London on May 4, 1607.

When they reached Fort James, they happily discovered that four of their ships arrived four days ahead of them. The *Blessing* with Captain Gabriel Archer, the *Falcon*, with Captain John Martin and Master Francis Nelson, the *Lion*, with Captain Webb, and the *Unitie,* with Captain Wood and Master Robert Pitt, also managed to make it through the storm.

On August 18, the *Swallow* appeared with Captain Moone and Master Matthew Somers, nephew of Admiral Somers. Then, on October 3, the *Virginia* found its way onto the coast near the mouth of the James River under Captain James Davis. Captain Davis's decision to stay with his thirty men at Fort Algernon rather than traveling inland probably saved their lives during the siege on Fort James by Powhatan Indians.

Distressingly, no one had seen or heard anything from the *Sea Venture*, which carried most of the supplies desperately needed by Jamestown's settlers. At that point, all assumed that the *Sea Venture* and the *Catch* lay at the bottom of the ocean.

Those arriving on this third supply mission were shocked to discover sixty emaciated people. In late 1606, 104 men and boys sailed with then Captain Newport to establish the colony. Two-thirds had died by the time the first supply mission arrived in

January 1608 with 120 additional men. A second supply mission followed four months later with seventy new colonists. Eighty percent of those who had ventured to Jamestown were dead from starvation or disease. A variety of factors contributed.

They based the location on the fact that it would sit at a strategic, defensible point in the river. Because of its isolation, fortification was critical. But the island was swampy. Unfit for agriculture. Mosquitoes infested the area. Drinking the brackish tidal river water contributed to disease. Between 1607 and 1612, the area suffered "severe drought."

Aside from poor judgment among leaders, including Captain Edward Wingfield (who was elected president of the governing council on April 25, 1607), other man-made problems plagued the newcomers. Many among them were English gentlemen unaccustomed to manual labor. Clearing land and planting crops proved to be a challenge, as did hunting and fishing.

Residents were accused of being idle or lazy. But others have since explained that people suffering from malnutrition "exhibit symptoms in their early phase which appear to be purely psychological, such as loss of appetite (anorexia) and indifference," or weakness and fatigue. Malnutrition can lead to diseases such as pellagra, beriberi, scurvy, malaria, and dysentery. During what became known as The Starving Time, fewer than one-fifth of those living in Jamestown colony in autumn 1609 remained alive by March 1610, primarily due to the consequences of insufficient food.

The low-lying plains of southeast Virginia are included in the Tidewater North Atlantic Coastal Plain Region. Living in riverside towns, the Indians of Tsenacomoco, a paramount chiefdom of twenty-eight to thirty-two Algonquian-speaking groups, greeted the new English arrivals, who first dropped anchor in the Chesapeake Bay on April 26, 1607. Powhatan Wahunsencawh, born around 1550, served as paramount chief to an estimated

14,000 people. Their territory ran from the south bank of the James (Powhatan) River, north to the south bank of the Potomac River, and was bounded to the west, by the fall line and on the east by the Chesapeake Bay.

Drought contributed to the inability of the Powhatans to aid in relieving the colonist's food shortages. Then, early friendly relations with the Indians soured. The new arrivals soon discovered that their adversaries possessed cunning and intelligence. Famine became a weapon. From November until May 1609, the Powhatans seized Fort James, thereby preventing the settlers from leaving the fort to obtain food by any means. The white men kept their hogs on an island a short distance from the fort, which the Indians slaughtered for their own use. Conditions within the fort rapidly deteriorated. People ate horses, dogs, cats, snakes, rats, mice, musk turtles, and even raptors. Tragically, future research confirmed reports of cannibalism.

A few colonists fled the fort and assimilated with the Powhatans in order to survive. To the horror of Robert and Judith Hill and all surviving passengers of the *Diamond*, especially Captain Ratcliffe met a grievous end the month after their arrival. He led fifteen men north to trade with the Indians for food. They were lured into an ambush at Werowocomoco, home of Chief Powhatan, on the York River. The narrow Virginia Peninsula separates the York River from Jamestown. Fourteen of his companions died in the ensuing assault. A single eyewitness gave this account of Captain Ratcliffe's torturous death:

". . . when the sly old King espied a fitting time, [he] cut them all off, only surprised Captain Radcliffe alive, whom he caused to be bound unto a tree naked with a fire before, and by women his flesh was scraped from his bones with mussel shells and, before his face, thrown into the fire, and so for want of circumspection, miserably perished."

To everyone's surprise, two remnants of the *Sea Venture* arrived in Jamestown on Sunday, May 23, 1610. Those on board were equally shocked at the spectacle of the starving survivors they encountered and at the conditions found within the fort.

The *Sea Venture* became separated from the other ships during the storm. In the surging sea, she began taking on several feet of water through new caulking in her hull. Most men took turns pumping and bailing water, desperately trying to keep her afloat. On the third day of the storm, Admiral Somers deliberately had the ship driven onto the beautiful coral reefs at Discovery Bay in eastern Bermuda, which would become Jamaica over four decades later. Although the ship became permanently disabled, all 150 passengers and crew survived.

It took almost ten months to salvage hardware from the wrecked *Sea Venture* and collect enough Bermuda cedar to build two light sailing ships, which they called the *Deliverance* and *Patience*. For one reason or another, eight of their number died, and two remained on the island. Therefore, 140 people sailed for three days, beginning May 10, to finally reach Virginia.

Surveying the deplorable conditions upon their arrival, *Sea Venture* survivors Governor Sir Gates and Admiral Somers, quickly decided to abandon James Fort. Many of the supplies brought for the colonists had been destroyed or used in Bermuda and they carried insufficient food for the total number of people now under their direction.

Captain John Smith returned to England and wrote a book about his adventures while in Jamestown during 1607 and 1608. This generated interest in a fourth supply mission. King James I promised investors with the Virginia Company of London more land to the west of the settlement. Soon, additional colonists, a doctor, food, and supplies were loaded onto three ships, *Blessing of Plymouth, De La Warr,* and *Hercules of Rye*, and readied for departure on March 10, 1610. Thomas West was appointed as the new governor of Virginia prior to his departure.

Meanwhile, on the other side of the Atlantic, on June 7, Governor Sir Gates oversaw the loading and boarding process of his two lightweight ships that sailed up from Discovery Bay, *Deliverance* and *Patience*, as well as the *Virginia* and the *Discovery*, one of three ships on the original mission to establish a settlement in the Virginia territory four years earlier.

On June 9, as the convoy sailed down the James River, they spied the three mission ships near Mulberry Island coming toward them. To the annoyance of most, the new governor insisted all ships return to the settlement.

The Hills were quite disturbed by the turn of events. They had buried Judith's father the previous week. William Atkinson never regained his appetite after the three-day trauma of the storm. He immediately started experiencing back pain, and he stayed fatigued. He also remained head-achy. Prior to arriving in Virginia, he developed a fever. For the last couple of days, he suffered with chills. They suspected he contracted yellow fever aboard the ship.

Judith and Robert both wanted to escape to the safety of their sons in Devonshire. This was obviously the wrong place and time to be where they were. They would go home, regroup, talk with others, and return to a more desirable location in the future, perhaps when they could come as a family.

Their opportunity came in September when Sir Gates, Admiral Newport, Captain Adams, and others from the colony returned to England on the *Blessing* and the *Hercules*.

♦ ♦ ♦

Judith and Robert Hill's oldest son, Edward, at the age of fourteen, married Elizabeth Boyle, the twenty-one-year-old daughter of Sir Richard Boyle, 1st Earl of Cork, in 1604. History presumed her mother was Sir Richard's second wife, Lady Catherine Fenton, Countess of York, and the mother of his fourteen other children. In fact, the "great earl," as he became known, did not marry his first wife, Joan Apsley, of Limerick, Ireland, until 1595. She died in childbirth, leaving him with a large estate, which was the beginning of his fortune. He then married Lady Catherine eight years later.

Lady Elizabeth Boyle, known as Mary, was born in Shropshire, England, in November 1582. She was six years old when Sir Richard arrived in Ireland and stayed by his side until her marriage. Her father never revealed the identity of her real mother. Both of her stepmothers loved Mary and treated her as their own.

Despite Edward Hill's young age, Sir Richard considered matrimonial prospects between the young man and Mary to be good. It would create an advantageous political alliance for him. Having his first child marry a line of British sovereignty bodes well for his plans of acquiring power and wealth. Besides, Edward appeared intelligent, mannered, and personable. Mary genuinely liked him, and that was a good beginning.

Before the September 1604 wedding took place, all agreed that Mary would live with the Hills in Devon. Edward would continue his studies until he turned twenty.

Richard Boyle was born in Canterbury, England, on October 3, 1566. By the time he was twenty, both his father, Roger Boyle, and mother, Joan Naylor, were dead. Finding himself without funds to continue his studies, he received work as an assistant to the clerk of the chief baron of the national treasurer.

Not seeing any future in this work, he decided to travel. He landed in Dublin in 1588. By his own account, all he owned was ". . . his wearing apparel, 27l. 3s. in money, and a diamond ring and a bracelet, which his mother gave him as tokens."

Quickly, the escheator general hired him. This legal officer looked after property reverted to the crown. Richard wrote memorials, cases, and answers, thus gaining much knowledge about the kingdom and the general state of public affairs. The experience proved invaluable.

It was not long after the death of Richard's first wife and his subsequent inheritance of her estate that he attracted the attention of distractors. Sir Henry Wallop, of Wares led the charge in a series of false accusations against Richard, including trafficking in forfeited estates, specifically to Spain, and being a Roman Catholic "in his heart."

After a series of misfortunes, he stood accused before Queen Elizabeth. At the conclusion of his account regarding his actions and his revelations of malpractice by his accuser as treasurer of Ireland, the queen exclaimed, "By God's death, these are, but inventions against the young man, and all his sufferings are but for being able to do us service." Her Majesty even gave Richard her hand to kiss before the whole assembly.

The proclamation changed Sir Richard's life. Sir Wallop was immediately replaced by Sir George Carew as treasurer. Within days, Sir Richard received the position of office of clerk for the Council of Munster. Sir Carew, who was also Lord President of Munster, sent Sir Richard on two missions to see the queen. On the second one, he came with a letter of introduction to Sir Walter Raleigh, who wanted to sell all of his substantial lands in Ireland. Soon enough, Sir Richard discovered that he owned 12,000 acres of "exceptionally fertile" land in the counties of Cork, Waterford, and Tipperary. The transaction was completed in 1604.

Sir Richard left his mark on the development of this property. He attracted manufacturers and mechanical artists from England. From his ironworks, he built bridges, constructed harbors, and founded towns. Thirteen strong castles sprang up in different districts. He kept at least 4,000 laborers on his vast plantations. Jobs became available for all who wanted to work.

On July 25, 1603, the same day he married Lady Catherine Fenton, Sir Richard Boyle was knighted. On March 12, 1606, he was sworn in as Privy Councilor for the Province of Munster, and then, six years later, as Privy Councilor of State for the Kingdom of Ireland. As such, he became part of a private body that advised the monarch on state affairs. On September 29, 1616, he became Lord Boyle, Baron of Youghal, and on October 6, 1620, Viscount Dungarvan and Earl of Cork. On October 26, 1629, he was appointed one of the Lord Justices of Ireland. On November 9, 1631, he was designated Lord High Treasurer. That office became hereditary in his family.

Lady Catherine grew up with an administrator of public affairs in Ireland. Her father, Sir Geoffrey Fenton, was born in Nottinghamshire, England, in 1539. Highly educated as a young man, he spent his early years interpreting and transcribing renowned foreign literary authors.

In 1580, Sir Geoffrey Fenton followed his oldest brother, Edward Fenton, into the Province of Munster, Ireland. Edward had joined Sir William Pelham's English forces in an effort to subdue Irish rebels in what was known as the Second Desmond Rebellion. Whether or not Sir Geoffrey participated in the fighting, he impressed Sir Pelham enough that he later recommended him to new Lord Deputy Arthur Grey de Wilton, Queen Elizabeth's secretary in Ireland.

Later that same year, the lord deputy sent him to London with messages for the queen. Apparently, his performance inspired Her Majesty's trust and confidence. He remained Ireland's principal secretary through a succession of lord deputies. In 1603, he became Privy Councilor of State for Ireland. He consistently supported English interests and Protestantism in Ireland.

Sir Geoffrey married Lady Alice Weston in June 1585. Her father, Sir Robert Weston, known for his dutiful service in executing of justice, had been chosen by the queen to become Lord Chancellor of Ireland in June 1567.

When Sir Geoffrey died in October 1608 in Lismore, located in Munster, where he and Lady Alice made their home, his body was transported to Dublin. There, he became entombed alongside Sir Weston in St. Patrick's Cathedral. When Lady Alice passed away twenty-three years later, she chose to be buried in Lismore, where she and her mother, Alice Jennings, were both born and died.

❧ ❧ ❧

Extremely weary but thankful travelers debarked from the *Blessing* and the *Hercules* in mid-November 1610. When the Hills walked into their large estate, not far up the coast of Devon from Plymouth, all three of their sons, plus daughter-in-law, Mary, and a handful of servants, greeted them with disbelief and much relief. The sudden transition stunned Lady Judith. She cried. As often as she prayed over the past year and a half, in her heart of hearts, she never thought she would lay eyes on her sons again.

"God is merciful," she exclaimed as she flung her primitive-looking fur hat to the side. "You have no idea how gracious He can be if you just have faith. Your grandfather is lost to us. But your father and I return from trials and tribulations that, by all rights, we should not have survived.

"I love everyone so very much. The compulsion to get back to our boys motivated us to hold on."

With that, their two younger sons, John and Henry, rushed to their mother for a long embrace. Edward, now twenty, strode over to his father and extended his hand. Sir Robert at first shook his son's hand while staring into the handsome, mature face, then grabbed him tightly and buried his teary face in his neck.

Their cook, Meida, said, "Sir Hill, let me feed you something now. It's early afternoon. I can send Chelsea out to the market for supper. There must be something special you would like me to prepare."

"No, Meida, that is not necessary tonight," replied Lady Judith. "Believe me, anything you set before us will be special and much appreciated. I just want to get out of these clothes and into a hot bath."

"Yes, m'Lady. I already have hot water heating for your bath," Edith, the maid, said as she appeared in a doorway.

"Meida, you can bring a sandwich and an ale upstairs while I get more comfortable," Sir Hill said as Edward helped his father out of his poorly tailored fur coat and took his leather hat.

When the senior Hills sat down with their family and explained in detail the attempted founding of Jamestown and the subsequent struggles due to the drought, poor judgment by leaders, lack of hardiness by selected settlers, starvation, disease, and, at best, unstable relations with area Natives, their sons expressed distress that the Virginia Company of London could allow such a disaster to occur. However, Edward, particularly, immediately recognized the potential for trade once the situation stabilized.

They agreed as a family to monitor events and return when the time seemed right. The brothers liked the idea of building a business from scratch. They would start from where they were with plans to connect with land in Virginia.

Edward and Mary heard that a group of five men received a land grant from the Virginia Company of London in 1618 for about eight thousand acres on the north bank of the James River near Herring Creek, downriver from Jamestown. After gathering details about Berkeley Hundred, as the plantation would be called, Edward asked that he and his wife be among the approximate forty settlers chosen for the venture.

On the first of October 1619, the entire Hill family took the couple to Bristol, which sits on the southwest English coast across the Bristol Channel from Cardiff, Wales. Captain John Woodlief Sr., of Bristol, who had sailed to Jamestown in 1609, loaded thirty-eight passengers in the ship *Margaret*. They arrived in Charles City on Wednesday, December 4.

The newcomers commenced with what would be the first annual Thanksgiving on the shores of America. Captain Woodlief declared:

"Wee ordaine that the day of our ships arrivall at the place assigned for the plantacon in the land of Virginia shall be yearly and perpetually kept holy as a day of thanksgiving to Almighty God."

Sir Robert Hill had briefly encountered Captain Nathaniel Basse of London on a couple of occasions. Edward corresponded with the captain as a possible future business resource. He wanted him to know he was now in Elizabeth City and asked the captain to contact him should he come into the area.

Captain Basse wrote that he arrived in Jamestown in April 1619 with about one hundred settlers. They were immediately situated on the south side of the James River from Jamestown in an area known as Lawne's Creek, the first settlement in Isle of Wight County. Edward sensed this was the right path for him to follow. He liked the idea of being associated with a smaller, more intimate operation until he could get his feet under him. And Captain Basse and he were the same age.

The captain said he would be returning to England to secure a patent on 400 acres in the same vicinity on the James River and Warrosquoyacke Creek to establish a plantation to be named Basses Choice. He would return with his family and more English settlers.

John and Henry Hill were chomping at the bit to join their brother in Virginia. Edward thought now was the time for them to secure passage. He suggested to his parents that they wait a couple of years to follow. By then, Basses Choice should be well under construction, and he and his brothers might have a couple of houses finished.

The Hill brothers arrived in the summer of 1621, along with Reverend Francis Hill, an uncle. There was much work to be done and Edward was grateful to have his brothers available to share the exhausting load. Surprisingly, Captain Basse, and his wife, Mary, made another trip to England early in 1622. However, the settlers demonstrated resolve and showed much progress in readying the land and starting construction under Captain Basse's partner, Arthur Swayen, and a pair of good craftsmen.

All hell broke loose at midday on Tuesday, March 22, 1622. Chief Opechancanough, paramount chief of the Powhatan Confederacy, led his Nation in a series of coordinated attacks against white settlers along the north and south sides of the James River, from the mouth nearly up to the fall line. There were 1,240 English inhabitants in the state of Virginia at the time. The Indians killed 347.

Native hostilities had intensified in the months leading up to the slaughter. Everyone expected an attack somewhere, but no one dreamed of anything so widespread and vicious as what took place. The Hills had discussed what they would do if an attack came. None were trained fighters. Since coming to Virginia, they practiced shooting because they needed to secure meat for their table. But, as far as Edward was concerned, going against these renegades, who were skilled masters in fighting, seemed out of the question. He would not leave his Mary a widow in this wild country if he could possibly avoid it. Uncle Francis at forty-seven, would present no challenge in a physical altercation. So they developed a plan.

That fateful Tuesday, when they heard shots and distant screams, everyone at Basses Choice did what they felt they needed to do. John and Henry Hill refused to hide. They would use two guns. One of them would fire and the other would load. They knew they stood no chance in hand-to-hand combat with a knife, although each kept one sharpened hunting knife on him, which came in handy for multiple tasks.

Edward tried to use Shakespeare to quell their intent. "You know, 'Discretion is the better part of valour,'" he said.

Henry countered, "Sir William also said, 'The valiant never taste death but once.'"

"Damn it, brother, we are not in the Middle Ages. Remember, we are trying to build a life here. I need both of you. You have no idea what you will be facing. You are not prepared."

Uncle Francis shocked them when he said he would join the hogs in their pen. "Aye, it is deep in there. I'll roll around. Cover myself completely with their shite. Pray the good Lord I can breathe, and the animals will hide me."

Edward and Mary knew there was a natural culvert just over a small bank leading down to a field outside the village. It was big enough for a man to crawl in and long enough for two people. If they were careful not to disturb the surroundings by getting in, and carrying a dead piece of brush to place over the opening, they thought luck might see them through.

The attackers burned the Basse's house under construction and killed their seven-year-old son, Humphrey. His younger brother, John, six, escaped into the forest. Friendly Nansemond Indians, fleeing from the hostilities, rescued the boy. He ended up being raised by the tribe. When he was twenty-two, John Basse married Princess Keziah Elizabeth, fourteen, daughter of Chief Robin the Elder. They added eight children to their family, who would produce many descendants.

Miraculously, all five of the Hills survived the day of the attack on Basses Choice, but it immediately let them know exactly where they were. The experience toughened their resolve to become mentally sharper, to learn skills needed to last in their new environment, and to physically become men equal to whatever challenges they might face. It tortured Edward to know his younger brothers may be getting butchered while he was holed up, yet, if they were all killed, their goals, hopes and dreams, would be for naught.

When Sir Robert and Lady Judith Hill learned about the extent of the Indian massacre in Virginia, they decided not to wait another year to cross the ocean again. The first week in October, they set sail on one of Edward Bennett's ships, *Gift from God*. They arrived twenty-four days later and discovered that survivors of area plantations, including Basses Choice, had moved temporarily to Jamestown for protection. Memories rushed back as the Hills traveled up the James River. They made it to a still traumatized Jamestown, much to the surprise of their family.

Late in November, Lady Judith developed a nagging cough. Many area residents experienced various sicknesses, so no one expressed surprise. By the first of December, the cough was accompanied by breathing difficulty and a fever. A doctor on-site suspected what would become known as pneumonia, but he was helpless to administer effective relief. Soon, chills started. Sunday, December 11, Lady Judith Atkinson Hill died on her fifty-fourth birthday. The family buried her beside her father, William Atkinson, who was laid to rest in June 1610, just prior to the Hill's departure to England.

The Hill men relocated to Basses Choice in February 1623. They wanted to prepare the ground for spring crops. Edward wanted to meet their nearest neighbor, Edward Bennett, a London merchant who owned Bennett's Plantation, or Bennett's Welcome, on the south side of the river. Mr. Bennett remained in London. His brother, Robert Bennett, managed the large estate that year, which was heavily damaged during the Powhatan raid in March.

Their first year as agriculturalists coincided with a season of crop failure for the area. But between 1624 and 1637, the Hills expanded their production of tobacco for export, continually hired workers, and did, indeed, become successful planters on the fertile ground along the James River.

One sunny April morning in 1631, Sir Robert's horse, Captain, came trotting into the barn without his rider. None of the other Hills were around., The stable boy, Alton, jumped on the horse and rode toward the lower field. He saw John first.

"Alton, where's father? Why are ye on Captain?" John asked.

"Something happened I's afraid, Master John. Don't know where Sir Hill be. Say he be going to Bennett's place this mornin'.'"

At that, John whistled loud enough to get Henry's attention. Then he ran toward a line of trees where his horse stood in the shade. He asked Alton to go find Edward.

John took off toward the barn. Henry rode up a minute behind him.

"Henry, did father not say he was going to ride over to Bennett's Welcome this morning?"

"Aye. He did. Captain came back without him?"

"Does Edward know where he went? Something is wrong. Let's ride in that direction. Edward can catch up," said John. "Got your gun?

"Of course," replied Henry.

The Hills rode down the rough road toward the Bennett's at a full gallop. In less than five minutes, they found their father stretched out practically in the middle of the road. Barely coming to a full stop, they jumped off their horses and leaned over his body. Thankfully, Sir Robert opened his eyes. His face looked splotched. Both hands clutched his chest.

"Water," he whispered.

Henry quickly retrieved a leather water bag he kept attached to his saddle. Meanwhile, John wiped his face with an extra kerchief he pulled from a pocket. Henry lifted his father's head and slowly tipped the water to his lips. When he removed his hand from behind his father's head, he saw blood.

After taking a couple of sips, Sir Robert looked up and lightly thumped his chest twice with his clutched fists. "Heart," he said. "Horse did not throw me."

Right then, Edward rode up.

"Do not dismount," John instructed. "Go to Bennett's and get a wagon back here as fast as ye can. If there should be a doctor there, we need him. If not, we need one as soon as possible. It's his heart. Go!"

Robert Bennett accompanied one of his wagon drivers within fifteen minutes after Edward left. Edward returned five minutes earlier with a blanket to discover that his brothers had moved their father out of the middle of the road.

They accompanied Sir Robert to the Bennett's large house and helped get him situated in one of the bedrooms. A messenger had left for the doctor. But no one appeared certain where he would be.

As it turned out, it did not matter. Within a half hour of getting him into the Bennett's house, Sir Robert Hill passed away as the result of an apparent heart attack at age sixty-one with his three beloved sons around his bedside. Before he took his last breath, he looked into Edward's eyes and thanked him for Elizabeth, now eight, and Nicholas, almost one, his grandchildren. They buried the body outside of Jamestown next to his wife and father-in-law.

A royal land grant in 1613 resulted in Virginia's first plantation, located on the north bank of the James River, where Charles City would soon stand. In 1616, two years after John Rolfe married Pocahontas, daughter of Chief Powhatan (Wahunsenacawh), he documented that Captain Isaac Madison commanded twenty-five indentured white men who started planting and curing tobacco on the Shirley Plantation.

Edward Hill assumed ownership in 1638 and began farming operations on the original 450-acre plot. It began what would become the oldest family-owned business in North America.

When the House of Burgesses (the elected representative portion of the Virginia General Assembly) was created in 1642, Edward became a member. In 1644, he was again elected as a burgess, and also chosen as speaker of the house. He proceeded to serve as speaker of the house the following year.

William Claiborne, twenty-one, immigrated to Virginia in 1621. The enterprising young man came from a family in Kent, England, which did not lack for funding. Almost immediately he was appointed Surveyor General of Virginia. Soon, he became the first secretary of state and served as Virginia's treasurer. Along with his political achievements, he developed economic success.

In 1629, Mr. Claiborne became a partner in a joint stock trading company and established a base for trading on Kent Island. He received a license from King Charles I to trade for corn, furs, or other commodities "in those parts of America for which there is not already a patent granted to others for the sole trade."

King Charles I granted George Calvert, Lord Baltimore, a charter establishing the Colony of Maryland in 1634. Mr. Calvert approached Mr. Claiborne and advised him that King Island now belonged to the Colony of Maryland. Angered by the action, Mr. Claiborne, who the Virginia General Assembly backed, refused to acknowledge Mr. Calvert's authority.

Military action forced Mr. Claiborne and his supporters to leave the island. He retreated to England and returned to Virginia in 1643 after developing close ties with leading Puritan English businessmen.

As Civil War broke out in England in 1645, Mr. Claiborne took the opportunity to ally himself with Captain Richard Ingle who was an English colonial seaman, ship captain, tobacco trader, privateer, and pirate in Maryland. With supporters, they launched a successful attack on St. Mary's City, the capital of Maryland. Lord Baltimore fled to Virginia for two years.

The Virginia General Assembly bestowed the rank of captain on Edward Hill in 1654 and ordered him, along with Captain Thomas Willoughby, to go to Maryland to intervene in the participation of rebel Virginian Protestants who were attempting to reclaim Kent Island yet again. Edward inadvertently found himself in the middle of a contentious early chapter of Maryland's history.

Rather than successfully intervening in the attack, Edward agreed, at the insistence of the insurrectionists, to stay and serve as governor of Maryland. Supposedly, he held a commission from the Council of Maryland dated July 30, 1646. Once the Calverts were back in office, Lord Baltimore issued a proclamation saying, "Captain Edward Hill (the Governor in 1646) was only his 'pretended' lieutenant of said province, but never fully authorized by or from him."

Most of the rebels received amnesty when Governor Calvert returned to office, but not Captain Richard Ingle. He failed to get a release. Instead, at age forty-four, he was used as an example and executed.

When Edward returned to Virginia, he assumed his seat as a burgess in the General Assembly until 1654. He was then, again, chosen as speaker of the house.

Edward served as commander-in-chief of militias from Charles City and Henrico counties in the early to mid-1650s. In March 1655, the General Assembly asked him to lead a dangerous mission to the west. Inland Indians created perilous conditions for white settlers around the Falls of the James River, about fifteen miles west of what would become the city of Richmond. A little over one hundred men, including colonists and Pamunkey tribe members under Captain Hill's command, took on an estimated 600 members of combined tribes on a small creek in Hanover County, with a predictable outcome.

Because of the defeat, Captain Hill received the censure of the General Assembly in 1656, which suspended him from all civic and military functions. But, in April 1658, he again became a member of the General Assembly. A year later, he was a burgess for Charles City and, again, speaker of the house.

Mary Hill celebrated when her husband returned from the fight at the Falls of the James River with his scalp intact. Edward was sixty-four years old when he led those troops into a situation in which they all could have been killed. Mary begged him to lay down his weapons and step aside from military duties. She was thrilled when the General Assembly made that decision for him the next year,.

A surprisingly heavy snow fell during the night on Monday, November 24, 1659 in Charles City. Edward got up, and put a couple of big logs on the fire in their bedroom and noticed furious flakes falling outside the large windows. He opened the curtains all the way and woke his wife because she loved snow.

Mary did not feel like getting up in the cold. She puffed her feathery pillow up as much as possible so she could prop it up a bit, pulled the quilt over her chest, and watched the big flakes coming down. She thought how miraculous it was that each flake was supposedly, different. Beautiful! With Edward's hand in hers, listening to his deep breathing, and staring at this wintry scene, she suddenly felt extremely serene.

This had not been the life intended for her, but she would not have had it any other way. When she moved with her husband and his family to the new country, her father was so upset at the idea of her going to live among savages that he cut her off. She had not seen her Boyle family since she left the English shore forty years ago.

She was never quite sure what had attracted her to the boy who came in the spring of 1603 with his parents to visit friends. They were also neighbors of the Boyles in Youghal, County Cork, Ireland. There was no pretense about him. He loved to have fun. He laughed a lot. He beat her brothers with clever moves when they played chess in the evenings. The adult conversation did not seem to intimidate him. Despite his age, when the Hills left after two weeks, she realized she wanted to see him again.

Life with Edward Hill and his family had been one adventure after another. Not much came easy. Yet, she did not mind the work. They had ten children, who learned to contribute early, and neighbors were more than willing to pick up the slack when needed. They did not just survive; they thrived as their tobacco export business became increasingly profitable.

Mary felt a deep sense of satisfaction as the fire popped and crackled. She and this man she grew to love and admire laid a foundation for growth, something their children and grandchildren could take into a future that should be a little more secure because of what they accomplished.

The falling snow soon mesmerized her. She fell into a contented sleep from which she never awoke. Lady Elizabeth "Mary" Boyle Hill passed away sometime before daylight at the age of seventy-seven .

Thursday, May 15, 1664, Edward rode with his son Edward II, around the perimeter of their large tobacco fields at Shirley Plantation, talking about how clean everything looked as laborers worked to finish weeding the little hills around each plant. By the next week, they thought they should be able to start topping off the plants, which would allow the lower leaves to spread. Skies were partly cloudy, temperatures in the high seventies. Comfortable compared to what would come soon.

All of a sudden, Edward felt debilitating pain on the left side of his chest. It doubled him over. Instinctively, he knew this was what his father experienced back in 1631. His son rode virtually beside him, so he witnessed Edward's distress. The younger man jumped down and rushed to his father's side.

Edward could hardly get breathe enough to gasp, "Help me down."

A water bucket for the workers sat nearby and two men ran to retrieve it. One of them handed young Edward the dipper, but his father choked when he tried to swallow.

"Run to the house for help," Edward II instructed one of the workers. "Take my horse."

"My heart. Stay here," whispered the senior Edward.

Father and son clasped hands. Edward knew this was the end. He could say nothing more. He lifted a hand up to his son's strong face, hovering above his own, and wiped a tear. Within fifteen minutes, Edward Hill I lay dead ten days before his seventy-fourth birthday.

Edward Hill IV, sixteen, died of tuberculosis in 1708. In October 1723, his father passed Shirley Plantation along to his thirty-three year old daughter, Elizabeth, and her new husband, John Carter, as a wedding gift.

That year, construction began on the mansion, called the "Great House," located near the original house. It would be completed fifteen years later. Surrounding the Georgian-style home were outbuildings, including a two-story kitchen with living quarters for slaves, a two-story laundry with living quarters, a smokehouse, a stable, an ice house, a large storehouse, and a dovecote.

John Carter came from a family which some said was the wealthiest in Virginia. His father, Colonel Robert "King" Carter, was born on Corotomon Plantation in Lancaster County, as were all fourteen of his children by two wives. John's mother, Judith Armistead Carter, died in 1699 when he was just four. Two years later, Robert Carter married widower Elizabeth "Betty" Landon Willis, an immigrant from Herefordshire, England.

Robert Carter earned the nickname "King." When he died on Corotomon Plantation in 1732, he owned about 300,000 acres of land in the Northern Neck of Virginia and west of the Blue Ridge Mountains, 1,000 slaves, and 10,000 British pounds of cash. He stayed politically active most of his adult life. Between 1694 and 1732, he served as a member of the King's Council. He was speaker of the House of Burgesses from 1695 to 1699 and treasurer from 1694 to 1732. He also served as a rector for William and Mary College. The Carter family joined Christ Church when it was erected in 1714 on a narrow peninsula between the Rappahannock and Piankatank rivers. One-fourth of the church was set aside each Sunday for the Carter family and their slaves.

When the elder Carter died in 1732, son John started dividing his time between Shirley and Corotomon plantations and a townhouse he owned in Williamsburg. He did a great deal of the work assisting his half-brothers in administering his father's enormous Corotomon estate. During those years, Shirley Plantation included about 52,000 acres on which tobacco and grain were raised. He also managed hundreds of tenants and slaves who resided there. And, like his father, he held various public offices.

✯ ✯ ✯

Edward Bennett headed the other family, which would directly connect with the Hill family. The Bennetts were one of the earliest families to establish a plantation in what became Isle of Wight County. In 1621, Edward first named his 20,000-acre plantation Warrosquoake, after the river. He received the land patent from the Virginia Company of London on the condition he settled 200 people. He proceeded to sponsor 120 settlers, who came over on the *Sea Flower* in February 1622. Leading the group was Captain Ralph Hamor, a Virginia Council member, who first arrived in

1609 with the third supply mission of the Virginia Company of London aboard the *Sea Venture*.

Edward married Mary Bourne, born in Stanmore Magna, Middlesex, England, in 1605, twenty-eight years after Edward became a member of the Bennett family in Wiveliscombe, Somerset County. They married in London in April 1619. The Bennetts fled to Holland with other Puritans who wanted to leave the English Anglican Church. There, Edward facilitated the departure of more than 600 people who would make their homes in Isle of Wight County, Virginia. Most became indentured servants. Because of his wealth as a London merchant, he owned a fleet of ships that traded in Virginia and the Netherlands. He served as Commissioner of Virginia at the Court of England.

When Edward first ventured to Virginia to establish his plantation, also known as Bennett's Welcome, his associates included his brother, Robert Bennett, his nephew, Richard Bennett, Thomas Ayes, Thomas Wiseman, and Richard Wiseman. Nephew Robert Bennett, soon followed, as did their brother, Richard Bennett. Edward and Mary returned to London. They never planned to live in Virginia.

Only a month after the *Sea Flower* brought new arrivals to Warrosquoake, the Powhatan Nation attacked white settlers along the James River. Of the 347 English murdered that March day, fifty-three lived and worked at Bennett's Welcome.

Revenge by the settlers took various forms over the next year. One incident effectively used poisoning. On May 22, 1623, Captain William Tucker took twelve men up the Potomac River to meet with the Paramount Powhatan Chief Opechancanough. Their pretended mission was to negotiate for the release of prisoners. In the process, they brought an ample supply of poisoned liquor to distribute to the Indians.

Robert Bennett wrote details of the mission on June 9, 1623, in a letter to his brother. An excerpt follows:

Edward Bennett, London, England
Robert Bennett, Bennett's Welcome, 9th of June, 1623
    Loving Brother,

". . . Soe thene the kinge with the King Cheskacke (near Yorktown), their sonnes and all the great men, were drunk how many we cannot wryte of but yt is thought some tooe hundred were poysened and thaye coming back (we) killed som 50 more, and brought home part of their heads. At ther departure of Opechancanough the worde beinge geven by the interpreter which stode by the kinge on a high rock, the interpretour, the worde being paste, tumbled down, soe they gave in a volie of shotte and killed the tooe king's and many also as ys reported to the cownsell for serten. Soe this being done yt wil be a great desmayinge to the boldye infidelles. We purpose Good willinge after we have weedid our tobacco and cornne with the help of Captain (John) Smythe and others to goe upon the Waresquokes and Nansemones to cute down the corne and put them to the sorde."

Although Robert Bennett survived the massacre, he died two years later. His other brother, Richard, who came from England to replace him as plantation manager, passed away in 1626, not too long after his arrival.

Edward returned to his Virginia property the following year to supervise Bennett's Welcome. In 1628, he represented his plantation in the House of Burgesses. He then returned to London, and his nephew, Richard, nineteen, came over to further develop Bennett's plantation and the colony. But the young man held high aspirations for himself. He began to acquire property and became a large landowner in both Virginia and Maryland. He became governor of the Colony of Virginia from 1652 to 1655. In 1628, his cousin, Richard Bennett, twenty, son of Thomas, Edward's brother, arrived in Virginia and assumed management of their uncle's plantation.

All six of Edward and Mary Bennett's children, who survived past young childhood, ended up living in the colonies. Their youngest surviving daughter, Sylvestra, named after her maternal great-grandmother, was born in October 1630 on Bennett's Plantation. Five months earlier, Nicholas Hill had been born to Edward and Mary Hill on Berkeley Plantation on the north side of the James River.

In 1653, Sylvestra and Nicholas married. Thus began centuries of descendants in Virginia, which would become West Virginia, Kentucky, Tennessee, Alabama, Texas, Arizona, California, Michigan, and states in between.

Nicholas and Sylvestra Hill's granddaughter, Margaret Loyall, married into the Early family in 1682 in Christ Church, Middlesex County, Virginia. John Early immigrated as a twenty-seven year old from County Donegal, Ireland, to Maryland in 1669, seven years after his father, William, sailed to Virginia.

John and Margaret Early's granddaughter, Judith Early, created quite a legacy when she and General John Thomas Buford married in the early spring of 1735. Both were from Middlesex County. That same year, they settled on a wilderness tract of land, which runs off of the Rappahannock River in Culpeper County in the north of the state.

All six of their sons fought for America's fragile freedom: the oldest, Captain Thomas Buford, thirty-eight, was killed on October 10, 1774, while leading militia from Bedford County against attacking members of Shawnee and Mingo tribes at Point Pleasant on the Ohio River.

This skirmish proved to be a prelude to the Revolutionary War in which the other five Buford sons participated. Captain James Buford, Sergeant William Buford, Colonel Abraham Buford,

Captain Henry Buford and Ensign Simeon Buford collectively brought acclaim to the family.

Colonel Abraham Buford found himself in crucial battles when sent South to relieve the British siege of Charleston, South Carolina. He subsequently, and tragically, came face-to-face with British Lieutenant Geneneral Banastre Tarleton in an incident that became known as the Waxhaw Massacre. Many of his men were slaughtered as they tried to surrender. But it proved to be a turning point for the Continental Army. From then on, the battle cry, "Tarleton's quarter," rang out around the Southern theater. It meant, "Give no quarter!"

The great-great-granddaughter of John and Judith Early, Nancy Batson, twenty, married James Henry Currey in November 1825 in Harrison County, Virginia. Growing up, James was the oldest of eleven children. He had seven children by his first wife, Rosanna Finley Currey, who died earlier in the year of undetermined causes. Nancy and James proceeded to have nine more.

Eleanor, a daughter of James and Rosanna, was born in 1816 and married Benjamin Currey, son of Jonathan, a younger brother of James's. William Currey, the grandson of Ben and Eleanor, married Velma Tucker in 1923 in Grafton, West Virginia. Velma was the granddaughter of Palmyra Tucker and Fenton Currey, son of James and his second wife, Nancy Batson Currey. Therefore, James, Ben, Eleanor, and Fenton Currey, all being immediate family and intermarried, or the result of intermarriage, provided strong Currey influence to the six children of William and Velma Currey since James contributed to both sides of the family through two wives.

Not an unheard of situation for large families in nineteenth century rural northwest Virginia, which became West Virginia. Probably, Lady Judith Atkinson Hill would have admitted that the British Royals living in Westminster Palace knew a little something about marrying within the family in days of old.

Remarkable Courage, Strength, and Endurance

Ashcraft (Currey)

Living a life between two worlds never became easy. John Snider's soul struggled with a decision made as a twenty-one-year-old in late 1764 when he was released by a Seneca Indian tribe back into his Native white world. He remained conflicted for his remaining sixty-five years.

In the late 1740s, young John moved from Maryland with his parents, older sister, and three younger brothers to western Virginia on Scott's Run, just west of where Morgantown would be founded thirty years later. The government enticed migrating German families to occupy land west of English settlements to serve as a buffer against malicious Indian activity. Moving into this wilderness presented dangerous challenges. The Natives were decades away from ceding these hunting grounds to white interlopers.

Athalia Minor lived near the Sniders. One late summer day in 1754, Will and Lawrence Minor, her oldest boys, asked if John, eleven, wanted to go hunting with them. Both mothers were nervous, but the weather had been coolish for a couple of days, and the boys said they were going out for the day. The next morning, after the small hunting party left, the weather turned warmer, and Susanna Snider feared this might draw Indians into the area.

A Seneca war party raided settlements in the area that day. They encountered the small, young hunting party and attacked. The Minor brothers walked toward the agreed upon meeting place, when they heard war whoops and screams and realized the plight of their friends. Wisely, they took cover. Horrified, John Snider watched as the other three boys were tomahawked and scalped.

When a warrior died or was killed, customarily, war parties went out to bring back people to replace the dead. They either retrieved the scalp of a dead enemy, or they returned with a live prisoner who was allowed to live and replace, in a social role with the tribe, the one whose death precipitated the raid. Many white children were kidnapped to replace a Native child who had died.

John found himself among other prisoners who were herded into a forced march northwest. The first day, he felt dazed with fear. But the boy was strong, healthy, and comfortable in the woods. There were a few older adult captives, but most were children from about nine to twelve years of age. By the second day, all of the captives who the Indians did not believe were strong enough to survive the pace or whose temperaments suggested problems were killed and scalped.

John kept thinking about his friends smartly concealing themselves when they heard the attack rather than foolishly trying to come to their rescue. Had they done so, they would have lost their lives. He did not think his father and other men of the community would attempt a rescue. Eighteen warriors in the raiding party surely presented too much of a challenge. He guessed he was on his own now.

Instinctively, the boy suspected these warriors respected others who exhibited strength. He observed everything they did. Although little daily food was offered, he ate every bite. At every opportunity, he drank as much water as possible. He paid attention to where he stepped. He understood an injury might mean death. As much pain as he was in, he told himself he had to walk through it, if he was going to live. When one of the Indians infrequently spoke to him, John looked him directly in the eye, even though he did not yet understand the language. He hid his fear as well as he could.

The Seneca were one among the Five Nations in the original Iroquois Confederacy. The Finger Lakes area between Seneca Lake and the Genesse River, in what would become New York, served as the Seneca Nation's home territory. Fortunately, John and the other captives did not have to walk nearly that far.

The Indians took them toward Fort Duquesne, located at the confluence of the Ohio River, flowing from the west, and the Monongahela River, coming up from Virginia. The French controlled the fort, which they burned and vacated in 1758 in anticipation of advancing English troops claiming the Upper Ohio River Valley. The English then built Fort Pitt near the site of the original fort.

The French were in alliance with the Indians and sanctioned an Indian camp very near Fort Duquesne when John's group arrived. Many white prisoners initially found themselves there.

John knew about the gauntlet. An adult captive was made to run through two lines of warriors who attempted to beat down the runner in order to judge his character. If he failed to make it, he would be given a second chance. If the tribe approved of his performance, the man would be invited to join the tribe. If not, it amounted to a death sentence.

To John's great relief, children did not have to run the gauntlet. Maybe they ran through a gauntlet of squaws and young braves, but it was a game. Perhaps a scary experience for the child, but certainly not one with serious consequences.

Shortly after arriving, John followed a few others several miles to a Seneca camp where he was adopted. Right away, his new mother, Owatah, understood his weariness and the trauma of his experience and tended to him as if he were her own son.

Owatah dressed in broadcloth skirts with flannel underskirts and leggings. Her overdresses were light flannel dyed in greens, reds, and blues and hand-beaded. She wore moccasins.

The differences in the Indian culture surprised him, but he never objected to his new life. A woman led the clan. Children belonged to the mother's clan for life. Boys were not expected to work. They were to become hunters and to engage in other activities designed to develop them into brave warriors. He quickly learned the language. All tribe members treated him with kindness and respect as if he had been born among them.

By 1756, many Indian tribes in the area increased attacks on settlers coming into the area. Seven years later, Lieutenant Colonel Henry Bouquet of the Royal American Regiment of the British Army attempted to calm agitated tribes, which planned a combined assault on border settlements, by assuring them that white settlements would cease west of the Allegheny Mountains. This official policy was virtually ignored by both sides.

Pontiac's War broke out in 1763. The Ottawa war leader urged area tribes to unite in removing the British from their territory. They first sieged Fort Detroit on the Detroit River in French territory in May, then rapidly overran several other forts. That August, Colonel Bouquet and a force of 500 mostly Scots Highlanders coming from Philadelphia were attacked by warriors from four tribes near Bushy Run in southwestern Pennsylvania. The British troops prevailed to save nearby Fort Pitt.

Colonel Bouquet assumed command of Fort Pitt in the fall of 1764. From there, he led a force of 1,500 militiamen and British Regulars into the northeastern section of the Ohio Country to the Tuscarawas River, a tributary of the Muskingum River.

Soon, representatives from the Senecas, Shawnees, and Delawares came to Colonel Bouquet to negotiate for peace. The troops moved to a site on the Muskingum River, which placed them even closer to the Native's villages.

The colonel's stipulation for peace involved white prisoners. He demanded, by October 29, that the Natives deliver to his camp "all white prisoners whatsoever who were in their hands, whether they be English or French, women or children, whether they be adopted by a tribe, united by marriage, or held on any other pretense."

Each chief capitulated, much to the sadness of people within the tribes. Parents lost children, children lost parents and siblings, wives lost husbands, husbands lost wives, and most everyone all lost friends. Many had been with their new families for years and had no desire to leave. It was with great reluctance that John Snider and eighty other men, along with 125 women and children, walked with their Seneca family representatives to Fort Pitt on November 9 to be reunited with their families of origin. Many tears flowed.

After living a Native lifestyle for ten years, John's family did not recognize him. Brothers Henry, George, and Rudolph, or Dol, as they called him, were there upon his release. His father, Michael Snider, died in May 1759 of a fever. Mother Susanna then moved her family back to what she felt was the relative safety of central Maryland. Included were youngest sons, Jacob, who had been less than a year old when John was kidnapped, and Adam, five, who he'd never seen.

The brothers took John east to reunite with his mother. She refused to believe he was her son when she saw him.

"Don't you remember the year before I disappeared when I was on the porch roof?" John asked his mother. "You were in the yard hangin' up clothes. For some reason, instead of slidin' down the post, I thought I could jump down. I did. And the underside of my right arm, just under my elbow, caught that sharp rock. Lucky hit missed the bone."

Susanna Snider just stood with her mouth open, listening to her son.

He walked over to her and rolled up his sleeve. "Here, see the scar? You took me over to the Myer's cabin because she had cat gut to sew up all us young'uns along the crick."

With that, John's mother immediately embraced and accepted him back into the family.

In 1768, the British and representatives from each of the Six Nations signed a treaty designed to end rampant frontier violence on the one side and to create a permanent line intended to hold back British colonial expansion on the other. The Treaty of Fort Stanwix was signed on November 5 in New York. The line ran close to Fort Pitt and followed the Ohio River down to the Tennessee River, which effectively gave the Kentucky portion of the Colony of Virginia to the British, as well as most of what became West Virginia.

Shawnee and Delaware nations occupied these lands. Representatives were present at the negotiations, but they did not sign the treaty or have any role in the sale of their homeland. It would spell much trouble in the coming years for white settlers moving west as far as the banks of the Ohio River.

John never forgot his journey northwest as a captive fourteen years earlier when they overnighted in a place of exquisite beauty. He did not know it, but they were at the southeastern boundary of the Seneca Nation, not too far from Fort Pitt. The Treaty of Fort Stanwix made that land available for white settlement. His brothers and sister, Mary, and their families, along with several other families, decided to move back west with him.

🖋🖋🖋

John Evans Sr. and his wife, Sarah, brought their children to southwest Pennsylvania along with the Snider families in 1769. They settled on Dunkard's Creek, which weaves along the border of Pennsylvania and Virginia before flowing into the Monongahela River. They found the land fertile for farming and eventually acquired 306 acres.

Nine Evans children came west with their parents. One more was born in their new home. Dorcus, fifteen, their third daughter, married John Snider the year after the two families arrived in what was then Washington County. Perhaps because of John's intimate knowledge of Indian ways, he and Dorcus created a life together at Indian Camp Farm without being molested by the Shawnee and Delaware, who continued to invade and harass white settlers in the area.

John learned from his Seneca tribe that the wife conducted family business. Young Dorcus saw right away she could not take care of a farm and manage a house and future children. She told John he needed to build a second house because he had to find two slaves to work the fields if he expected to have a farm. He immediately consented.

By the time the land was cleared and a barn, smokehouse, and two houses were constructed, summer drew to a close. Fall beckoned John back to the woods, where he and his brother, Dol, spent the next two months hunting. He dressed himself and his brother as Indians. He planned to teach Dol the ways of the Natives in the wild. They would bring back meat for the winter. In his mind, as a man and a husband, that was his job.

Fortunately, Dorcus came from a family of intellectuals. She fell right into the role of supervisor. She was not afraid to ask for help. She knew how to use all kinds of guns. She expressed gratitude for John's willingness to venture into the wilderness to hunt food for their table. Many men were hesitant to stray far because of Indian hostility.

Some in the area questioned John and Dorcus's arrangement, including a few within their immediate families. They failed to understand John's hesitancy to work and his desire to spend so much time in the woods. They did not, however, argue over the years with a shield of strange protection that seemed to surround not only his immediate family but Snider and Evans families living in the area.

Whatever the marital agreement between John and Dorcus, it apparently worked well. They raised six daughters and eight sons on Indian Camp Farm. Dorcus lived there fifty-nine years before passing away at age seventy-four from pneumonia in February 1829. The next year, in May, John, eighty-seven, died in his sleep.

When the Sniders moved back west, much to their delight, they found the offspring of their friend, Athalia Minor, now living in close proximity. After the tragic killing of the three boys and the kidnapping of John Snider by Indians in 1754, Athalia felt extremely fortunate to have gotten back her sons, Will and Lawrence, uninjured. She lost her husband, Stephen, in 1750. She decided not to push their luck. She moved the family back east to Winchester, in Frederick County, Maryland, the following spring.

John Minor, born in Winchester just before the Minor's first move west, was seven years old when the traumatic murders and kidnapping happened in Virginia. When he was barely eighteen, he arrived in Mapletown, one mile west of the Monongahela River in the southeast section of Washington County, Pennsylvania. He immediately joined the local militia. He made "tomahawk improvement" on hundreds of acres of remote wilderness around Whiteley Creek. There, he built a cabin, which became a fortress in battles between the French, British, and local Indian tribes.

John made a separate claim for his oldest brother, Will. He then returned east for his brother and family, which followed him back. They brought mill equipment and proceeded to build the first flour mill west of the Monongahela River. The Minors built docks and a boat yard at the mouth of Dunkard Creek on the big river, which created business.

The other Minor siblings followed their brothers to the area as the Revolutionary War began. In April 1777, John was commissioned as a captain to assume command of Statler's Fort on Dunkard's Creek, and Garards Fort on Whiteley Creek. There, he oversaw supplies and enlisted soldiers to help defend the local population from Indian attacks coming from the Ohio Territory. He later became a colonel under Colonel Zachariah Morgan.

Captain Minor supervised the construction of boats for Captain George Rogers Clark who was known for his exploits during Lord Dunmore's War and then, as Lieutenant Colonel Clark during the Revolutionary War. In 1778, Captain Minor led a ten-boat flotilla of 150 militia and more than a dozen settler families into Illinois Country, near what would become Lexington, Kentucky, to repel British Regulars.

When the war ended, Washington County, where the Minors lived, was largely unsettled. John became a justice of the peace in Cumberland Township. The road he took to do business in the county seat of Washington was little more than a bridle path. Services from the federal government were virtually nonexistent. Residents saw no need to pay a federal whiskey tax because they considered the tax structure to favor the rich. Trouble ensued.

John began the drive for a new county in 1791. Five years later, his petition was finally approved. Greene County, named after Gen. Nathanael Greene, came into existence. General Greene became one of General George Washington's most dependable officers during the war in the Southern theater.

By 1796, John Minor had built a large two-story log house with a separate log kitchen. He lost wife Cassandra, three years later. He spent his last years in Greensboro with his family. Dying at age eighty-five on December 5, 1833, he developed a legacy as the "Father of Greene County."

❦ ❦ ❦

The Evans family crossed paths with the Ashcraft family, from Connecticut, southwest through Pennsylvania, and into Virginia throughout the 1700s. John and Sarah Evans' oldest child, Charity, was born in what would become Fayette County, next to Greene County, Pennsylvania, in 1739. She married John Ashcraft, the seventh out of nine sons of Daniel and Elizabeth Ashcraft, in 1762.

John's namesake and great-grandfather, Captain John Ashcraft II, a mariner, arrived in Mystic, Connecticut, in 1662 from Barbados. He made numerous trips in the shipping lanes from England to the Caribbean and North America, stopping in Virginia and Connecticut with rum, molasses, and slaves.

Court records show twenty-year-old John had a few wild oats to sow once his feet hit these shores. He, along with his friend, John Carr, were arraigned with various misdemeanors. For one thing, they endeavored to entice women from their husbands by hiding themselves in houses, writing letters, which were intercepted, and defaming said women. The offenders received fines. The wives were solemnly warned and ordered to "take care."

To circumvent his early legal troubles, John Ashcraft II moved just to the east on the coast of Connecticut to Stonington. There, he met Hannah Osborne and married the thirteen year-old in September 1670, with her parents blessing. The newlyweds lived on the property for a year, rented to them by the pastor who married them. They then moved to property owned by John Osborne, Hannah's father. John Ashcraft III came along on August 14, 1671. A month later, the couple left the farm and relocated on another property owned by Mr. Osborne.

John immediately realized that this new country would not be won without armed conflict. Europeans were, after all, invaders. The current occupants, who had, in all likelihood, inhabited these lands for centuries, were unwilling to turn their vast property over to newcomers without compromises that had, thus far, not pleased either side.

In 1676, John set the stage for decades of Ashcraft participation in warfare against Indians while helping to gain a foothold for settlement. At age thirty-two, he served as a volunteer soldier under Captain George Denison Sr. who commanded New London County troops in King Philip's War against the Narragansetts in Rhode Island.

Captain Denison, an English immigrant from Northamptonshire, also settled in Stonington. With the possible exception of Captain John Mason, who devastated the Pequot people in a surprise attack on the Pequot fort in Mystic on May 26, 1637, Captain Denison had no equal in any of the colonies for conducting war against the Natives. He earned a reputation as a brilliant soldier.

After hearing of Captain Denison's success against the Narragansetts the previous year, in what was known as the Great Swamp Massacre near Kingstown, Rhode Island, John did not hesitate when the call went out for additional soldiers. He and his Connecticut troops made a series of successful excursions into Rhode Island and then up to Massachusetts. In the process, they captured the celebrated Narragansett Chieftan, Canonchet, who was brought to Stonington. Members of the Pequot and Mohegan tribes were allowed to first shoot, then quarter him.

The year after John returned from King Philip's War, he moved his young family to Groton, a seaport town at the mouth of the Thames River to the west of Mystic. He did, after all, know more about ships than anything. He figured he could find regular employment around other mariners.

On June 6, 1732, John Ashcraft passed away after suffering for several months with a disease he knew was terminal. Son, John III, was nine when he lost his father. His infant sister, Mary, had been born three months earlier but died when she was a year old. Thus, Hannah Ashcraft became a twenty-three year-old widow with just one of six children having survived.

Daniel Ashcraft found himself in a position that would have seemed all to familiar to his grandfather sixty-five years earlier.

The now twenty-two year-old son of John Ashcraft III sat in a jail cell in New London, Connecticut, located on the west side of the Thames River, west of Stonington, where most of his large family lived. Consequences for Daniel loomed large. He was charged with the murder of the son of a Wampanoag. The court considered his case to be an example of how the laws of King George II applied to both Indian and Englishmen alike.

The young man, named Pas-ka-hant, died after Daniel hit him on the forehead with a stone. An Indian squaw luckily came forward during the trial and testified that she witnessed the victim load a pistol and threaten to kill Daniel. A jury acquitted Daniel in 1720, but hard feelings toward him lingered in the community.

It was not the last time Ashcraft's sons wound up in the New London courtroom. Joshua Hempstead, a local lawyer, related that he made bail for Jedidiah Ashcraft, thirty, on January 19, 1733. Then, he spent all day in court with Uriah Ashcraft, twenty-five, on March 14 of that year, as he was tried and acquitted for killing a stranger.

Daniel left the coast of Connecticut and moved to the Philadelphia area for the next several years after his father, who died in 1732, left him money in his will. There, he successfully made land transactions. In 1735, he met and married Elizabeth Lewis. She was reputedly a cousin of the Warner Hall Lewis family of Virginia.

The grandsons and great-grandsons of John Ashcraft III inherited his adventurous spirit. They recognized the need to push forward despite the obstacles and dangers in exploring and expanding this new country. They chose women willing to take risks.

Daniel and Elizabeth moved to extreme northeast Virginia in Berkeley County and settled along Sleepy Creek in 1753. In addition to son John, who would marry Charity Evans in 1798, eight other boys and two girls had been born in the family. The youngest, Absolom, was nine when the Ashcrafts transitioned into the wilderness.

Shortly after that, Thomas Townsend, an Indian trader, arranged with Daniel Boone, a young explorer who became renowned, to recruit settlers for lands in Kentucky. On a trading expedition into the Ohio Territory, he passed the message along to William Hibbs, a partner in the venture. Mr. Hibbs talked Daniel, Ichabod, Richard, and Uriah Ashcraft into a trip southwest. They mounted and led pack horses up the Monongahela River, up the West Fork, down the Little Kanawha River, and to the Ohio River, where it meets the Scioto River. The next morning, after crossing the Tygart Valley River, a fierce storm forced the men to take shelter in an abandoned cabin. Thomas Townsend found them there. So did a group of Shawnee warriors. Mr. Townsend and two other men were killed in an ensuing battle. Their trip toward Kentucky ended that day.

In early October 1755, not too far from their home in Berkeley County, Daniel Ashcraft, his son, Jacob, Abe Johnson, the brother of Jacob's wife, Mary, and James Lowrey, a peddler known in the area, was murdered by Delaware Indians. The blood bath took place on Conococheague Creek. The area that drained into the watershed of the creek, continued to be the scene of hostilities between the Delaware tribe and white settlers until a peace treaty was concluded in 1758.

Carnage lay ahead. Richard Ashcraft became an Indian scout, a spy, land owner, and entrepreneur. He demonstrated "remarkable courage, strength, and endurance" at a time when the Indian wars were rampant. Some said he was driven by revenge for the brutal killings of family and friends.

Loyalties between Indian tribes were being aligned with either the British or French as the French and Indian War, as it was known in the colonies, dawned. It lasted from 1756 to 1763. On May 24 and July 3, 1754, the first skirmishes of the war were fought around Uniontown, Fayette County, Pennsylvania, practically in the backyard of settlers living in northern Virginia.

Richard Ashcraft and Captain Thomas B. Carr, brother of his wife, Betsy, first served together as trackers and spies in the French and Indian War fought between the Ohio Territory and Lake Erie and Lake Ontario. They were still on expeditions in early 1764. The pair served under British commanders Colonel John Bradstreet and Colonel Henry Bouquet, young John Snider's rescuer that same year.

Richard was quite fond of all the Carrs. He liked their Irish spunk. He loved the feistiness in Betsy the first time he met her. Somehow, she knew she could keep up with a house full of children. And Thomas was not only tough, physically but as smart as anybody Richard knew. Their father, John, immigrated from County Cork, Ireland, as a Kerr. He changed his name upon arriving in New Jersey and heading to the frontier.

During the American Revolutionary War, Richard served as an Indian scout close to home. He knew their language, and he was intimately familiar with the territory. He scouted western Pennsylvania all along the Monongahela River, detailing the movement of Indians allied with the British. He reported to Captain Basil Bowell's Company operating out of Ashcraft's Fort in Fayette County, built by his brother, Ichabod Ashcraft. The fort was constructed as protection from the Indians on John Evans' farm in 1770 at the crossing of two Indian trails.

Ichabod and his brother, Daniel, one year older, would soon be involved in a conflict that would become a precursor to the Revolutionary War. The Ashcrafts suffered another tragic blow as a result.

The Ashcraft family had been close friends with Colonel Thomas Cresap, land surveyor, landowner, explorer, and Indian fighter in Maryland, Pennsylvania, and Virginia. The families had been neighbors for several years in Fayette County, Pennsylvania.

In early spring 1774, the Ashcrafts heard that a son, Captain Michael Cresap, owner of a trading post at Redstone Old Fort on the Monongahela River, was actively involved with groups on the Ohio River combating escalating Indian violence.

John Murray, Lord Dunmore, Governor of Virginia, declared war on the Shawnee and Mingo tribes, which continued to ignore the terms of the 1768 Treaty of Fort Stanwix. The Iroquois Nation ceded land south of the Ohio River to the British in the treaty. Other Ohio Territory tribes refused to recognize the treaty and continued to defend their hunting rights while killing white settlers.

A volunteer militia was needed to turn the tide. When Ichabod and Daniel Ashcraft heard that Colonel Andrew Lewis called for troops to rendezvous with him at the mouth of the Kanawha River in late September, they cleaned their guns, grabbed plenty of powder and shot, sharpened their knives, and proceeded south.

"What ya reckon we're gettin' ourselves into," asked Ichabod shortly after the brothers crossed into Virginia, following the Monongahela River into Morgantown.

"I think the mayhem has to stop. The stream of families comin' over the mountains a wantin' to settle in western Pennsylvania, northwest Virginia, and purty soon, on into the Ohio Territory won't be slowin' down. These damned Natives might as well accept hit. The numbers ain't in their favor," Daniel responded.

'Yep. They's liable to be a mess of us gathered when we get down yonder. We've got Colonel Lewis, and a Captain Clark, who knows this area, is 'pose to be leadin' another group. But we're sure to run into a hornet's nest. Those Shawnee 'il foller Cornstalk off a cliff."

The men rode silently for miles in the cool, sunshiny fall weather. Neither had fought in military combat. They both considered this to be a cause for which they would sacrifice their lives.

"Brother, if I don't make hit back up this way, know that I'm at peace with givin' my life for the cause of freedom," Daniel said. "They's bound to be a war fought soon, and this might well be the start."

"I am proud to have ye by my side," answered Ichabod. "The Ashcrafts surely won't have nothing to be ashamed of."

When Colonel Lewis reached the headwaters of the Kanawha River, his force nearly numbered one hundred strong. He proceeded downriver to the Ohio River, where he established Camp Pleasant on October 6. He received word that Lord Dunmore wanted to meet at the Shawnee towns on the Scioto River.

On the morning of October 10, just as Colonel Lewis and his troops began crossing the big Ohio River, they were surprised by an estimated 500 Shawnee and Mingo warriors led by Chief Cornstalk. A fierce battle raged all day and eventually turned into a hand-to-hand maelstrom. By all accounts, the killing was vicious, and both sides took scalps. Late in the day, Captain George Mathews directed a flanking maneuver that resulted in Chief Cornstalk's retreat.

The chief lost his life with an undetermined number of his men. Colonel Lewis's army suffered 215 casualties, including seventy-five deaths. Daniel Ashcraft died after being shot in the neck. The next morning, Ichabod buried his brother and was among those crossing the river with Colonel Lewis to meet up with Lord Dunmore and his troops.

What became known as the Battle of Point Pleasant eliminated Native Americans as a force on the western frontier for the first three years of the upcoming Revolutionary War. It cleared the way for peaceful settlement of the region, which is exactly what Lord Dunmore gambled on when he requested the Virginia legislature to authorize general militia forces and to fund a volunteer expedition into the Ohio River Valley.

The year after surviving the Point Pleasant Battle, Ichabod Ashcraft was recruited by Captain Cresap as one among 130 frontier sharpshooters to fight as irregular militiamen. Some marched 800 miles from North Carolina, Virginia, Pennsylvania, and Maryland to Boston. They were reportedly a formidable-looking outfit from the mountains and backwoods painted like Indians, dressed in hunting shirts and moccasins, and armed with tomahawks and what would become known as their "Kentucky" rifles. They were called the shirt-tail men.

When they reached Massachusetts, they organized into small, independent units. Their orders were to pick off British officers during lulls in action around Boston after the Battle of Bunker Hill on June 17, 1775, during the very early stages of the Revolutionary War.

One day in February 1792, Richard Ashcraft rode toward home in Fayette County from Chambers Mill in south-central Washington County west of the Monongahela River. Between Ten-Mile Creek and West Ten-Mile Creek, his horse fell through ice into the creek. Richard, fifty-two, froze to death.

Seven years later, Betsy Ashcraft, his wife, gathered those family members who were not already there and followed Carr's relatives to Nelson County, Kentucky, and then on to Hardin County. She died at age ninety-six after seeing eleven children survive to adulthood.

A young, newly appointed Lieutenant Colonel George Rogers Clark recruited Jedidiah Ashcraft, among other volunteer militia, in early 1778 for a secret expedition to capture the British-held villages at Kaskaskia, Cahokia, and Vincennes in the Illinois Country. They arrived at Captain Michael Cresap's Redstone Old Fort on the Monongahela on February 1, where preparations were completed. In July 1778, about 175 of the Virginia state forces of the Illinois Regiment were led south by Lieutenant Colonel Clark.

Kaskaskia and Cahokia surrendered without firing a shot. Vincennes surrendered in August.

Jedidiah stayed with the militia into 1779. It became necessary to retake two of the forts in an arduous overland winter march under miserable conditions. Lieutenant Colonel Clark's ultimate goal was to destroy British influence among their British allies and open Kentucky up to settlement. But reinforcement from Shawnee, Delaware, and Wyandotte warriors kept British expectations high.

Jedidiah moved with his family, along with other families, to Phillips Fort in Hardin County, Kentucky, in 1780. After participating in the Northwest Campaign of the Revolutionary War, he received a land grant of 560 acres in Jefferson County, Kentucky, on the North Branch of Ashcraft Creek, "being the first south branch below Little Clifty." He received notice of the grant in April 1783.

Eleven years later, at the age of sixty-one, Jedidiah died under an Indian tomahawk near his home in Clifty Hollow, Hardin County. The last Indian fight in Hardin County happened in 1794.

When Charity Ashcraft, wife of John Ashcraft, passed away at age seventy-four in 1813, he moved off of Dunkard's Creek in Fayette County, Pennsylvania, south to Harrison County on Bingamon Creek in Virginia. Six out of seven of John's children ended up living in Harrison County.

Sarah McIntire was the youngest child and only girl in a house impossibly full of boys. She met Uriah Ashcraft, twenty-five, John's oldest son, in late 1787. They married the following October when she was fourteen. Her oldest brother, John, and his wife, Rachel, liked Uriah Ashcraft and happily hosted a wedding reception at their cabin.

Sarah's parents, Charles and Eleanor, who were known as Elender Alexander McIntire, both immigrated from County Donegal, Ireland. Charles died on an October 1783 hunting trip in Frederick County, Virginia. Elender, at age eighty-four, contentedly slipped away on December 29, 1815, rocking five month-old Mary Ann Ashcraft, her thirteenth grandchild from Sarah and Uriah, who lay in a sling across her chest in front of the fire.

One day in mid-May 1791, John and Rachel McIntire returned home about two miles above Bingamon Creek after rounding up a few stray cows. On the way, they passed through the yard of Uriah Ashcraft. When they got in the house, one of John's dogs started aggressively growling. When he stepped to the door, he saw an Indian in the yard. He told the children to lay low, then ran upstairs and attempted to fire on him, but his gun jammed. When he observed more Indians, he yelled loudly for help. Three of his brothers, Levi, John Jr., and Zekiel, arrived shortly to find Uriah Ashcraft at the house and Charles McIntire, thirteen, John's second oldest son, out on the porch. The boy said his parents had gone after the invaders.

"What the hell?" Levi shouted. "Even if they's just a handful, why did he take off after 'um without waitin' for help? He knew we'd be here right quick."

"And why on earth did he take Rachel with him?" asked Zekiel. "I know she can shoot 'bout good as any of us, but still. I don't like the odds."

"Boy, you git in that house and bolt the door good," his Uncle Uriah instructed him. "If they come back, do not engage them. Load all the weapons, but don't shoot 'lessun they break the door down, which ain't likely. If they do, fire away. Get the little 'uns hid under the floor. You hear me?"

"Yes, sir."

"Come on. Let's git," Zekiel said.

About a mile off, they found the body of John, who had been tomahawked and scalped. Since Rachel was missing, they assumed she had been kidnapped. Zekiel and John Jr. rode to Clarksburg for assistance since, now, an assumed rescue would be required. The brothers rode back with Colonel George Jackson, Colonel John Haymond, and his brother, William Haymond, Major Benjamin Robinson, John Harbert, Nicholas Carpenter, and his son, Christopher Carpenter (who would lose their lives four months later in an Indian attack while driving cattle from Clarksburg to Marietta for soldiers at Fort Harmar).

In a letter more than fifty years later, William Haymond shared the details of what the scouts encountered searching for the Indians after the attacks on the McIntires.

"Palatine Hill, Va. April 10, 1842

Luther Haymond, Colonel George Jackson proposed that six men be chosen who should strip as light as they could and go ahead on the horses. He also asked for the privilege of choosing them and going ahead, which was granted. I then thought, chosen or not, I would be one of them. George Jackson, Benjamin Robinson, Christopher Carpenter, John Haymond, John Harbert, and myself, the sixth one, were the number. We stripped ourselves as lightly as we could, tied handkerchiefs around our heads, and proceeded to travel as fast as we could. The Indians appeared to travel very carelessly, broke bushes, etc. It was in May. The weeds were young and tender. We could follow a man very easily. We went about seven or eight miles, past where the Indians had stopped to eat. Arriving on a high bank, Jackson turned around and said: "Where do you think they have gone?" With that, he jumped down the bank, and we proceeded down on the beach a short distance, when one of the Indians fired. I think we were about forty yards from them, we on the beach, they on the bank, on the same side of the creek. We started on the run and had run ten or fifteen yards when the other three fired, then we were in about thirty yards from them. At the first gun, Jackson wheeled around and said: "Where did that gun come from?" John Harbert and brother, John, discovered them first running up the hill. They fired. Benjamin Robinson and myself ran and jumped on the bank where the Indians left their knapsacks. I fired the third shot, the Indians were sixty yards off. They had to run up a very steep hill. Robinson shot at the same Indian that I did. I heard him or one of them talk after I shot. Jackson and Carpenter had run up the hill. I was the first on top, with the company I was with (the other men had joined us and two or three went around the hill in another place).

We then turned down to where the Indians had got on the top of the hill; there, we found a blanket, belt, knife, scabbard, and blood. The Indian had bled considerably. He went about a quarter of a mile and cut a stick, which we supposed was to stop the blood. We followed him about a mile when we then thought it dangerous to follow, thinking he had his gun with him and would hide and kill one of us. To my mortification, we returned. We could have trailed him anywhere. On our return, we found his shot pouch. Had we found it first, I think we would have overtaken him. About ten years after, his gun was found. After we fired, I wanted to run down a creek as I could see that a run came in just below, but the rest would not. If we had, I have no doubt we would have met them again as the wounded Indian crossed the point and run not very far from its mouth. The other Indians we did not follow, but the Indians' place of attack where we found all their knapsacks, one shot pouch (having previously found one) four hatchets and all their plunder, including the woman's scalp. Here on examination we found that brother John had been shot through the handkerchief just above his ear, and Jackson through the shirt sleeve near his wrist. Had we looked, we would have found the Indian's gun. We ought to have expected that the Indian would have thrown away his gun before his shot pouch. I have since heard that one of the Cunninghams who was a prisoner with the Indians at that time, on his return, said that an Indian came home and said that he had been with three others on Muddy River (West Fork), killed a man and a woman, and they were followed, and they fired on the white men and killed two, and the white men fired on them and wounded three, one of whom died after crossing the second ridge at a run. We were on the second ridge and near the second run. The other two died between that and the Ohio River. If this account is true and the Indians we followed were the same, we must have shot well. We thought at the time we had wounded two. We sold our Indian plunder for about twenty dollars along with what were some curious affairs.

Yours, William Haymond"

In the fall of 1791, Ephraim Ashcraft, sixty-seven, lost his life to marauding Indians on Little Bingamon Creek near Shinnston in Marion County. It was near where his brother's daughter-in-law's brother and wife, John and Rachel McIntire, had been killed in the spring. Ephraim, the eldest son of Daniel Sr., owned land on Decker's Creek in Monongalia County near John Evans's plantation.

After that year, there were no more murders of whites by Indians in Harrison County. Depredations would not end in northwestern Virginia until the new century. Native aggression continued across the country, though, as families of European origin flooded westward to make their homes.

This is the story of one family and branches of that family, and the violence suffered because they sought to help develop this new country, giving themselves the opportunity to live without undue taxation and worship without harsh penalties. They wanted their children to own land, to grow crops, to become self-sufficient, and to have a chance at freedom.

Hundreds of such families endured thousands of unimaginable losses for more than two long centuries. They are unsung heroes who sacrificed everything to move this country forward.

Freedom to Become Whatever They Wanted

Lambert (Currey)

Josiah Lambert, thirty-four, knew he wanted to fight this war on the sea as part of the American strategy to disrupt British trade. He could go one of two ways. Join the Continental Navy, which had few vessels and offered low pay and rigid discipline. Or, become a crew member on a privateer ship where officers and crew shared all money collected after the sale of a captured prize vessel and its cargo.

Either way, risks loomed. As the Revolutionary War began in earnest in 1776, Britain's navy was the world's most powerful. American forces were not equipped to go head-to-head with it. Yet, all realized the importance of disrupting the enemy's supply lines. General George Washington's troops desperately needed supplies, particularly firearms, gunpowder, and ammunition; he recognized British ships as a ready source.

On March 23, 1776, the Continental Congress resolved: "That the inhabitants of these colonies be permitted to fit out armed vessels to cruise on the enemies of these United States."

Josiah talked it over with his wife, Joannah, at their home in Hopewell, New Jersey, in Mercer County, just northeast and across the Delaware River from Philadelphia. He decided to join a privateer vessel. Riches were possible. On the other hand, capture might mean death since the British would likely consider captured American seamen to be traitors.

In early August, Josiah said goodbye to Joannah and their five children before riding to Philadelphia, a major port on the eastern seaboard with dozens of shipyards. Philadelphia was one of thirteen home ports for those operating as privateers in this country. He discovered that a privateer sloop, *Retrieve,* had been commissioned by William Paul of Philadelphia. Captain Joshua Stone was in the process of hiring a crew of eighty.

A delay in departure gave Josiah time to learn more about the enterprise. In America, privateers most often used two-masted schooners and brigantines. The government legally sanctioned these privately owned and armed ships to attack the merchant vessels of a nation with which the sponsoring country was at war. During the March 23, 1776 session of the Continental Congress, it formalized the commissioning process with an act that granted these ships the right to be armed and outfitted for these types of missions. Congress often stipulated the vessel size, crew number, and basic rules they had to follow in order to have a legitimate claim on captured vessels, known as prizes. Prize courts, or vice-admiralty courts, determined whether or not they were legitimate. When found to be legitimate, the value of the captured ship and cargo was shared by the owners and crew.

The *Retrieve* sailed from Philadelphia with fifty-five sailors, including Ensign Josiah Lambert. Captain Stone headed down the Delaware Bay and around to the New Jersey coast, where he picked up twenty-five more. On Thursday, August 29, 1776, the sloop, armed with ten cannons, headed north up the coast from Little Egg Harbor.

The British ship of war, *Milford,* had been cruising the coast between New Jersey and Maine, disrupting fishing and shipping. It was a full-rigged ship with twenty-four, nine pound cannons on the upper deck, four three pound cannons on the quarter deck, and twelve half-pound swivel guns. It carried 200 officers and crew.

Mid-morning on Monday, September 30, the *Retrieve's* lookout signaled a big British ship heading toward them from the north. It popped out of the mostly dissipated fog. They were sailing through Casco Bay off the coast of Maine, just east of where the town of Falmouth had been. The British Royal Navy burned it the previous year. Portland would be established on the site eleven years later.

If it was a warship, they certainly could not fight. The sailors were ten to twelve miles offshore. With her sails full, the approaching vessel would easily be able to track down the *Retrieve* in a race for the coast. Besides, charts showed no safe inlets for them to enter if they did make it from where they were. But that is where Captain Stone immediately headed.

When the crew of the *Milford* spotted the smaller vessel, two commissioned officers and the captain discussed whether they wanted to bother chasing down this enemy boat. Did they want fifty to seventy-five prisoners on their frigate right now? Of course, they had just left Canada and stocked up on provisions, so there was plenty of food and water. They could accommodate them in the hold of their big ship until they reached New York.

When they saw the *Retrieve* suddenly tact to her port side, the chase was on. The captain of the *Milford* knew he would catch the smaller vessel long before they made it to safety.

Captain Stone hoped the larger ship would not fire on them broadsides and simply take them down. On the other hand, he wondered for a minute whether he might not prefer swimming with sharks in the water rather than surrendering to the sharks he knew were on that ship. Early reports of prisoners being held on old ships in New York harbor sounded ominous.

"Captain, are we going to make it in?" asked a young crew member.

"Probably not, son, but we have to at least make a run for it."

"Can we not turn and fire on them or something?"

"With the firepower they have on that Man of War, they would blow us to kingdom come. Is that how you want to go?" the captain asked.

"No, sir. Does it mean we're about to become prisoners of war?"

"Do you believe in prayer? If so, I believe I'd spend the next little bit asking for peace," said the captain. Josiah scanned the now mostly clear horizon, hoping to see another American privateer or warship. He did not know how else they would get out of their predicament. Winds were favorable, but still, a monster bore down upon them.

In a little less than thirty minutes, Captain Stone ran up the white flag. He peacefully surrendered his ship and crew, who had quickly gathered their few personal belongings. Not a man was injured because no fights occurred. No conversation took place. They happily received only abusive language from their English captors. The men figured the Brits must be in an unusually congenial mood because of their brief stopover in Canada. Maybe they found women and liquor to their liking. And Captain Stone had rehearsed desired behavior in just such a situation. They were transferred to the dark, dank hole at the bottom of the *Milford*.

Nearly two uncomfortable weeks passed, and the cold set in until, on Friday, October 12, they were all transferred from the *Milford* to the prison ship *Hostage*. It sat in Wallabout Bay, off the shore of Brooklyn, New York, along with fifteen others.

On August 27, an expeditionary force of over 32,000 British Regular troops, along with ten ships of the line, twenty frigates, and 170 transports, had defeated General Washington's troops at Kip's Bay, an inlet on the East River. Afterward, they invaded Manhattan Island. On November 16, British troops secured Manhattan when they forced the fall of Fort Washington and the evacuation of Fort Lee, which sat on the Hudson River's western shore of New Jersey. They held the city for the next seven years.

Josiah and his mates discovered conditions aboard their prison ship worse than they could have possibly imagined. Guards harassed and abused prisoners. By the end of 1776, disease and starvation were killing at least half of those taken on Long Island and maybe two-thirds of the men captured at Fort Washington. Thousands of American soldiers and sailors found themselves crammed together in the dark, airless hulls of these ships. Human waste mingled with the smells of sickness and death. Some corpses were tossed overboard. Others were buried in shallow graves along the eroding shoreline, which local residents found and reburied in years to come. Four out of five men who were held in captivity suffered death. More died on British prison ships than were killed on battlefields.

One prisoner who survived was Philip Freneau of New Jersey, a poet, sea captain, and editor of the *National Gazette*, sometimes called the "Poet of the American Revolution." He wrote the following poem after being held in a prison hulk as the result of the British capturing the vessel he sailed on in 1780:

"Hail dark abode! What can with thee compare —
Heat, sickness, famine, death and stagnant air —
Pandora's box, from whence all mischief flew,
Here real found, torments mankind anew! —
Swift from the guarded decks we rush'd along,
And vainly sought repose, so vast our throng;
Four hundred wretches here, denied all light,
In crowded mansions pass the infernal night,
Some for a bed their tattered vestments join,
And some on chests, and some on floors recline;
Shut from the blessings of the evening air
Pensive we lay with mingled corpses there,
Meagre and wan, and scorch'd with heat, below.
We look'd like ghosts, ere death had made us so." (Green, vii)

Prisoners were allowed on the top deck for air and exercise every four days, so there would not be more than one hundred at a time. Josiah always listened to conversations among the crew. In late spring of 1777, he heard someone refer to one of the new officers as Lieutenant Horton. He knew it was a long shot, but his paternal grandfather immigrated from Wiltshire, England, to New Jersey in 1677. His mother had been Eleanor Horton, also from Wiltshire. Josiah's father told him that his grandfather was Thomas Horton, and following him, Thomas II and Thomas III joined the family. He thought he must talk to this officer.

Toward the end of that summer, the lieutenant walked by him on deck.

"Excuse me, Lieutenant Horton. Allow me a personal question," Josiah said.

"How personal?"

"It's about my family in England. My grandmother was a Horton. The family came from Wiltshire. May I ask from where you hail, sir?"

"I, too, come from Wiltshire. What is your name?" asked the British officer.

"Josiah Lambert from New Jersey. My great-grandmother Eleanor's father was Thomas Horton. There has since been a Thomas in the following two generations, which means Thomas III would be my grandfather's age."

The lieutenant, who Josiah figured to be about his age, straightened up, tilted his hat back a tad, looked Josiah square in the eyes, and then smiled. "Well, my grandfather does, in fact, have a brother who is Thomas Horton III. Both still live. Say your grandmother was Eleanor? Let me look into this, and I'll get back to you, Josiah Lambert."

With that, the officer discreetly reached into a pocket and handed Josiah a packet of wrapped walnuts before turning and walking away.

Nearly two months later, the two again met on the upper deck.

"We are, indeed, cousins, Josiah Lambert," Lieutenant Cedric Horton revealed in a lowered voice.

"What? Surely . . . you jest," replied Josiah.

"Shhhh. This must stay between the two of us. Thomas Horton of Wiltshire did have a daughter, Eleanor, who married a Roger Lambert, and they immigrated to the new country, to New Jersey, around 1660."

"Yes, they were my great-grandparents," Josiah said. "So Eleanor and your great-uncle Thomas . . . were brother and sister. My grandfather and your grandfather would have been first cousins, correct?"

The lieutenant laughed softly. "I do believe you have it right." With that, he pulled out a packet of venison jerky and slipped it to Josiah. "Over there sits a water barrel. I'll walk with you. Drink plenty of it. Stay as well as possible. I'll get food to you as I can, but it is dangerous. I'll speak with the captain and make sure you are on the list for the next exchange of prisoners. Do not know when it will be. No time soon. Be patient. And stay smart."

Sadly, Josiah lived under harsh conditions for nearly another two years. The best his new-found cousin could manage was for his early release when some American prisoners of war, who survived their incarceration, were exchanged for British prisoners of war in late October 1779. Although Lieutenant Horton received a transfer a year before the release, he kept a bug in the ear of a superior about his promise for Josiah Lambert's early release. But Josiah missed his cousin, who he considered a godsend. He enjoyed their brief encounters and the extra food, which boosted his energy somewhat.

Josiah found himself among about fifty soldiers released. Privateers would typically be among the last released after the war ended in 1782 because the British saw these Americans as rebels who they equated with pirates. He would never forget the grace shown him by his British cousin.

The group received transportation out of New York south to New Brunswick, located along the King's Highway and situated along the Raritan River. There, they were cleaned up, clothed, and fed by Continental troops and community members.

Once they walked off their god-forsaken prison onto land, friendly soldiers escorted them onto wagons for the relatively short ride into New Jersey. Every day he had remained on the ship, he made himself remain conscious in order to get up and walk despite the tight space. He loved his family. He would live. But now, as he was jostled around in a wagon, what very little energy he had dissipated, and he slumped against the man beside him.

It was a short distance from New Brunswick to Josiah's home in Hopewell. How he got there, he would never know for sure. He knew someone had carried him in a wagon. But who, when, how — details remained a blur. All he remembered was waking up one day and Joannah's teary face looking into his. Then he heard children. Next, he smelled cooking. And he knew it was real. God had delivered him from hell itself. He received a second chance at life.

***

To Josiah's surprise, his family had increased by one when he returned home. When he left that first week in August 1776, tiny Anna was just a month old. Nine months later, Suzanna, who the family called Sukey, arrived. Their oldest, Joe, twelve, assisted his mother, as did Richard, who was two years younger.

Right after Josiah left for Philadelphia, Joannah had sent word to her father's spinster cousin that she needed help. Mary Stevenson lived in Chesterfield, located south of Hopewell, just over the Mercer County border, near the Delaware River. Mary, the youngest child out of ten in her family, was nine years older than Joannah. She always said she was available in a crisis. Joannah liked the woman and took her at her word.

Almost six months went by before Josiah cleared the cobwebs from his head. He figured the nightmares would diminish over time. As he ate, his frame began filling out, and his strength slowly returned. He started cleaning up the farm when March arrived.

Josiah intended to lay low until the war officially ended. He could not imagine the carnage on battlefields being any harder on a man than he had experienced over the past three years. He wanted to stay as far away from all of it as possible.

When the British suffered a major defeat at Yorktown, Virginia, in October 1781, the nation rejoiced. But the end turned into a long process. The following November, preliminary peace articles were signed and drafted. It was not until the Treaty of Paris was signed on September 4, 1783, that the war formally ended. The U.S. Congress ratified the treaty on January 14, 1784.

In spring 1784, the Lambert family decided to head southwest. The new country had a preliminary Constitution in place, and it grappled with who and what it was to become. Josiah was now forty-two, but he thought he had never felt better. He wanted to take his seven children into the western frontier, where he hoped they would have the freedom to become whatever they wanted without anybody looking over their shoulders.

To his surprise, Josiah received a 221-acre land grant in Greene County, Pennsylvania, which was located in the extreme southwest corner of the state. It would one day be absorbed into Virginia.

The timing proved fortuitous. One of their neighbors in Hopewell had set his sights on western Virginia, as did his brother's family, who lived in New Hope on the Pennsylvania side of the Delaware River. Robert and Patricia Coughlin, long-time neighbors, had four boys older than the Lambert's oldest sons, who were by then fifteen and seventeen. The other Coughlin family also had two older teen boys. Josiah was greatly relieved to have strong young men along. All could shoot. The more help and protection crossing the Allegheny Mountains, the better.

During the French and Indian War, British forces built a rough road westward from Philadelphia in order to gain access to the interior. It was one of three routes used by a swelling migration moving toward the Monongahela River basin in western Virginia. The Lamberts planned to settle in a bordering county in Pennsylvania, and the Coughlins would travel down into Virginia.

Each family took one wagon apiece pulled by oxen. Horses carried people, limited feed for humans and animals, and other supplies. Four mules, much to the displeasure of one, hauled crates of chickens. A half dozen hogs and twelve cows completed the convoy.

The little caravan rolled through the towns of Lancaster, Yorktown, Gettysburg, and Chambersburg in southern Pennsylvania. Once they reached Bedford, they sold their wagons and packed what they could on extra horses. From there on, footpaths led them where they wanted to go. The Coughlins headed down Jacob's Creek, which flowed into the Monongahela River. The Lamberts traveled further west and located to newly-established Waynesburg in Greene County. Their property lay on the South Fork of Ten Mile River.

In the mid-1770s, Josiah's brother, Jonathan Lambert, had relocated to Clarksburg, Virginia, in Harrison County. In 1781, he acquired 1,400 acres on what became known as Lambert's Run. In 1786, Josiah and his family left Pennsylvania and move to Harrison County, too. They stayed for sixteen years, and the people they met influenced the rest of their lives.

After selling their property in Greene County, the Lambert family, including nine children, loaded up and headed seventy miles south to Clarksburg. Josiah was five years younger than his brother, Jonathan, but they were the closest in age to William Lambert's boys. An inseparable bond had existed between the two as youngsters. When Jonathan received word that his brother wanted to live close to him and his family, he welcomed them to move onto part of his ample property.

Harrison County was created by an act of the Virginia Assembly just two years before the Lamberts arrived. It extended over a huge territory, from the Maryland line to the Ohio River. The French and Indian War and subsequent Revolutionary War slowed migration. Indian warfare against the settlers would not stop until the early 1790s. Yet the people who settled in this mountainous northwestern territory of Virginia were organized, determined, and fierce against the odds.

One of the first families who befriended the Lamberts upon their arrival to Clarksburg was the Hulls. Samuel Sr. and his wife, Martha Glover Hull, arrived in the mid-1760s from Maryland. In April 1790, Samuel Hull Jr., nineteen, plowed a field for Major Benjamin Robinson, about three miles west of Shinnston. A small party of Indians shot, tomahawked, and scalped the young man. Mistress Robinson discovered his body when he failed to come to the house for dinner. The field where this killing occurred became known as "Hull Field."

In January 1791, Joe Lambert married Ruth Hull. Two months later, his sister, Mary, became the wife of Charles Hull. In 1798, the third marriage between the families took place as younger sister, Hannah Lambert and James Hull said their vows. James died two years later after he was attacked by a wild boar on a fall hunting trip with two brothers and a couple of friends.

In 1801, Hannah married Jacob Barnes, whose family came from Maryland in the late 1770s and settled near Fairmont. They would become the progenitors of the Currey family in the future West Virginia.

Marriages kept the Lamberts occupied for three consecutive years in the late 1790s. Sukey joined one of the best-known and most numerous families in the county when she married John

Davisson in 1796. His father, Amaziah Davisson, was one of the earlier settlers near Clarksburg, when he arrived in 1774. Jonathan Lambert wed Margaret McFarland the next year. In November 1798, Anna Lambert and Noah Clark united in marriage. Noah's father, Watson Clark, would serve as sheriff of Harrison County from 1801-1803.

The new century saw an exodus of Harrison County families who sold their property and hauled their possessions west to Holderby's Landing, which would soon become Huntington, on the Ohio River. There, they helped build flatboats to carry them south along the river. These sturdy boats were box-shaped, fifty feet long, and twelve feet wide. Most families traveled in groups. Danger lurked from unpredictable Indians and pirates.

In the spring of 1800, Josiah and Joannah Lambert, along with most of their children and spouses, joined a large contingent of Davisson family members heading southwest. Joe Lambert and his wife, Ruth, and Mary and Charles Hull went west with the Hull family and settled in Licking County, located in the remote interior of Ohio.

The Davissons decided to stop on the river in Scioto County. The Lamberts continued on to Maysville, Kentucky, where there was a natural harbor at Limestone Creek. A blockhouse in the new settlement and a frontier fort three miles inland were added attractions. Daniel Boone, the famed frontiersman, and early founder, established a trading post and tavern there, where he owned most of the land. Two years later, the Lamberts made their final move. They went back up the river to Upper Township, Ohio, which, at the time, was in Scioto County. There, they discovered the Davissons, who had settled in the developing river town.

By this time, Ben and Elizabeth Carpenter and family had moved to Ironton, along with the McFarland family, including daughter Margaret and husband Jonathan Lambert, from Harrison County. Luke and Mary Kelly and family came west from

Shenandoah County, Virginia, in 1797 and first purchased fifty acres on the Clinch River near Hanging Rock.

Surveys were conducted of Scioto County in 1799, but the lands did not become available until three years later. Before that time, settlers were considered squatters. In 1802, Luke Kelly entered a section of 640 acres at $2 per acre, $9 for surveying, and $12 for the patent.

Early entries in the Ohio River's rich bottomland in Scioto County, when land became available for sale, included Josiah Lambert, John Davisson, and William Carpenter. Below the Union Landing, John's father, Amaziah Davisson, and two of his brothers, Nathan and Andrew, secured land.

John and Sukey Lambert Davisson brought their three children to their new land on the south bank of Storms Creek, where it then followed the Ohio River south. It cut due east to Upper Township and what would be the town of Ironton. He cleared timber, built a log cabin, set fruit trees around it, and farmed. He continued clearing and cultivating land, and in 1812, he built a bigger, more substantial log cabin for their growing family. By 1822, as one of the more prosperous farmers in the area, he constructed the first two-story brick house ever built in that part of the country.

John served as a squire for many years before the new county of Lawrence was organized in 1817. He then became presiding county judge and later served three terms in the state legislature between 1821 and 1826. Located in Columbus, Ohio, he made the trips on horseback and stayed all winter throughout the sessions. He intended to stand for the state Senate in 1831. But John Davisson died of consumption on February 3 that year at the age of thirty-five.

In September 1804, Abigail Lambert decided to marry Reverand John Kelly, a son of Luke and Mary Kelly. He served as the first sheriff of the county. He was an expert rifleman and

hunter, and in his early days, he became known for his ability to gig fish with a
fifteen-foot-long spear with three heavy bearded prongs.

He built a horse mill below Union Landing, using the stones from a floating mill constructed in 1799 that had broken loose and been purchased by his father. He bought a bolt from Chillicothe and made the first flour in the region. (Bolting means the miller can sift out the desired parts of the grain and discard the rest.) It improved the baking qualities of his flour.

Union Landing sat opposite Ferguson's Sandbar in the river. The old settlers had always heard about marauding Indians who entrapped flat boats heading downriver at this point. The bar forced boats close to the bank, and sometimes, whole families lost their lives and possessions to the attackers.

John and his brother Joshua Kelly, located below Union Landing. Joshua's farm sat very near Union Furnace Landing. Both brothers found many human skeletons on their farms, including under their houses. Indian mounds were in the area. Rumor had it there used to be an old Indian town just below John Kelly's farm where many were killed and buried on a nearby battleground from the early days.

The following month, October 1804, Richard Lambert, thirty-five, married Nancy Carpenter, who everybody called Linnie. She was the fourteen-year-old daughter of Ben and Elizabeth Carpenter. Linnie gave birth to two healthy boys over the next two years. She failed to survive the birth of her twin daughters on December 29, 1808. Mary Kelly, a skilled midwife, delivered the babies. She suffered over the loss of the mother because the two families were close, but she nurtured the babies to health. They buried young Linnie in a graveyard just below Hanging Rock, near the Ohio River. Sadly, a subsequent flood washed it away.

Richard Lambert worked as a blacksmith. He greatly benefited from the location of his family's property, which backed up to coal banks. Josiah Lambert built a small log cabin up a road that ran directly down to his son's place on the bank of the Ohio River. They hauled coal on carts pulled by oxen to the boat landing. This coal supplied Richard's blacksmith shop. The Lamberts sold what they could to river traffic, which carried it away on keelboats. It would be 1811 before the first steamboat plied the waters of the Ohio.

In 1820, Josiah Lambert passed away in his sleep at seventy-eight after seeing ten children live to adulthood. Their youngest, Priscilla, born in Harrison County, Virginia, was the only member of the family to return to her parent's home state of New Jersey to live. Never married, Priscilla died in April 1825 of unknown causes at age thirty-four. Her mother, Joannah Lambert, eighty, suffered a head injury in a fall the following month and was lost to the family before hearing of her daughter's passing.

# # #

Jacob was the eighth child out of seven sons and three daughters, produced by William and Mary Marietta Barnes. When he and Hannah Lambert Hull married in October 1801, he already had thirteen nieces and nephews.

Hannah fit right into the Barnes family after she wed Jacob, who helped her overcome the shock of her first husband's death. He moved her to his home on Tevebaugh Creek outside of Fairmont in Monongalia County, Virginia, north of where the Lamberts lived. Once there, she was close to a large, loving family much like hers.

William Barnes descended from tough Massachusetts stock, beginning with Thomas Barnes II, who sailed on the *Speedwell* in 1656 from Barking in Essex County, England, to Marlborough. During King Philip's War, between 1676 and 1678, his son and William's great-grandfather, Thomas III, lost his house and all his possessions to the Indians. On April 23, 1734, at age seventy-two, in Brookfield, he was fatally gored by a bull.

William Barnes, a millwright, moved to Monongalia County, Virginia, sometime before 1782. By then, there were eight of his children in his household. He operated a mill on George's Creek in Allegany County, Maryland, where he was born, before heading west. Upon arrival, he found five or six acres of level land on the east bank of the Tygarts Valley River at the mouth of a small branch that rose at the Fairmont reservoir and drained into the Pleasant Valley Basin.

William built a mill a short distance above the mouth of this branch where there was a forty-foot waterfall. He constructed a house of hewn logs well above high water and cultivated a garden sloping down the river. His mill ground corn and thrived for decades until the railroad arrived and divided his garden in two. Other mills later opened in Fairmont.

Beautiful Mary Marietta Barnes was born in Maryland to Johann Marietta. He started calling himself Samuel once he left his parents as a young man in Torino, located in the Province of Piedmont, Italy. He immigrated to Maryland in the mid-1700s. Mary's mother, Elizabeth Sabin, was raised in Newport, Rhode Island. Mary married William Barnes in Maryland on George's Creek in 1762.

After a few years and five babies, Jacob and Hannah Barnes moved to a farm at the head of Pleasant Valley in Virginia, where they lived for about forty years. By the time Amanda, the last of their fourteen children, was born in 1840. Whatever family remained in the house, moved to the old Shinn farm between the village of Shinnston and Maulsby's Ford on the West Fork River.

Jacob and Hannah raised their family to be devout Christians. They belonged to the Methodist Episcopal Church, and their home remained open to all ministers of the gospel. For more than fifty years, family worship was maintained morning and night. All children made public professions of faith in Christ before they were fifteen years old.

Every Barnes child lived to adulthood. Abe was the youngest to experience tragedy when he drowned in the West Fork River in late May 1852 at age thirty-two. They had just lost their father one month previously to apparent heart failure. He was seventy-three. Daughter Ara, born in May 1813, outlived her entire family. She surrendered to old age in June 1903 at the home of her daughter, Slyvina, in Ravenswood, West Virginia, on the Ohio River.

Ara Barnes, who most people called Ary, married Aaron Vincent in 1833. It was one of three marriages between the Barnes and Vincent families. Aaron's sister, Francis, or Fanny, as she was known, and John L. Barnes became man and wife two years earlier. Then, in 1846, Jesse Barnes and Susannah Vincent followed suit.

The Vincents originally came from France. They moved to England during the religious uprising in the sixteenth and seventeenth centuries, seeking religious freedom. Soon, they became disillusioned with the restrictions they found there.

There were three brothers in the Vincent family. Zedekiah left for America around the turn of the nineteenth century and began working for a farmer in Bridgeport, Virginia. His family soon lost track of him. Brother Edward wanted to come look for him, but first, he planned to marry Rebecca Wisby.

"My father will not allow me to marry ye," fourteen year-old Rebecca, said. "I don't know how I'll get away."

Edward, ten years older, refused to be deterred. "Put a very few clothes and what ye absolutely cannot get along without in a sack. Hide it in the southwest fence corner tonight. I'll have someone retrieve it in the morn. Put on your bonnet and say ye ere going to visit your mate, Clara. Then, meet me at the boat."

To their dismay, they found there was room for only one passenger. They decided Edward would take the boat. Rebecca agreed to wait on the next one. One month later, she arrived in New York City to her anxiously awaiting beau. They bought two horses and commenced riding south. When they reached Gapplus Tavern in Geneva, Pennsylvania, Edward explained that they were not married but wanted to be as soon as possible. The accommodating host and Edward rode for a day to bring back a preacher. They were then united in marriage on Sunday, March 6.

They arrived in Bridgeport only to discover that Zedekiah had left unannounced. But they settled there in Harrison County. When the War of 1812 broke out, Edward joined the Pennsylvania 58th Regiment Infantry in Fayette County just over the state line on September 4, 1812. One day, he and a few fellow soldiers entered a nice house near Charleston, Virginia, to find something to eat. To his complete shock, he found it belonged to his long-lost brother. The two brothers sent money and brought their younger brother, William, to join them.

Edward was discharged on March 23, 1813. He was granted 187 acres of bounty land for his war service near Bridgeport near the Tygart Valley River. There, he preached in the local Methodist Episcopal Church.

The Vincents' oldest son, Aaron, and wife, Ary, lived nearby in Harrison County, as did most of their thirteen children. Aaron farmed, and he also practiced healing in the community as a doctor. In 1849, at thirty-seven, he received the fruits of faith, hope, and love through a Christian conversion. From that point on, he spent his life ministering to the people.

The Vincents and Barnes connected with the Currey family when Ellen Vincent, fifth out of seven daughters of Aaron and Ary Barnes Vincent, married John Currey in 1866. The Curreys rapidly multiplied in Harrison and Taylor counties after John B. and Eleanor "Nellie" Welsh Currey moved from Fauquier County, in eastern Virginia, to Harrison County by 1785.

This family represented the mix typically found in communities in the new state of West Virginia as the nineteenth century headed into its final decades: seven parts British Isles — five English, one Scottish, and one Irish and one part French.

Journey 'Cross the Mountains

Carder (Currey)

John Carder rocked on his front porch while surveying land accumulated around his northwest Virginia mountaintop over five decades. The day approached late afternoon. Cool temperatures came on a little early this year. Late September showers continued into October. The result was a brilliant display of orange, crimson, burgundy, and yellow on wooded slopes down through the valley where a small herd of cows grazed. An ideal birthday present, he thought.

The Carder patriarch would turn eighty within days. The only thing missing was his Mary, who he lost forty-five years earlier.

Mary Shingleton came from English immigrants. Both families lived in Culpeper County, located in the northeastern section of the state. John and Pricilla Shingleton made the journey from Berkshire in the 1740s, just as the county was being established. Mary, the Shingleton's eldest daughter, and little John Carder knew each other as classmates beginning in 1774. They were soon joined by Jonathan Shingleton and Lucy Carder, all within a year apart in age. Citizens of Culpeper started contributing to a schoolhouse and salary for a school mistress ten years earlier.

As evening shadows moved across his fields, which had been carved out of hilly, forested land through years of toil and sweat by man and animal, John's mind once again traveled back to the day Mary died. A decade after it happened, he felt certain the details would one day fade. He now knew that day would never come.

John and his oldest son, John R. Carder III, twenty then, who was a twin to Lucinda, one of two sets of twins among his eleven children, drove one of the wagons into Grafton early morning, October 12, 1807, with a load of cushaw squash and pumpkins. Lucinda was helping a neighbor make cheese. In return, she usually brought home delicious course-textured cow's milk cheese.

The other boys, age seventeen and the fourteen year-old twins were at the lower end of the property gathering large stones to construct a wall. Three slave field hands worked with the boys. The oldest field hand, Jake, an excellent stone mason, used his sons, Rufus, twenty, and Cleo, eighteen, to help him in the construction. A good-sized stream, known as Carder Run, bordered the south end of the property.

Liz, eleven, was the oldest of the Carder girls at home that day. Two house slaves, Lila, Jake's wife, and their daughter, Rhea, twenty-three, minded the children. Since it was Monday, they collected laundry for washing when they heard Mary scream. Both women ran out and around the side of the house just as Mary halfway stumbled out of the garden.

"Mistress, what wrong?" asked Lila as she took Mary's arm to steady her.

"I didn't see it. A big copperhead. It got me good down on my leg."

"Oh, Lawd, I sho do see da bit marks. Um, um. Did you kilt hit?"

"No. Nooooo!"

"Girl, go ring dat bell loud an' long. Get da mens up here. Can't have no bad snake up 'round da house with da chillens. Let me get Mistress in da house," Lila said.

"Then, Rhea, you run to the barn. Put a bridle on Blondie. I know you can ride her bareback. Hurry over to the Powell's place and tell Lucinda I need her right now," ordered Mary as she and Lila headed toward the front door.

"Yes, 'um, I be right quick," Rhea replied as she reached for the rope attached to a big iron bell hanging from a post in the yard.

It signaled meals were ready if rung six times or an emergency if rung continuously.

Lila's people in mountainous Greene County, North Carolina, learned the role of plants in medicine from the Cherokee. She knew that cinnamon fern was used for snake bite by the local Cherokee and the Iroquois, who came into western Virginia from across the Ohio River. It was a common plant. She immediately collected a few from the woods. She had Mary chew on the fern's root before swallowing some of it. Then Lila applied the rest to the bite just below her right calf. By that time, there was redness, swelling, and warmth around the wound.

As soon as the boys came up from the field, Mary told Isaac and Thomas to saddle two of the horses and ride into Grafton to find their father and brother. Meanwhile, Jake killed the copperhead, which he found stretched out in the sun on a large flat rock bordering the garden. Lucinda arrived shortly after that in a twirl.

By the time Mary's family returned from town around noon, muscle pain had set in. Soon, she became nauseous and commenced to vomiting.

John, Lucinda, Jake, and Lila stepped outside the door while Liz attended to her mother.

"We stopped by Doc Quillan's. Told him what happened," explained John. "He said not to raise up the leg. Not to apply any pressure to it, so you done good, Lila. He said if Lila knew an Indian remedy, it wouldn't hurt nothing, although it might not help neither. Said in his two decades of practice here in Harrison County, he hears of right near a dozen copperhead bites a year on average. Generally, two or three of those people fail to pull out of it. Whereas, they's almost exactly the same number of bites by rattlers. Four of those folks every year don't live to tell of it."

"Oh, Papa, couldn't the doctor of come back with you?" asked Lucinda. "Ain't there nothing he can do for Mama?"

"No, daughter, evidently they's nothing to do but let her run hit's course. Let's pray your mama is strong enough to outlast hit. She is surrounded by love and the best care we and Lila can give her. Hit's up to God above now I reckon."

John glanced to his right at his youngest sons, Isaac, Joe, Thomas, and Will, who were seated on log porch benches. "You boys hear that?"

"Yes, sir," they replied in unison.

"If none of you has prayed in earnest, now would be a good time to do it. Your mama's in a bad way."

Rare silence surrounded the brothers for a minute. Then, Will, one of the twins, said to Issac, "You don't really think God's gonna take Mama away from us, do you?"

"That's hard to ponder. But if He needs her in Heaven for some reason, I reckon He will. I don't rightly understand death. I know the savages leave our family alone 'cause they trust Pa. He's built up goodwill with 'um. But folks in these parts still don't know whether or not they'll get a tomahawk in their head when they walk out 'n their door."

"Remember two years ago when the three Kitts brothers and their pa traveled down to Leadville to visit their papaw," Joe asked.

"Yeah, I remember," replied Isaac.

"He took 'em up on the Cheat River to fish," continued Joe. "And Cooper, the youngest, I think he was thirteen, got bit by a rattler sunning on a river rock. Stuck his hand out to balance hisself and it got him on the arm. Never saw it nor heard it, I reckon 'cause of the rushin' water."

"He was a goner before they made it back to Leadsville," added Isaac. "His mamaw must have had a fit. They brung the body on back to Grafton to bury him in the family's cemetery. Good thing his ma already passed on. Saved her the sufferin'."

By late afternoon, Lila realized that Mary was becoming still. Her breaths were shallow. She had seen this before when she attended the victim of a rattlesnake bite in North Carolina. The woman soon passed away. She stepped away from the bed, then whispered to John that she did not believe Mary would hang on long into the night.

Lila and Jake headed to their cabin to give the Carders privacy. Lila realized that nobody had eaten since breakfast. A meal became her next mission. But as soon as they walked through their front door, she smelled that Rhea, bless her heart, had it covered. Two big cast iron pots of soup heated over the fire. A good bit of leftover brown beans from yesterday went into the pots, along with carrots, onions, fennel, cabbage, tomatoes, oregano, and thyme. She threw in ham bones since they had butchered a hog just days earlier. Then she filled each pot three-quarters full of water. The soup slowly cooked for the better part of the afternoon.

"Ma, I can slide cornbread batter in da coals anytime ya think peoples be ready to eat," said Rhea.

"Oh, chil, I do thanks ya," replied her mother. "I 'spect da angels guine come fur Mistress any time. But them chillens gots to eat. You cook da cornbread. Pap and yo brothers can tote hit over yonder."

"Rufus and Cleo done et," Rhea said.

"Good. We all needs to sit down and eat. Where da boys?"

"Da barn I 'spose."

"Yo pap 'il go find 'um."

Mary slipped away just after the sunset on that beautiful October day. Two days later, the family laid her to rest in the John Carder Cemetery in Williamsport. John's brother, Henry, had also moved west to Harrison County with his wife, Nancy. He became an accomplished furniture maker. The coffin he constructed for Mary was of chestnut, a thing of beauty to match her own.

John had bought his slave family in 1803, four years after he crossed the Shenandoah, then the Allegheny mountains, to reach his first 247 acres in the Lost Run section above Williamsport, where he established the Carder homestead. He purchased the land from John Prunty. The town's name would be changed to Pruntytown in 1843 to honor this early pioneer.

He realized his family would face various dangers in relocating to what was still a virtual wilderness. But no white settlers had been murdered in the county by Indians since 1791 when John and Rachel McIntire were tomahawked and scalped near their home down on Bingamon Creek. A granddaughter of John and Mary, Lucinda Carder would marry Samuel Ashcraft Tucker in 1849, a grandson of Sarah McIntire Ashcraft, who had been a sister of John McIntire.

It took various members of the Carder family almost two months to make the arduous journey across the mountains to their new home in 1799. There were no roads. What trails existed were not wide enough to accommodate wagons. It required many horses, most ladened with the family's essential household goods. The twin boys were four, and little Lizzie just three. The youngsters spent the trip doubled up on horseback with their oldest siblings or one of the adult women. Mahaly was barely a year old. She stayed in a sling on one of the adults, much to her consternation. Seems an excessive amount of squalling went on and, thus, more stopping than any of the parents would have liked. They did not sneak up on anybody when they occasionally ran across fellow travelers. They negotiated rivers, avoided calamity, and found their way.

The previous owner of Jake, Lila, and their family, Clay Edwards, 61, had no heirs. His wife had recently passed away in western North Carolina. She made him promise to take the family out of North Carolina up into the Virginia mountains, thinking the further north they went, the safer they would be. She wanted him to find a Christian family who were not likely to mistreat Jake and Lila and who would not separate them from their teenage children.

Mr. Edwards and company arrived in Grafton on a Saturday in early April 1803. He inquired as to the location of a local meeting house for Negros. To everyone's relief, he was told to take the road heading west out of town about two miles, then to turn right by the bridge. The building would be about a quarter mile up that road after passing the Baptist church. When he turned the team of horses by the bridge, he noticed a good-sized stream running under it. They arrived at what he took to be the meeting house. The stream ran just behind it. A level area made an ideal camping spot.

They awakened at daybreak, stoked the fire, made coffee, and ate fresh bread and ham he purchased while in town. The preacher arrived just as Mr. Edwards and Jake got the team harnessed.

Reverend Matt Rawlins turned out to be a free black man. He was the first free Negro that Jake and Lila had ever met. He also operated his blacksmith shop in Grafton. Reverend Rawlins heartily welcomed Jake, Lila, and her family. He assured Mr. Edwards that they were in excellent care. Said if Mr. Edwards had not returned when the service ended, he would personally transport them down to the Baptist Church.

By the time Mr. Edwards hitched his team back down the road, horses, other wagons, and a few buggies rimmed the churchyard. People stood in small bunches, and children ran and yelped. A middle-aged preacher warmly greeted those entering the door to a smallish but well--maintained building. Wooden benches provided adequate seating for perhaps fifty worshippers.

Mr. Edwards did not know it, but the hand of Providence directed him to his seat. To his right was a couple with what appeared to be twin boys and another boy a little older. He shook hands with a man who introduced himself as John Carder and his wife as Mary. Directly in front of them sat little girls with a couple of older boys.

Strolling back into the yard, Mr. Edwards took the opportunity to further introduce himself. He explained to the Carders what had brought him to Grafton. Told them that Jake, Lila, and their offspring were at the meeting house up the road. John invited them to their place for lunch. He asked John and Issac, who had ridden their horses, to follow Mr. Edwards to the other church and then lead him and his slaves back to the house.

Lunch stretched into a week. John badly needed labor. There were not enough hours in a day to get everything done that needed doing to start a farm from scratch on wooded land. The two oldest Carder boys were sixteen and thirteen. Son, John, provided good help already. Issac was big for his age and getting stronger all the time, but he was not yet a skilled worker. With help from William Bennett, John's brother-in-law, they had a log cabin half-finished in anticipation of hiring slave labor.

Mary objected, but she admitted that assistance in and around the house would be much welcomed. However, she drew the line when it came to attending a slave auction. She said if there were some other way of finding, preferably, a family to go to work for them, then she would acquiesce. She knew her husband could not keep trying to do the work of two men.

After lunch, all were invited to stay the night. Mary handed out flour sacks for towels, and soap. She pointed the new arrivals toward the stream for baths. Mary, Lucinda, and Liz went out to the small, temporary barn with a lantern and extra quilts and created a space for sleeping. Mr. Edwards would sleep in their recently completed two-story log house.

The next morning after breakfast, John, his two oldest sons, Mr. Edwards, Jake, his two boys, and four dogs toured the property on foot. John wanted them to get a feel for what was there, what he planned to do with it, and what adjacent land he planned to acquire.

Meanwhile, back at the house, Mary talked to Lila and her poised nineteen year-old daughter, about managing ten children and their chores while cooking, churning butter, gardening, canning vegetables and fruit, making soap, cleaning, and sewing. Lila claimed to have helped butcher about every kind of animal and said she knew how to cook meat, too. "Til hit drop off da bone," she said.

The next day, the two men negotiated on a price. The previous evening, John and Mary agreed that this family appeared to be an ideal solution to their labor problem. Mr. Edwards even offered to stay on for a few days to assist with construction on the cabin. Said he had built several cabins in his lifetime and knew something about working with wood.

John figured this family was the best investment he ever made, aside from the land. All were good workers. He and Mary grew to trust every one of them. The Carder's children listened to what Jake and Lila said and never back-talked. They made sure their children understood the essential Biblical message that commands us to: "Do unto others as you would have them do unto you." The relationship evolved into a lifelong blessing.

Ten years after Mary's death, John turned fifty on October 8, 1817. As a tribute to his late wife, he filled out the paperwork and legally gave his slaves their freedom. He knew that is what Mary would have wanted.

Besides, John discovered Rhea had been courting Reverend Rawlin's younger brother, Lucus, who worked with him in his blacksmith shop. He was also a free man. Rhea would not marry him until she was free because she refused to bring children into the world as slaves.

John told the five family members that they were free to go or they were welcome to stay. Told Jake and Lila they could stay in the cabin forever if they would work another ten years for room and board. They told their grown children they could each have twenty acres of their own, with papers, so they could build their own places if they would give him ten years of work. Rufus and Cleo chose to stay on the seemingly protected Carder land, while

Rhea quickly jumped the broom with Lucus Rawlins, and the couple moved into their own small home in Grafton.

*** *** ***

One June morning in 1803, four years after the Carders arrived in Harrison County and two months after Jake and Lila's family found their way to the mountain, John looked down toward the creek and, much to his surprise, he saw four of whom he thought to be Iroquois standing on the bank beside their canoes. In front of them, they had stacked piles of animal furs.

He called for Mary. When she opened the door, he said, "Tell the boys no guns. And keep them up here. I think they want to trade. I'm a going down to meet with 'um."

They did, indeed, want to trade. John had looked forward to this day. The family grew tobacco on their land in Culpeper County. Three of the horses they brought with them over the mountains carried big bundles of cured tobacco. John hoped to use it to trade for Indian furs if the opportunity presented itself before they could get crops in their new ground. Mary thought he was crazy, but he knew it would be a readily tradable item with the Natives.

In 1767, Thomas and Sally Bennett immigrated from Derbyshire, England, and settled in Culpeper. Five years later, their son, William, and his twin sister, Mary, came along. Their two older sisters never made it past childhood, nor did their three younger siblings.

Thomas Bennett tailored men's clothing, as had his father. His wife worked alongside him after developing exceptional sewing skills in her teenage years in Holmesfield, England. When William and Mary turned sixteen, they started working in their family's shop, which thrived. But young William longed to be outdoors. He realized this big, new country lay open for exploration.

The Bennetts knew the Carder family. About half of them had scattered, including the parents, William and Sarah, who mysteriously relocated smack in the middle of what would become Ohio, truly a barren wilderness. Daughter Lucy and her husband, Frederick Bray, went with them. John and Will Carder Jr., who they called Henry, had invited William along on a couple of hunting trips over the past year. Henry was ten years older and John five, but it did not make much difference. He thought maybe they felt sorry for him not having any brothers. Whatever the reason, William was grateful. He learned about guns and shooting. He was also becoming proficient in skinning deer and smaller game. He enjoyed every minute he spent in the woods.

In the spring of 1792, John Carder came into Bennett's Clothier. William stepped outside with him. John told him that his oldest sister, Patty, had divorced her no-account husband. Said Mary and he were celebrating with an early supper for her Saturday. Would William like to come? There would be a half dozen other friends there. Of course, William accepted. John told him not to be shocked. Said Patty was within weeks of giving birth. The ex-husband had signed away his parental rights.

To William's surprise, pretty Patty Carder, as she called herself again after immediately dropping her married name of Duncan, spent quite a bit of time that evening talking with him. After all, she was thirty-four, and William was twenty, so he did not expect her to pay much attention to him. He most certainly didn't conceive of the possibility that the two of them would be married before the year was up. But that is exactly what transpired.

William and Patty Bennett traveled over the mountains to Harrison County in 1799 to establish their new home, along with John and Mary Carder and their brood, which numbered seven at the time. William and Patty had four children together when they arrived; the youngest, Betsy, an infant, older sister Tabitha, plus Patty's two sons from her first marriage. They found a house just outside Grafton, close to three neighbors, since Patty did not want to be isolated.

Shortly after John's first successful barter with the Indians for furs in 1803, he recruited an all-too-willing William Bennett to go on an exploratory water journey to find a buyer.

The Iroquois originally lived in New York near Lake Ontario on the Mohawk River near what became Ithica. Around 1650, they moved into the Ohio Country between the Great Lakes and the Ohio River. They sought more land for access to deer, beaver, and bear. To acquire this land, they fought and conquered various other tribes occupying the area in the Beaver Wars between 1650 and 1700. They first traded their furs with the Dutch, then with the English.

These Iroquois, with whom John traded, paddled east on the Ohio River to Pittsburgh, then came up the Monongahela River, running out of Pennsylvania into its confluence with the Tygart Valley River, which runs through Harrison County. From there, they approached Lost Run and found Carder Run, where they located the Carders place.

John reasoned he and William could reverse that course, and it would lead them straight to Pittsburgh. The growing town sat at the confluence of three major rivers. The Allegheny River runs from its headwaters just below the middle of Pennsylvania's northern border. It flows south to meet the Monongahela and Ohio Rivers in Pittsburgh and the Mississippi River a little further west.

Many among what would soon become a flood of settlers heading into the western frontier traveled through Pittsburgh. John thought he would receive a better price for his furs in this highly populated place.

The journey presented challenges. In John's mind, the water route suggested greater safety than traveling by wagon on what rough roadways existed. They needed two well-made canoes. An acquaintance in Grafton referred John to a boat builder in

Morgantown, located about twenty-five miles north on the Monongahela River.

John immediately sent a letter to Ralph Cardiff, who had immigrated from Swansea, Wales, in 1778 as a twenty-six year-old. The young man found himself sailing up the Chesapeake Bay to Baltimore. Previously, he had worked alongside his father and two uncles building wooden vessels on the southwest coast of Wales. He stayed in Baltimore for fourteen years, honing his craft. Then, the western frontier called. He intended to reach the Ohio River. Moving across the northern edge of Virginia, one day, he looked out from a ridge over the Monongahela River flowing through Morgantown. In an instant, he determined this was where he wanted to stay.

To John's surprise, Mr. Cardiff replied to say he had two large canoes ordered by a man from nearby Barrackville, which he never picked up. Nor had Mr. Cardiff received a reply to his inquiry. John explained why he needed the canoes. Mr. Cardiff claimed his craftsmanship would withstand travel on small and large rivers. He said he would hold them until September 1 for John.

They decided to take one of the wagons up to Morgantown. John's brother, Henry, and Mary's brother, Jonathan, would accompany them on horses. Morgantown was bigger than Grafton, so Henry and Jonathan planned to pick up supplies for the return trip. John and William then faced about a seventy-five mile paddle up the north-flowing Monongahela River to reach Pittsburgh.

Mr. Cardiff gave them the name of a reputable merchant in Pittsburgh who paid cash for furs. John intended to use proceeds from fur sales for the purchase of land.

The men paddled north into Pennsylvania under sunny skies in late August. Each guided a loaded canoe. Since neither had much experience negotiating rivers, they welcomed the relatively broad, mostly easy-flowing water. On the morning of the fourth day, they arrived in Pittsburgh.

Mr. Cardiff referred them to a reasonably priced inn operated by the brother of a neighbor. William stayed with the canoes and cargo. John made arrangements with a boathouse to store the canoes for several nights. The owner sent a wagon to pick up the two men and their supplies.

They found the inn a couple of blocks from the water. The proprietor, Mr. O'Shea, agreed to let them keep their furs in a secure storage area until they could connect with the buyer. Then, they enjoyed a much-needed hot bath in a tub on the property despite having to pay extra. Mr. O'Shea directed them to a tavern up the street for supper. He said to follow the smell, allowin' as how they were smoking pork.

After a quick breakfast of coffee, graham muffins, and soft-boiled eggs the next morning, John and William strolled toward where they thought the merchants were. The streets seemed crowded with people. A buzz of excitement inexplicably hung in the air.

They entered a door under the sign saying, "Erwin Meyer & Sons." A musky but not quite pungent smell permeated the wide, two-story building with double, sliding, heavy doors in the rear. For the most part, it appeared to be empty. A not-quite-grown boy attacked the floor with a large broom. Turns out, he was the youngest Meyer, Conrad.

A smiling young woman, probably in her early twenties, walked toward them and introduced herself as Eva Meyer.

"Mistress Eva, I am John Carder, and this is my brother-in-law, William Bennett. We have paddled up the Mon with two canoes full of furs. We're hopin' to talk with your father."

"Well, I'm certain he would want to speak with you, too," Eva said. "We are about to close up, along with the rest of the town. Everybody wants to go down and see Captain Lewis off this morning when he leaves on his exciting adventure."

John and William looked at each other and then looked back at Eva, obviously befuddled.

"Oh, President Thomas Jefferson commissioned Captain Merriwether Lewis to lead an expedition to explore and chart the western United States. Their mission is to find a navigable water route across the continent. I think, in the long run, to improve and increase commerce."

"Well, I'll be," said William. "And they're starting from here?"

"Ja. We hear Captain Lewis asked a man named William Clark to lead with him. He is supposed to be a skilled riverman and a geographer. They're meeting him and additional crew when they reach Indiana."

At that moment, all six feet four inches of Erwin Meyer walked through his front door. "Ah, gentlemen, if this concerns business, I assume daughter Eva told you about the excitement down at the wharf."

"She did," John replied. "This expedition comes as news to us."

"I plan to be back here right after dinner. Shall we talk then?" Mr. Meyer asked as he showed them to the door.

John and William did not want to miss out on the fun. They followed the crowd heading to the river.

No sooner than they reached the water, the extent of the celebration became obvious. The Corps of Discovery, as it was being called, must have attracted the entire town of Pittsburgh. Crowds stretched from where they stood at the confluence of the Allegheny and Monongahela rivers and beyond, down to the left or southeast to Fort Fayette. The fifty-five-foot keelboat, which would carry Captain Lewis and a few men along the Ohio River toward the Missouri River, was supposedly commissioned and built at this fort. Within an hour, it would launch from the Monongahela Wharf.

Entire families attended the event despite it being the middle of the week. Picnic baskets topped many quilts on the ground, undoubtedly awaiting hungry family members after the launch. Boys carried American flags through the crowd. A fife and drum corps added to the exuberance. The sounds undoubtedly took a few men back to the war they fought for independence. It was, after all, hardly two decades past.

As John and William ambled down toward the wharf, they picked up bits of information. Evidently, Captain Lewis chose two Pittsburgh men as crew members. One, George Shannon, eighteen, became the youngest member. The other, John Colter, twenty-nine, came as an experienced backwoodsman. They learned that the keelboat would carry the majority of supplies for the Corps. They also discovered the number of men leaving from this starting point for the expedition: eleven hands, seven of whom were soldiers, a pilot, and three younger crew members, including George Shannon.

When departure time arrived, Captain Lewis stepped back onto the empty wharf. After waving his hat to quiet the crowd, he thanked the people of Pittsburgh for their warmth and generosity. At least, that is what John and William thought he said. It was difficult to hear with the large crowd still humming.

The captain then re-boarded. He entered the boat's cabin. A few minutes later, a priest left the cabin with him. A soldier helped the elderly man of God onto the wharf. Ropes were untied. And, although no one in attendance realized it, the most extensive and significant exploration of the country ever undertaken began.

When the Carders sat down with Mr. Meyer, they discovered that his four oldest sons, Simon, Werner, Otto, and Felix, departed mid-month for Philadelphia with a load of furs. Twice a year, the brothers made the difficult and dangerous journey cross-state to reach a tannery. Once processed, the furs went to a Philadelphia furrier whose reputation remained unmatched in this country.

With three major rivers running through Pittsburgh, Mr. Meyer sought to attract an experienced tanner to the growing town. He felt a profitable business opportunity awaited the right person. More money would go into his pocket. But his primary concern lay in the safety of his sons. Eliminating the long, risky journey remained at the top of his agenda.

The Iroquois traded John otter, fox, and wolf skins. Mr. Meyer expressed satisfaction with the quality of his furs.

After a successful transaction, the pair headed home. Their two days in Pittsburgh proved altogether satisfactory.

John and William stood on the threshold of history in more ways than one. The Northwest Territory included all land west of Pennsylvania, northwest of the Ohio River, and east of the Mississippi River below the Great Lakes. It had been created as a territory by the Northwest Ordinance on July 13, 1787. Many lives were being lost in the ensuing wars between white soldiers, as well as settlers, and Indians both within the contested territory and in the surrounding fledgling states.

A Shawnee Village, Chioudaista, called Upper Shawneetown by white people in the area, sat at the confluence of the Ohio and the Kanawha rivers. It became known as Point Pleasant just after the ferocious battle on October 10, 1774, between Shawnee Chief Cornstock and his warriors and American militia forces directed by Colonel Andrew Lewis. It was later thought to be the oldest English town on the east bank of the Ohio River. In 1788, Marietta, located on the west bank of the Ohio River, became the first permanent settlement in the new territory.

Wagon roads through gaps in the Allegheny Mountains in central Pennsylvania were opening to accommodate streams of settlers heading toward the new frontier territory. The Carders knew trails would soon be widened and roads built through the Alleghenies in Virginia to more easily access the western part of the state, as well as the Ohio River.

John figured on a five-day return trip since he and William would be paddling against the current of the Monongahela River. As the miles flowed by, he thought about ways to capitalize on the fur trade. After all, they lived in a forested wilderness – a land of plenty. Neutralizing the danger posed by the Natives, who did not want to share their hunting ground, represented the most significant obstacle. If the Treaty of Greenville, made and ratified in 1795, truly did signal peace in the Northwest Territory, things would change. The treaty was signed eight years ago. At best, it remained an uneasy peace.

As John paddled up Carder Run, he anticipated a good homecoming. But he was not prepared for what he got. He floated within sight of his property and saw a boy skipping stones across the water. Glancing up towards the house, he noticed several people.

"Are you my Uncle John?" asked the boy as he approached the bow of the canoe.

"I reckon I probably am. And who might you be, young man?"

"I'm John Wesley. My papa is your brother, Henry."

John leaned his head back and laughed big. It felt good. "Is that right?"

"Yes, sir, it is," grinned the boy.

John knew then he could not belong to anybody else. That crooked grin was exactly like Henry's. He gingerly stepped out of the boat. Then he turned around and pulled William's canoe up next to his.

"You must be about ten now, John Wesley."

"I was nine years old in March. Are you my other uncle?" he asked as William gratefully exited his boat.

"I am your Uncle William, boy, and it's mighty good to see you."

These visiting Carders lived on the south end of Harrison County near Jane Lew on Hacker's Creek because that is where the Lowthers located, and Henry did not figure he could find a more secure locale to raise his family. As the nineteenth century approached, little took precedence over safety for settlers coming into the frontier.

William Henry Carder Jr. preceded John by five years. They called him Henry to distinguish him from several Williams in the immediate and near family. In 1784, Henry, twenty-two, married Nancy Lowther, eighteen, in Harrison County.

Nancy's parents, Robert and Aquilla Reese Lowther, both immigrated from County Westmeath, Ireland, to Pennsylvania. They married in Philadelphia in 1734. Robert's father disowned him for renouncing his Quaker origins. The couple soon headed south, first to Albemarle County, Virginia, where the last five of their six children were born, then to the South Branch of the Potomac River. In 1763, they ventured west over the mountains to Hacker's Creek.

Robert and Aquilla had five sons before Nancy came along, their last child and only daughter. One of those sons was destined for infamy during one of this country's most crucial chapters.

John and William commenced pulling gear out of the canoes. John turned to see Henry and Uriah, another brother who lived in the county, striding down the long hill from his house. Just then, the solution to his future in furs hit him. How could he have missed it? Undoubtedly, no white men knew this territory east of the Ohio River and now west of the big river into the state of Ohio, which had been founded just five months previous, better than his extended family.

"Papa, look what I found paddlin' up the crick," said John Wesley. "You know these men?"

The brothers and William all embraced. Uriah uncorked a jug of local spirits, held it high, and said, "Here's to Destiny. May she not forget us in our time." Every man took a long, thankful drink.

♦♦♦

Henry Carder's wife, Nancy, was the sister of Colonel William Beamer Lowther Sr. In his early twenties, William met Sudna Hughes when the families lived in the Eastern Panhandle of Virginia. Sudna was a short, dark-skinned woman whose ancestor, Hugh Hughes, came from Wales and settled in Pennsylvania in the 1630s. They were married in 1763 in the Hughes' home near Moorefield, where they remained until they moved west ten years later to Harrison County. He built a cabin one and a half miles below West Milford on the Clarksburg Road.

With the Treaty of Fort Stanwix in 1768, the British acquired land south of the Ohio River from the Iroquois, which would become West Virginia ninety-five years later. Many other Ohio Indians refused to abide by the treaty. They continued to hunt and defend what they considered to be their land. Bloodshed followed as white settlers flowed into the region. William quickly became a staunch defender of this frontier against hostile Indians.

By 1774, Lord Dunmore, or John Murray, governor of Virginia, had heard enough about raids, attacks, and massacres up and down the Ohio River and along the Virginia frontier. He asked the legislature to authorize volunteer militia forces. One group headed down the Ohio from Fort Pitt, which would become Pittsburgh.

William Lowther joined the second group as a captain under Colonel Andrew Lewis. They were supposed to meet Lord Dunmore's group at the mouth of the Great Kanawha River. Fate stepped in to, undoubtedly, shorten the conflict.

Colonel Lewis's troops continued down the Kanawha until they reached the Ohio River on October 6, where they established Camp Pleasant, soon known as Point Pleasant. Four days later, as Colonel Lewis began crossing the big river to meet up with Lord Dunmore at the Shawnee towns, they were astounded to hear war cries coming from a large contingent of Shawnee and Mingo warriors led by Chief Cornstalk.

What transpired over the day would stand as a turning point in relations between the settlers and Indians. Some historians later considered it the first actual battle in the American Revolutionary War. Very late in the day, after grisly hand-to-hand combat, a flanking maneuver by the Virginia troops resulted in Chief Cornstalk's retreat.

For William Lowther, his brother-in-law, Elias Hughes, and others fortunate enough to get out of the battle with their skins intact, it clearly defined the stakes for what would soon be written into this very young country's Constitution as "life, liberty, and the pursuit of happiness." Seventy-five of the volunteer militia died, including the brother of Colonel Lewis, about 140 suffered wounds. Shawnee and Mingo losses could not be determined.

In 1781, Gen. George Rogers Clark commissioned William Lowther as a major for his service in the militia during the Revolutionary War. During the latter years of the war, he accepted responsibility for the line of scouts along the Ohio River, who covered approaches to the Kanawha Valley. Perhaps it was this vigilant defense of the territory during the war that earned him undying respect among the colonists.

Probably no other white men knew the Little Kanawha and the Hughes River valleys and what would become Ritchie County, Virginia, better than William Lowther, and his brothers-in-law, Elias Hughes and Jesse Hughes—three fearless adventurers whose names would remain prominent in pioneer history. In the fall of 1772, they ventured into this pristine wilderness and put their stamp on it.

Minnie Kendall Lowther, born in Ritchie County, West Virginia, in 1869, William Lowther's great-great-great-granddaughter, introduced that initial expedition by the trio of her ancestors in her book, *The Discovery of Ritchie County,* as follows:

"Leaving the place where Clarksburg now stands, they steered their course up the West Fork of the Monongahela River to its headwaters and, crossing over the dividing ridge near the present site of Weston, pursued their journey down Sand Creek to its confluence with the Little Kanawha. Here they found a beautiful mountain river upon which the eye of civilized man had, perhaps, never before rested, and being filled with delight at this discovery, and lured on by their desire to explore, to penetrate this dense wilderness, and to find the destination of this river, they followed its tortuous course, its meanderings like a silver thread; naming the tributaries as they passed along."

Few, if any, claimed to be a better rifle shot on the western waters than Elias Hughes. Generally known as "Ellis," he served as a frontier soldier from 1774 until the Treaty of Greenville was signed in 1795. He patrolled the settlements bordering the Ohio River as a spy or scout, protecting the people from hostile Indian activity.

In 1778, Thomas Hughes Sr., the father of Elias, Jesse, and Sudna, along with Jonathan Lowther, a brother of William Lowther, was killed by Indians on Hacker's Creek. At about that same time, a young woman whom Elias intended to marry died under an Indian knife. These deaths, in particular, set the stage for what would become a lifetime of retribution by Elias Hughes. He became an unrelenting Indian hater. Reputedly, he killed an untold number of those he considered to be the enemy.

Jesse Hughes also mastered the rifle and the tomahawk. He never farmed. He hunted exclusively for a living and served as a scout. He, too, became legendary as an Indian fighter.

A detailed description of this mountain man comes from Lucullus V. McWhorter's *The Border Settlers of Northwestern Virginia*. He writes:

"Jesse Hughes. He was of Welsh extraction, slight in his proportions, and light and active in his movements. He possessed a form as erect as that of an Indian and an endurance and fleetness of limb that no man of his day surpassed. His height was about five feet and nine inches, and his weight never exceeded one hundred and forty-five pounds. He had thin lips, a narrow chin, a nose that was sharp and inclined to the Roman form, little or no beard, light hair, and eyes of that indefinable color that one person would pronounce gray, another blue, but was both — and neither. They were piercing, cold, fierce, and as penetrating and restless as those of the mountain lion.

"He was of an irritable, vindictive, and suspicious nature, and his hatred, when aroused, knew no bounds. Yet it is said that he was true to those who gained his friendship."

On December 5, 1787, four days after Martha Hughes turned fourteen, she and her older sister, Nancy, were rounding up cows on Turkey Run, which enters the Ohio River a mile above Ravenswood in Jackson County, when a party of Indians snatched the younger daughter of Jesse Hughes. They were raiding and killing whites that day. Martha was lucky. They kidnapped her. She lived with her captors for two years and nine months. Then, her father ransomed her release. He realized she had the grit to survive her ordeal, and he was willing to do what it took to get his daughter back. No one ever knew what he sacrificed in the exchange, not even his brothers.

When Jesse first saw Martha upon her release, he did not recognize her. She dressed as an Indian, with rings in her ears, mouth, and on all of her fingers. Her face and body were smeared with paint. And she carried a bow and arrows, which she soon proved more than capable of using. Her father forever considered her to be a Hughes through and through.

Martha Hughes married Jacob Bonnet, and they lived out their lives in the Jane Lew community in Lewis County. They raised six girls and three boys, one of whom, Jesse, lived to be 105 years old.

John Carder discussed with his brothers, Henry and Uriah, the practicality of supplementing animal skins traded with the Indians. Since Henry's wife, Nancy, was William Lowther's sister, he figured finding a guide should not be a problem. After William and his brothers-in-law, Elias and Jesse Hughes, first forayed into the Little Kanawha Valley in the early 1770s, the families used the territory for hunting. Although William stayed consumed with efforts to protect the white population, open the territory to further settlement and fulfill political appointments, four of his five sons stayed in northwestern Virginia.

In the fall of 1804, John ventured into the wilderness for a month. John Carder Jr. wanted to accompany his father, but John decided to have him watch the homeplace for a couple of years until his brother, Issac, turned sixteen.

William Bennett went with John. His wife, Patty, lost an infant boy earlier in the year, shortly after he was born. The previous year, two year-old Betsy died. But their oldest two boys were now in their teens, and their daughter, Tabitha, was a somewhat useful ten year-old. Patty conceded she could do without her husband for another few weeks.

Robert Lowther, a son of William, who lived nearby in Harrison County, offered to take the pair west to Ritchie County, where his brother, Will, lived. Will Lowther graciously agreed to take John and William on his annual hunting trip into valleys south stretching to the Ohio River?

John hunted for the next decade without any major injuries. The Iroquois annually supplied him with furs in exchange for his tobacco. His relationship with Erwin Meyer & Sons continued to be reliable. He progressively purchased land surrounding his original mountain top bit by bit. Some said he accumulated close to 4,000 acres.

Before he passed away on June 15, 1854, on the Carder homestead, John sat on his front porch, and all that his eighty-seven year-old eyes surveyed belonged now to his children and grandchildren. He thought his Mary rested well with such a legacy.

Keeping it All in the Family

(Currey)

The mountains and hills of northwest Virginia reverberated with violence through much of the 1700s. Howls from Native aggressors mingled with screams of horror by their white victims. Settler families were torn apart. Tombstones, most made illegible by the weather, attest to lives lost.

Early explorers ventured into the unknown because they heard that the Iroquois, Delaware, and Shawnee Indian tribes, as well as others, were being removed from their hunting grounds. English and French soldiers vied for dominance in the eastern Ohio Valley. Prior land occupation east of the Allegheny Mountains served as a warning to the Natives of the inevitable movement west by Europeans.

Bringing a family into the western frontier proved to be a supreme challenge. Those who stayed became resilient, resourceful, and community-minded.

Another wolf stood at the door as their descendants prepared for what they did not know. Now, one hundred years later, there was about to be a war between the Northern and Southern states. It would be the catalyst for more violence than this new country ever imagined.

Adaline Currey, eighteen, picked wild lettuces and creasy beans She also found the first poke sallet of the season, woolen britches, and she spotted wild garlic. She loved spending time in the woods by herself. Her soul needed restoring after seeing the look on Sam's face when she told him she would not become his bride until he returned home from the war.

She loved Samuel T. Currey. She'd known him among her many cousins and always liked him. His father, Israel, was a brother of her paternal grandfather, Jonathan, and her maternal grandfather, James Henry Currey. When she married Sam, she'd be a double Currey, just like her mother. She laughed and said out loud, "Nothing like keeping it all in the family."

The approaching war brought entirely too much uncertainty to commit to such a life change, Adaline thought. She figured all their lives would be altered in ways they never dreamed of. She was unwilling to risk carrying Sam's baby, not knowing if he'd ever return.

The talk was that Virginia probably would be in the crosshairs of this conflict. She knew one thing. People in this rugged western area of the state reached no consensus regarding the war. Some favored the Confederate cause, as her family did, somewhat reluctantly. Most, however, went with the Union, in large part, it seemed, because of their not-very-distant roots. Others said they would not wear either uniform, but would fight to protect their families and home turf.

Adaline feared for the safety of all. She thought if the Northern armies marched South and the Southern armies advanced North, they would meet in the middle — Virginia. If men could not sit down and figure this thing out somewhere besides on the battlefield, there might not be anything left when they finished. Or anybody left to enjoy what our forefathers meant for us to have. It did not make sense. None of it.

As far as Adaline knew, there had not been much participation by her families in past wars, probably because they were busy protecting home and hearth. She did know that her maternal grandmother, Rosanna Finley Currey's grandfather, Lieutenant Archibald Finley, served in the Revolutionary War.

Adaline turned back toward the house with her sack full of greens. Various shades of April green were beautiful under a clear sky. White and pink dotted the forest as dogwoods and redbuds showcased their palettes. She passed a patch of yellow trillium after seeing lots of white trillium all over the hillside. There were also flowering spring beauties and jack-in-the-pulpits. She had spotted a colony of mayapples not yet in bloom. She topped a small ridge, and the bushy tail of a big red fox down by the creek caught her attention. At least two warblers were carrying on a conversation while a woodpecker drummed on a tree not far away. She always hated leaving this sanctuary.

When she reached the good-sized garden about fifty yards from the house, she checked the asparagus. Sure enough, it snapped in the middle when she tested it. She'd add it to the salad she was about to make.

Benjamin and Nellie Currey lived on Booths Creek, one of many creeks running through Taylor County. Adaline was their oldest child. She had, thus far, three sisters and two brothers. Ben and Nellie's fathers were brothers. Their father was John B. Currey. His parents were John H. Currey and Margaret Adams from Lanarkshire, Scotland.

All the Currey men farmed. Ben's land ran in a long, relatively narrow strip bounded by the creek on one side, a 200-yard level expanse on the other side that then ran up a moderate incline. He planted an apple orchard on the small ridge, peach trees below those, and corn and Irish potatoes on the level ground. Of course, they raised chickens for their eggs and meat. A couple of cows for their milk.

There were always many mouths to feed because, invariably, at least a couple of cousins gathered around their table. But food was plentiful even in winter months. The family hunted year-round. Ben and his brothers went on an extended hunting trip to Pennsylvania every fall. The girls helped their mother can produce from their garden: dry beans, peaches, and apples, as well as make quarts of applesauce and apple butter and make jelly from berries.

Ben's brother, James, lived down the road on Booths Creek with his wife, Mary, who was Nellie's close sister. James and Mary married in 1851 after their first spouses unexpectedly passed away.

James had raised hogs successfully for the last fifteen years. He ran out of room in his smokehouse. He asked Ben if he would consider building a smokehouse for meat on his property in exchange for some product. The brothers commenced to build a good-sized smokehouse near Ben and Nellie's house. Every late fall, Currey family members gathered at James's farm for the hog killing. Then, James and his sons placed his hams in large containers, completely covered them with salt to start the dehydration process, and left them for thirty days on shelves in his cool smokehouse. At the end of that time, they wiped off the salt and rubbed the hams with whiskey. After this, the meat was wrapped in cotton gauze. Around the end of October, they brought a wagon load of hams to Ben's smokehouse and hung them, along with cured pork bellies from which bacon would be cut. On a cool spring day, Ben lit a smoldering fire. The pork bellies were smoked for a couple of weeks, and the hams a few weeks more.

Whiskey, or moonshine, was not hard to come by. By the late eighteenth century, Scots-Irish from Ulster in Northern Ireland, as well as others from Wales and England, brought their recipe for "water of life" into the mountains of western Virginia. They came with their distilling equipment and a recipe that easily adapted to the use of corn. Small distilleries abounded. Also called mountain dew or white lightning, this one hundred-proof whiskey was made without aging. It quickly became an efficient and profitable way to market corn. People used it to barter for all the necessities, even property.

Adaline noticed a two-seater carriage as she rounded the corner of the house. She walked in and smelled beans cooking that sister, Nancy, thirteen, put on early that morning with a ham hock. Visiting were cousins Elizabeth, eighteen, Prudie, sixteen, and their mother, Aunt Polly, wife of Uncle John Currey, who was Mama's brother from Webster (south of Grafton and west of Tygart Lake).

"My, 'tis a wonderful surprise," said Adaline. "You sure picked a beautiful day to drive a right smart distance."

"We was goin' a little stir crazy. We wanted to get out and visit with all ya'll and see James and Mary," explained Aunt Polly.

"Well, I have a whole sack of wild greens I've gathered this morning I need to wash, and I found the first asparagus in the garden tender enough to eat. I've been hankerin' for fresh greens. We'll have a big ole salad, and Nancy has soup beans cooked."

"Yes, and I had John go to the smokehouse earlier and cut off a big chunk of ham, which I'm fixin' to fry up," Nancy said as she used two hands to pull a big cast iron skillet off a shelf.

As Adaline poured water into the sink to wash the greens, Prudie said, "Here, let me help you trim up those greens. Did you see any wild mustard yet? Or ramps?"

"Wild mustard, no. But ramps, yes. In fact, sister, we need to get everybody together sometime in the next week and go to our spots. They'll be more plentiful up on the mountain. I don't want nobody beatin' us to 'um.

"Nancy, you got the oven hot?"

"I do. But I've not mixed batter yet. Eggs are in the bowl."

"Elizabeth, come over and mix up some cornbread batter for us. I'll go ahead and put the skillet in the oven with bacon grease," said Adaline as she pulled down another iron skillet. "They's buttermilk in cool storage downstairs."

"Soon as that cornbread goes in the oven, I'll go out and ring the dinner bell," Aunt Polly said.

"I don't know where everybody is. By the time they get to the house and wash up, that ought to be good timing," said Adaline. "I thank ya."

"I sent Prudence and Patsy down to Aunt Mary's a couple a hours ago to tell her and Mama to come on up here to eat dinner with us. Don't know where they are. They should be here by now. Guess they'll hear the bell and hurry if they're not here before,"

Nancy said as she slid fried ham streaks out of the skillet and added more.

The family all seemed to appear at once, including Uncle John and Aunt Mary, along with Nellie, her two younger girls, and Elihu, her three year-old son. Ben came in with his son John, soon to turn sixteen. It made for a full table.

"To what do we owe this pleasure," Ben asked, looking toward Aunt Polly. "Everything alright with John?"

"It is. He had a potential buyer comin' today to look at some heifers he's a wantin' to sell. I was afraid with this dad-burned war getting underway that, if we didn't come now, Lord knows when we might be able to get out again. Oh, Benjamin, things is so up in the air. We all have things to do to prepare. But let's not talk about any of that right now. Let's enjoy this food our girls put together for us."

After the dishes were cleared and washed, the three women and the girls settled in to talk. They were anxious to hear what Aunt Polly had to say.

"A couple months ago, the ladies in our church got together to decide on a project to help the soldiers," she said. "We figure their needs are goin' a be many out there in the field. Well, as of last week, we've commenced making quilts to send with boys who need one and also to send to the military field hospitals. We'll meet once a week to work on quilts."

"Polly, what a good idea," said Nellie.

"They are three homes with overhead quilt frames that eight to ten can sit at," Aunt Polly continued. "We'll rotate amongst those. And the son of one of the ladies made a mobile quilt frame that we're a keepin' at the church. That one we'll use every week.

"You know, our people are awfully split in their politics. It's a sight. I'm afraid we're going to have brother fighting brother in some cases. Anyway, these quilts will go to either Union or Confederate soldiers. We don't believe God has nary a favorite in this war. I believe He wished man had better sense than he does. And so do I."

Brother against brother would strike much closer to home than any of the Currey women imagined. Reverend Aaron Vincent and his wife, Ara Barnes Vincent, who everyone called Ary, lived just north in Fairmont, in Marion County. Aaron had a sister, Mary, who married Daniel Riblett. Like many of his comrades in the northern counties, Daniel fought for the Union, serving in the 6th Regiment Virginia Cavalry. However, his brother, George, enlisted with the Confederacy, serving with the 20th Regiment Virginia Cavalry. Both brothers survived the war and continued operating their mills on Shinn's Run. Aaron and Ary's daughter, Ellen Marie, would marry John Currey, Ben and Nellie's oldest son.

"Polly, this sounds like a real fine way to help meet a need and to unite those left at home worryin' and wonderin'," said Nellie. "We have a lot of kin scattered around these hollers, as you know. Most all the women sew. I feel certain we can organize quilt makin' between family and neighbors. What do you think, girls?"

"Yes, Mama. This is like a godsend, ain't it? Sam is going to be out there in the field, and he can let us know what his regiment needs for blankets," Adaline said as she got up and hugged her aunt.

Aunt Polly proceeded to share details with her eager listeners. The military had requested that quilts be made about seven feet by four feet, a convenient size for a bedding pack and a military cot. Sometimes two bed quilts could be cut up and sewn together to make three cot quilts.

According to directions, simple quilt patterns should be used, such as a nine-patch or a churn dash pattern. Fabrics would generally be cotton, but they could come from many sources, including men's clothing, old blankets (which make excellent batting), feed and fertilizer sacks, wool weave, old uniforms, suits, coats, twill flannel, sleeves, pocket-flaps, and pants legs.

"The store up at Monongah has bins for flour and meal, and they sell in bulk. Next time we go, I'll ask Mr. Dunlap if'n he'll save all his flour sacks for us and explain what we're a doin'," said Adaline.

"Yes, any fabric from any source you can think of, you need to start collectin'," Aunt Polly said.

"Grandma Nancy has a hanging quilt frame," said Nellie. "She may be over seventy, but there aren't many who can stitch any better than she can. Sally and Catherine both inherited their mother's sewing ability. Both of their families also live nearby. I'll bet they'd be glad to help."

"Both of her daughters married Lawler brothers, didn't they?" inquired Aunt Polly.

"Yes, Sally married Joe maybe thirty years back," explained Nellie. "Then, in 1852, Catherine married Jehu. Their grandfather came over to Lost Run from Fauquier County.

"I'll tell ya somebody else who has an overhead quilt frame, and that's Matilda Dunham. She's my brother, Nathan's, mother-in-law. She enjoys havin' people over to quilt. Nathan's wife, Elizabeth, has sewed since she was little."

Once the Curreys started spreading their excitement among family members and neighbors, the project took on a life of its own. Grandma Nancy and two of her daughters enthusiastically agreed to use their quilt frame and recruited several neighbors. Also, the Dunhams said they would be tickled to host quilters who focused on making quilts to send into the war.

Nellie and Adaline were in the Dunlap's Monongah store one day and ran into Gladys Miller. The Millers had an extended family, which lived up on Hustead Branch. She said two of her sons planned to join the Confederate Virginia infantry in June. She wanted to help and pledged to bring finished quilts to the Dunlap's store when they made their monthly supply runs. ` Mr. and Mrs. Dunlap graciously agreed for their store to serve as a collecting center for all area finished quilts. Mrs. Dunlap said she had a sister, Beatrice Phipps, in Shinnston, who worked from a quilt frame. She felt this opportunity to contribute quilts to the war efforts would please her. Within a couple of months, Nellie heard that word reached Pleasant Valley, and a group of women at a church up there was also working on quilts as well.

From the Dunlap's store, Currey men would pick up the quilts and take them to Grafton every two or three months. Aunt Polly said the women in Webster agreed that, as the county seat, it presented a central location for distributing the quilts. A church in Pruntytown, a few miles west of Grafton, had started their own quilt group. Undoubtedly, women in Grafton would follow suit when they heard about the collective effect going on.

While talking about helping with the war effort, the women discovered that a family member already contributed in a much-needed way. It came as no surprise.

Ben's younger brother, Silas, and his wife, Sarah Jane, lived less than two miles along Booths Creek. He was in the right place at the right time when this piece of land came up for sale. It featured more open pasture than any property in the area. Sarah Jane wanted sheep and convinced her husband that there was money to be made in their wool and meat. Silas said she could start with a dozen sheep and one ram on twenty acres of pasture to see how the grass held up.

In the fall, when they sheared the sheep and washed what wool Sarah Jane wanted to keep, she carded it. On September 15, 1855, her parents, Samuel and Arsenah Ashcraft Tucker, who people called Sena, presented her with a beautiful Old Salem spinning wheel for her twenty-fifth birthday. Then, to her utter surprise, Silas installed a loom in their house on Christmas Eve day, while

Sarah Jane and the children spent the day with her extended Tucker family at her parent's home. It transformed her artistic world.

In January, she spent five days with Ruth Carroll, who lived on Bingamon Creek in Harrison County. Sister Ruth, as she wanted everybody to call her, had long been known as a master weaver. She took right to her new student. And Sarah Jane was awed by her mentor's knowledge, patience, and generosity.

Sister Ruth came from Henrico County in eastern Virginia. Her family grew a lot of cotton, owned many slaves, and expected their seven daughters to marry well. However, the last thing Ruth, the middle sister, wanted to be was a belle. She knew she had to be presented at a debutante ball by the time she was eighteen. But that June, after leaving a note explaining her feelings and desires to a father who adored her, she left home to come to the mountains of western Virginia. She arranged transportation with someone in Charles City whom she trusted. That was forty-four years ago. Her father secretly sent her money every month, which she collected at the bank in Fairmont. Before his death, he designated her brother, Stephen, to continue the payments. Her correspondence with Stephen was friendly. The siblings were just twenty months apart and had been close as children.

Ruth never married. She planted a garden every year. She owned a buggy, a wagon, a horse, a mule, at least two dogs, six goats, about a dozen chickens, two roosters, and a comfortable four-room house with a large porch. And, of course, her spinning wheel and loom. She loved the beauty, simplicity, and creativity of her life.

When Sarah Jane saw a government list of clothing needed by soldiers, she immediately realized she could provide socks. Even though gloves were not on the list, she wondered why not. Without gloves, their hands would surely freeze in the cold winter months. She knit socks and gloves for family members. After experimenting years ago, she'd figured out the exact ply or thickness of yarn for making socks. Not too thin. Not too thick.

Her beloved spinning wheel and loom would have to rest. She decided to focus on knitting socks and gloves for the duration of this cursed war. Her sister, Susan, volunteered to help. They thought three sizes – small, medium, and large – would be needed.

≢ ≢ ≢

Ben knew there was no easy way to break the news. He heard all the arguments. He'd turned it all over in his head. He tried to add it all up. Nobody could provide him with an answer. He had prayed more than once and asked the good Lord to direct his thoughts and actions. After not being able to sleep, he walked along the creek under a full moon and clear sky in the early morning hours of April 24, 1861. He stopped, looked up, closed his eyes, and felt peace.

He would join the Confederate army. Not because he believed in secession, certainly not because he supported the institution of slavery, not because he thought the rights of Southern states were being infringed upon. He was born in the western mountains of Virginia. He assumed Union soldiers would not show mercy toward the people he loved. He could remain at home and help those who stayed behind fight as guerrillas. Or officially go into the service of Virginia and help beat back the bastards as a member of a much larger force. Most of his family had elected not to join either army. They would protect his family while he was gone.

Nellie knew something had burdened her husband's mind over the past few months. Ben chose not to talk about it. She decided not to pry. After breakfast that morning, Ben asked her to walk with him, and he appeared relaxed. Serene even. He told her he would be joining the 31st Regiment Virginia Infantry within the month and explained his rationale for doing so.

She suspected he might be tempted to guard the home front as a member of the Confederate forces. She prayed it would not come to pass. But now it lay in God's hands. Her job was to help him get the farm ready for his departure and to prepare the children for what might lie ahead. Everything was about to change.

Ben sensed Yankee soldiers were approaching the area. His concern was securing his family. He and John took all his guns apart and cleaned them. He would take his best rifle and pistol with him. That left five rifles and two pistols at the house. Two rifles would stay upstairs and two downstairs in the house. Both pistols would be kept in the cellar. One rifle was kept in the barn. Nellie and the four oldest children knew how to shoot. But every day, he took them all out to a practice range for target shooting. Their accuracy with those guns could now save their lives.

They stored water down in the cellar, where their food stayed, and put a series of heavy locks on the underside of the door. They had let the smokehouse dwindle to almost nothing when war became a certainty. They knew if soldiers came demanding meat, they would undoubtedly lose their chickens, but that was a risk they'd have to take.

Ben did not leave alone. Young Sam Currey, his cousin, would enroll with the 31th regiment, too. Also, Jacob Tucker, thirty-two, Sarah Jane's cousin, joined the pair as they headed south to Camp Allegheny in Pocahontas County. At least they could keep an eye on Sam. And Adaline felt better knowing her father, future husband, and another cousin joined forces.

On June 3, a mere ten days after reporting to camp, Ben's regiment found itself engaged in what was the first organized land action of the war. They were practically on their home turf. With virtually no preparation, they skirmished at Philippi in Barbour County, just south of Taylor County. Union soldiers fought under the command of Maj. Gen. George B. McClellan who had returned to the Army after the commencement of hostilities at Fort Sumter in South Carolina in April. The Confederates fled the battlefield with little resistance.

Unbeknownst to Ben, a cousin, Melville Currey, son of his father's brother, James Currey, had joined the 19th Regiment Virginia Infantry and was also in the Battle of Philippi. Melville's regiment headed south from Philippi and crossed the Allegheny Mountains to the hills overlooking Beverly. Melville was among those who contracted typhoid fever. He died of the disease on July 1. His brother, Milton, and cousins, brothers Silas and Emory Currey, both brothers of Ben, came down and buried him at Beverly. At the conclusion of the fighting in 1865, Fenton Currey, another son of James, along with Ben, and his brothers, James P. and Cornelius Currey, traveled to Beverly, retrieved the body, and buried it with family in Taylor County.

When the 31st regiment retreated from Philippi, they headed south to Beverly, then twelve miles further to Huttonsville. Confederate Gen. Robert S. Garnett had seized vital turnpike passes at Laurel Hill in Barbour County, the northeastern extension of Rich Mountain in Randolph County. General Garnett believed these two passes to be the "gates to northwestern Virginia." He established headquarters at Laurel Hill, which he fortified in anticipation of the advance of Federalists into the Tygart Valley. Realizing they likely faced Union troops twice their size, the general asked for reinforcements due to the poor conditions of his troops.

Letter from Gen. Robert S. Garnett to Adjutant General Cooper Camp Laurel Hill, Virginia, June 18, 1861

> "The force . . . here is in a miserable condition as to ammunition and equipment. As regards to the latter, they are actually suffering. Many are without blankets, and I may say nearly all are without tents. The nights are cold, and there is much rain in this mountainous region. Sickness is, therefore, to be apprehended. In addition to this, they are

obliged to carry their ammunition in their pockets, and that which escapes the rain is ruined by the perspiration of the men and the wearing out of paper cartridges. I simply want something to protect arms and ammunition from rain."

A couple of days later, he wrote again, urgently requesting more cavalry and additional artillery pieces and rifles. Even though he doubted that combined Union forces at Philippi and Grafton were as large as indicated, he knew his troops were too small to push heavy scouts as far to the front as he wanted.

On July 11, General Garrett's troops were forced to retreat from Laurel Hill across the mountain via Cheat Ridge. The next day, they reached Kaler's Ford on the Cheat River. According to reports, they bivouacked in heavy rain. On July 13, they continued their march through rough country, over roads deep with mud. The 31st regiment formed the advance. They reached Carricks Ford on Shaver's Fork, and General Garrett posted his rear guard around approaches to the swollen river crossing. When the enemy was within fifty yards of the ford, they shot the general in the back. Reportedly, he died as the Federals reached his position.

Ben had crossed the river and lay in a copse of small trees when he saw the general fall. It was the first instance of extreme bravery by a Confederate officer he witnessed.

Once again, Gen. Garrett's charges escaped. Exhausted and disheveled, they made it to Monterey, which was under the command of Brig. General Henry R. Jackson.

Letter from Gen. Henry R. Jackson to Colonel George Deas, Assistant Adjutant-General, Confederate States Army, Monterey, Virginia, July 19, 1861

"Our present position in this village, the only one in the vicinity fit for a deposit of supplies, is exposed and wholly untenable unless the routes approaching it from the west be guarded at considerable distance. I have been restless in the consciousness that, were the enemy appraised of our real condition, he might make sad havoc among us and at least destroy what they might not be able to hold. The debris of General Garnett's command are constantly pouring in, and what is left in anything like organized form will be here on tomorrow or the day following in a more forlorn condition. I fear that, while they must be cared for, they will be almost useless for any military purpose."

Sam Currey was hardly impressed with what little military warfare he had experienced. When the Confederate forces at Philippi were surprised by a dawn artillery bombardment in that first action, it was so helter-skelter it could hardly have been called a battle in his mind. When the opposing sides organized in straight lines and shot at each other, he considered it suicide. He understood it to be a remnant of English military strategy. It was not at all practical for fighting in western Virginia. He knew he was young and inexperienced, but he did not consider himself stupid.

Sam had hunted most of his life with his father, uncles, and cousins. He had been taught to focus and drop the deer, or any animal, with a single shot so as not to inflict injury and pain. He became known at home as a dead-eye shot. His first kills in battle were at Laurel Hill, not on the battlefield, but on their flanks from behind a large tree on the very edge of the field where he could hide, focus, and take down his target cleanly. He had a friend, Wilson McGregor, from Harrison County, with him. He would reload, pick another target, put him in his sights, and squeeze the trigger. Then he reloaded while Wilson took his shot. All the while, they watched as bodies crumpled out on the field with no cover to reload.

Sam did not sign up for this war to die. In fact, he fully intended to survive. He had to get back to Adaline. It did not take him long to figure out what his job needed to be.

By the end of August, the 31st regiment moved a little further south and met up with other troops under the overall command of Brigadier General Jackson at Camp Bartow in Pocahontas County. It was there Sam dropped by Captain Robert Bradshaw's tent for a discussion.

"Captain Bradshaw, I'd like a word with you, sir."

"And who am I talking with?" the captain inquired.

"Private Samuel Currey from Taylor County, sir."

"Alright, come in, Private."

"Since I came in with the 31st regiment, I've been with General Jackson, as you know. I have thirteen kills, and it's not by obeying orders."

"Exactly what do you mean by that soldier?"

"I'm going to be perfectly honest with you, sir. I aim to survive this here war. And the way it's being fought on the few battlefields we've been on so far does not bode well for the average soldier's survival. I was reared in these mountains. I was taught to hunt, trap, track, and survive in the woods by men who learnt those skills from their fathers and grandfathers, who learnt them from their fathers and grandfathers, and so on. Those old people learnt much of what they knew from the Indians, who tormented the settlers when they first moved into these parts. But those Natives was smart. They was very cunning warriors. They didn't fight out in the middle of fields. They fought behind trees, logs, and other cover. And, sir, that's what I've been a doin'.

"You know I could write you up for disobeying orders."

"I do. I'm also fairly certain, among soldiers in our regiment still healthy enough to fight, few are better shots then I am, nor are they likely to have as many kills as I do, which I believe is the reason I am here. I'm a thinkin' I could serve a valuable purpose."

The captain sat back and looked over this brash young man, thinking he had brass balls coming in here questioning military strategy. It reminded him of himself twenty years ago. He struggled not to smile.

"Go ahead, Private Currey. If a man has a valuable purpose, I want to know what it is."

"What if you sent me, and maybe one other man, out to locate Union pickets? Dispose of them before they could get back to their troops with information on us? Probably wouldn't want to use guns because of the noise. Could use bows and arrows. I'm deadly with those, too."

"Our advantage has been reduced because our numbers have been so diminished by sickness," said Captain Bradshaw. "For this expected battle here on or around the Greenbrier River, we could use any advantage we can find. Let me run this idea by the general. Check back with me in two days."

"Yes, sir, I will," Sam said.

For the past week, rain had fallen incessantly. Surprisingly, for this time of year, there was a chill mixed in with the dampness. Soon, nearly half of the still relatively unseasoned troops lay in poorly provided hospitals. A letter from Colonel Henry R. Jackson to his future wife, Florence King, Camp Bartow, Virginia, September 1, 1891, reads:

> "Many men are sick. They have every disease – measles, mumps, jaundice, dysentery, typhoid fever. Out of about five hundred men present, I have this morning only 231 men fit for duty. There has been so much hardship and exposure. The mortality rate became very high. Since supply trains had difficulty reaching the camps, the army was short on rations for weeks. This was a terrible ordeal for the troops, but they bore it uncomplainingly. Their chief concern being why they did not advance against an enemy who was only one days march away."

One of those sickened in recent days was Ben Currey. He was among those afflicted by an outbreak of measles. He felt run down before getting sick. This was hot, dirty, uncomfortable, tiring work. He wished he were twenty years younger.

They remained in western Virginia, but still, they had been nearly constantly on the move. Not knowing what lay ahead stressed him. He kept waiting for the man on the other end of his rifle to be someone he knew. In his mind, he tried to make enemies out of them. But, realistically, they were not enemies. For all he knew, they could be relatives.

Ben was glad to lay up and recover. The doctors offered little other than coffee or whiskey to keep him hydrated. He took the rank coffee because, with the associated headaches, whiskey held no appeal. He had been shocked at the number of others who were sick. He prayed that no serious diseases snuck into camp. Rumor had it that typhoid fever claimed the lives of soldiers in Beverly, just north of Bartow. If it was here, they were keeping it quiet.

Captain Bradshaw told Sam that his request had been denied. He was, however, being given an opportunity to join their pickets, which provided security for the rest of the army. They warn the army when the enemy approaches to keep them from observing and interfering with its operation at rest, on the march, or in a battle. They are part of light infantry.

"They are known as petite guerre by the French," explained the captain. "Their task is a critical one and often puts one side or the other at a serious disadvantage before the battle even starts. It may result in small-scale battles or formidable resistance conducted away from the main army.

"We expect to remain in western Virginia at least through the end of the year. We've ordered a case of Enfield P53 series rifles and a case of Whitworth rifles. Once we get those, we'll start using sharpshooters, which is, in effect, the role you have unofficially taken upon yourself. But you're going to have to start taking orders, young man. If we see you can do that, in the spring, we will look at you as one of our sharpshooters. If you cannot obey orders, you're liable to find yourself court-martialed. That is not a position you want to be in."

Although these were small mountain battles, the effects produced lasting results. The Union seized control of western Virginia for the duration of the war. Union presence provided protection for leaders who met in Wheeling to establish a new state, which was destined to become West Virginia on June 20, 1863. Based on his performances in those very first land battles, Union General McClellan became a paramount figure in the course of the war.

∥ ∥ ∥

Even though dark clouds looked determined, Nellie figured to go down the road to Sarah Jane's on this early July morning. Sarah Jane usually knits on Wednesdays, and extra hands would be welcomed. Adaline decided to go with her mother. They both wanted a break from farm chores, and they needed a good walk. Son, John, agreed to mind the children.

When they arrived, they found Mary there also. Silas had taken his brother, James, into Grafton the previous morning to pick up supplies. On the way, they were going to collect quilts at the Dunlap's store in Monongah to deliver to a drop-off in Pruntytown, where there were supply wagons going out every couple of weeks with food for the Confederate Army. When it became known that Grafton was entrenched on the side of the Federalists, the women from Fairmont to Shinnston agreed that they did not want all their quilts going to Grafton. The women in Pruntytown said they would gladly distribute the quilts to their Confederate sources. The men were due back late that afternoon.

George, fifteen, Silas's only child from an early marriage, left at sunrise to hunt grouse for dinner. Jesse, who was a month shy of being ten, came into the house and told his mother that one of the cows in the upper pasture was lying down and seemed to be having trouble breathing. The boy led his mother, Aunt Mary, cousin Adaline, and his Aunt Nellie up into the pasture. As they walked, they heard thunder rumble in the west.

"That doesn't sound good," said Sarah Jane. "We could use a good soaking, but we don't want a storm while we've got a cow down."

"She's over here," hollered Jesse. "She hasn't moved."

"Oh, me. That girl is labored with her breathing," observed Mary. "We're not up in the day, so she's not overheated. Has she been sick?"

"Jesse, this cow's been healthy, hasn't she, son?" asked Sarah Jane.

"Yes, mama. We haven't had Doctor Mason out here for any of our cattle since spring, I don't reckon."

"It could be a respiratory infection, maybe diphtheria or emphysema, or some kind of bacteria or virus," Mary said. "I doubt if it's weed poisoning because I know Silas stays on top of that, and the rest of the cattle seem alright."

"Mary, your sons didn't go with their pa and Silas, did they? Are they on the farm?" asked Sarah Jane.

"Yes, my George and Joe are both at home."

"Jesse, why don't you high tail it over there and see if they might know where to find Doc Mason? We can use him. Have one of them go after him if they can.

"Those rumbles are getting close. You three go on back to the house. I'm going to move water and a little feed out of that hay manger close to this sick cow so she can get to it if she has a mind to."

"I'll help you," Mary said.

As Nellie and her daughter started back down through the pasture, they saw the sky light up when lightning flickered behind them and to their left. Raindrops began to fall.

Adaline remembered walking maybe five paces behind her mother. Suddenly, there was an intense white light and the loudest noise she'd ever heard. The next instant, she lay on the ground. She could not hear, and she experienced extreme dizziness. She didn't remember how long it was before she gazed up into the face of Sarah Jane, who looked panic-stricken.

Sarah Jane heard Mary say, "I don't know whether her heart is beatin'. It looks like it hit her in her upper back."

Adaline struggled to sit up. She looked over at her mother and realized, with horror, that she had suffered a direct lightning strike. That's why she, herself, had been knocked to the ground because she was so close to her.

Mary had her head on Nellie's chest. Adaline crawled to her mother, held her face in her hands, and talked to her. Mary's mouth did not move. Her eyes were transfixed.

"Have mercy. Sarah Jane, come over and help us try to find a heartbeat," Mary said breathlessly as she sat back on her heels.

"We need to pick Nellie up and carry her into the house," replied Sarah Jane, just as a lightning bolt hit the edge of the forest. "We don't want another one of us to get hit. Adaline, are you up to carrying your mother's feet, or do we need to get one of the horses up here?"

Eleanor Nellie Currey, forty-five, died of heart failure on July 2, 1862, a day forever remembered by female members of her family who witnessed the random and deadly power of an electrical storm. Her body was transported to Grafton for burial in Ironside Baptist Cemetery near her father, James Henry Currey Sr., who predeceased her by seven years.

Ben did not find out about his wife's sudden death until nearly three weeks later. It came as his regiment recovered from its participation in the brutal Seven Days Battles, the climax of the Peninsula Campaign in eastern Virginia.

His 31st Regiment Virginia Infantry, along with other Confederate troops that had been engaged in skirmishes in western Virginia, crossed the Allegheny Mountains around the first of May 1862. For most of the next two months, they fought west and north of the Shenandoah Valley in Harrisonburg, Winchester, Front Royal, Strasburg, Woodstock, Cross Keys, and Port Republic.

Then, they were commanded to travel south to join Gen. Robert E. Lee's army of 92,000 Confederate soldiers, battling an estimated 103,000 who fought in General McClellan's Union ranks. General McClellan attempted to capture Richmond, the Confederate capital, in the Peninsula Campaign. The Seven Days Battles, fought from June 25 to July 1, 1862, were the culmination of General McClellan's unsuccessful Peninsula Campaign.

Despite General Lee's Army of Northern Virginia suffering a terribly high number of casualties (3,494 killed, 15,758 wounded, and 952 captured or missing), the Seven Days Battles were considered a Southern victory since Richmond held. As a result, Confederate morale finally escalated.

On a trip into Grafton in March 1864, Silas Currey discovered that a Union regiment was forming in Ohio for a short-term assignment involving garrison duty. He had not wanted to engage in battle for either side. But he did want this wretched war to end. If he could lend his service in making that happen any quicker, he was now willing to do so.

The news came as a surprise to Sarah Jane. In her mind, the only thing good about it was that it would qualify him for a pension after the war. Their two oldest boys were now seventeen and thirteen. They, along with their three sisters and baby, Thomas, born a year ago, were virtually surrounded by family. She knew there would be help to keep things running.

Silas enrolled at Camp Dennison near Cincinnati on May 2 with the 146th Ohio Infantry. His guard unit left for Charleston, West Virginia, on August 17, then moved to Fayetteville for garrison duty until August 27. While in Fayetteville, his company had numerous minor skirmishes with small Rebel forces. On the 27th, they left for Camp Piatt, just south of Charleston, where they received transportation back to Camp Dennison. The 146th regiment mustered out on September 7.

Everybody had gathered at Sarah Jane's house for dinner around noon on May 28. Jesse was walking by a front window when he noticed the group of six riders coming off the road toward the house.

His mother saw they were in raggedy Union uniforms, and they carried weapons. Somehow, she immediately sensed danger.

"Okay, stop what ya'll are doing. Everybody get down in cold storage. You each know the plan. Hurry! Cynthia, grab the honey off the table to keep the baby quiet. Both those pistols down there are loaded, aren't they, George?"

"Yes, Mama."

"If somebody breaks the locks on that door, Jesse, you let the first man come all the way down the steps before you shoot him and make it count. George, you kill the second man coming down the steps. Let's pray that does not happen. Do not come out of there until they are gone. You hear me?"

"Yes, Mama."

Sarah Jane set the pot off the heat, hurried over to the rifle, leaning against the wall to make sure it was loaded, and took a deep breath. "God help me," she muttered under her breath.

"Hello, the house," sounded from outside.

After steadying herself, Sarah Jane picked up the gun and walked out onto her porch.

"Afternoon, ma'am. I'm Captain Ross. We're meeting up with a company in Randolph County. We've come down out of the Pittsburgh area and got separated from some of our regiment. Don't suppose you have any extra food you could share with us?"

"There's nothing left in my smokehouse, and there are no chickens anymore. The garden's producing a little bit, though. It's still kind of early for tomatoes. You are welcome to go look."

"I'm going to have a look around the barn and the smokehouse," said the captain. "You men stay put."

A couple of the soldiers were talking to each other. Two more seemed at ease looking around. The other one had not taken his beady eyes off of Sarah Jane. He dismounted and took three or four steps toward the porch.

"I'm thinking it's about dinner time, and I may be mistaken, but I believe I smell something cooking," he said. "Surely you have enough in there to feed six hungry soldiers. I hear this is pro-Union territory."

"I do not," Sarah Jane replied as she raised her rifle above her hips.

"Newton, leave the lady alone," one of the other men said.

"How 'bout I come on in and see how much you do have in your pot?" Newton asked as he took three more steps toward the house.

At that, Sarah Jane quickly raised the rifle into a shooting position and pulled back the hammer.

"Take another step toward me, and you'll eat this musket ball," she replied.

Before anybody knew what happened, Newton reached under his jacket, pulled out a pistol, and fired a round into Sarah Jane's chest. At the same time, she fired a ball that tore off most of his left ear.

"What in the bloody hell have you done?" asked Pvt. Alan Proctor who immigrated from London with his parents as a young boy. All four men jumped off their horses.

Captain Ross darted from around the corner and stood dumbfounded. He stepped upon the porch and confirmed his worst fear. Sarah Jane Currey lay dead.

"Goddamn, Newton."

"The bitch shot off my ear."

"Do not speak," ordered the captain. "Don't say another word. You have been nothing but a liability. You lie. You cheat. You steal. Now you've committed cold-blooded murder. Stand up. Look at me."

Captain Ross then drew his pistol and shot Newton square between the eyes.

"The right thing would have been to haul his sorry arse back for a court martial. But we don't have the time, and I had no more patience for that lousy excuse for a human being. Now, somebody was bound to have heard those gunshots. Get him tied up on his horse, double quick. We've got to get out of this county as fast as we can. We'll dump the body on down the road."

"Sir, what if somebody is in the house and can identify us? Shouldn't we check?" asked one of the soldiers.

"We're through here. We've done quite enough damage. We are riding out."

After much discussion between family members, they decided not to notify Silas about his wife's murder. Mary and Adaline felt that Silas would not handle the news well. James agreed. He knew his younger brother could be impetuous. Having just enrolled in the Army, James didn't know if Silas realized the severity of desertion. The fact was, deserters were shot. And everybody agreed that if Silas knew about Sarah Jane's death, he would try and come home.

Son George, now seventeen, could keep the family's scaled-down farm afloat until his father's return, with the help of brother Jesse, nearly thirteen, and family and neighbor men, who would be available for consultation and occasionally needed help with work. However, at age eleven, Cynthia, the oldest of three girls, required assistance with cooking and with her younger siblings since there was a one year-old in the house who was unhappy about the disruption of his milk when his mother disappeared.

Aunt Rachel Ashcraft Newbrough, sixty-one, younger sister of Sarah Jane's mother, Sena Ashcraft Tucker, agreed to live with the siblings until their father's return. Aunt Rachel's husband, Abel, had been killed during a robbery at age thirty-two in 1830. She never remarried. She lived with her only daughter, Levina, and her family near the Curreys on Booths Creek.

The children rallied around Aunt Rachel, who provided good meals from vegetables in the garden tended by Jesse and Cynthia and game hunted by George, including squirrel, rabbit, muskrat, groundhog, and an occasional deer, as well as quail, dove, snipe, and grouse. They got milk from their remaining cattle, and made butter, which required help from family members.

Martha Ashcraft, twenty-one, a cousin of Sarah Jane's, was a niece of Aunt Rachel. She had been coming to the Currey's once a week to help her aunt with the children, bringing along her three year-old son, Jefferson, who they called Jeff. She lived on Booths Creek with her parents, Levi and Charity Ashcraft.

Silas returned in mid-September to discover that his wife had been shot dead, his children had been living without a parent, and the farm was in worse shape than he imagined. However, he thanked God for his family. Just over two months before he left, the person he was probably closest to left this earth. His Papa, Jonathan T. Currey, died in his sleep on March 26, 1864, at age seventy-five. He wished the old man was here now. But his faithful mother, Nancy Mason Currey, seventy-three, was at his house when he walked in. She was the one who broke the news to him. Nancy Currey had been there periodically, doing what she could to help Rachel and the children. She would live another twenty years to become the family matriarch on Booths Creek.

What on earth had he been thinking? His enrolling in the Union Army did not make one iota of difference. Why would a man leave his family to go into an Army he had no allegiance to? Where he could be killed? Silas was plagued by these thoughts, especially at night. If he had not left home, his brave wife would still be here with him. George said he was almost certain he had heard two simultaneous shots that day. Blood found in the yard indicated that Sarah Jane had shot one of the intruders.

By the end of November 1864, the 31st regiment found itself back in the mountains of western Virginia. They camped outside Beverly with no anticipated action until after the first of the year. The weather was proving to be particularly brutal early. Already slim rations were barely above a level of sustenance.

Ben decided that he would not continue as a soldier into 1865. He had enrolled and served from the beginning of this miserable war. It was time for him to leave. He would not be going back east with his regiment to fight another day. Sam agreed they should muster out since they were so close to home. Gen. Jubal Early did not like losing two healthy men, but the Confederacy had retained their services for nearly four years. He signed their papers for release.

Although General Early did not know it when he released the Curreys from their military duty, he performed a favor for family members. Ben's uncle, James Currey, married Nancy Batson in 1825. Nancy's great-great-grandmother, Judith Early (1710-1787), was the sister of Jeremiah Allen Early Sr. (1705-1787), Gen. Jubal Early's great-great-grandfather. Judith married John T. Buford Sr. Jeremiah wed his sister, Elizabeth Buford. The Early lineage in the country started when William Harley Early immigrated from County Donegal, Ireland, in 1662. He settled in Middlesex County, Virginia, after his father, Thomas Early, died at sea off Sulawesi, Indonesia.

When Ben arrived on Booths Creek, he found his son, John, a grown man. Nancy, sixteen, had grown into a lovely young woman, and Prudence was now in her teens. John had been courting one of the Vincent daughters, Ellen, eighteen, from Shinnston. She had been spending quite a bit of time at the house helping Adaline and Nancy manage all the work since they lost their mother.

Adaline hardly recognized Sam when she first saw him. He and her father looked like they had not bathed in a year, and the smell rolling off them was horrendous. They both had beards nearly down to their chests. Their scraggly hair lay almost to their shoulders. And they needed meat on their bones.

"Oh, my . . . Papa, Sam, don't stand there letting the heat out. Step in," said Adaline, who opened the front door. "Girls, fill the biggest pots we have with water and get them to heatin'. I love you both. But do you have any idea how bad you smell? John, take their coats and throw them outside. Nancy, get them something hot to drink. Make a place in front of the fire."

"Papa, I didn't hear horses come up," John said.

"No, son, no horses. We've walked most of the way from Beverly. We caught a wagon ride outside of Buckhannon for maybe twenty miles, but other than that, it's been on foot."

"Oh, no, look at your boots. Your feet must be tore up," said Ellen.

"You have no idea," Sam replied. "You'd think after four years of marching, feet would get tough as nails. But human feet, without good protection, ain't made for constant pounding. Ever winter, feet freeze, get gangrene, and men have to have their foot or feet amputated."

Nancy brought over a plate full of bread with butter and hot tea for the men.

"We don't have coffee right now, Papa," she said "It's hard to come by. But we do have a big ole pot of burgoo cooking. Ya know, you can shoot squirrels anytime."

"Boy, does that sound good," said Ben.

"By the time you two clean up, supper should be ready," Adaline said.

"What about cousin Jacob," asked John. "Did he not come home with ya?"

"Jacob's alright. For some reason, he decided to see this thing through. I think it'll end before long. I need to go let Uncle Booth know what Jacob decided," said Ben as he got up and turned his backside to the fire.

Sam asked, "What day is this? It must be getting awfully close to Christmas."

"Sure is. Just three more days," Ellen answered.

"I reckon tomorrow I better be gettin' over to Orange. Maw will likely think I'm a right fine Christmas present, don't ya think?"

"You are that, Sam," said Nancy. "Havin' you and our Papa home safe is the best present any of us could possibly ask for. God has answered our prayers fer certain. And your Maw will be overcome with joy to see ya walk in her door."

"John, go back there and set me up with a strap razor and shaving cream. I'll go ahead and get this beard off while the water is heating. I'll take a little out of the kettle. Maybe tomorrow, one of you females can cut my hair short. And somebody, find us two sets of clean clothes, including socks and whole boots, if there are any around there. Everything we have on is going in the fire."

"Not this fire. We'll build a fire outside special fer those clothes," laughed Adaline.

✦ ✦ ✦

The year 1865 was a time for recovery, re-acquaintance, inventory, and plans for what normal might look like again. Almost everything had changed since 1861. Miraculously, most homes in the northern mountains of what was now West Virginia had been spared by the carnage of war. Many farms were raided for what food could be had, which was expected. A few lives had been lost, but activity by guerrillas served to protect much of the area. Railroad supply lines had been cut off, and the people went without much of what they normally purchased in stores. But as soldiers started returning home, farms slowly began returning to order.

Weddings marked 1866 for the Currey family. John and Ellen postponed getting married after the arrival of John's father. John knew he would need his help in starting to move the farm back toward stability. And the Vincents had a homecoming of their own in June. James Barton, husband of Ellen's oldest sister, Mary, returned in June after serving three years in the 12th Regiment, West Virginia Infantry.

John and Ellen decided to have their wedding on Saturday, January 20, in the church outside of Clarksburg in Harrison County, pastored by Reverend Aaron Vincent, Ellen's father. It would accommodate both large families. Ary Vincent, and three of her daughters, Mary, Melissa, and Ema, demonstrated their cooking skills by creating a delicious post-ceremony wintertime meal with winter vegetables, including apples, beets, carrots, celery root, garlic, leeks, onions, sorrel, spinach, sweet potatoes, winter squash, as well as herbs, such as mint, oregano, parsley, and sage. Adaline and Nancy Currey made loaves of bread and rolls. Aunt Mary Riblett, Reverend Vincent's sister, agreed to make cakes. Silas slaughtered one of his last cows in honor of his nephew and new wife. Men had two fires going outside the church. Over one hung a large iron pot into which cut-up oxtail, bone-in short ribs, and fatty brisket cooked, along with an assortment of summer vegetables pulled out of cold storage to make a stew. Metal racks laid over the other fire held various cuts of beef to grill. It was an overcast, cold day, but no precipitation fell. Everybody agreed it could not have been a better start to 1866.

Aunt Rachel agreed to stay at Silas's place until New Year's 1866. He needed time to get his feet back under him. Martha Ashcraft had grown close to the children and said she would be glad to continue coming once a week to help. By this time, Ben's daughter, Prudence, was fourteen years old, but she had grown up fast since they lost their mother. She was sometimes at her cousin's house helping Aunt Rachel cook or weeding the garden, taking her turn churning butter or whatever needed to be done.

In December 1865, the women in the family got together. They decided it would be good if teams of two females spent two months each cooking and taking care of Silas's house and smaller children until a permanent solution could be found. He readily agreed.

Martha Ashcraft and her younger sister, Minerva, sixteen, volunteered to stay January and February. Cousins and sisters Elizabeth and Prudie Currey offered to come for the next two months. Prudie was engaged to Singleton Wilhite, a Union soldier who returned from the war in July of the previous year. They wanted an October wedding in Webster since both families lived there. But she agreed to take time for Uncle Silas's little ones. Nancy said she would stay for a couple of months with her sister, Prudence, which would leave Adaline short-handed at her father's house.

Adaline claimed to be okay. On the far side of their ridge, their closest neighbors were twin spinster sisters Mattie and Mavis Holmes and their bachelor brother, Richard. All were in their forties. They farmed close to 200 acres. The Curreys considered themselves lucky to have such good neighbors covering their backside. The women quilted with the Curreys and other neighbors during the war. When they heard about Silas's dilemma, Mattie told Adaline she would be happy to help her while her sisters were gone.

As it turned out, fate stepped in to alter everyone's plans. It was mid-February. Minerva was in the kitchen finishing the dishes with Prudence, who had come up to visit. The younger children were quiet for once. Silas and Martha sat in front of the fireplace. He felt her eyes on him. He looked up into a young twenty-three year-old face that featured the McIntire freckles of her maternal grandmother and blue eyes of both McIntires and Ashcrafts. If Martha could look back in time, she'd see that she looked exactly like her fifth great-grandmother, Lady Katherine Gifford, born in 1600 in Ulster, Ireland. What Silas saw deep in her eyes, for the first time, was an old soul. It made him smile.

"What are ya smiling at, Silas Currey?"

"Wisdom I never noticed before," he said.

"Aye, and don't ye be forgettin' it."

This made him laugh. It felt good. There was an eighteen-year difference between the two. But what the hell, he thought. He was ready to live again. If this war had taught him anything, he knew there may not be a tomorrow. He needed a life partner. He needed a wife.

Silas and Martha took their wedding vows one month later, on March 17, in front of that same fireplace, as immediate family and a handful of friends gathered at noon. Aunt Mary made a couple of cakes, which she served with good coffee. Somebody surely paid too much for fresh citrus fruit in Grafton, which they used in a tasty punch. Some other families made big pots of soup, and others brought their specialty bread for dinner. Martha's mama, Charity, came with her other three girls. They had lost Papa Levi four years earlier in a hunting accident. However, his only remaining brother, Aaron Ashcraft, from Marion County, who would turn 60 the following month, came down to visit family and honor his brother's daughter and new husband. Emory Currey, Silas's youngest brother, and his wife, Jennie, surprised the bride and groom. Jennie's parents, Tom and Lucinda Hughes, owned Valley River Farm in Monongalia County. They had an old, refurbished log cabin on the property, which they offered to the newlyweds. Nancy and Prudence quickly volunteered to stay with the children. As soon as everyone ate, Silas and Martha happily rode northwest to escape for a couple of nights.

It seems like joy is inevitably interrupted by sorrow in the hills. Martha's sister, Mary, did not survive her fifth pregnancy. In the early morning hours of May 12, she went into labor much earlier than expected. The midwife arrived, and hours later, she delivered the tiny baby. Soon after that, Mary began to hemorrhage and then died late afternoon. The infant lasted barely twenty-four hours.

Ben knew Julia Riley because her cousin, John Riley, was the father of Palmyra, who would marry Ben's cousin, Fenton Currey. Fenton lived on Booth's Creek not far away. (Two of Julia's brothers served in the Confederacy. Ben crossed paths with Captain Jonathan Riley in a battle at Cold Harbor in early June of the previous year.)

Fenton planted a good-sized sugar cane field in the late summer of 1864, which was risky in West Virginia. The crop needs hot, dry weather to prosper. Thankfully, the good Lord provided just those conditions the following summer. By fall, it was ready to cut. He sent word that he would host a cane grinding the next Saturday. He received plenty of help.

Friends and family gathered for a good time. People took turns running the pre-cut cane through metal grinders turned by a mule. The raw juice went into a pan set over hickory wood. It was stirred and strictly monitored until it reached an exact temperature. Then, it was skimmed and run through a thin, mesh cloth. Finally, the beautiful, dark, thick sorghum was poured into glass jars.

Ben noticed Julia setting jars out on a work table. She did not look much different than she did ten years ago when he had last seen her. She had Riley's red hair. Three of her father's great-grandparents immigrated from Ulster, Ireland, while his paternal great-grandmother, Eleanor Jewell, came from County Cork. All grew various shades of red locks. Julia thanked her mama for tempering the bright red of her papa's hair. Ben thought hers was a beautiful auburn color.

"She's our oldest at twenty-seven and still not married," said Margaret Riley, who stepped up beside Ben. "Says she can't see herself tied down to any of the men 'round here."

"Margaret, it's been a while. You and Harrison survive the war in one piece? I hear both your sons returned intact."

"Thank God for that. Yes, I reckon we have much to be thankful fer."

"I expect lots of women are a lookin' for love. Julia's probably not found her a man who's captured her heart." Ben said.

"Well, now, that's exactly what she says," laughed Margaret.

"I'll just bet you can relate to that, too."

"I do understand. I was sixteen when I started courtin'. Met Harrison Riley at a cousin's wedding when I was twenty-one. We fell in love and married the next year. I still am crazy about that man."

"I was born in 1816," said Ben. "We're all about the same age, aren't we?"

"Yes, I'm one year behind you, and Harrison was born in 1813."

Ben wandered into his cousin's kitchen just as a pan of biscuits came out of the oven. He took a seat at the table. Julia measured flour into a large bowl on the counter as women prepared more biscuits.

"Julia Riley, can I interrupt you a minute, please?" Ben said.

Julia looked up from the bowl and said, "Yes, just let me finish mixin' this dough, and I'll get Annie to come roll hit out for me."

Julia washed her hands and walked to the table. "Mr. Currey, I hope you fair well. It's been a while. Good to see ya."

"You're lookin' fine, Miss Julia. Would you mind gettin' two plates with a couple of biscuits on each? I'm goin' a grab a jar of sorghum and hep myself to some coffee. And, if you will, we are goin' to leave out of here and talk."

It was the start of a ten-month courtship. On Thursday, August 9, the third 1866 wedding in the Currey family took place. Harrison and Margaret Riley hosted the ceremony at their farm in Valley Spring. Ben and Julia tried to beat the heat with a simple outdoor morning service in a small grove of persimmon trees.

Sam Currey returned from the war a changed man. He was quieter and somewhat withdrawn. Adaline noticed a dark side to him. She discovered the source when she saw he carried a flask everywhere.

Sam refused to talk about his experiences in the war. Adaline didn't understand his reluctance. Ben advised his daughter to avoid the subject. He told her Sam would talk about it when and if he ever got ready. He explained that, as soldiers, they experienced horrible things on those battlefields, and none of them would recover overnight. Each man would have to deal with it in his own way.

Adaline knew one thing. She would not marry a man who drank as much as she feared Sam did. She intuitively knew it was not the solution to any problem. She reasoned that if a person drank enough today to make the demons go away, tomorrow, they would be right back in their head. Then, they'd drink enough again to make them go away. And the next day, there they'd be. That vicious cycle could go on forever until a body drank itself to death. No, God knew we would all wrestle with the devil. Through His Word, He gave us ways to avoid his traps and win those battles. That thought gave her an idea.

Harrison Riley, her new stepfather, had been a devoted, life-long Bible reader. Since two of his sons recently returned from the war, he was already intimately familiar with the mental struggles of the war-weary. Sam knew the Rileys since they lived close-by in Taylor County. Of course, they hosted Ben and Julia's wedding.

Adaline paid the Rileys a visit and explained Sam's situation. She asked Mr. Riley if he would intervene on her behalf. She invited the couple to an early supper the next week. She said she would also ask Sam and his older spinster sister, Amelia, with whom he was staying.

After a meal of fried trout, custard corn pudding, and slaw (made of cabbage, carrots, and onion, with a dressing of egg yolks, water, vinegar, and butter, which was heated), the three men went out on the porch to smoke. Ben quickly excused himself and came back into the house to give Harrison and Sam time to talk.

To Sam's surprise, Mr. Riley invited him to stay with his family in Valley Spring.

"Jonathan and Mordeci are helping to get the farm back to where it needs to be, but we could use another pair of hands," Mr. Riley explained. "I know you're recovering from a bad time, Sam, and there's nothing like connecting with the earth to help the process of healing.

"You did not ask for my help. Often, we men won't ask when we need something. It's just how we are. Frankly, I don't know anybody amongst us who cannot use help right now. We've all been through a terrible ordeal these last five years. Doesn't matter whether a body was out there fighting or here at home, we've suffered mental anguish, and many people have known gut-wrenching loss.

"Adaline is a special young lady. I'm a guessin' here, but I'd say she's a big reason you made it back home."

"I thought of her every single day," Sam confessed. "I was determined not to die out there so I could come home and marry her. And, believe me, that took some doin'. Now, she says she don't even know who I am anymore. She won't become my wife 'til I find my way back."

"The Scriptures say in Romans, chapter 10, verse 11, 'Whoever believes in Him, will not be disappointed,'" Mr. Riley said, looking the younger man squarely in the eye.

"That's a right powerful message. I hope you'll keep it in mind. And I hope you will consider our offer of a place to stay and work to help get our harvest in, which we're in the middle of. There will be plenty to do this fall, for certain."

Sam did not have to mull it over long. He felt the need for a safe haven, and the Rileys farm might provide the security he sought.

His sister, Amelia, agreed. She heard sounds of distress coming from his bedroom at night and knew these nightmares originated on the battlefield. She also realized she was powerless to intervene.

Adaline was thrilled at Sam's decision. She didn't know what Mr. Riley said to produce such action. She only knew that hope now replaced despair in her heart.

Sam and Adaline would not marry until April 28, 1870. Adaline wanted the ceremony to be in the forest as spring burst forth. Mid-morning, family and friends walked a quarter mile up Booth's Creek from Ben Currey's house to a flat area carpeted by Virginia bluebells. "Sarvis" trees, redbuds, and pink and white dogwoods framed nature's panorama, just as Adaline hoped. Sam asked Harrison Riley to bless the union using the same Bible that the pair had spent the preceding three years reading and studying. It became the couple's wedding gift.

People from the counties of Taylor, Harrison, Marion, and Monongalia remained tight- knit from the time of settlement. Intially, their lives depended on an effective communication system between families. Through the years, lingering apprehension about their physical security created natural suspicion of outsiders. Locals tended to close ranks. Trust was at a premium. Marriages, for the most part, stayed between families well-known to each other and, often, within individual families themselves. In addition to marrying cousins, the Curreys often found life partners among the Ashcraft, Riley, Tucker, and Vincent families.

It would be another two generations before people started leaving those counties of mountainous northern West Virginia and moving to other states. Economics provided the impetus. Many return to honor ancestors who rest in cemeteries that dot the landscape. If they reach an age when travel becomes impossible, those men and women surely remember the unbelievable stories of old about the ones who survived the odds to pass along their genes.

It is through the sharing of such stories that we know from whence we came.

Acknowledgments

My profound thanks go to my book club members. These intelligent, diligent women rallied around my project. They accompanied me to Townsend, Tennessee, outside the Great Smoky Mountains to read, critique, and make suggestions. Thank you Gladys Church, Becky Emmerson, Elissa Evans, Diane Hicks, Sandy Miller, Kathi Parkins, and Mavis Ziegler. Also present were the late Ginny West Case and Kay Dillard.

As a young man, my dad wanted to become a journalist but went to law school instead. When I majored in journalism and started writing, he was delighted. Late in life, he told me countless times that I needed to write a book. I wanted to but the stronger inkling came as I began my genealogical research. Dad wanted to learn about his Byrne ancestry, which he explored on a trip with Mom to Ireland. He would be over the moon discovering the information I have since gathered. I am indebted to my late, beloved daddy, Arthur D. Byrne, for driving the process.

Cover art work provided by Melanie "Mimi" Eichholz, a juried member of the Townsend Art Guild in Tennessee.

About the Author

J. Laurie Byrne spent her career as a writer and photographer at a newspaper and at a state university. This is her debut book. A native of Knoxville, Tennessee, she lives near the edge of the Smoky Mountains in retirement writing, reading, quilting, and cooking.

www.ingramcontent.com/pod-product-compliance
Lightning Source LLC
Chambersburg PA
CBHW070400310726
48977CB00003B/509